This collection of short stories is taken from the Michael Terence Publishing Summer 2020 Short Story Competition.

Entries were received from across the world – which perhaps helps to explain the wide and stimulating range of subjects covered.

We extend our sincere thanks to the judges for their hard work and diligence. The panel was, as always, truly impressed by the overall high standard of the submissions – so it's a big thank you to all of the wonderful authors.

Here we publish the three prize-winning stories plus works that were highly commended by the judges.

Each has been published as it was received, without further editing.

We hope you will enjoy reading them all.

About Michael Terence Publishing

In the past, the founders of MTP experienced the frustration of having a great manuscript but meeting a brick wall when trying to find a traditional agent/publisher.

Quite simply, MTP was founded to give worthy authors a platform to publish their works, earn 100% royalties and to achieve the best sales for print books and eBooks.

Today, submissions of new works in all genres are being gratefully received via our website.

Find out more about publishing *your* book at:

www.mtp.agency

Contents

1st PRIZE:
Anthony Buck -
All Those Things That You Never Thought Mattered 1

2nd PRIZE:
Rosalind Thomas -
Iron 9

3rd PRIZE:
James Hancock -
VORTAK: Evil Wizard 15

HIGHLY COMMENDED STORIES (in alphabetical order):
Aiden Furey - Conor McCloskey is Not Dead 23
Benny Allen - Maya Woke Up Late for The End of The World .. 30
Beth Roberts - Her Last Temptation 37
Carrie O'Leary - The Book 45
Christopher Kerr - All In The Mind 52
David Bell - The Dark Suit 57
David Challenger - Samui 65
Doris Allimadi - The Priest & I 73
Eddie Woods - Cattle Fodder 81
Helen Lawrence - The Affair 89
Ian Craine - Two Sisters At Their Windows 96
Ian Goh Hsien Jun - The Art and Science of Predicting Cherry Blossom Showers 101

All Those Things That You Never Thought Mattered

An Anthology from
Michael Terence Publishing
September 2020

Michael Terence
Publishing

First published in paperback by
Michael Terence Publishing in 2020
www.mtp.agency

ISBN 9781800940376

To writers and readers everywhere…

J W Voyce - Hold On 110

John Buckley - The Fitbit 120

John Sandry - The Man In The Dark 128

Karmen Špiljak - The Assistant 132

Kate Bramhall - Another Lost Day 138

Malina Douglas - The Secondhand Smile 146

Matt McCabe - The Token 154

Michael Noonan - The Mystery Tour 159

Mike Tibbs - Hibernation 166

The Ruminant Kind - M.E. Hills 173

Neil Walker - Rebecca & William Zero 180

Patrick Eades - What Lies Beneath 189

Peter Hankins - Glimpsing Her 195

Philip Charter - Ludgate Circus Crossing 202

Rachel New - Compliments and Appreciative Platitudes Season Two 210

Richard Hooton - The Secret of My Success 217

Rob Dorey - Past Imperfect 227

Ros Levenson - So lucky 232

Rosemary Barry - Ivy, Mary and Me 235

Sagamba Muhira and James Page - Out of Africa 242

Samiha Ali - Cave of Anguish 246

Sean Sheehan - Insects 256

Stephanie Rybak - Transmogrification 265

T.H. Kunze - Ionisation 271

Yvonne Barker - 3 Syllables 280

1st PRIZE: Anthony Buck - All Those Things That You Never Thought Mattered

Rupert slumped forward onto the steering wheel, pain racing across his chest, completely baffled as to what was going on. The last thing he saw was a tree zooming toward him at over fifty miles an hour over the dashboard.

Everything went dark. And then a small dot of white appeared in the far distance, slowly growing until Rupert could resolve it as a single rectangular block of pure white marble. Soon afterwards, it stopped in front of him, or he stopped in front of it. He kicked at the oblong, he tried to pick it up, he sat on it. Nothing happened. Eventually, he had the bright idea of standing on it, and immediately a second block appeared next to but just above it. For want of anything more sensible or constructive to do, he stepped up onto that one. A third block appeared, and so on until he had followed the mysterious set of steps all the way up to a flat white walkway, that he had failed to notice initially, suspended a long way off the ground.

It was starting to become apparent that he had died. He liked the special effects but he was worried that the afterlife seemed a bit boring so far. He hoped that something exciting would happen soon.

He shuffled lazily along the walkway, without any particular motivation to get a move on. He peered over the side, but found that without anything visible on the ground it was impossible to judge how high up he was. Even the steps behind him had now disappeared. He had a sudden urge to step off the walkway to see what happened, but he had already managed to die once today and it had hurt. He didn't fancy going through all that again.

After what seemed like an eternity of walking he eventually reached a door. Just a plain white door, with a handle and a white glow spilling out from all around the sides of it. Had Rupert been of a more practical disposition, he would have noticed that there were no breaks in the light around the door where hinges might be. But he wasn't, so he just opened it and walked through.

He found himself in a waiting room. As he had come to expect, everything was white, including the skin on the half dozen faces of people sitting around the room. He wasn't really in the mood for standing around gawping at everything, so he skipped further inspection and lolloped over to the desk to be greeted by the albino receptionist. He noticed, without much interest, that her eyes were pure white around the small black pupils. Not much colour around here, he thought to himself.

"If you would like to have a seat, Saint Peter will call you through shortly," she informed him sedately. He shrugged and chose not to reply, instead turning to do as she suggested. As he sat he looked around for a magazine to read, but couldn't find any. The pages would probably have been totally white anyway, he thought to himself morosely.

He had no idea how long he sat there waiting to go in. A few of the others in the room were called by name and went through, and another pair of dead people walked in through the same door that he had at some point. He just stared at one of the walls impassively, thinking about the life he had left behind. His five-a-side team would probably be a man short now, he realised. Which was a shame as it was a big game this weekend, the semi-final. Maybe they would be able to get his cousin to play instead. He found himself wishing that he had hidden his pornography more carefully before dying, as his Mum would almost certainly find it while sorting through his personal effects. That would be embarrassing. He also wondered, with a little irritation, whether he would ever get to see the end of the film he had been halfway through watching before he left the house.

Eventually he was pulled away from his thoughts by his name being read out. "Rupert John Barnstable," was what the receptionist said. "Saint Peter will see you now." Rupert wondered what this Saint Peter guy was like and what he wanted from him.

Whoever Saint Peter was, he certainly kept a tidy office. The whole room was white, of course, and everything seemed to be in its own specific place. Rupert had never seen a room so tidy, not even his Mum's bedroom.

Saint Peter was stood behind his white desk, beaming and rocking backward and forward between the balls of his feet and his heels. "Rupert!" he bellowed cheerfully as Rupert entered the room. "Or may I call you Rupe?" he continued, leaning forward as if to create a feeling of camaraderie between them.

Rupert shrugged, uninterested in what Saint Peter called him.

"OK, Rupe it is!" Saint Peter continued. "Great to meet you, Rupe." Rupert couldn't think of what to say to this, given that Saint Peter was essentially telling him how glad he was about his death.

"Hi," he decided upon, and accepted Saint Peter's outstretched hand to unenthusiastically shake it. "Can I call you Pete then?" he mumbled, feeling like something more was needed.

"No, you may call me Saint Peter," Saint Peter replied, without a break in his nauseating enthusiasm. "Saint Peter will be fine."

"Right, Rupe, take a seat, and we'll get down to business," Saint Peter continued. Rupert sat down, a bit annoyed at not being allowed to call him Pete.

"Now, you're dead, I'm afraid." Saint Peter explained, momentarily dropping his voice to a sympathetic tone.

"Yep," Rupert agreed, after realising that Saint Peter was waiting for a response.

"A heart attack, unfortunately," Saint Peter continued. That explained the pain in the chest, Rupert thought to himself ruefully. "Aged… thirty," Saint Peter confirmed, looking down at his notes. "Oh dear! Bad luck, Rupe!" He looked Rupert directly in the face, and inclined his head to one side in sympathy. "Don't worry though, plenty of fun still to be had on the other side! I'll let you go and join in with it just as soon as we've scored you."

"Scored…" Rupert began, but Saint Peter was in full flow now.

"I'm going to take you through the scoring process step by step," Saint Peter explained patronisingly. "If at any stage I tell you anything that you think is inaccurate, just let me know. Sometimes my notes do get mixed up!" Saint Peter chuckled to himself at this. "You wouldn't believe some of the laughs we've had over the years," he explained, shaking his head and laughing still more. Rupert sat opposite in stony silence.

"Anyway, back to business," Saint Peter said, coming over all serious again. By now, Rupert had decided just to sit and wait until Saint Peter eventually got onto the subject of what the hell he was going on about.

"First of all, we get a starting score based on the wealth that you had accumulated at the time of your death," Saint Peter explained, looking down at his notes once more. "Looks like you had accumulated debts amounting to… thirty-two thousand pounds." Rupert began to protest, but Saint Peter interrupted. "Don't worry, we take into account the value of your possessions before scoring you. It would be a very foolish scale otherwise!" Rupert felt an absurd sense of relief at this. "So that brings you to… negative twenty eight thousand in the wealth category."

Rupert was horrified. His mother had told him all his life that money wasn't really important. What a bloody fool she was.

"Surely all my stuff together is worth more than four thousand pounds?" he asked incredulously.

"Afraid not, Rupe," Saint Peter insisted, abruptly. "To be honest, four thousand might be a bit on the generous side. But don't worry, plenty of opportunities for you to improve your score. Money isn't everything!"

Rupert was relieved to hear this. He wondered what the other scoring opportunities might be. Amount of time spent helping people maybe? Or possibly kindness to animals? Perhaps total donations to charity? If any of these counted, he was screwed.

"Now, Scrabble," Saint Peter began, surprisingly. "You played fifty-eight games of Scrabble in your life. How many do you think you won?"

Rupert couldn't believe he had played that many. He couldn't remember most of the games, so he guessed "I dunno, about half?"

"Eight. And two of those were because you cheated." Saint Peter confirmed. "So that's fourteen per cent." Once again, Rupert had cause to curse his mother, who had been responsible for nearly all of the defeats. He had always felt that she had held him back in his life, and now she was causing him to underachieve even after death.

"Scrabble is the main one, but we do allow for other games…" Saint Peter began, looking down at those notes once more. "Trivial Pursuit, twenty two percent success rate. Connect Four, fifty one percent wins. Snakes and Ladders, forty per cent."

"But Snakes and Ladders is total luck!" Rupert insisted.

"Everyone says that," Saint Peter replied, furrowing his brow in confusion. "You must all be playing it wrong. Anyway, Pro Evolution Soccer (various versions) thirty three percent." He scanned further down the list. "You did complete the first two Tomb Raider games – it's a shame you didn't quite finish the third as you would have got a bonus for that."

"I didn't complete it because I got the job in the warehouse!" Rupert protested.

"You still had the evenings, didn't you?" Saint Peter chided him, lightly. "Anyway, I don't think you played any other games enough to give a fair sample, so we'll ignore the results of those, I think." He put down the list and smiled at Rupert benevolently.

"Now, sexual partners," Saint Peter bellowed, rather more loudly than Rupert thought was really necessary. He looked around, hoping that there was no-one else nearby to hear, but actually he was quite pleased that this had come up as he felt that he had done quite well.

"Fifteen full sexual partners," Saint Peter announced. "Twelve partial." He looked up from the list and winked at Rupert. "Good going, Rupe! Lots of points for that." Rupert beamed, glad that he was finally starting to do well in this nonsensical reckoning.

"But… oh dear." Saint Peter continued, his smile fading. "You failed to generate a single orgasm for any one of your partners."

Rupert went crimson (if such a thing was possible in this monochrome environment). "That can't be right!" he protested loudly. "You've definitely got the wrong sheet of paper there!"

Saint Peter looked down again at his notes, flipped them over to look at the reverse, and then looked back up at Rupert. "I'm afraid that isn't possible in this case, Rupe." Rupert accepted with a sinking heart that it was probably true. "For heaven's sake, Rupe! It really isn't all that difficult!" Saint Peter exhorted, rather unnecessarily in Rupert's view. After all, there wasn't much he could do about it now, being dead.

"Oh well," he continued, placing the sheet of paper back on the desk. "I won't lie to you Rupe, that isn't going to do your score any favours at all. But you mustn't lose hope just yet."

There was a short awkward silence between the two men, which made Rupert lose hope far more effectively than anything Saint Peter could have said. Then Saint Peter piped up again.

"Now, Rupe, it won't surprise you to hear that popularity has a great bearing on your score," he explained kindly while looking up from his notes, in a way that suggested he usually wore glasses that he could peer over but wasn't today for some reason.

Rupert didn't know how to feel anymore. Maybe everyone had secretly hated him? Secretly loathed him while beating him at Scrabble, exaggerating the value of his possessions and faking orgasms left, right and centre?

"You received a total of three hundred and twelve Christmas cards, excluding those from immediate family, and elderly extended family members," Saint Peter summarised. "For a male of your age, that's pretty decent going. You score well for that." Rupert could sense Saint Peter breathing a sigh of relief at finally having some good news to impart. "However," Saint Peter continued, to a man who should have known that it was too good to last, "that doesn't compare well with your total of five hundred and seventy-six cards sent. I'm afraid there's a similar story with phone calls made and received, and with text messages." Text messages? Rupert could hardly believe his luck at Saint Peter being the only guy over fifty years old to understand what text messages were. On top of the misfortune of dying of a heart attack aged thirty, this was almost too much to take.

"Not much more to get through now," Saint Peter continued rapidly, now obviously keen to wrap this loser up and get onto his next appointment. "The last section is conflict. How have you performed in this area, I wonder?" Rupert didn't dare guess.

"Now, you've only ever had three fights," Saint Peter began. Rupert felt a small thrill of pride in his pacifism – after all this was a rate of only one fight per decade. "Your record is won none, lost two. The other we'll call a draw."

"A draw?" Rupert protested, his peaceful nature suddenly discarded. "He ran away crying!" he insisted, recalling the fight vividly.

"Yes, Rupe," Saint Peter conceded with the air of someone trying to explain to a child how to run without falling flat on their face. "But only in horror at having broken your arm. To be honest, I think you're lucky to get a draw out of that one."

"Look, I'm a lover not a fighter," Rupert explained, immediately ashamed at himself for using such a corny line. But not as ashamed as he was after Saint Peter's reaction, which was to flick back a few pages in those blasted notes and look back up at him with his eyebrows raised.

"Anyway, your fighting career is hardly a points bonanza," Saint Peter clarified unnecessarily after the awkward moment. "How about the arguments?"

"Oh, it's probably terrible!" Rupert replied testily, getting a bit sick of this nonsense now. OK, so he had lived an unsuccessful and undistinguished life. Everyone he knew had too. But how was he meant to know that he should have been soliciting Christmas cards and finding someone awful at Connect Four that he could beat time and time again?

"Now, come on," Saint Peter chided. "There's no point in getting cross with me. These are exactly the same criteria that are used for everyone who comes through here."

"OK then. How many arguments have I won?"

"Well, as usual, it depends on who the arguments are with." Saint Peter began. "Against your first girlfriend, Claire, you were on sixty four percent success. Pretty good." Rupert smiled wanly at this rare compliment.

"Against Sasha, your second girlfriend, you won seventy-six percent, although your score for that is reduced because English wasn't her first language. And with Trish, your most recent girlfriend, you were in the sixties again."

"However." Saint Peter began, and Rupert's heart sank once more. "Against your sister, your argument success rate is sixteen per cent. Against your Mum, it's four per cent." Rupert started to wonder whether his Mum might have known about this system all along and been using him to bump up her score. "Against your father, twenty two percent."

"How do you even decide who wins an argument?" Rupert asked exasperatedly.

"It's usually obvious," Saint Peter shot back, clearly not in the mood to get drawn into a long justification of his methods. And neither was Rupert, really. He had the feeling that nothing he said would change his points total. He just shrugged in response.

"And now, you have a zero per cent argument success rate against Saint Peter," Saint Peter concluded smugly, sticking the boot in somewhat.

"So…" he then began, with the air of someone about to finally get to the point. "Overall, that's a score of two thousand, six hundred and eighty-eight." Rupert wondered whether that was decent or not. "I should point out that the scoring system isn't totally accurate, but it's the best I can do without spending hours on every person," Saint Peter explained patiently.

"OK," Rupert agreed, wondering what would happen next.

"However, based on this scoring system, you ended up in the ninth percentile of the human race." Rupert frowned, thinking that sounded unexpectedly good. "That's really very poor," Saint Peter concluded, shaking his head sadly at how incompetently Rupert had done at life.

"Oh." Rupert replied, morosely. He was feeling pretty cross with things, all in all. Dying had been bad enough, and then to have to endure this character assassination was almost too much to take. "Sorry," he added, wondering abstractly what the consequences of this result would be.

"I'm afraid that there is only one course of action available to me," Saint Peter explained. "You'll have to go back and try again."

2nd PRIZE:
Rosalind Thomas - Iron

The interview room was cold. Deliberately made cold. Bare walls. Lino floor. One large, serious policeman.

Mrs Birdie Dunlop was not intimidated. Instead, she sat across from the detective, her face a study in sangfroid.

If you knew Mrs Birdie Dunlop from Number 6 Jacaranda Crescent, Beecroft, you'd know she was quite capable of manufacturing calm. You'd also know she was once an actress, an actress who once received a telephone call from The Queen, congratulating her magnificent turn as Lady Macbeth at the Aston Street Theatre.

Birdie Dunlop would have told you this herself, possibly more than once.

Sometimes, she forgot which neighbours she'd told and which she hadn't and proceeded to give you a second (or even third) reminder of the royal stamp on her theatrical curriculum vitae.

Of course, this required the verbal dexterity to squeeze a mention of 'The Queen' and 'my role as Lady Macbeth' into any kerbside exchange of pleasantries between neighbours, even if you happened to be dragging your bin to the verge or emptying your mailbox.

The fact that there was never a theatre on Aston Street, and that Birdie Dunlop was never an actress, let alone a Lady Macbeth, is not important. What *is* important is that no-one, not even Her Majesty, corrected her. (Long ago, Birdie Dunlop convinced herself that behaving like an actress was not a pretence if it led to self-realisation).

So it's not surprising that if you were observing Mrs Dunlop now - a suspect being held for questioning at the Eastwood police station in Sydney - you'd be impressed by her performance.

You'd notice how still she was. The only discernible movement about her was the swell and fall of her considerable bosom under the soft cowl of her lambswool knit. She sat with the straight-backed carriage of a woman who considers posture a measure of class.

Unlike the usual demeanour of police suspects, Mrs Dunlop was composed. Serene even. You might also observe that Mrs Dunlop was hinged forward on her seat, knees pressed together so she could align the toes of her sensible maroon lace-ups with a join in the lino tiles. From this, you might conclude that Birdie Dunlop liked symmetry and uniformity and took pleasure in creating order as a kind of moral uplift.

You'd never guess, then, that on the inside, Birdie Dunlop was seething with indignation, and that it was the heat from this internal outrage that enabled her to remain unstirred in the frigid interview room.

She rested her eyes lightly on the large, serious policeman. Detective Gordon Quiney was absorbed in the file before him, beating time on the desk-top with a 2B pencil, which was tied to a string and nailed to centre of the desk.

"Are you worried I might steal your 20-cent pencil?" said Mrs Brown, her supercilious tone clipping the silence.

She assumed Detective Quiney would draw from her pronunciation of 'pen-ceal,' that he was dealing with a woman of superior community standing who did not belong in a 'poh-lice' station.

The detective looked at her blankly, then flipped to a clean page in his file: "I must inform you," he said in his policeman's drone, "that I am recording this interview on Wednesday August 6, 1996. You do not have to say anything unless you wish to do so, but what you say may be given in evidence. Now Mrs Dunlop, before we start, are you on any medication?"

It was not a question Birdie Dunlop was expecting. Her hands, until now resting demurely in her lap, sprang into motion. One brushed conspicuously at an invisible crumb on her skirt so the other could fly to her top lip to check for perspiration.

"Well, yes," she said with obvious annoyance. "I'm on Hormone Replacement Therapy actually. But only," she added hastily, "as a precaution. My husband agrees I'm far too youthful for such a mid-life ailment."

The detective scribbled something on the page.

Mrs Dunlop let her gaze drop from his broad ruddy face to a patch of dust on the desk, lit by a weak shaft of sunlight from the high window.

A few lazy sunbeams waltzed above the tabletop.

Without thinking, she lunged forward and – using her sleeve as a duster - swept her arm across the desk. The sunbeams now leapt into a frenzy of cavorting and cartwheeling. Mrs Dunlop frowned at the now visible chaos she had created, wishing she had a damp cloth and a bottle of Mr Sheen.

Detective Quiney appeared unfazed by her commotion.

"Mrs Dunlop, could you please explain what happened to your husband this morning?"

He waited, pencil poised.

"Well," said Mrs Dunlop, taking a deep breath and making a mental note to project her voice, "It was like any other morning. I was very busy getting my husband ready for work. It was cold outside, so I had already been out to the garage to get the car warmed up for him. He's a bank manager, my Robert, you know. A good head for numbers. Has his sights set on the corner office. With my help," - she was quite enjoying herself now – "I expect Robert will take over the branch one day."

She paused a moment to allow Detective Quiney to be suitably impressed, then ploughed ahead.

"I often tell my Robert," she announced loudly, " 'Screw your courage to the sticking place, darling, and we'll not fail!' " She snorted at her own joke, but it was lost on Detective Quiney, who was pining for a cigarette.

"Mrs Dunlop, please answer my question."

"Oh. Yes. Well, Robert usually irons his shirt around 7.30am. Actually," - she doubled back – "first I make him a cup of coffee - black, one sugar - then he fetches the ironing board from the laundry cupboard. He's very particular about his shirts, you see, and, despite my protests, insists on ironing them himself. And this morning, like every morning, I say to him, 'Robert, dear, if you've finished with the ironing board, could you please return it to the laundry.' And every morning, he leaves the house with the ironing board still in the middle of the kitchen floor.'"

The detective raised one eyebrow.

Mrs Dunlop took this as encouragement. "As you can well imagine, I find my husband's domestic neglect quite infuriating." She had no doubt a policeman, wedded to the management of order and chaos, would feel the same.

"But what happened *after* he ironed his shirt this morning?"

"Well *this* morning, my husband overslept. Being the power behind the throne," - she tittered at this – "I offered to iron his shirt."

Sensing he was now getting somewhere, Detective Quiney humoured her by stretching his serious mouth into a tight smile.

"I do appreciate a super crisp look in a business shirt. In the rag trade," - she guffawed at her ironic usage of the slang – they call it a 'double press.' You turn the shirt inside out and iron it that way, then turn it back the right way and iron it again. It's a trick I read about in *Woman's Day*. And let's face it, there's nothing more disappointing than a gentleman lacking the courage to dress for success."

She gave a short derisive laugh then craned forward to give Detective Quiney another insider's tip.

"I also recommend you do not press the turn of a French cuff. It steals the life and body from a smooth fold."

The detective sighed.

"Mrs Dunlop, I'm going to ask you one last time. What happened to your husband this morning?"

"Goodness me, I was getting to that," she said, visibly put out. "Where was I? Ah yes. I had almost finished double pressing his shirt when Robert emerged from the shower. While he waited, he took it upon himself to offer me some advice."

"Advice?"

"Yes. Advice. If you could call it that. I doubt he was thinking properly, owing to the fact he'd overslept and was now running late for work."

Detective Quiney wondered if he'd have time to put a buck on the last race at Randwick.

"My husband suggested that I was ironing his shirt *in-co-rrectly*." She paused for dramatic effect, which Detective Quiney failed to acknowledge.

Mrs Dunlop forced her voice into a low register to deliver her husband's line: "Don't you know you always start with the collar, woman, never the sleeves! Everyone knows that!"

Detective Quiney stared intently at her.

"So I said to Robert: to whom are you referring when you speak of 'everyone?"' She adopted her gravelly baritone once again: "Well, it's just common sense isn't it?

Birdie? If you iron the sleeves first, they get in the way and then you have to do them again. It's not rocket science, is it?"

"And then what happened?" said Detective Quiney, beginning to feel tense himself.

"Well," said Mrs Dunlop sweetly, "he got dressed, fixed his tie, took up his briefcase and made for the front door so I said, 'Robert, dear, will you be putting the ironing board back in the laundry before you go?' He mustn't have heard me because he took a step towards the hallway and that's when I tripped over the cat – little rascal - and the hot iron in my hand made contact with the back of poor Robert's head and down he went in a crumpled heap. And I remember screaming, 'Robert, my darling Robert, are you hurt?' and the next thing I knew the room began to spin wildly and I lurched to one side and then the other and I must have fainted, because when I came to, my darling husband was in the back of an ambulance."

"Did you call the ambulance?" "Yes, yes of course."

Detective Quiney looked down at his notes and began to read:

"Ambulance officer Luis Hernandez reported that it was your neighbour, Mrs Beverley Lipman, who called the ambulance at 7.50am because smoke was emanating from your garage. Officer Hernandez said that when he and his colleague arrived at your house at 8.05am, your husband had no pulse, your neighbour Mrs Lipman was attempting to perform CPR and you, Mrs Dunlop, were on your hands and knees scrubbing at the bloodstains in your carpet?"

"That Lipman woman always was a nosy parker," said Mrs Dunlop through clenched teeth. "I mentioned to her one day that Robert had a bad habit of leaving the ironing board out, and I clearly remember her saying: 'Well, he's asking for it then, isn't he?' There's your motive right there!"

With a flourish, Mrs Birdie Dunlop snapped shut her handbag and scraped back her chair to stand.

"To think only last week I made cumquat marmalade for my husband's murderer!" She took a tissue from her purse and dabbed at her dry eyes.

"Well dear," she said, as Detective Quiney wrote furiously in his file.

"I guess you'll be arresting Mrs Lipman shortly. If you have everything you need from me, I have an appointment at the podiatrist."

3rd PRIZE:
James Hancock - VORTAK: Evil Wizard

Vortak was an evil wizard. He had a tower at the edge of the black forest in Mortissia, and twenty minions to guard it. He had fifteen magic items in his treasury at the top of the tower, and a princess from Elandar locked in the dungeons below. He was on the verge of defeating Duke Laminar of Brightmoor, when a party of hired adventurers broke into his tower and set upon his minions. The princess was rescued, there were deaths on both sides, and Vortak was forced to quickly open and flee through a magic portal. The spell didn't go as planned. A fumbled casting when he really didn't need one, and Vortak was transported to an unknown world and without the means to open a new portal. Trapped! But he had survived. Now he lives in a one bedroom flat in Brighton, England, and earns his keep in the only way he can… Vortak The Incredible: Wizard For Hire. Degrading himself at music festivals and children's parties in the Sussex area.

Three months in his new life; a life of gas and electricity bills, buying bread and milk from the local shop, and making small talk with his eccentric neighbour, Graham.

***

Graham knocked on Vortak's door, beamed a big smile, and held it fixed ready for when Vortak answered. He waited. A minute passed and his jaws began to ache. He dropped the smile and reached up to knock again as the door opened. Graham quickly smiled again as Vortak stepped into the doorway and lifted a lantern to illuminate the area. Deep blue eyes under a heavy frown, pale skin, jet black hair, and robes to match. Vortak stared at Graham… fake tan, brilliantly white teeth, skinny and weak looking; Vortak considered how easily he could crush him. Graham held up a plate of freshly cooked homemade brownies.

"I thought you might like some homemade brownies. Fresh out the oven." Graham continued to beam his exaggerated smile.

Vortak looked at the brownies and then back at Graham, thinking for a moment. "I accept," Vortak said, took the brownies with his free hand

and slammed the door shut with his foot. Graham waited for two minutes, but Vortak didn't return.

Vortak walked into his living room. All the modern furnishings yet lit by several lanterns and dozens of candles. He placed the lantern on a small table, and sat in a comfortable chair with brownies on lap. He picked up the first brownie, and a vibrating buzz sounded from under him. He jumped, startled, and dropped the plate of brownies on the floor.

"Son of a witch!" he yelled and instinctively unleashed flames from his hands at the scattered brownies. He quickly calmed himself as the buzz sounded again, and reached under his robes to pull a mobile phone from his trousers pocket.

Vortak placed the phone to his ear whilst stamping out the small carpet fire near his feet. "Who calls me at this hour?" Vortak spoke with an intimidating tone.

He listened. "Yes. Next Saturday at one o'clock. Let me check my diary." Vortak paused, leaned forward and picked up a non-charred brownie. "I am available. What age will your daughter be, and how many infants should I expect?"

Vortak took a bite of the brownie, nodding as he listened to the information.

"Send an electronic message to this device after the conversation has ended, and specify your address. I shall be there on time. I accept cash and cash only!" he ended the call.

Vortak got up and walked across his living room, taking another bite of the brownie and making a noise of appreciation as he entered his kitchen. He lifted a Brighton Pier fridge magnet, and pulled a sheet of paper free from his fridge door. A thermometer style goal chart, with four thousand as the objective and just under one hundred coloured in. A long way to go. Vortak mused over the words at the top of the page – *Minions required to conquer the lands of East Sussex.*

Vortak shook his head, disappointed. "Eight-year-olds. Damn them and their weak bodies! Oh how I despise children and their…" his phone buzzed and vibrated again, causing him to drop the sheet of paper and last of his brownie.

"Damn this cursed communication device!" he yelled as he pulled the phone from his pocket and checked a text message. His rage calmed.

"Oh good, that's just around the corner."

***

An eighth birthday party for Maisie. 'Hire a wizard' Muriel's friend had advised, and that's what she did. Hopefully it would be a party her daughter would remember. Ten children sat on the living room floor, staring up at the black robed individual before them.

"Who knows what a Necromancer is?" asked Vortak. Three hands went up.

"Ugly child at the front." Vortak pointed at a spotty child. Half of the children were shocked by Vortak's comment, and the other half sniggered, covering their mouths to stop themselves from laughing out loud. The spotty child was understandably embarrassed.

"Someone who can summon skeletons," the spotty child said, worried he might get ridiculed again.

Muriel had been making sandwiches in the kitchen, and unsure of what she had just heard, moved to the living room doorway to keep an eye on things.

"Sort of," said Vortak. "It is someone who can animate the dead. Zombies, ghouls, even wraiths if the Necromancer is powerful enough. Now, does anyone have a dead pet with them?"

Muriel frowned and crossed her arms, edging into the room a little to let Vortak see she was there and watching him. Seeing where this was going. None of the children raised a hand, and all looked understandably confused.

"Never mind," said Vortak, thinking for a moment. "Any live pets? I can still make it work."

Maisie's hand went up. "Spoiled girl." Vortak pointed at Maisie.

"My cat died. Jemima. She is buried at the bottom of the garden," Maisie was unsure of herself.

"Excellent!" said Vortak, and waved a hand through the air. "Shovel." and a shovel appeared in his hand. The children gawped and gasped in amazement. Vortak passed the shovel to Maisie, who gave a grin of importance and put it on the carpet beside her. It was too big to keep hold of.

Vortak rubbed his chin, thinking. "The ground is a bit hard this time of year. Pickaxe," he said, and a pickaxe appeared in his hand. The children all clapped.

"You'll need to choose a friend to help you." Vortak passed the pickaxe to Maisie, who placed it with the shovel. She looked back to see all nine of her friends looking at her, with their hands up, and desperately trying to get her to attention. Pick me!

"No. Sorry… can we move away from this please?" Muriel interjected.

Vortak nodded. "Maybe you'd like to help me. I need an assistant for my next trick."

As Muriel made her way around the gathering of infants, Vortak rummaged in his holdall bag of props and produced a fist-sized rock. A rough and uncut gemstone that glistened with shades of gold and purple. Muriel stepped up beside Vortak as he pulled a coffee table closer to him and placed the gemstone on top. All ten children gazed at the stone in wonder.

Muriel leaned in close to whisper so only Vortak could hear her. "This is a child's party. If you want to get paid…" Vortak cut her sentence short…

"Paralyse," Vortak said, and waved his hand in front of Muriel's face. She collapsed to the floor, stiff as a board and unable to move. Vortak turned his attention back to his mesmerised audience.

"This is the shard of suggestion," Vortak said. "You will hear my words and remember them, for they are important to you." The children continued to stare at the shard of suggestion. Muriel continued to lie paralysed on the carpet by Vortak's feet.

Vortak returned to his holdall bag as he spoke, rummaging through it, looking for something, "You will take these purple sashes and… Oh crap! I've forgotten the bloody sashes." Vortak stopped looking and thought for a moment.

"The next time you get the opportunity to do some craft activities with friends or your parents, you will make a purple sash. Then you shall put it in a safe place and await the trigger words." The children remained under Vortak's spell, staring at the shard of suggestion. "You will hear them on the radio, or on the television. Or someone might read them in the newspaper. And you will hear my name, 'Vortak'. And you will hear of magic and death. When you hear these three words together, you will don your purple sashes, arm yourselves and rise up. You will come to me. Seek me out, and kill anyone who gets in your way. Joining with other purple sashes along the way. Minions of Vortak, do you understand?"

"Yes, Vortak. We understand." the children spoke in unison and without emotion.

"Now repeat the trigger words back to me," Vortak commanded.

"Vortak! Magic! Death!" the children spoke the words loud and clear.

"Good," said Vortak in an upbeat manner, and picked up the shard of suggestion. "Now then. None of you will remember this spell. Including you, Mum. You will all think I was an excellent wizard and tell your friends they want to hire me. And you're back!" Vortak clicked his fingers and everyone became themselves once again. Including Muriel.

"Took a bit of a tumble there, Mrs Barker." Vortak helped Muriel to her feet. "That will be one hundred pounds please." Vortak held out his hand. The children burst into applause and whooped cheers of appreciation.

Muriel smiled. "Let me get my handbag."

Six years later

Vortak stood in the lantern light of his kitchen, leaning over the worktop and colouring in the top of his thermometer chart. Four thousand minions, ready and waiting to be activated.

"It is time! Time to venture forth and make myself known. Time to strike!" Vortak bellowed a sinister laugh… "Muahahahahaha!" There was a knock at his door.

Graham waited, with lamb hotpot in hand and a smile on his face, as Vortak opened his door. "Lamb hotpot," Graham said cheerfully.

"Really Graham? It's been six years. You don't need to keep doing this." Vortak studied the Pyrex dish and inhaled the aroma. It looked and smelt good.

"Just making sure you get a hot meal once in a while. And not one from a microwave," Graham said. "You look happy today, Vortak. Something good to report?"

Vortak smiled. "Yes. This afternoon I achieved an important goal. A task which has taken six years to complete." He thought for a second and then nodded a confirmation of his decision. "In fact, I can think of nobody better to be my first."

"Ooh," said Graham, excited. His dazzling white smile widened.

Vortak waved his hand in front of Graham's face. "It is time for you to get your purple sash, Graham. Vortak! Magic! Death!"

Graham's smile dropped, but he didn't move. Both men stared at each other. Vortak frowned, unsure how Graham was unaffected by the spell.

"It's true. You are the one," Graham whispered.

Realising the potential threat facing him, Vortak quickly waved a hand before Graham, and began uttering magic incantations, but was stopped as Graham threw the contents of the Pyrex dish into Vortak's face. Vortak screamed!

Graham dropped the dish as Vortak wiped lamb hotpot from his eyes.

"Aargh! It burns!" Vortak cried.

The door to number twenty, opposite, opened and old Mrs Crabtree appeared in the doorway. The nosy neighbour listened to many a corridor conversation behind her closed door, but this one needed to be seen.

"The Shadow! Archmage Hemlock said you would come." Graham quickly moved aside as Vortak cast a spell.

"Disintegrate!" Vortak bellowed, and waved his hand at Graham. Due to his blurred vision, Vortak missed his target. A pile of ash fell onto the welcome mat where Mrs Crabtree had been standing.

Graham lunged forward and slammed the palm of his hand against Vortak's chest. "Death!" Graham yelled, and Vortak fell. Lifeless. Killed by a powerful counter-spell. The wizards' duel was over in a matter of seconds.

Graham pulled out his mobile phone and quickly made a call. "Put me through to the Sussex Wizards and Warlocks Guild. Archmage Hemlock." Graham picked up his Pyrex dish as he listened. He rubbed his fingerprints from it, and threw it down beside Vortak's body. "Then give him a vital message. Extremely important. Tell him Master Mage Graham Goldcrest has confirmed his suspicions, and The Shadow is no more."

Graham ended the call, closed Vortak's and Mrs Crabtree's doors, and headed back to his flat.

***

Graham cracked an egg and added it to the bowl of flour, sugar and raisins. He picked up a spoon and started mixing the contents. His attention was drawn away from his recipe as he heard something of interest from his television in the next room. He left the kitchen, stirring the bowl of ingredients as he walked into his living room. Graham always had the news on, and Robert and Jill were sat side by side as always keeping him up to date with recent events. Young, attractive, fashionable… a great double act who timed their alternate lines to perfection.

Robert's piece had caught Graham's ear. "And in local news, the people of Sussex were shocked at the sudden death of much-loved wizard, Vortak The Incredible, who died on Thursday. He suffered a heart attack whilst at his flat in Brighton. His magic will be greatly missed." Robert paused and looked at Jill. It was her turn, yet she stared ahead blankly.

Somewhat thrown by the unexpected mistake, Robert continued where Jill should have taken over, "The funeral will be held tomorrow at Saint Bartholomew's…" Robert was distracted by Jill, who had put her handbag on the news desk and was removing a long piece of purple cloth from within.

Robert gave an uncomfortable laugh and looked off camera for help.

Standing up, Jill placed the purple sash over her shoulder and reached into her handbag again.

"Is everything okay, Jill?" Robert asked, and looked back at the camera with a smile intended to reassure the viewers. Without emotion, Jill pulled a can of mace spray from her handbag, turned to Robert, and sprayed him in the eyes. Robert screamed!

As Robert coughed, cried out in pain, and tried to rub his eyes clean, Jill produced an extendable police baton from her handbag, swiped down to fully extend it, and hit Robert across the back of the head with a great deal of force. Robert slumped over the news desk… Unconscious.

Graham's jaw dropped in shock as he watched Jill casually walk off screen and the television channel blip to darkness as it went off air.

Stunned, Graham's attention remained fixed upon the blank TV screen. Moments later, he snapped out of it; a screeching car from a nearby street pulled him back into the here and now. A distinct smashing sound followed the screech.

There was a scream from somewhere in the building, followed by a car alarm and what sounded like a gunshot from outside. Graham hurried over to his window and looked down at the streets below. A dozen youths wearing purple sashes were smashing a police car with bricks and bats. In the distance, a tall building's windows shattered and flames licked through. A flash of light followed by an explosion echoing from miles away, quickly followed by the droning whir of a police helicopter as it flew overhead. Horrified, Graham stared from his window. Stared at the escalating chaos. The beginnings of Vortak's uprising was underway and moving fast.

"Son of a witch," Graham whispered.

Aiden Furey - Conor McCloskey is Not Dead

When they lowered you into the ground, I knew that you weren't dead. We'd played that game a thousand times. This one time, you played it so well, they took you to the hospital for three whole days. My dad told me that you had just fallen asleep. But, if you ask me, I think you're being mean. Your mum cried like a banshee the whole summer long. Everyone kept asking me if I was okay and I just looked at them like they were crazy. I knew you just playing around. After they put that box in the ground I yelled, 'Conor McCloskey, you quit this messing, no one finds it funny anymore!' But you always were a stubborn one.

In August, Mum and Dad brought me on my first ever holiday. They said that it would be good to get away from everything. We went to a place called Dunquin and you would have loved it. There was a great big pier for jumping off or fishing from. I didn't feel like swimming though, I was so worried about Mum. She looked nervous, like she was carrying the weight of the world upon her shoulders and it was about to fall off. So, I kept close to her. I even took to sleeping in her bed. They kept on asking me if I was having fun and I kept on telling them that I was. But maybe I was and maybe I wasn't. I wish you could've come too.

By the time I went back to school, I'd gotten pretty mad at you. At first, I thought it was a mean trick to play on your mum, but I began to think that it was a mean trick to play on me too. And everyone kept acting strange around me, sometimes all quiet when they stumbled across me in the hall and sometimes all friendly when they never used to be. And they'd always be blabbering about how much I must miss you and asking if I was okay. I took to eating lunch by myself, just to get away from them. Miss Mullen said that it wouldn't do any good to spend so much time by myself. Maybe she was right, but I couldn't stand all the yelling and laughing that went on at that school. It was too much.

I don't know why, but I got to thinking about my old dog Buddy a lot. You remember Buddy, don't you? When I went anywhere, he would sit at the window and watch me go, like he was sad not to be coming too. And when I returned, he'd jump up and down like a kangaroo on a trampoline and he'd run in great big circles around me, his eyes nearly popping out of his head and his ears pointing toward his tail. Then, one morning I woke up and he wasn't there anymore. Mum said that he would turn up somewhere, but he never did. Dad told me that he'd probably went to a farm, somewhere up the country. He said that's just what dogs do, one day they just move on – it happened to every dog he ever had. Maybe that's what boys do too. Maybe that's what you did.

I still go over to your house nearly every day. I sit on the swing in your back garden. Your mum used to come out and say "Hi" and sometimes she'd bring me a coke and a slice of that red cake that you like, but she must be busy because I haven't seen her in a while. So, I just sit and rock back and forward and I look at your bedroom window and I know… I know that when you're ready, you'll open those curtains and yell out at me. I'm mad at you though, but I know you'll have me laughing about it soon enough. I could never stay mad at you for long.

Last week, I asked Miss Mullen if she knew any nice places that were up the country and had good fishing and she looked at me funny and then handed me a map book. I studied it carefully and I found a place called Fish Quay in Sligo. If I know you, that will be the sort of place that caught your eye. It doesn't look that far away, maybe an afternoon's walk, and I think that is where you might be.

I wait until Mum has gone grocery shopping and Dad is asleep in his chair. I empty my backpack and then fill it with two peanut butter sandwiches, a bag of Tayto and a Diet Coke. I tell Dad that I am going to Macy's and he opens one eye and grunts something. Then I step out of the house, excited at the thought of seeing you again.

I walk to the end of the street, nodding and smiling at everyone that I meet. I walk to the end of the town, giddy at the thought of the adventure that is to come. And then I realise that I have no idea of where Fish Quay is. I sit down by the side of the road, feeling like I've failed before I even started and wishing that I'd brought that stupid map book.

'Does your mum know you're out here?'

I turn around and see a man standing behind me. He does not look at me but instead glances up and down the empty street. He is as old as Dad. His clothes are unwashed, as is his hair, and his face is covered by a clumpy beard. He takes a step toward me and I become aware of his smell, like a damp dog.

'I won't hurt you,' he says.

'I'm not supposed to talk to strangers.'

'I know your mum and dad.'

'How you know my mum and dad?'

He scratches his beard and looks up and down the street again.

'We went to school together. Long-time ago.'

'What's their names then?'

He sighs and then is quiet for a moment.

'What you doing out here all by yourself?' he asks.

'I am looking for my friend Conor McCloskey. I think he is in a place called Fish Quay in Sligo.'

'And this Conor boy, why do you think he's there?'

I can feel my cheeks flush and I look down at my feet. My eyes begin to mist over, and I bite the inside of my cheek hard to make them stop. You taught me that.

'Now, now,' he says. 'No need for the tears. I'm sure I can get you to where you need to be.'

'You know how to get there?' I say, and I look up at him excitedly.

'I guess you take the N4 out of town,' he replies.

His thumb points to the left and I immediately get up and begin to walk. He follows, a few steps behind me. I hear his heavy boots scrape along the pavement and his breath, like a groan, each time he moves.

'You sure this is the way?' I ask.

'Just a little more,' he grunts.

He doesn't say anything else for a while, but I can almost hear him thinking.

'You don't sound too sure that he's up in Fish Quay.'

I think about the map and I begin to wish that I had studied it longer. Maybe I would have found someplace else where you might have gone – maybe Fish and Coca-Cola Quay or Fish and Cake Quay.

'He'll be there,' I say.

The sun looks like it is melting into the long road ahead and I wonder if I will get to you before it settles down for the night.

'Anyone know you're out here?' asks the man.

'Lots,' I say.

I think about Mum. She will be making the dinner soon. I can picture her asking Dad to shout for me. When I do not come, she'll begin to worry and start cursing at Dad and then calling at the neighbours and then… I don't know. I hope she doesn't cry, but I know she will, and I start to feel bad.

The footsteps behind me stop and I look back to see the man scratch at his chin. My eyes move down over his dirt-smeared clothing and arrive at his boots which separate at the sole and the leather, making them look like the open mouth of a thirsty horse.

'What if you make it all the way up there and this Conor boy isn't there?'

I have to try. I can't think of where else you'd be.

'Are you gonna show me the way or not?' I ask.

'I suppose,' he replies.

We come to a junction where our little town road meets a dual carriageway full of traffic that zips by faster as a dog licks a dish. A sign points right to Collooney and left to Boyle.

'Which way?' I ask.

I turn around and get the feeling that he is examining me.

'We cut through here,' he says, and for the first time, he walks ahead, taking us down a narrow, overgrown path that runs parallel to the carriageway. Bushes flank us left and right and the man bends down to get through. We push on, the bushes get thicker and thicker and the noise from the road gets quieter and quieter. I look back, and the path behind has disappeared, overrun by the trees and bushes. I look forward and it looks the same. The raggedy man has disappeared too, but I can hear him grunt and breathe heavily somewhere through the bushes ahead. I look back once more and decide that the only thing that I can do is follow his sound. I push ahead slowly, becoming aware of each branch and leaf as they touch my arms and face. Finally, I push through the bushes and into a wide opening. The man is waiting for me, still as a statue, his old eyes staring at me.

I know this place.

'What you bring me here for?' I ask.

He remains quiet.

'What you bring me here for, Mister?' I repeat.

Still, he does not speak. All he does is stare at me with those big old empty eyes. Then, he turns his body slightly to the side, inviting me to enter the place. Inviting me into the cemetery.

'He's not in there,' I say.

He no longer looks at me. His head drops to his chest.

'That's the whole point, Mister.' I say.

...

'Why'd you bring me here?'

...

'You stupid?'

...

'It doesn't make any sense.'

...

'Fine,' I say, and I shake my head and begin to walk. I leave the silly man and his wild goose chase. I know that if I walk through the cemetery that I will come out at the other side of town and I could be home by bedtime.

The cemetery is quiet, and my angry feet kick up tiny stones that scatter before me along the crisscrossing pathway. Above me, yellow leaves fall, spinning slowly downwards until they silently touch the ground. It is very quiet. Death is quiet. Row after row of quiet. Death is broken stone and rusting metal, weeds and collapsed earth, faded letters and faded numbers.

I begin to slow. I do not know why, but my legs guide me left and right and then right again. I am tired. I am dead tired.

A few metres from your grave, I stop, my feet locked by the ground beneath me. And I stand there, unable to take the final truthful step.

The stone is black, the writing gold. I stare at your name, Conor McCloskey. Under your name, there are two dates with a dash in between and there is something about that dash that makes me mad.

Twelve years is not a life.

Do you remember how we met? How you pushed in front of me in the lunch line? You remember how I put manners on you that day? But if you hadn't, maybe we would never have met. It's strange… don't you think… the moments? And then your mum knowing my mum and we just seemed to fit, like peas in a pod.

You can't be in there. It only seems like yesterday that we were laughing together. You had the widest smile. It was as if you had four extra teeth in your mouth. And you always pulled those silly faces, sticking out your tongue and turning in your eyes. And your mum always told you that the wind would change, and you'd be stuck with one of those faces. I smile just at the thought of it.

Your life was not a dash.

And you were always there for me. When Niall Kelly wanted to kill me because I stood on his brand-new Hot Wheels Criss-Cross track, you fixed him. And when I fell and hurt my ankle in the field over by Mr William's place, you piggybacked me all the way home. You always seemed to be what I needed, when I needed it.

A breeze blows and I take a single step closer to the grave. How could you be in there? You don't feel dead, not to me. It doesn't make any sense. How can a person be here one day and then not? How can a twelve-year-old boy just not be here anymore? How?

And I just keep staring at that dash and thinking that it should be longer or bigger. Your life was not a dash!

The sun begins to sink low behind me, and I take a seat right by your headstone and I crank my face to feel the last warmth of it. I don't know how long I sit there, but it feels nice. It feels peaceful. It feels like it is where I am supposed to be. Then, just before the light dies, I get myself up. I place my hand on the cold stone tablet and I know that when I take it off… that will be that. You will be gone. I hold on, my hand getting cold as the sun dips below the horizon. But the sky does not go dark; light hangs in the sky, long after the sun has gone. It flashes brilliant red and orange. My hand slips from the gravestone and I stare at the sky for a few seconds longer and I smile.

When I get to the exit, Mum and Dad are there. The old trampy man is standing a little behind them. When Mum sees me, she lets out a yelp and runs to me. My feet lock to the earth like they have been nailed there and I feel too tired to go on. I begin to cry and cry. I can not stop. I do not think that I will ever stop.

Benny Allen - Maya Woke Up Late for The End of The World

You know the feeling. You wake up with sunlight peeking from the blind and you wonder if you're late for work. Keep snoozing and you end up missing your dentist appointment. Your manicure session. The world spinning half an hour too long and you there, with a drooling mess edging on your pillow.

Sometimes you count up. Sometimes you only need to count down.

Twelve minutes.

I woke up with a banging coming from upstairs and someone knocking at my door.

At the door, a motorbike helmet. A blue suit hanging loose, choked up in a yellow tie. Eyes hidden behind a matt black shield reflecting my face. He could be a burglar. A mannequin. The helmet says, "Did I wake you up?"

Water's running in the hall from the flats upstairs. People rushed away leaving their front doors open and running taps overflowing sinks. Unflushed toilets and TVs left on with nothing to watch anymore.

The last broadcast said whatever God people believe in, he probably won't do his magic this time. An asteroid as big as the moon would hit soon. They said do your prayers and forget about your unpaid bills. Then millions of black and white dots were flickering on the screen and a countdown appeared.

Eleven minutes.

A man's screaming outside. He says the end is near and he's available for sex. At my door, the helmet ducks his neck and the shield reflects my blue pedicure with my toes sunk in the carpet. My legs look distorted and ginormous. Back to my face, the helmet says, "This is for protection." He taps his knuckles on the shell and says, "From the blast."

Inside the helmet is Ivor. He usually wanders around with yellow crocs and white socks tingling inside. Like a patient without a hospital. The suit and the tie he's wearing now, he's trying to make an effort for the big ending. Blowing up in fashion.

Ten minutes.

Ivor shuffles his feet in my kitchen and his head slams against the cupboard. He lands both hands on his helmet and says, "How could you still be asleep?"

When the asteroid hits, that island of plastic we tossed in the Atlantic Ocean will no longer matter. The recycling we do to save the planet. Green bin. Blue bin. Brown bin. It'd all be wasted.

To Ivor, I say, how could you not sleep?

All those vegan diets you've been on for years, they will all have been for nothing. All those cows farting methane. They will win.

Then Ivor's sitting at the table, the helmet still on. He lifts the shield and wipes his face with four fingers. His cheeks are covered in stripes of cream. Rugby-player style. Motivational make-up. He says, "The sunscreen is for protection from the radiation."

Tell everyone the end is near and all those folks will show you their real selves.

Gina pictured herself dying with pleasure. Just before everything's reduced to a mushroom of smoke. The bang, bang, banging from upstairs, that's her sex party still going on. She asked if I was interested.

The last thing you want to do is to be hit by an asteroid with an STD. A thousand years from now aliens with seven toes and three eyes, they'll find what's left of your body and question your contraception approach. They'll point at your gonorrhoea. Those crabs you caught. Syphilis. Chlamydia. Or worst, you could die pregnant.

No thanks.

Nine minutes.

Outside, a circle of people holding hands. They're praying. They say, "This is our last day on earth." They shout, "You must be born again. Salvation is for everyone."

Ivor drums his fingers on the table and says, "In case I survive and you don't"—he leans forward and my face on the shield turns watermelon big—"I won't hold your hand while you're all dead and covered in blood. So you know."

The point of the impact shouldn't be far from here. Teenagers and families drove all the way there. Pitching a tent and getting stoned. Waiting to get killed with the impact.

This is like a war movie. Only this is for real and there's just one single bullet the size of a planet. Grandad always said that the secret to surviving in the trenches was to think of yourself already dead. He said, "The fear of dying kills you way before you get shot."

Outside, cars are left on the street with engines still on, stacked up in an endless queue. There are no ambulances anymore. Get a heart attack, a stroke, and you're ahead of the game.

Think of yourself as already dead, my grandad said, and you become fearless.

He was at the front long enough for Grandma to give birth and stop breastfeeding. Then one day at the front they were playing cards, just to kill time before someone killed them. And one of his friends shot him in one hand. It was an accident. Paul Carnie was a good laugh but terrible at holding a rifle. Grandad had to eat soup with a spoon between his thumb and pinky until he died. Paul Carnie felt so guilty that he paid off his remorse letting me stay in one of his apartments for free. This flat I live in, I pay my rent in morning teas with his wife. Widowed Mrs Carnie pops in every day with a new reincarnation of her husband. Poor Paul's been a teapot. A chandelier. A pillow.

Mrs Carnie living with the dead and waiting for her turn to pass away.

Seven minutes.

All the shop windows outside turned into broken spiderwebs, leaving a carpet of glass for everyone to parade on. All those grocery stores, hairdressers and vaping shops. No one will need them any more.

Ivor asks if there's anything I regret. And he says it rocking on the chair so much he's giving me seasickness.

Then there's the jiggling of a thousand cats' necklaces in front of my door. The ding-dinging is Mrs Carnie shuffling her feet in slow motion with a giant bunch of keys dangling on her hip. The jiggling stops and a voice yells, "Maya. Open up, I've no hands."

What Mrs Carnie is holding is a plant. This is what her husband turned into, today. Her face peering between the leaves, Mrs Carnie takes a big sniff and says, "It's an acacia." She says it's like her Paul, only it snores less and smells better.

One of the several upsides of reincarnation.

Outside a security alarm is squealing, deafening everyone. Winking flashes of red inside my kitchen. A herd of zebras is galloping between cars. A family of elephants is stepping on trash and plastic bags. Someone opened the cages at the zoo.

The giant acacia spurts yellow buds all over the floor and Mrs Carnie glances at the helmet with Ivor inside and says, "Are you dating a rapist or just a delivery guy?"

Outside the window the world is getting ready to die and Ivor sneezes. His head snaps forward and he says, "What plant is that again?"

The clouds and the sky get darker. A shadow casting on everyone's cirrhoses and bone cancer. A queue of penguins is waddling away, direction nowhere. Monkeys are ripping off car wing mirrors and climbing on lamp posts.

Five minutes.

Mrs Carnie says that this will be everyone's fresh start. And she keeps caressing the reincarnation of her husband, brushing it against her lips and says, "No more pain to suffer. Isn't it, Paul?"

Ivor lifts his shield and he must be having an allergic reaction because his face is all sweaty and swollen. With his lips turning purple, he says, "Is she talking to the plant?"

I tell Ivor that the acacia is Mrs Carnie's dead husband. Ivor sneezes again, drops his chair back down and his helmet slams on the table.

And Mrs Carnie says, "I found him dead. Surrounded by porn magazines. God bless his soul." Ivor clears his throat inside the helmet and Mrs Carnie says, "Now you can find all that sort of thing on the internet."

Four minutes.

Then it's night in broad daylight. The solar eclipse you don't expect. Once the asteroid enters the atmosphere it will catch fire like a giant burnt marshmallow.

Mrs Carnie says, "Some people are dead longtime before they die."

And Ivor says, "Has anyone talked to any explosion survivors?" He says, "Is it painful? Like waxing or something?"

I tell Mrs Carnie that she'll finally meet Paul again. And a monkey jumps in from the window. Ivor springs up from his chair and yells, "Get out of here."

With her face inside the acacia, Mrs Carnie says, "Paul was hiding." She says that after he came back from the front he couldn't sleep. She says, "He had one of those things doctors call with long words ending with 'phobia' no one can ever pronounce."

The monkey jumps on Ivor's lap, arms around his helmet. And Ivor holds her baby-style and says, "Look, she thinks I'm her mama."

On the street, a man's shouting to save all women and children. And a woman tells him to go to hell. Mrs Carnie says, "Paul liked this building for the hidden room downstairs." Her eyes on me while Ivor's playing with the monkey forgetting about our death. Mrs Carnie says, "Not even rats could sneak in there. He felt safe."

Three minutes.

I say, he was hiding porn magazines in a basement?

Mrs Carnie shrugs. She pinches a leaf with two fingers and says, "He called it his cave."

And Ivor opens his shield. All eyes rooted with blood and steaming sweat, he says, "Do you mean a bunker?"

Mr Carnie the batman. Sinking with his iceberg of feeling back from the war. Hiding away from everyone.

Then Ivor stands up. The monkey still hugging his neck and from inside the helmet, he says, "What are we waiting for?"

I say, what?

And Ivor says, "A *bunker*. I really don't want to die."

Mrs Carnie says, "Oh sweetheart. The end comes when it comes. It's alright."

The monkey on his neck, Ivor grabs the plant and presses it on my chest and says, "You take this."

Two minutes.

And we're all walking down the stairs. All the way to the basement. Mrs Carnie in front. I'm holding the plant and Ivor keeps sneezing holding the monkey.

The corridor's stairs flooded. All those doors left ajar. The open museum our next lives. Our Chernobyl for the next generations of tourists to visit.

Mrs Carnie's limping all her way down the stairs, holding the handrail with one hand. Ivor says, "I don't want to be rude, but could you walk a bit faster?"

I'm only wondering if there's a toilet in the bunker.

Mrs Carnie stops. She turns her head back at us and says, "What, love?"

One minute.

The monkey jumps on Ivor's shoulders, clutching his helmet, screaming in fear. There are voices of people coming from everywhere. They say, sixty. Fifty-nine.

This is the New Year's Eve of the end of our lives. The beginning of our death. No more bad movies or TV presenters to complain about.

We reach a giant metal door at the bottom of the stairs and Mrs Carnie grabs her bunch of keys and says, "Now." Checking the keys one at a time, she says, "Which one is the right one?"

And Ivor says, "Oh God."

Outside people are counting. Forty-eight. Forty-seven.

The bunker in front of us. Our Noah's ark. Our ship of salvation.

The monkey sneaks inside Ivor's suit, jerking his yellow tie.

Mrs Carnie looking through her million keys.

The atrocity of war, my grandpa said, the problem is always for those who survive.

Outside the crowd is singing. Shouting.

Twenty-one. Twenty.

There's a roaring. Like a plane taking off. The asteroid entering the atmosphere.

You can hear people sobbing. Crying for the moments they never lived, washing all their regrets away.

Mrs Carnie says, "Maybe it's the blue one."

Ivor says, "Seriously?" And he's jumping on his toes, the way you wait for your turn at the bathroom.

Sixteen. Fifteen.

Someone's whining. Shrilling. A scream echoing in the flight of stairs.

Thirteen. Twelve.

I smell the acacia on my hand. The smell of Paul Carnie.

You can dodge death only a handful of times.

Eleven. Ten. Nine.

Grandad said that the problem with memories is that you never remember them the way they are.

The crowd outside shouts, eight. Seven.

Six.

Your sad memories become nightmares you can't get out of your head.

A kid is crying somewhere. On the street. Behind a wall.

Five.

Grandad said that what's worse than dying is dying alone.

Ivor says, "C'mon."

Mrs Carnie grabs a key and sticks it in the door lock.

Four.

Grandad said that when death sits next to you, only wish you have a window seat to look outside.

Mrs Carnie says, "Maybe this is the one."

Three. Tw—

Beth Roberts - Her Last Temptation

It was the Great Exhibition of 1851. I was famished. Excruciatingly so. Every part of my body felt plagued with atrophy, riddled with decay. The years had finally begun to catch up with me.

Of course I did not need to attend such an event. I could frequent balls or soirees, but I have always struggled to keep my lips tightly sealed. An event in which I would be allowed to express an opinion, despite being of the supposed fairer sex, was always welcome. Besides, the monarchy would be there. What self-respecting socialite would miss such an opportunity to win favor?

In the days leading up to the event, I had wandered the cobbled streets of London town and flitted from one dingy streetlamp to another in an attempt to find something to satiate my hunger. The pursuit of temporary fulfillment tired me; so much effort for a small instance of relief. It fatigued me to simply raise my hand and flick away the desirous, stray hand of a thieving child. It must be said that to wear four layers of fabric is to be most constricted and I do not miss the caged fashion of Victoria's reign.

A prostitute would last the week. Maybe a few days for a beggar. I needed something more substantial. Life as a bottom-feeder was exhausting. I could no longer even bring myself to abduct a newborn babe. My anger had waned. I no longer needed to punish the world. I simply needed to survive.

The relative health of human beings determines how many encounters they will survive. Those who smell the sweetest are the best targets – that is the best indicator of health, the scent of a person's aura. They are always more difficult to acquire, that is a certainty. There are fewer of the sweeter smelling in general society and Victoria's reign met me with an infestation of various pungent scents. But I had been doing this for millennia and the chase, the danger, the hunt still managed to thrill me.

The glass observatory, the Crystal Palace as they called it, was rife with the hustle and bustle of well-dressed couples flitting from exhibit to exhibit like the butterflies of Eden, on a journey across a path of flowers. I do not think I have ever seen so many waistcoats and bodices – one must look the part to be accepted in society. It was like being a child in a sweet shop where every sweet treat was wrapped in twelve pieces of paper foil. I was spoiled for choice. I went through the motions. The woman in the red corseted dress was a definite no. If she eventually disappeared too many people would notice. Indeed, I also made sure to avoid the inventors, too much like celebrities.

My methodical approach was interrupted by a rich scent and I sought out the perpetrator across the room. I was quite shocked, for she was quite ordinary – no older than twenty-two, I would have thought. Petite. Everything about her was so unremarkable that it became quite remarkable; brown eyes, brown hair, black dress, black hat, a symbol of the times. Except for the scent. She smelled like my favourite Babylonian dessert wine, the type so overwhelmingly saccharine that the sugary residue remains on your teeth for hours to come. I had not smelt the sweet scent in such an unspeakably long time. I was intoxicated.

I slalomed around the exhibits and over to her. I stood just behind her, she was fixated with the Colt Navy prototype. Samuel Colt himself fiddled with the firearm, unloaded of course, to exhibit the intricate chambers and facets that made up its body. I took a step forward.

"Quite beautiful for machine of death, is it not?" I asked, soft enough that only she would hear. She jumped. I wondered if she was startled by my sarcasm or the mere fact someone had addressed her. Her cheeks flushed a vibrant red.

"Oh, yes, well. Of course," she said. It endeared me that she struggled so much for an answer.

"Lily De Montserrat." I held out my hand.

"Annie Williams." She shook mine. Her hand was soft like a newborn's, untouched.

"Enjoying the exhibition?"

"Oh it's rather splendid, isn't it? It is rare that I have the chance to attend something so… so new," she said. She seemed to have somewhat forgotten her surroundings in a flurry of enthusiasm and gesticulated rather wildly. A man I assumed to be her husband approached and wrapped his arm around her waist; immediately she stiffened. The smile on her face evaporated.

"Well, if you would ever like to discuss these silly newfangled experiments as ladies do, you are most welcome to visit me," I said. I had raised the pitch of my voice slightly and played into his hands. Silly women, discussing things their silly brains cannot fathom. I ripped a page out of my journal and jotted down my address. She took it with a gentle nod of the head.

"Thank you," she said.

"We have to go, Annie," her husband said. He placed a protective arm around her waist. He smelt like cabbage. Not quite rotting, not quite fresh either. A perfect pair.

Annie smiled and bowed her head to me before she was led off. I hoped she would take up my offer.

A week after the exhibition, Annie began to visit me often, once or twice a week in the early evening. Sometimes she stayed the night. She blossomed before me like a delicately watered rose in bloom. With each visit, I taught her about worlds she had not previously been privy to: philosophy, literature, art. A real intellect began to thrive. She was eager, hungry to know more. It was the least I could do, everything to come considered.

I took my time before initiating anything sexual, but I was growing impatient. I was starving and her aura called to me. All I desired was to have a taste. I knew where one small taste would lead and yet I was desperate for her innocent life force. She was pure in a way I had never quite seen before. Purity in character and emotion, not the base sexual purity your Bible would have you believe.

A few months after our first meeting in the Crystal Palace, Annie sat in my parlor and read Jane Austen's *Emma* whilst I wrote in my journal.

"I find it amusing that Emma believes that she can force love upon two people," she said. She put down the book and looked at me with furrowed eyebrows.

"And why is that?" I enjoyed her small queries. They were so utterly human, so innocent and bursting with folly.

"Is love not natural?"

"How do you define love?" I quirked an eyebrow at her. She pursed her lips together and looked to the sky as if looking for divine intervention.

"That is just it. You do not define love, my dear Lily. You experience it." A sweet smile spread across her face, the type a grandmother would wear whilst providing cookies to a grandchild, warm, comforting. She genuinely believed her claim, it seemed. I found it both endearing and pathetic.

"I will humor you, Annie. Then how would one know they have experienced love?" I asked. Annie stood up, walked over to me and perched on the sofa next to me. She reached over and placed her palm on the outside of my hand, which rested upon my lap.

"A surge of magic, shooting through your body," she said. "Do you understand now?" He eyes were wide and pleaded for me to understand. She urged for my agreement, the way a child begs for reward.

I raised my hand and cupped her face. My thumb caressed her cheek as softly as a whisper rides the wind. Her eyes closed. Her lips parted slightly and when my lips touched hers I knew that she was mine. She let out the breath she had been holding and I gladly collected it, for it is important to cherish life's smallest markers.

A faint blush remained upon her cheeks when I pulled away. Her eyes flickered open and her gaze immediately met mine. I stood up and strode to the door. With a turn of my head and a raise of my eyebrow, I beckoned her to follow me. Of course she did.

I took a small sip from a cup of English breakfast tea, whilst Annie lay in bed after our first intimate encounter. I did not particularly appreciate how the English had bastardized tea and I greatly missed the leaves of the Shang dynasty. What a shame it had been to let it go.

I felt energized. I had desperately needed this encounter; my hair had started to thin and now it was as luscious as it had been the first days I spent in the Garden. I knew I was physically stronger too. Perhaps as strong as I had been during the Battle of Mazikert, the strongest I had been in centuries. Annie must have been an incredibly healthy source. I heard the rustling of bed covers and chuckled.

"Are you still tired, dear?" I asked. I took another sip of the foreign tea and raised my eyebrow. She groaned slightly.

"I am exhausted, Lily," she said. Her voice was quiet but content. Of course she was exhausted – the Babylonian wine had faded slightly. I am ever so glad that I obtain my strength through sexual intimacy since it is so innocuous. Everyone is exhausted after sex.

I enjoyed the first few weeks. I finally began to feel strong again, revitalized. Her life force flowed through my body and replenished me. The atrophy went away. I almost felt human once more. I had not felt human since I spurned Adam and chose this path. This small, insignificant woman had given me more than the fabled first man. And she seemed happy. And for the first time I was content that someone else seemed happy.

A month passed. With each encounter, she became weaker and her aura faded. I missed the saccharine wine. And yet she had lasted longer than any human I had taken before. I was suitably impressed. And equally perturbed. I did not take pleasure in watching her fall in the same way so many others had before her. She deserved better. Yes, she was a daughter of Eve, but I could make an exception in this case. I did not understand how she had captivated me so. Perhaps it was my age. Perhaps I was growing softer.

Her face gradually became thinner, hollow, as if she were preparing herself for death. Her eyes had sunk deeper into their sockets and the bones were now visible under her skin. It was the grey pallor upon her skin that affected me the most. The vibrant blush I had grown accustomed to, that I had noticed immediately, had disappeared. Gone without a trace. I had taken every essence that made her human to better myself.

And yet she seemed content. I sat in my bed and gazed down at her sleeping features, a subtle smile spread across her face. Even with her newly slim face, her dimples sat in her cheeks like little valleys. The left side of my mouth quirked up into a half smile. It faded as soon as it appeared. I knew I had two choices and I did not know which was kinder.

I was startled one morning by a knock on my door. I was not expecting Annie so early and I wondered if something terrible may have happened. I rushed to the door and swung it open. And there he was. George Williams. Face as dower as ever. Holding himself with all the pomp and circumstance associated with traditional manhood. The stench of cabbage filled the air.

"Mr. Williams, how can I be of assistance?" I tried to keep the sarcasm out of my tone of voice. He narrowed his eyes. After a small period of silence, he pushed past me and strode into my house. For propriety's sake, I could not react indignantly. He took a seat in my living room without invitation.

"I think you could begin by elaborating on my wife's current condition." The pitch of his voice was low and I noted the serious expression in his eyes. George may not have been the most caring of husbands but he had every reason to question me.

"I do not understand why you think I would know more than you about your wife's condition, Mr. Williams," I said. I kept my voice steady. His fist clenched slightly and then released.

"It has come to my attention that, since Annie has made your acquaintance, her physical health has been suffering greatly." His voice grew slightly louder.

"What exactly are you accusing me of?" George stood up from his seat and strode over to me. He lifted his finger and pointed it in my face.

"I think you're poisoning her," he said. I stared at him in disbelief and he took that as an indication to continue. "I don't know what your game is or what you are getting out of this but I want you to stay away from my wife." He dropped his hand and leant in near my ear. "I will not hesitate to use any connection I have to run you out of London town."

With his threats uttered, George Williams straightened his black coat and black hat and, with the neutrality of an undertaker, left the room. I stood where I was and heard the door slam in the distance.

When you speak of the Devil, he is sure to appear, and when you think of a lover, their attention will turn to you. Annie's eyes fluttered open and her smile grew, her slightly crooked teeth appeared in her open grin.

"Did I fall asleep, my love?" she asked.

"As you usually do." I looked away and took a deep breath. "It is nearing six, you should be getting home, Annie."

She did not say anything for some time. At last I felt a weight leave its place on the mattress. I walked her to the door once she had readied herself, as I usually did. Nothing different. Nothing suspect. She stopped in front of door and turned to me.

"Until next time," she said.

"Next time." After a gentle press of my lips to hers she was gone.

I had made my decision. There would be no next time. I would never see her again. I knew that in my heart. I did not need Annie to survive and survival was truly my only goal. She could live. I honestly did not know if she would be able to get better because I had never allowed anyone I had fed from to live. But I had to hope. The good parts of humanity had to survive.

I wandered the streets of Paris a couple of years after my desertion. My life had taken on a cyclical nature; dying, dying, dying, healthy, a period of the sublime, dying, dying. The monotony was exhausting. I considered flitting from city to city, to only target the rich. Less effort, less faces appearing to me in my dreams.

I turned the corner and saw a homeless man sat against the wall. He didn't have a leg. Water damage, mold. That is what he smelt like. My stomach churned. I didn't want it. But I needed it. I gulped.

I was about to engage when the aroma of something else breached my senses. Dessert wine. Sweet Babylonian dessert wine. The scent was as mesmerizing as I remembered it. Perhaps she had once again grown stronger. Perhaps there was an opportunity for me to see her once more.

I walked back into the main courtyard outside of Le Pavillon De La Reine. I had been there before, courting a courtesan of the French court. Fitting.

There was a performance of some sort. A circus act? A street play? I do not remember anymore. I was fixated on the crowd gathered around the performers. I could still smell the wine. She had to be here.

I weaved through the crowd with my usual precision and scanned each face with scrutiny. With each passing individual I grew more frantic. Was I hallucinating? I wondered if I was just so incredibly starved that my mind was paying tricks. I turned around sharply.

And there was Annie. She had not improved since I had said goodbye. Skin still pallid, eyes still sunken. I was reminded of why I had left. And yet the smile returned, bright as ever, the moment her eyes met mine.

"I knew it was you," she smiled. "I do not know how, but I could feel you."

I swallowed. Tears filled my. I should have stayed away. I tried to stay away.

"I should leave you," I said. I turned in preparation to make my escape.

"Lily, I forgive you," she said. I halted. "I am not angry you left. I am just so happy to see you again, my dear." I bowed my head in defeat and squeezed my eyes shut. "George is not here, if that is what you are wondering? He sent me away for a retreat. You see, he does not think I am well." She looked down at her feet before meeting my eyes once more. "He thought that if I were away from you, I would get better. I had not the heart to tell him you had already left."

She would never be well. I had taken that opportunity, that certainty from her. I could not speak. There was nothing I could say to make Annie better. I turned away with the honest intention to leave. She grabbed my wrist with her delicate hands, skin as soft as a baby's.

"Stay, Lily."

Carrie O'Leary - The Book

I wouldn't normally expect a knock on my door at four o'clock on a Sunday afternoon, and planned to ignore it. When the knock came again, I had a feeling that something wasn't right. My anxiety grew when I was confronted by two policemen on my doorstep.

"Are you Miss Elaine Cassidy, the daughter of Mrs Margaret Cassidy?"

At my nod they asked to come in. I led them to the lounge, inviting them to sit, but they just stood, looking awkwardly at one other.

"Miss Cassidy, I'm Sergeant Jameson, my colleague here is Constable Blake. You might like to sit down."

A burst of adrenalin surged through me. I flexed my fingers as the tips tingled. My heart quickened and my breath caught; the familiar flight or fight response. I never dealt well with confrontation.

"Miss Cassidy, I'm sorry to have to inform you, your mother was involved in an accident this afternoon."

Tears pricked the corners of my eyes and my throat constricted, choking away my words. Was she okay?

"I'm so sorry Miss Cassidy, this was a very serious accident. Your mother, was pronounced dead at the scene."

The tears flowed. My tense fingers clutched my chest as I felt my world collapse.

"I know that this will be extremely difficult for you, but we do need you to come and formally identify the deceased. Is there anyone we can call to be with you?"

I shook my head. My thoughts ran in wild, incoherent circles around my head. I should never have opened the door; if I'd ignored it, Mum would still be alive. But, in my heart, I knew that she was gone.

Mum's funeral was a quiet affair, with mourners in the single figures. She'd had a small group of friends; I had no one and stood alone, no family, no friends, tears pouring down my face. Life as I'd known it was gone.

I cleared out Mum's flat quickly, she had so little that I wanted to keep. All I brought home with me was a small box of personal possessions, which I placed on a side table and forgot about for several weeks.

My sleep pattern had always been a bit haphazard, so I wasn't surprised to wake in the early hours one morning. It was a few weeks since Mum died, but I woke with a sense of urgency, sure that someone was either watching me, or watching over me.

The streetlight shone through a crack in the curtains, giving a good enough illumination to show that there was no one in the room with me.

"Mum," I whispered, "Mum, is that you?"

I felt a sudden urge to retrieve the box. Was Mum trying to tell me something? Pushing back my duvet, I grabbed my cardigan from the chair by my bed, pulled it on and headed for the stairs.

Taking up the box I took it into the lounge and curled up in my favourite chair. Darkness surrounded me as I sat for a while with the box on my knee. Could I bear to open it? Yes. I had to. I took a deep breath. It was time.

I switched on the table lamp, lighting my little corner of the lounge and flipped open the lid. The box was full of knick-knacks; the crystal guardian angel that mum hung in her lounge window, the evening sunshine casting prismatic rainbows across the walls and ceiling which danced with the breeze. The remains of a faded, pressed-flower bookmark I'd made at school. I hadn't realised she'd kept the pieces. Shells and pebbles we'd collected on the beach. My first tooth and a curl of my hair. Others may have thought it rubbish, but to her they were treasures. It made me miss her more. I set her jewellery box to one side. Too many memories there.

Tears glazed my vision as I pulled out a couple of framed photographs of the two of us together. I stroked her lovely face through the glass; this was how I wanted to remember her, not how she'd looked after the accident.

There were some less significant items, but then my fingers brushed across the soft, leather binding of a book and I knew, instantly, that this is what had been calling out to me. I pulled it out, caressing the cover. I inhaled the scent of the leather, opened it and flipped through the pages. All but the first page were empty. I scooted over in my chair so I could read the words more easily by the dim light of the lamp.

Jenny's Journal

I'll always be here when you need me the most

And that was it. So many conflicted emotions; confusion, hope, uncertainty. I hadn't thought about Jenny for years. But this had to be a coincidence. Jenny had been my imaginary friend as a child. My only friend when I was a child, truth be told. The very last time I'd 'spoken' to Jenny, before I'd let her go, those were the very words that she'd said to me. The day I'd said goodbye to Jenny was the last time I'd felt complete. And now, here were her final words to me in this book. It seemed quite impossible.

I rubbed my head, aware for the first time of the dull ache that refused to leave me alone.

When the headaches became worse, I ignored them. Reaching for the paracetamol, I hoped they'd settle. When the headaches were accompanied by flashing lights and tinnitus, I wrote them off as migraines, added ibuprofen to my drug cocktail and went to lie down in a dark room. But it never truly went away. Over the weeks, I just got used to the pain being my constant companion, subsequently ignoring it all.

I started forgetting things and missing deadlines, but put it down to the stress of Mum's death. I treated the nausea and loss of appetite with the same dismissal. It wasn't until I started missing chunks of time that I began to feel anxious. I was still in denial until I collapsed whilst out shopping. I knew the time had come to visit my doctor.

The night before my appointment, I was woken again by a whisper in the air. "Laini, I'm here if you need me now." I sat bolt upright in my bed, heart skipping a beat. No-one ever called me Laini. No-one but Jenny. I dived out of bed and down the stairs. I opened the book with trembling fingers, heart stuttering as I looked at the page.

Today my favourite person in the whole world noticed me for the very first time. I call her Laini and she calls me Jenny. Laini is very lonely because all the other kids are mean to her. They don't know her like I do because I'm half her and she's half me. But now she's seen me and we are going to have so much fun together. Laini's mum looked surprised when she said she had a new friend called Jenny. She shouldn't have though. She knew about me before Laini did.

How? How could a friend who had been in my imagination write in this book? Half of her, half of me? The cryptic message tickled something at the back of my mind. I'd been about five, maybe even six when I first met, or concocted Jenny out of my child's mind. I had been so lonely. The other children at school found me strange, I was on the outside looking in and was too shy to do anything about it. Until I found Jenny. She accepted me for who I was. But this writing was making her look real, and my brain just couldn't work out how it was possible. I was so tired, far too tired to think and spent the rest of the night curled up in my chair.

My visit to the doctor did not go as expected. *Some pills for the stress and depression, perhaps something stronger for the headaches?* I thought. Not this very solemn expression as he said that he wanted to admit me to hospital… immediately. His comforting pat on the shoulder as I left the surgery told me he didn't anticipate good news.

I walked home feeling completely disconnected from everything around me. In a complete daze I packed what I felt were essentials, including the little leather-bound book.

I was admitted. I answered questions. I lost count of the number of times I had to repeat my name and date of birth. They gave me stronger pain killers that made me feel woozy and I was scheduled for an MRI the following morning.

I didn't sleep. Other patients snored, grunted and cried out. Nurses whispered as they clumped up and down the ward attending to patients. Sighing, I switched on the bed lamp, wondering… hoping Jenny might have added to her journal, and was relieved to see another couple of entries.

Do you remember, Laini, when we made hobby horses from some of your Mum's old socks. We stuffed their heads using a whole packet of kitchen roll, and mounted them on bamboo canes from the shed. We sewed buttons on for eyes, used an old belt for reins and then galloped and jumped them round the garden in our own gymkhana, sure that the stuck up girls from school never had so much fun on their real ponies. Your mum never did figure out what happened to her kitchen roll, she thought she forgot to buy it, and we didn't dare tell her.

Oh, and the old spinsters next door, the Misses Fraser and Finley. They were a right odd pair of old ducks. Frumpy Fraser and Finicky Finley. Those apples just looked far too good to resist, so we squeezed through the fence to help ourselves. The two of them came flying down their garden, shaking their broomsticks at us, because we'd trampled their prize begonias.

The MRI scan was another completely new experience. They secured my head in a brace to ensure minimal movement. As the table moved, panic overwhelmed me, my heart racing. "Jenny, I need you," I whispered, trying hard to hold back the tears.

"I'm here, Laini."

And she was. A comforting pressure squeezed my hand and it remained there as the radiographer's voice called through the earphones to say she was starting the procedure. Feeling reassured, I almost fell asleep to the hypnotic knocking and burring.

Later, back on the ward, I opened the journal once more and wasn't surprised to find more from Jenny.

One of the very best days was when we found Scraps. Do you remember our puppy? We called him Scraps because all we could find to feed him on were the leftovers from your dinner. We hid him in the garden shed for two weeks before your mum found out. She was so cross. It was when old Finicky Finley died. Your mum gave him to Frumpy Fraser to keep her company. When she died, your mum took him home for company.

The doctor came to see me later that afternoon. The expression on his face looked tired and wary telling me that the news wasn't good.

"I'm sorry to tell you Elaine, and I'm not going to beat about the bush. You have a particularly aggressive tumour in your brain."

My body tingled with apprehension, but the feeling of Jenny's hands supporting my shoulders steadied me. "Go on," I said.

"I could try to operate, but the tumour is so convoluted that it's unlikely I can remove it all. Of course, we could follow this up with radiotherapy or chemotherapy, which could give you a little bit longer, a year at most. There is, though, a relatively high risk of some damage being caused by the surgery. This could be as slight as a little weakness to, well, something far more severe..."

"And, if I don't have treatment?"

"I'd say, you have no more than two months."

It wasn't a hard decision. Tired of this life, of being alone and feeling incomplete, I felt more relieved than anything. When it came down to it, I didn't want to be prodded and poked for the sake of a possible extra few months of life. No-one needed me or relied on me. No family or friends; I barely even existed. It would be easier to just let go and allow things proceed as they would.

So, I went home. The hospital wasn't happy with my decision as I had no-one at home to look after me, but once we'd arranged with an agency for me to have twenty-four hour nursing care and that my doctor could visit regularly, they allowed me to go.

I got my affairs in order. And then it was just a waiting game. There was constant, nagging pain, nausea and dizziness, all dulled only slightly by the medicines. My four rotational nurses were incredibly kind and attentive. And then there was Jenny. I always felt her comforting presence, and throughout that time I read many more tales of what we considered our derring-do. It reminded me of how I'd felt then. Cherished. Loved. Complete. I knew I was reaching the end of our adventures together when I read this one:

I remember the day I saw your heart break for the first time. We climbed the tree to watch your new neighbour, Jonathon, who had just started in your class at school. You thought he might be your friend, but then Britney the walking Barbie walked into his garden and claimed him, turning him against you, the same as the rest of the school.

But it was the next entry that had me sobbing into my pillow.

Today Laini said goodbye to me. I knew it was coming, and I know it's not her fault. She believes me to be an imaginary friend who she should have grown out of by now. But I'll always be here because I know that one day she's going to need me again. I do so love you, Laini.

I completely lost track of time, it wasn't important anymore. One morning, I was helped downstairs and into my favourite chair with a promise of tea and toast 'in a jiffy'. I tiredly pulled the book to me and was astonished to see a new entry for the first time in several days.

My darling sister, today will be the day that you let loose from this mortal coil. We will finally be together like we were always meant to be.

I know you have never felt that you quite belonged in this world; you have always felt that half of your soul was missing. I've always been here, waiting for you, Laini. Mischance took my life in our mother's womb, but spared yours. The truth is that you should have died too, so our shared soul could remain complete. You shouldn't have been pushed out into this cruel world. No-one but I could ever truly understand you, love you; not the way I would have done if I could have lived my life. I should have been your older twin, but it wasn't to be; we were torn asunder. It won't be long now, dearest Laini. When you are ready, just close your eyes and I'll be waiting for you.

I felt no fear. Gently closing the pages, I placed the book on my knee, my fingers caressing the cover.

So, now I knew the truth of it. I was supposed to be, had always been, a twin. Jenny was my sister, not the imaginary friend who I thought had been writing in my book. All those adventures with her, when I was a child, had really been with the ghost of a sister I'd never known I had, but with whom I shared a soul. Why had Mum never told me?

It was no wonder Jenny had always seemed so real; she was the missing part of me. Pulling the book closer, I cradled it close to my heart, remembering all of those adventures we'd shared, just as though she'd really been with me. There was also a feeling of vindication; those girls at school should never have tormented me for my belief in my imaginary friend, my sister.

I closed my eyes for a moment and, when I opened them again, she was there. I saw my Jenny for the very first time and she truly was the image of me. The same, wayward, brown hair that frizzed slightly round her face; her green eyes met my own and her face lit with a radiant smile as she held out her hand. My own smile was a little tremulous. I reached for her, my fingers straight, expecting my hand to pass through hers, as though it was moving through mist. But her hand was firm and warm as our fingers linked. I suddenly felt great joy in my heart as she gripped my hand more tightly, pulling me up from my chair.

Laughing together, immediately comfortable in one another's company, we left the room, and then the house, to go on our next grand adventure… together.

Epilogue

Nurse Garoway looked around the house to make sure everything was neat and tidy before leaving and locking up. She'd brought back the breakfast for Elaine, only to find that she had already gone, just drifted off and died peacefully, and much more gently than they'd expected. She picked up the book that seemed to give her patient so much comfort over the last few weeks, hoping to read some of the words that had given her solace. She opened the cover and flipped through the pages.

Every single page was blank.

Christopher Kerr - All In The Mind

It was the little touches he was so good at. He had the knack of knowing intuitively how she was feeling and what she wanted to do. If she felt like going for a walk, he would suggest it before she did; he could sense when she wanted a coffee, when she had had a row at work and often even with whom; he knew instinctively – and this was why she loved him – when she didn't feel like making love but simply wanted to lie beside him; and when she had to leave to go home to her husband.

It had taken her some time to work it out. As their affair continued – developed would be to give it too much weight - they had evolved, as lovers do, a gentle telepathy for what the other was thinking. They loved each other and each was still selflessly concerned for the other's welfare. As they became more familiar it became easier to guess the other's fears and desires and, before long, she began to realise that he was better at it than she. He seemed to have a greater sensitivity to her moods and anxieties. It was almost as if he had the key-book to her personal code; she realized guiltily that she felt that there was something slightly unnatural about his ability to read her. It was more than intuition.

One day, while they were sitting companionably having a drink in a pub, he answered a question she hadn't asked. She had been thinking, as she often did, about their relationship, worried about the fact that they worked together. Perhaps it would be better – and safer – if she left and got another job.

"I think that would be a bad idea" he said.

"What?" she asked.

"It would probably arouse more suspicion than if you stay. People would be bound to wonder."

"What?"

"If you left the job now."

"How did you know I was thinking about that?"

He hesitated. "You were very quiet. And I know it's a worry for you."

"Mm."

So could he really read her actual thoughts? She began to study his manner, especially his responses to her. When he poured her another coffee was it from simple human courtesy or did he really know she wanted more? When he smiled and nodded at her across the pub table was it a simple declaration of affection, or encouragement to say what he knew was in her mind? It was unsettling: she was happy with the love and support, less happy with the thought that he might be permanently inside her head.

She was afflicted by the realisation that to challenge him directly was out of the question; she could not let him know that she was suspicious. There were thoughts she wanted to keep private. And when it came down to it she simply didn't want to know that she was right to suspect him. If he really did have this ability, he was clearly aware of it and, since he had never mentioned it to her, she could only assume that it was because he didn't want her to know. Why? To spare her the sense of exposure, the loss of privacy and individuality? Or the sheer power it gave him? Whichever, she could not let him know she knew or let him suspect she suspected. She realised that even thinking about it could alert him and she set her mind to the challenge of controlling her thoughts when he was around; could she, she wondered, develop a poker mind, that neutralised her thoughts and gave nothing away? It was like a heightened form of meditation where the mind has constantly to be brought back from its wanderings to a single object or idea. Only, for her, the exercise was to divert her thoughts away from anything she wished to keep private, to build a mental quarantine around them or to put them in a coded form that only she could understand.

She began to experiment. She sent him test thoughts to see if he would respond. Simple at first, along the lines of 'I feel like a walk' or 'how about the pictures this afternoon?'. He usually did. Then they became more complicated, about politics or shopping, and he mostly didn't. She wondered whether his ability was limited by range; how far away, for instance, did she have to be? Could he only read her if they were in the same room? From her careful trials it appeared that they had to be together. When she was in bed with her husband she once or twice sent her lover a taunting message 'guess where I am now?'. When he didn't mention it she refined it; lying with him in his flat one afternoon she flashed him a vivid image of herself and her husband but there was no reaction. She wondered, as it were, aloud whether she should break off their affair. As before, there was no reaction. It proved nothing of course. He might not be getting the messages or he might know precisely what she was up to and, too smart to rise to her bait, be blocking them or simply choosing not to respond. There was no way for her to tell.

They talked one afternoon about their regrets. She said how sorry she was that she hadn't listened more to her mother, asked more questions and discovered the truth behind those half-told stories. He agreed. "But regrets are what life is made of. You didn't ask because you weren't interested then. That was how life was, how you were then. The question is do we learn from our regrets? No, because by the time they're regrets it's too late. The dead are dead, there's no talking to them now. Regret is what gives life its poignancy."

And all the time she was thinking that what she really regretted was their old familiarity based on affection and instinct. For one partner to be able accurately to read the other's mind was a kind of cheat. It devalued the shared link.

She wondered if he could read other people's thoughts. Colleagues at their work place would surely have noticed something, but even to ask a casual question about him could lead people to wonder why she wanted to know and perhaps to guess at their relationship.

She tried to confuse him by leaving random thoughts about, like Post-it notes then, later, she began to send him false thoughts, deliberately outlandish inventions, to see if he would react. But this progression in the relationship brought its own problems. Before, when she first acknowledged to herself that he could in fact read her thoughts, she had known that he would know that she knew. There had been the feeling of connection, sensed more than felt, like clicking on a web-page with her mouse. She had been more or less happy for him to know what she was thinking if it brought them together. And she was content to feel that he knew that she knew; unspoken, mysterious, extra-sensory, it was a magic bond between them.

After a time he seemed to retaliate to her smokescreen by no longer responding to her. He ignored everything she thought, not responding even to the smallest things like the refill of coffee. But this too was confusing; was he trying to hurt her by cutting her off? Or trying to reassure her by seeming not to be able to read her any more?

Now there was nothing, no sense of connection, no contact. He was a blank wall. She could not tell whether he knew that she had cracked his secret.

It occurred to her that perhaps it was not so much a matter of her lover's perceptiveness but of her own openness. Perhaps others could read her thoughts as he did. She practiced on her friends, teasing them with thought messages. When, unaware of her experiment, they showed no sign of receiving them she made the messages easier and easier, closing her eyes and groaning as she willed them to ask if she had a headache. Obtuse or uninterested, they volunteered nothing.

What made it more painful was having no one with whom she could discuss it. With him, unavoidably, it had to remain unspoken. She could not talk about it to friends since her liaison was supposed to be secret. And she knew that if she mentioned it to the few who were in the know they would ask her what she had to hide? She should be so lucky to have such an attentive lover. And there was always the chance that somehow it would drift back to him on the breeze.

She found it increasingly hard to behave normally with him. It was like being watched all the time only more intrusive. There was no hiding, no possibility of switching off her thoughts; she felt that even the most trivial harmless whispers were exposed to his scrutiny. For all she knew he could read her dreams too. It was like having an incubus in her memory. She was torn between her need for him and the urge to protect herself. If she started to see him less often he would want to know why; did she not love him any more? She asked herself the same question, no longer so convinced of the answer.

She tried to read his mind back; after all telepathy was meant to be a two-way thing. It didn't work.

She suppressed her natural chattiness, reducing their talk from relaxed conversations to the essential trivialities. "Damn you" she thought. "If you know what I'm thinking why should I bother to say it?" When he asked if she was happy, she replied with a smile. He, anxious to be conciliatory, matched her reserve with his own. But this was still unfair, she thought, since she had no way of knowing what he was thinking or wanting. He had always been easy-going, placid even and silence did not oppress him.

They met, they smiled, they sat together, they ate and drank, they went to bed, they dozed, they parted. If she did not want to talk, it seemed, that was fine with him. Yet, of all people he was the one she most wanted to talk to: about everything, but especially about this indefinable link between them. Exercising her poker mind was exhausting and she longed to relax with him as before, open her mind and be herself again. Was the abandonment of her privacy too high a price to pay for a return to the reassuring comfort of their love for each other? She considered. They sat together one afternoon in the sunshine of his sitting room. "I do love you" she thought, almost without thinking. He turned to her, smiling. "And I love you." She sighed and put her hand to his cheek. "I give up" she thought. "You win."

He smiled at her. "I know" he said.

And she knew, as she watched him smile, that it was a price she would not pay.

David Bell - The Dark Suit

Rupert Pringle did not find it easy to make up his mind. He had his definite likes and dislikes that never caused him any trouble in deciding: if lasagne was on the menu, he always ordered it. If a sauce had tarragon, he rejected it. But when it came to desserts he agonised over choosing between crumble and lemon sorbet. He had more than once thought of changing his name. Rupert sounded a bit weak, he thought and the two 'P' sounds coming close together somewhat stuttery. In the end, he did nothing about it.

Worst of all was when it came to buying clothes. His wife Celia had tried to help at first but had finally become exasperated by his dithering (her word for it) and now left him to keep on wearing the old blue thorn proof tweed jacket she'd bought for him. The cuffs were frayed and the pockets sagged but she'd given up saying anything. She did look, however, and sigh. Perhaps it was that sigh, because he was fond of her and didn't want her to think too badly of him, that finally made him decide. He would go out and buy a suit. This time, he really would.

He knew exactly where to go: Styles in Canal Row. Styles sold second-hand clothes and there was nothing wrong with that because only the very best in quality and condition, all cleaned and freshly pressed were on offer. Styles was no charity shop: no jeans or bomber jackets or trainers, oh no. Styles' suits and hacking jackets and Crombies came from country houses and aloof Victorian villas in the exclusive part of the city, most likely after the funerals; true but never mind about that.

In Styles he didn't feel uncomfortable as he did in other clothes shops. The two middle-aged women who ran the place didn't ask could they be of any help, or what it was you were looking for. They left you alone to look, feel, turn over the price tag and browse (dither, Celia would have sighed). They just said goodbye when he left, yet again without having bought anything. This time he was going to surprise them.

He had seen the suit on his last visit but one and it was still there when he had dropped in for another look two days later. It was a dark navy pinstripe, with a waistcoat and two pairs of trousers. Two pairs of trousers meant it was bespoke. It was exactly his size: 42 chest, 36 waist, 30 inside leg. That's what the pinned-on label said. But the tailor's label inside was the clincher. Silver copperplate stitching read Hunter and Son Savile Row, London W1: *Savile Row* and only £175. Rupert reached for the coat hanger and then hesitated. Although it looked pretty well new, it must have been worn and hung up in a wardrobe. Perhaps he should see if there were any moth-holes.

"There was another gentleman looking at it this morning, tried the jacket on, he did. Said he might be back later."

"Oh, well, I think, yes now, would you mind taking a cheque?"

"Yes, sir, seeing as it's you it'll be all right, if you put your address on the back. Shall I wrap it up for you?"

Clutching his bulky parcel outside the shop, Rupert felt a bit sick. He hadn't tried it on and he hadn't looked for moth holes. Still, *alea iacta est,* the die is cast; he knew a Latin tag or two. And if he found anything wrong with it when he got home, he could always take it back and stop the cheque. He turned round to head back to Styles and then pulled himself together: no, the die was cast.

He opened the front door as quietly as he could. Celia was in the garden so he was able to carry his parcel upstairs without her seeing. They had agreed to have separate bedrooms several years ago. It had been her idea but he hadn't seen any point in making a fuss. He laid the suit out on his bed. He knew very little about cloths but this one felt smooth and rich and not too heavy. He thought it might be worsted and the linings with their dark sheen, silk. As if he had done this sort of thing every day of his life, he took a white shirt with double cuffs and a dark blue tie with thin silver diagonal stripes from his wardrobe, fished his gold cufflinks from his drawer and dressed himself in his new, to him, finery. Black shoes, of course: in the rack, a bit dusty but soon brushed clean. He stood before the wardrobe looking glass and inspected himself, long and critically. His hair needed brushing. That done, he looked again: not bad at all. He felt a surge of self-confidence and stepped gravely downstairs to show Celia that he had at last kept a promise.

Celia was wearing her green gardening apron and holding a pair of secateurs as she studied a rampant montana clematis.

"Need any help?" he said to attract her attention.

"No, I think," she said turning to him. "Hm."

"What is it?"

"There's something different about you."

"It's the suit, my new suit."

"Yes, but no, there's something else. It's as if, no, I'm being silly."

"Go on, tell me what you mean."

"It's as if I recognised you but for a moment I didn't know who you were."

"Does that mean you don't like it?"

She came up close, took off one of her gloves and stroked his lapel, running her hand slowly down the front of his jacket as she looked up at him.

"Oh yes," she said. "I like it. Like I said, there's something different about you."

Oddly enough, he wasn't surprised by what she said. Something had happened.

He wasn't quite sure what or why.

"I'm going upstairs, she said. "Don't be long."

At breakfast the following morning Celia looked up from the newspaper and said,

"Don't forget: you have two appointments today."

"God, must have slipped my mind. "Who, where?"

"They're in the diary. No not there," she said as Rupert got up to go into the conservatory, "on the hall table."

'Doctor 11 am, accountant 2.30 pm', he read. "I'll have lunch in town; a sandwich somewhere."

He decided on his maroon tie with the suit this time and came downstairs to wave goodbye to Celia who was already at work in the garden. Unlike her usual slight wiggle of the fingers goodbye, she stood up, gave him the wide-eyed open lips smile he hadn't seen in years until yesterday and blew him a kiss. He bowed to her and put his hand on his heart.

In the doctor's waiting room Rupert became impatient. It was now twenty minutes past his appointment time. He got up from his seat and walked over to the window, skirting a small child who sat on the floor chewing at a yellow plastic duck. The view outside offended him: roofs spattered with bird droppings and dirty neglected windows. He heard the door to the consulting room open and turned to see a patient being ushered out. The door closed again before he could reach it. He sat down, trying to suppress his impatience: bad for the blood pressure.

Five minutes passed before the door opened again and the doctor spotted him and beckoned him in.

"Rupert, sorry you've had to wait. Had to make a couple of 'phone calls."

"Was one to the New Theatre and the other booking a table for lunch at the Saraceno? Joke. I've been waiting out there for half an hour watching a dribbling infant gorging a plastic duck. I've got a very busy day ahead of me, Andrew."

The doctor looked rather taken aback.

"Right, OK, sorry; better get on with it then. Jacket off, roll up your sleeve; quiet for a minute. Hm. Again. Hm. That's fine. Put your jacket back on."

"What does 'fine' mean?"

"It means fine, normal… for a man of your age."

"I meant what was the reading? I should like to know."

"One forty five over ninety, both readings."

"Isn't that a bit high?"

"Nothing to worry about. The pills are working."

"Well, I was going to ask you about that. Isn't it time I had a review?"

"Not for another month." The doctor looked at his computer screen and tapped at the keyboard. "I've had your blood test results."

"And?"

"Fine; nothing to worry about."

"You keep saying that. May I actually see my results?"

"Of course. Let me swing the screen round. There."

Rupert examined the graphs carefully as the doctor identified each one: cholesterol, sugar, blood pressure, potassium. They all showed pretty straight lines and low values. Except for one.

"Potassium's gone down. I've been feeling a bit tired recently."

"Not all that much. Still, I can prescribe a supplement if you like. It tastes bloody horrible. Anything else to tell me?"

"No thank you, Andrew."

"Rupert, do you mind my asking, is that a new suit?"

"Not all that new: haven't worn it much."

"I thought there was something different. Looks, well, very smart. Make another appointment at Reception for a blood sample: for the potassium. Just to check it, you know."

"Thank you, Andrew. I hope I'm not too late for my appointment now."

He was shown to his table in the new roof restaurant that had such a fine view over the city. The Italian waiter produced a thick leather bound folder with a flourish and laid it on the table before him. Rupert ordered a Manhattan, specifying Grant's whisky and no cherry and waited until his drink arrived before opening the menu. The waiter hovered while Rupert took his time, deciding finally on crusted rack of lamb with pesto and a little mashed potato with almond tiramisu to follow and a double espresso brought at the same time. No wine, only mineral water, yes, San Pellegrino.

He sat back and sipped the cocktail. Hm, a little too much vermouth, not quite enough bitters. Let it pass this time. He glanced round the room. A woman sitting alone near the window was looking back at him. She briefly raised two fingers of her left hand that was resting on the table. He got up and walked across.

"Have we met?"

"I'm sure I would have remembered."

"Can I give you lunch?"

"Let me think."

Still looking her in the eye, Rupert put up his hand beckoning to the waiter who hurried across.

"A menu for the lady and bring my lunch here."

"Si, Signore. La lista dei vini?"

"Cherto che si."

"I haven't said I will have lunch with you, yet."

"That means you will. The lamb is usually good."

"I'll take the salade niçoise, artichoke hearts, no fish," she said to the waiter.

Rupert scanned the wine list. "Tavel should suit that, do you think?"

"And Badoit: I don't normally drink before nightfall."

Rupert cleared his plate. The lamb was good today. The woman hardly touched her salad, a small artichoke heart, part of an egg and a leaf or two of the lettuce. She said yes to coffee.

"Care for a walk along the towpath?" said Rupert, sipping his espresso. "It's a fine afternoon."

"If you like. My flat is on the other side. There's the bridge. I must… see you at the door."

Rupert knew what she meant. He needed to go too. He looked only at the total on the bill and paid by card. "Order me a taxi," he said as he tapped out his PIN.

Subdued lighting, a faint scent of manly perfume: in the craftily tinted mirror the suit looked just right. He took off his jacket to wash his hands. Mustn't get splashes on the cuffs. This was going well. Smiling to himself he looked up at the mirror. Oh God, what was he doing here? Picking up strange women, er woman. What if Celia got to know? What if there was somebody in the restaurant who recognised him. Blast, he hadn't checked. Could he nip out before she, that woman, came out of the loo? Jacket, quick, quick. No, stop, haven't dried hands. Right, now: nip out quick. Oh, jacket. Right, quick look in the mirror: now, then, madam.

"Well, there you are again," she said. "And here was I thinking you'd run away."

"Not a chance. Come on. I've ordered a cab."

Her flat was in one of the old warehouses on the canal that had been given a lavish renovation and conversion a few years ago: very chic now and very expensive, even for this city.

"Penthouse," she said, pointing to the button on the lift. "There's a lovely view over the river. Should be able to see the Downs on a day like this."

Rupert looked round. Yes, she's right, a very nice flat. Just the sort of place for a…

She was wearing a dark green silk—Celia had one, so he knew the word—peignoir. And high-heeled shoes. And her hair was down.

"You're looking very formal. Are you waiting to be asked? Take your jacket off."

He knew how to treat women like her. Make 'em wait. Make 'em guess.

"Tell you what: let's play a little game," she said. "I take something off, then you do. Then I take off another and you, well, get the idea?"

"Deal: get on with it."

She made a slow wriggling movement and something white and frilly settled round her shoes.

"Your turn. Not shoes. Tie."

"OK, now hurry up."

"Turn round."

She didn't seem to know what he knew: that there was a mirror in which he could see her. The peignoir parted just enough for him to see one very shapely leg appear and a sheer stocking be rolled down followed by the other and then she stepped back into her shoes.

To hell with this. He swung round, pulling off his jacket and unbuttoning his waistcoat.

"Need any help with that belt?"

He rushed towards her and tore at the green silk. Then everything went black.

He had a terrible headache and felt a bit sick. Ooh, massive bump on the back of his head. He was lying on a bed with only his shirt, pants and socks on. His shoes were beside him. In one was a folded sheet of paper. It took a while for him to be able to focus on the writing.

Who do you think you are? There's an old jacket and some trousers in the cupboard. Oh, thanks for the cards and cash as well.

There was no sign of his suit or tie.

"Where's your suit," said Celia. You had it on when you went out."

"I took it back. Didn't quite fit. Bought these in exchange."

"Hm, pity: I quite liked you in it."

"Wasn't me, really."

"You're right. Those suit you better."

"Shall I make the tea?"

"Tell me, where is that place you bought the suit? Do they do women's clothes?"

David Challenger - Samui

Thailand, 2014

The Jet Ski thundered onto the shimmering white sand of Chaweng Beach and came to a halt. A Chinese tourist, iPhone camera-snapping wife in tow, jumped off, only to be replaced by another Mainland Chinese visitor, who roared away towards the horizon over the glassy turquoise waters.

Once more quiet descended, disturbed only by the tiny Gulf of Thailand waves lapping the shoreline, where little ripples smiled and frowned. It was 4pm and while the worst of the day's heat had passed, I was glad for the shade of a large umbrella. And for the 5-star hotel that provided said umbrella, along with the padded deck chair.

This was my third resort on this stretch of Ko Samui coast in as many weeks. What started as a self-dare had turned into a rewarding game. I'd choose high-class digs and pose as a paying guest, lounging around opulent pools or, as on this occasion, using guest-only beach chairs. I especially liked the resorts that delivered me free snacks and cold drinks. Had to be careful when I departed, though; I drove a 20-year-old Mitsubishi Lancer with more rust than metal. Just to be sure, I usually parked it around the corner under a big coconut palm.

Next to me an obese Russian father noisily debated a female beach vendor selling ice-cream, trying, in his guttural English, to knock off a few baht. His walrus-like wife looked on, throwing in the odd taunt. "Make lower, make lower," she'd bark, tusks jabbing. The kids were walrus-like, too. Dark pink and blubbery. The vendor finally caved and shuffled off sadly in her tattered black, long-sleeved Bon Jovi T-shirt, army pants and tape-wound sandals. The family of marine mammals slurped their icy sugar fix and grunted happily, another Stalingrad-like battle won.

Then I saw them, a couple. Still 30 meters or so up the beach, it was the woman who really caught my attention. The way she scuttled along the shore on those short, stumpy legs. In the office, her gait was unmistakable. Usually in three-inch platforms she'd totter about comically, hoping to convince all and sundry she was considerably taller than her five feet. But here, on sand, even sans high-heels, I knew who it was -- the fucker who cost me my job, and ruined my life: Sandra Bromby, my former boss.

***

Until a year ago I'd been a high-flying employee for a large bank in Singapore, but after a decade decided it was time for a change. I loved Southeast Asia, with its pungent scents, rich culture and unbeatable food. But I also appreciated pretty churches and cobblestone squares, so when I saw an ad for what looked like a great job in Prague, I jumped at the chance. Three months later I was living in the Czech capital in a 3rd-storey loft with a view of the Charles Bridge, and drinking the world's best (and likely cheapest) beer. What wasn't there to love?

As it happened, my new job.

Alarm bells rang from day one, with my mostly expat co-workers so self-absorbed they could barely manage a decent introduction. And you had to pay for your own coffee. It was all downhill from there. The office was stuffy and over-heated, the work pointless and dull. My fellow analyst, allegedly in charge of facilitating my smooth transition was a pompous berk from England who, at least in his mind, radiated cool. His name was Andy Great, wore white-framed glasses and often whistled tunelessly. He was persisting with a scruffy, beatnik beard but it looked as if he'd glued on the fluff of a Samoyed pup.

"You know, I don't own a TV," he'd once pronounced from his desk to no one in particular.

"Really?" I feigned, still hoping for a decent working relationship. "There's some pretty good stuff out these days, especially from HBO. Don't think I could live without a decent flat screen."

Stroking his puppy fuzz, his response was a blank stare. Seconds later I heard his fingers tap-tapping fast, and giggling. I looked up to catch a woman grinning at her screen, then she also began typing at speed. Despite his unsavory nature, it seemed Andy had at least one close friend in the office.

Sandra may have been vertically challenged, but what she lacked in height she made up for in arrogance, dullness and spite. Like Andy, she believed she possessed a razor sharp wit and chortled at the end of every perceived quip, her pasty face creased and chalky, uneven teeth exposed. Her fingernails were bitten down to the quick, which belied metaphoric talons used for stabbing underlings in the back.

I'll probably never know why she disliked me so viciously from the outset; it could have simply been good old-fashioned jealousy, having never worked at such a prestigious company as the one I'd left in Singapore. In the end it didn't matter. She was out for blood and knew how to draw it. And despite my renowned skill set, nothing impressed her. By the second month I was convinced she was setting unattainable tasks just to set me up for a fall. I became paranoid, stressed and, worst of all, began doubting myself.

Three months to the day an email from Human Resources dropped into my inbox, headed "Urgent: Scheduled meeting 3pm." Given it was 2:55pm I immediately dashed up to the 4th floor, knocked once and entered the HR manager's office. Already at the table was the head of HR, Jessie Choy, a similarly officious and grim-looking admin staffer I didn't know on her right, and on her left, bug-eyed and smirking uncontrollably, sat Sandra.

The next 10 minutes were brutal, as my "severe shortcomings" as an employee were listed Nuremberg style.

"After heavy consultation with Sandra, we've come to the conclusion this just isn't a good fit," Jessie concluded sternly. "You've continually made errors of judgment, which has resulted in your supervisors spending time correcting said errors. Then there's your attitude, which…"

I could feel my heat rise. "My attitude? Excuse me? What's that supposed to mean," I asked, through gritted teeth. "I've done everything possible to fit into this role, this team, including working unpaid overtime. As for errors, what errors? There are none. What is this, anyway? Why am I here"?

"Why not go back to your old job in Singapore?" Sandra asked, in a smug, patronizing tone. "You were doing well there, right? Might be a good move. This type of financing work isn't for everyone."

"Geez, thanks for your advice, Sandra," I replied. "Here's some for you: why not try and perform your duties as a boss professionally for once, and without stabbing anyone in the back you perceive as a threat. And while you're at it, maybe grow a few inches, you short-assed fuck."

Jessie gasped. Her officious colleague looked close to tears. But Sandra, as usual, smirked, in triumph; I'd fallen into her trap easier than even she could have hoped.

A few more insults were hurled, until I was formally fired and marched directly down to the foyer by two security guards. I wasn't even allowed back to my desk to fetch my "Czech Me Out" coffee mug. The only consolation was that, as it turned out, I hadn't been paranoid after all.

I took a massive hit financially. Not only now unemployed, I had to repay the company all the costs they'd spent relocating me, and forfeited a huge rental deposit. Despite a decade of high salaries, I'd been a spendthrift, had little savings, and only just managed to buy a ticket back to Singapore. Mentally, I was a wreck. I'd never taken rejection well, and was so stunned by my sudden downfall that the idea of a new job was inconceivable. After a month of crashing on friends' couches, I made my way to Ko Samui, took a 12-month lease on a thinly furnished, decrepit, but incredibly cheap bungalow, and began living like the people I secretly used to mock: scrimping and saving and crossing off lists.

***

I'd managed to bury all that horror deep in the back of my mind but it had come surging back like a tide of sewage. As Sandra moved closer, I pulled down my wide-brimmed hat until it was almost touching my sunglasses. I'd met her husband, Don, only once, briefly, at a rare after-work dinner in Prague, but recognized him immediately. He was a senior partner at a huge international law firm that specialized in European tax law, and likely its next president. My heart raced, my hands clenched, but mercifully they walked along the shoreline oblivious, before turning up and heading into the resort. Thoughts buzzed, emotions boiled. I looked out at the horizon to where the southern tip of Vietnam somewhere lay.

That night, in a cane chair drinking a Singha on my porch, I reflected on the day's events. The temperature had finally dropped below 25°C; just as well given I had no air conditioning. Mosquitoes buzzed my face, but I'd long ago become accustomed to their high-pitched singing. A chime indicated a newly arrived text. It was from Mint.

"Come see me," the message read. "Bored!"

Twenty minutes later, I was chatting to one of my few true friends on the island. Mint ran her own beauty and massage salon, called Fresh Mint. Clever. It was a simple place, but the location across the street from Don and Sandra's resort meant she attracted a steady stream of customers, especially in high season. We sat on the sofa outside the glass sliding door, drinking cheap Thai rum and coke. Mint was model material, 24 and stunning, a flawless complexion and taller than the average female Thai. Makeup always perfect, hair long and lustrous, hands and feet faultless from regular manicures and pedicures. And she reputedly had the biggest cock this side of Bangkok.

Living as a girl since the age of 12, Mint was a ladyboy. She moved to Samui at 19, escaping the small-minded attitudes of the Isan town where she was born. After a few years working as a hotel cleaner in the island resorts, she'd managed to save enough money to start her own business and send for her older sister, Goong, who also worked in the shop. To close the circle, I had started dating Goong a few months back.

The beers and rum had relaxed me, and I related the day's events to Mint as she periodically texted Goong, who was on the long bus journey back to Isan for a family visit. Her texting slowed and expression hardened as I related the story in full.

"Sandra sounds like a super bitch," Mint exclaimed. "Very bad woman!"

"You could say that," I laughed, Mint's bitch sounding like beach. "A day doesn't go by that I don't think of what happened in Prague, and the role she played."

Mint sighed and brow furrowed as she looked across the road towards the resort.

"Very bad woman," she repeated under her breath.

***

It was 1pm by the time I got out of bed the following day, the worst part of a Thai rum hangover gone. My cabin was already broiling, but I had no desire to hit the beach and chance an encounter with my ex boss and her corporate ladder-climbing financier husband. In the middle of considering my options, my phone chimed. It was Mint, once again requesting to see me ASAP. Christ, I thought. Not more rum.

She looked pristine and Zen-calm as usual. But her occasional furtive glance between me and her phone signaled something was awry.

"You OK, Fresh Mint?"

"Fine," she replied, "But I need to show you something. A big secret."

"Sorry Mint, I'm dating your sister. You know, the one without a penis."

She gave me her best deadpan look.

"Your old friends come here," she said. "Sandra and Don."

My jovial spirit vanished.

"They stop and chat with me," she continued. "Sandra want to go shopping, but he decide to stay for a massage."

Mint locked the shop door, pulled the curtains closed, and began tapping her iPhone screen. She looked at me once more, briefly, as if making a final decision, then handed me her phone.

"Press play," she said. "I go to take shower."

Like its camera function, the iPhone takes great video. I could tell from the angle that Mint's phone had been set up somewhere to the side, probably on the table below the window. It was a little dark, but certainly clear enough to easily identify Don laying face-down on a massage mat, face turned towards the camera, while Mint straddled his lower back and performed deep-tissue massage to his shoulders. It was then that I realized Mint's face had been digitally blurred, her features unrecognizable.

Fuck me, what the hell is she up to?

I felt flushed despite the air conditioner clunking noisily on full power. Mint occasionally looked towards the camera, every few minutes squirting oil onto Don's back. For his part, Don was snoring softly.

"More oil, Mr. Don?"

When he didn't reply, Mint unzipped her skirt and began masturbating. So the rumours are true, I thought, dumbfounded. Within a minute she shuddered, spurted onto Don's back, zipped up, and continued the massage seamlessly. His snoring continued unabated. The screen went black.

I stared at the phone, hands trembling. A memory of Sandra's despicable smug face from last year's HR meeting materialized. I opened Mint's Whatsapp and sent the video to my mobile. As I left her shop, I made a mental note: In future, only ever ask Mint for a haircut.

***

The next 48 hours was spent at home, analyzing recent events. Mint had taken the footage to help; a bizarre gesture and, given its content, almost certainly illegal. I'd partly convinced myself the video was simply a pointless but endearing exercise in loyalty, best deleted, then forgotten. But deep down I knew it for what it really was: a sheathed weapon.

My phone buzzed. "Don and Sandra leaving tomorrow," Mint's message said. "Don start job as new big boss."

So he was now officially the president at one of the world's biggest law firms, with all the trappings that went with it. I lamented the injustice of it all, grabbed my keys, and headed out.

***

They were sitting at the resort's restaurant, feasting on a dinner of extravagant seafood. Don's shiny bald head reflected candles from nearby tables, but no amount of soft lighting could mask Sandra's pasty complexion. Both were knuckle-deep in a large lobster, pulling at the white fleshy meat with vigor.

I pulled out a chair and sat down opposite without saying a word. Sandra's frenzied chewing slowed as realization dawned. Don looked from me to Sandra, then back to me, uncertain.

"Jesus," Sandra whispered, her usual bug-eyed stare even more pronounced. "You …"

"Hello Sandra, how's the lobster? Looks great, though I wouldn't know. Afraid I'm more of a canned-tuna kind of guy these days."

Silence.

"You guys celebrating something"?

"Don's just been promoted," she replied. "We're celebrating with a private dinner."

"Wow, congratulations Don," I replied with fake smile. "Thoroughly deserved, I'm sure."

He thanked me reluctantly, still uncertain what was happening. He'd obviously forgotten meeting me in Prague.

I quickly made a decision. I wanted out. It'd been a stupid mistake, one that'd take months of self-loathing to dissipate. I prepared to depart and slink back to my sparse room in pride-shattering defeat.

"We heard at the office you couldn't get your old job back in Singapore after you … left," Sandra said. "That must have been tough."

And there it was. Scarcely perceptible, but obvious nonetheless: that fucking smirk.

I waited a beat. Two.

"You know, it sounds grossly unfair in this myopic world of ours, but something tells me that ladyboys, jizz, and newly appointed CEOs just don't mix," I whispered across the table. "Maybe as a porn clip online somewhere, sure, but not in the corporate world of reality."

I pulled my phone out, pressed play, and slid it across.

Don picked it up, holding it so Sandra could also see the screen.

"What the… huh? What the fuck is this?" Don hissed.

Seconds later they gasped in unison: that'd be Mint exposing her python-like cock.

Which was quickly followed by another harmonizcd catch-of-breath: that'd be Mint blowing her load over Don's flabby back.

Both looked at me, stunned, a mix of shock and hatred.

"We need to talk," I said, casually picking up a crusty lobster leg and sucking out the flesh noisily.

***

Six months later

I paid the Bon Jovi-loving beach vendor for my coconut water and added a tip. She was still clothed head to ankles. I'd once asked her why, given the heat. "Don't like suntan," she'd replied.

I surfed my iPad, searching out Don and his firm. By all accounts his new position was going well. He and Sandra no doubt scarcely missed my monthly 10 percent cut from his vast salary. But it made a huge difference to me: I was now in a modern apartment on the water, and Mint and Goong were able to build an extra room onto their shop from the money I'd volunteered. I still occasionally pretended to be a guest at 5-star resorts, though. Some things money just can't buy.

I looked out to sea from under my umbrella, to where the southern tip of Vietnam probably still lay, but my reverie was interrupted by the whistling of a nameless song. On closer inspection, I noticed something vaguely familiar about the whistler's profile. And the haughty swagger. Surely not. But as he walked and warbled past, my suspicions were confirmed: Andy fucking Great.

I grabbed my phone, went to my address book and hit call.

"Fresh Mint … you free tonight"?

Doris Allimadi - The Priest & I

I was 19 at the time. Young, vivacious and perhaps a little wild too. Beautiful. I was a combination of so many things, like a wild berry; strawberries, raspberries, blackberries. It seems so long ago now but the memory of the priest is still so vivid in my mind as though it were yesterday.

My Heavenly sister Barbara, cousin Evelyn and I had gone to a wine bar, 'Slap Harry's'. It was a place we went to frequently. The music and crowd was great, the drinks a little pricey, but it was Central London, so it was to be expected.

On the night in question, we had been standing at the bar, waiting to order our drinks when we noticed a really handsome guy stood there. He was tall, medium build, short hair, hazel eyes. He was with an incredibly beautiful woman. They were drinking, talking and laughing. They looked like such a cute couple, but I also noticed him, noticing me! It is my small, innocent eyes, you see, they are very deceptive. lol. They seemed to have drawn him in. He said something to the woman and she turned to look at me. I smiled, and she smiled back. What a friendly couple I thought, I hoped they hadn't singled me out for a kinky evening, ala menage a trois! He ordered a drink in a tall glass with ice and handed it to me! It was coke. My all time favourite soft drink. How could he have known?

"For me?" I asked, feigning surprise as I took the glass from him. Barbara and Evelyn took his place at the bar and started a conversation with the beautiful woman. Turns out they were cousins. He was visiting and she had brought him out here. We talked for a while, exchanged the usual pleasantries like names, age, are you in school or work, single, did you come here often, you know, that sort of thing. Then we exchanged numbers, landlines. We also arranged to meet at a park the next afternoon.

We each had a small picnic bag. We sat under a tree and talked till the early evening when we said our goodbyes. He kissed me on the cheek.

There had been no mention of his interest in pursuing theology at university or the fact that he was a devout Christian whose ultimate goal was to be a church leader. He wasn't really a priest, but that was what we called him. We had many similar dates. He was incredibly romantic, always held my hands and kissed me often, always on the cheeks with my face in his hands. His hazel eyes were mesmerising. It was not long till I begun to feel nice about him. I am sure he was feeling nice about me too. Our dates were always simple but fun and meaningful. We were both students with not much money, but that was the furthest from our minds. We loved being in each other's company.

Most of our dates had been during the day because, he said "I want to get to know you, talk to you, hear you without any distraction". After a couple of months of breakfasts and picnics in the park, we met up for an evening stroll along the Thames Embankment. It was a mild summer evening, the lights on the bridges beautifully lit up the dark. We sat on a bench and he gave me a single red rose. I remember that a group of 4 middle aged men and women walked past us, and the women looked at me and said, "aaawwww". He made me feel so special. When he later walked me home, he kissed me goodbye on the lips. Oh, ok, it was just a peck!

I hadn't been back to 'Slap Harry's' since I met him, I found myself in an impenetrable bubble of happiness and absentmindedness that I didn't want to do anything but stay home and think about the priest. One evening Barbara and Evelyn were going back there and I am glad they insisted I go with them but to their annoyance I also invited the priest and met him there! I really shouldn't have because this was our evening together, a chance for our usual mischief. I was losing myself.

This time the priest got me brandy and coke and a coke for himself. We danced the night away. I laughed a lot, threw my head back and shook my weave from side to side, being all sexy and seductive. When the music was slow, we danced slow and close with my head on his chest. It felt right. In my head thoughts were running wild. It felt like tonight might just be the night.

Soon it was last call to the bar, last two songs on the dance floor and the crowd begun to file out. Another fun-filled night comes to an end. Barbara and Evelyn had said their goodbyes. We always left before the lights came back on to avoid the queue for cabs or a night bus home.

"What now?" he asked when we got outside. I was a little confused. Didn't he want me? Was I reading too much into nothing?

"Don't you find me attractive?" Oh, my God, I hadn't meant to say it out loud. It was just a thought in my head. But it was too late.

He took my hands and we walked silently for a while, I didn't know where to, but young, in love and lust, I would have followed him anywhere. He took me to McDonalds in Piccadilly Circus, it was always busy with revelers from clubs and wine bars. He had a big mac whilst I had McChicken sandwich.

"Why do you think I don't want you?"

I was so nervous and embarrassed at having to explain my question but I also felt grown up, talking about grown up emotions. I told him why. He laughed. He said partaking in pleasures of the flesh wouldn't prove that he wanted me, it would be just that. He finally told me, among other things, that he was reading theology at university, he was a Christian and didn't believe in pre-marital shenanigans. He was 23.

He stayed with his uncle and cousin when he was not at university. His aunty had long passed away. His parents lived in Zimbabwe. He was an only child.

After our late night junk food, he suggested that if I was uncomfortable taking a taxi by myself, I could stay with him and go home the next day. What he meant was, I could have his bed, whilst he slept elsewhere. He said he had never taken a girl home before! I believed him.

It was very late when we got in so we tiptoed and giggled to his bedroom where he gave me a T.shirt to wear to sleep. I used the bathroom, washed my face, rinsed my mouth and tiptoed back to his bedroom. We changed out of our clothes at the same time, like old friends!

I took my hooped earrings off and put them on his bedside table. I tied my hair up in a messy bun and turned back to face him. Then we just stood there, in the middle of his bedroom, me in his T.shirt and he in pajama trousers. There was undeniable chemistry, you could cut the tension with a butter knife. I could see the longing in his eyes and other parts of him. I longed for him too.

There was something in between us, a powerful force keeping us apart. We just stood there, looking at each other for what seemed like an eternity. Neither one of us knew what to do or say. My bosom heaved and dropped while his heart beat out of his chest. Is this where we say goodnight then toss and turn until daybreak?

In his mind a fierce battle raged on; a battle between my sex and his god, a battle between sin and virtue, a battle between my pert breasts and the Bible on his pillow, a battle between my tearful eyes that bore into his very soul and the door handle. I stood my ground and so did his god.

Finally, he walked towards me, slowly, apologetically, "I am sorry, I have to go", he said, as he approached the door and reached for the handle. I knew he didn't want to go, but he had to go. He pulled the door open and my heart sunk, If he could walk away from me now, stood here in his T.shirt, in the middle of his bedroom, fresh faced and messy bun, then we were a never. It was now or never. I do not believe in witchcraft, mediums or fortune tellers but in my moment of desire and weakness, I summoned my ancestors. The ones who gave me flesh, blood and breath!

"Your child needs you".

As the priest closed the door, lightning suddenly flashed across the sky, followed by the loud, slow rumble of thunder! I screamed and run towards the door. It is true that I am terrified of this act of God, but the timing terrified me even more. It had been a clear day with no hint of precipitation and yet now rain fell hard. The ancestors had answered. The priest was commanded back into his bedroom, into my arms and into his bed.

As we lay, I trembled with so much emotion.

Rain, lightning and thunder disappeared as mysteriously as they had arrived. Their mission accomplished.

Joy to my waist

As we lay side by side

With no distance between us

His hands linger at the meeting of my thighs, then trace every inch of my body

Bringing joy to my waist

His breath on my neck, a soft moan from my mouth

Sip me, drink me

Our bodies intertwine, the ride is divine

Our hearts beat rhythmically

We love slowly, we love discreetly

He speaks the language of love so fluently

The morning comes, we sleep blissfully

The only evidence of sin, the tangled sheets

They say it hits differently in the morning light: clarity, energy and sweetness all rolled into one, but I won't kiss and tell! The man of the cloth deserves my discretion, so create your own soft porn!

Our love story carried on in much the same way. It was the stuff made of movies. Breakfasts, picnics in the park, watching beautiful sunsets, walks along the embankment hand in hand. We were delirious for each other.

We didn't talk about that night nor the morning after. What could we say? What could I say? Your god lost and my ancestors won? I saw the pain of betrayal in his eyes. After all these years of being resolute in observing abstinence, everything had changed in a puff of smoke. But I also saw his deep love for me, so how could I gloat? How could I tell him that he had not betrayed his god, because it was I, his love, who had evoked the spirits of my ancestors.

The priest didn't mention God, church or the Bible ever again. I guess he didn't want to be a hypocrite. It crushed me. I knew that I had destroyed a special relationship between he and his god. A promise that he had made to his god and himself. I was riddled with guilt.

One evening, my door bell rung. It was the priest. It was an unplanned visit. He looked downcast. There was no usual kiss on the cheek or peck on the lips, just a simple hello. Had he come to his senses? Had the fishermen of God cast their net? My heart was filled with trepidation.

"Hello", I said, "what is the matter?", I nervously continued. We sat down next to each other, in awkward silence.

"You are scaring me". He took my hands into his and looked at me with those eyes, those hazel eyes and he took my breath away.

"My father has died", he said.

I put my arms around him. I didn't know what to do or say. Nothing I could say would make it better. Nothing I could do would take his pain away. I just held him close to me and allowed him the space to grieve, to cry, to be vulnerable with someone he trusted.

"I have to go to Zimbabwe"

"Of course", I replied. "When will you be back?" I regretted it as soon as those words had come out of my mouth. I shouldn't have asked.

"I don't know, but I am not sure if I will come back anytime soon". There was no hint of anger or disappointment at my question, just calm understanding. I literally begun to hyperventilate, the words, "I am not sure if I will come back anytime soon", hit me like a ton of bricks.

"Breathe", he said. "Breathe"

I took my hands away from his and begun to pace up and down. It had been five months of total bliss. This was my punishment. The ecstacy that the ancestors had indulged me came at a price and I hadn't read the fine print. I felt faint, like I was about to pass out.

"I need some air", I went to open the door to go out but he wouldn't let me. I had somehow managed to turn his tragic loss into my drama.

"No, girl", he said, "you just, need, to breathe". His words were slow and measured. I took a deep breath and told him that I was very sorry for his painful loss and that I understood he needed his family and they needed him. He smiled, but it wasn't a happy smile, it was an acknowledgment of my genuine sympathy. He would be leaving in a matter of days. I understood but it didn't stop tears welling up in my eyes. He curled his index finger under my chin and pulled my face towards him. He kissed me tenderly. He told me that he would miss me. I told him that I would miss him more. He told me it wasn't a competition. We laughed amidst the sadness.

He pulled down the zipper on my cardigan, revealing a lace trimmed, cream coloured camisole against my tanned skin. I shivered. He admired God's creation of woman. His hands traced my long neck and prominent collarbone which he deemed a sign of beauty. It made him desirous, he told me so.

Then I heard him say, "I can't".

My heart screamed no!

I heard him say, "I have to go".

My heart screamed please don't go!

An image of a naked woman, with a serpent draped across her neck and an apple in one hand, held out majestically flashed before my eyes. I shook my head. This time, I would not rally reinforcement from the spiritual world.

I heard him say, "breathe" as he backed away from me and out into the cold, dark night.

I went into the kitchen and poured myself a brandy and coke with two ice cubes.

I thought about him. I thought about that night and the morning after. Aye caramba!

Oh, what the hell! I will tell you about it.

We had the house to ourselves because obviously the priest wouldn't be joining his uncle and cousin for worship. My ancestors still held him captive and I, their child was still ululating.

T.shirt

He hugged me from behind, whispering good morning in my ears

He was so close I felt the warmth of his breath

I turned to him

My young breasts plump and taut body eager and ripe for the picking

He brushed strands of hair off my face

He begun to touch me

He reached inside the T.shirt and caressed my curves with such familiarity and once again lingered at the meeting of my thighs

May I?

I think he wrote a prose inside of me, I felt lightheaded

Legs parted like the Red Sea, waves thick with lust crashed against each other

Drowning in holy water, he worshipped like the believer he was

Our bodies aligned

With each thrust as delicious as the last he bellowed like thunder

The irony as we called out oh, god, oh god, oh god

In a matter of days my love was gone.

He called me when he got to Harare and again when he buried his father, then never called me again.

His cousin, the beautiful woman he was with the night we met, called me two weeks after. We arranged to meet.

She hugged me like an old friend. There was sadness in her hug. A sadness she would soon pass on to me.

She gave me a gift from him, it was a beautiful hand-crafted bracelet. I wore it immediately.

"He is not coming back", she told me. He couldn't bring himself to tell me. His mother needed him for now. For now? I heard forever.

This man who had given up everything for me. This man who had defied god to feel the smooth of my skin, smeared with shea butter, glowing in the dark, shimmering in the sun. This man who had defied god to find joy inside of a woman. This man who loved me more than any man ever would.

My heart was broken. I could not imagine not ever seeing him again, never hearing his voice again, never hearing him tell me I was beautiful and he loved me.

I couldn't imagine that we would never lay together again, feel his hands search me with such dexterity in every crevice, every contour, every receptive part of me. I just could not.

Through the years I have wondered about the priest.

His love had taken my breath away. For a while, I couldn't breathe. We were intense.

Like two ships passing in the night, our paths never crossed again.

Eddie Woods - Cattle Fodder

Andrew looked at the brown envelope. He didn't need to open it!

Not for the first time, he thought, this is shit! I was a student, I wasn't treated this way. I was taught, I learned and I respected those who taught me.

*

In early years Andrew spent time around farms. He'd had holidays on farms as a kid, those holidays had seemed endless and the memories were mostly good. He didn't know it then but he wasn't just having holidays, he was learning stuff. It was only with the benefit of hindsight that he'd realised this.

Livestock farmers especially were carers. They raised cattle, looked after their welfare, fed and watered their herds and flocks, treated their illnesses and ailments and raised them to be healthy adult animals. The animals gave them milk, cheese, eggs, wool and manure for the crops that fed the farmer's family, local villages and the animals. Some animals were for draught labour and were cared for the same as the flocks and herds. It seemed to be a symbiotic relationship, well balanced with equal benefits.

The bit he really didn't like was that after all that caring and nurturing the animals, the farmers who had been so good to them, killed them! Well technically, the farmers didn't kill them, they had a euphemism called, sending to market, which removed direct responsibility from the farmer and transferred it to - Them. Them were faceless individuals who paid the farmer and ensured his complicity in the slaughter!

There was little symbiosis at this end of the deal! What was, 'how it was' at the age of six, it was different at the age of sixteen and hideous at the age of thirty.

Andrew learned a trade, carpentry and joinery. There was less killing involved and he planted trees whenever possible to balance his use of them. He'd worked on an arable farm, rebuilding ancient brick barns using the technology that had created them. He created things most people could only dream of and planted a lot of trees in the process.

He knew stuff and there was another generation of wood workers that should know it too!

The solution presented itself when he was passing his old college one day. The solution was staring him in the face, an F.E. Technical College. Andrew was going to get a job there and pass 'the knowledge' to the next generation.

**

Getting the job was easy he was well qualified and had thirty years of trade experience. The interviewers liked him and the job offer was made within hours of the interview.

The enrolment process, Andrew realised, had nothing to do with aptitude. Anything that came through the door got on the course. There was no selection and in most cases no employer either. How could you be an apprentice without a job? Something was wrong here, nobody was saying what it was but they all apparently knew.

Hindsight kicked in and Andrew realised that the aim was enrolment and the objective was retention. Everything else, including the trade, was a bolt-on inconvenience. These kids had nowhere else to go and the government was funnelling them, like coffee beans, into a hopper for grinding. It didn't matter what they did as long as they weren't an unemployment statistic! These kids had choices, get on a course or live in poverty. Even the parents wanted their kids on a course. They had little in the way of education and came from cash strapped families. If the kids weren't on a course there were no state benefits. There were no options apart from menial jobs. They couldn't get trade jobs without college training and they couldn't be trained properly without a job. This had an air of futility about it in Andrew's opinion.

F.E. Andrew realised, was about having over subscribed courses and maximising grant and government funding. The students were just a necessity to balance the financial spreadsheet. The aim was enrol them and the objective was retaining them. The ethic was - prove with statistics that they were actually doing the job they were not doing while collecting wages from employers who were paying them to do a job they didn't want done!

Awarding bodies put courses together but did not put all the required learning in them, how could you get the student back for the next year if you gave them everything in one go? Awarding bodies stipulated guided learning hours. Colleges did everything possible to rhetorically re-interpret what G.L.H. meant. They delivered courses in half the time and ran two courses a year and got double the government funding. The learning had become ring-fenced.

***

The barrel is a simple but amazing invention. It has flat ends it can stand on, parabolic curved sides to allow rolling it with minimum resistance and turning it on the spot. It's virtually indestructible and its contents stay inside, sanitised and unaffected by external influences. Another feature of the barrel is that it was designed to roll along tracks until the wear caused by friction lead to disintegration.

What, Andrew wondered, would be the outcome if a number of barrels contained education? The information in one barrel relates to barrels. It contains all the information required to make a barrel.

The only way to learn all of the barrel's contents is to enter that barrel on its tracks and stay there until the information it contains is learned. On leaving the barrel one would be aware of two things, how to make a barrel and that there are tracks. The information related to the barrel would be complete. The information related to the tracks would not. If at this point a student wanted to learn about tracks, there was a barrel that contained all the information related to tracks.

This would create a continuous system of barrels of information. The choice of how much of the barrels' content is learned should be an individual one.

That would be, 'neat and tidy', and unlikely in education today. Imagine a system where everyone in it knew everything about something and something about everything.

Andrew was trying to compare his hypothetical barrel system to present education systems, starting with the first barrel, the one that contained all the information for making the barrel.

He saw that a governing body had decided to take parts of the barrel information and place them in separate barrels, without keeping records of their whereabouts. After a time the situation would arise where somebody would be under qualified and under educated to deal with all the contingencies related to barrels and have no idea where to find the relevant information.

That individual's progress would have been documented and relevant boxes ticked. When all the boxes were ticked the individual had learned all of the contents of the barrel, this would leave the individual qualified to do anything with a barrel because the documentation says so. However, there is the slight drawback in that all of the information was not in the barrel. In practice and reality the individual would be under qualified and could not competently perform the task for which it has been certificated.

The ramifications for the system seemed obvious. History after all, is littered with debris of similar collapses. The pyramids, Troy, Ephesus, Victorian drainage and London underground were all examples of lost education. The human race was capable of such wonders - but not anymore!

Right there and then systems of relevant information were being stripped to the barest minimum. He could teach only what he was allowed to teach, when he was allowed to teach it. He'd been manoeuvred into a position where he couldn't teach. Education was being ring-fenced into compact, watered down, packages and sadly inadequate.

Unintentionally he'd become complicit in the deception. He was playing a part in destroying education, the thing he trained to do, because he had to accept the confines of the ring-fence he found himself contained within.

Andrew had learned a third of what his teachers knew and his students would be lucky to be allowed to learn a third of what he knew.

He also knew that politicians practise collective crowd teaching. If a politician can get a crowd to do something completely opposite to the public face of political desire by making the crowd think it is their own idea, then the politician has been successful in making the crowd conform and thinking that they are making their own decisions.

This is a cleverly played battle of wits and wills bordering on insurrection. It's dangerous but can be highly productive.

On the down side the crowd learn that they have been played when they see the political benefits are not for them. If this type of manoeuvring is employed it must be balanced for the greater good or the crowd will react to it. Students are no different, if they think they have been tricked into a path for which they are only sub-beneficiaries, they also will react. This way disharmony lies. The crowd will unite in opposition to the politician or the teacher and will not be duped next time around.

A battle field in the classroom does not work, how could it? It has never worked in the last 5000 years. Asking, 'who won the war?' is like asking, 'who won the eruption of Vesuvius?'

Putting it, Andrew thought, more basically, the nature of how a student learns is highly subjective to the way that the subject that is allowed to be taught - is taught.

It was the student that he was ultimately there for. He should not lose sight of this by becoming bogged down in the politics that govern the learning environment.

Well, he thought, this is shit!

The kids were treated like a herd and government ministers were the farmers. Andrew knew too well, what farmers did with the livestock they apparently nurtured to maturity - they milked them and used them up until they were dead!

The remit of any teacher should be to question the received wisdom. Andrew had been in this job for ten years now. He had been totally retrained in that period to be a teacher not a lecturer. From his point of view they had effectively given him the tool kit to talk to them in their own language. Andrew began to ask questions. "Why are we doing it like this when it is clearly ineffective?"

"Why do we accept this system?"

Nobody failed, that wasn't reality, everybody completed and passed because if they didn't funding would be withdrawn and the next year would be under funded but still bounded by the same full success expectation. Some students did not deserve to pass and they were leaving with the same accolade as those who did deserve to pass but neither type of student was actually prepared for the reality of what they were going into out there in the real world. Equal opportunity was one thing, equal success was quite another!

Andrew knew this, as did every other lecturer-converted-to-teacher. Ninety eight percent kept their heads down and complied with the deception required by the financial management of the college. Andrew had his head up above the parapet as did a few others but he was basically flying solo. This was a shit state of affairs and it needed changing!

Andrew looked and poked and found. The watchdog was behind this. They were the people who were turning education into edutainment. The figures were easy to access. In the space of under four years the watchdog had taken the country from having 427 self governing colleges to having 280. A lot of people were on the scrap heap and 147 colleges were gone. Eighty percent of it was type B mergers or, in plain language, hostile takeover. It was driven by failing statistics due to the watchdog setting unachievable targets, those who failed were only told after an inspection that they had not met the inspection criteria - and even then they still weren't told what those criteria were.

Good teachers just didn't turn into bad teachers in the space of four years but inspection reports said they did and the H.R. bastards took care of the rest, with the blessing of the watchdog and, performance managed them out! Essentially they threw out all of the experience in favour of lower paid, educated in the barrel young blood.

The light came on. Andrew thought, 'follow the money'. That was not such an easy matter but social media, being voluntarily populated and all intrusive as it is, provided many hyperlinks. The hyperlinks put many antagonists together in various settings in previous years. One way or another, dirt-bags knew shit-bags. It was like a travelling circus of hatchet folk.

Predominantly two or three of them got employed in the same college to maximise systems. They cut facilities, increased course and class numbers (but not class room dimensions). They sold assets and performance managed the higher paid staff and those with a decent pension pot out of the door.

The next phase was that interims, from the same travelling circus, were brought in to 'save' a failing college. They got three times the wages the post commanded, trimmed the ship to lean, mean and disabled but afloat and generally didn't stay above a year.

Then a new principal (with tentative but tangible links to the travelling circus) on extortionate remuneration but with an excellent proven track record of mergers, acquisitions and asset stripping came in and did just that. Two colleges became one and six million quid disappeared in constructive accounting.

The question was pretty obvious to Andrew, what did they want all that dosh for? A hundred and forty seven colleges at colleges at six mill a pop. It seemed to him that the watchdog had a puppet master!

The puppet master was a scary proposition. It was above the watchdog and the watchdog was government sanctioned. People turned up, or often didn't, missing for looking into things of this of this nature. Was it worth being 'disappeared' for?

Then he hit pay-dirt. A new college had opened, dedicated to super fast trains, costing as much as dissolving 147 colleges saved, with a bit left over. A coincidence obviously, one that didn't explain which back pocket the collective colleges' average four million quid each bank account had gone into. Interims were an expensive business, apparently! It was staffed by the travelling circus associates, funny how this stuff works out. Well, not really, it was orchestrated from higher up than the watchdog that thought it was in charge!

Surely our democratically elected government, 'Them', wouldn't treat its citizens like that! He was suffering from a misplaced trust in management. We, are, the herd!

"Quis custodiet ipsos custodes?"

****

Ten years ago it seemed so much better. Even eighteen months ago it still seemed viable. Eighteen months was how long it had taken corrupt management to destroy ten years and get him to where he was!

Andrew sat in front of the H.R. bitch, she was still licking her wounds from having been beaten by him on previous occasions and, still had an axe to grind! His trade union rep was not going to be any help due to having been performance managed out of the equation by the H.R bitch. He was on his own - the replacement rep was looking for an amicable agreement but was not disposed to fight for it. It had taken 'them' eighteen months to get to this point and it was relentless all the way. The last one had been another win for him but it came with a two year warning from the court of kangaroo. Basically if he put a hair out of place anywhere for the next two years it would be classed as gross misconduct. Gross misconduct was an instant dismissal offence and they were going to re-suspend him with immediate effect so that they could investigate matters that had come to light in the course of the present investigation. They had lined him up for another six months of investigation and instant dismissal all in one shot.

Oh the bitter irony, they had him over his own analogy, a barrel. Time to bite the bullet as the union was no use to him now. He had been manoeuvred into a position where he had no other choice. So Andrew put it straight to the H.R. bitch. "You want me out of here and so do a number of other people. I am prepared to go so let's talk money. If I pursue this I will tie you up in litigation for at least two years and it will cost you around 200k by the time I'm finished with you. You know I will do it and you know I have nothing to lose by pursuing this and, I will win

- so what are you offering?"

The bitch immediately replied, "Twelve grand."

Andrew smiled and said, "I'd get double that for voluntary redundancy."

The bitch said, "This is not a V.R. situation."

Andrew said, "Double it and add a zero plus any outstanding holiday pay and a decent reference, otherwise I'll see you in court."

The bitch called a recess and was back in five minutes. The offer was tripled, plus holiday pay, with a gagging order.

The gagging order was irrelevant. Nobody wanted to listen so far, so nobody would want to listen in the future either!

Andrew took the settlement - he took the pay off for his silence knowing that this would not be silenced.

Andrew went to his workshop and began making things from wood. He never returned to teaching in an educational setting ruled by the watchdog puppets - but that didn't stop him teaching. His barrel had all of the information and people came to him to learn.

*****

The brown envelope had its uses!

Helen Lawrence - The Affair

David glances at the date at the top of the newspaper and realises with a start that today is his wedding anniversary. 43 Years, he thinks. What was 45 again? Ruby? No, Sapphire? He wonders if he and Rita will make it that far. There is a good chance they won't.

David is 68, and was a bank manager before he retired. Rita is two years younger, and had worked in the local library until she had been forced to take early retirement at 55. Theirs had been a happy marriage, marred only by Rita's ill-health. They have two children; Eric lives in Canada with his wife and two daughters, Charlotte still lives in their village with her husband and young son.

They had planned to visit Eric regularly once they retired, staying for a couple of months at a time so they could get to know their grandchildren. But Rita cannot travel long distances these days, and will never do so again. She had a major heart attack a couple of years ago, and underwent a heart bypass, which had been a qualified success. However, there had been significant damage, and she has several other chronic illnesses that contribute to her poor condition. David has asked her cardiologist several times for a prognosis, whereupon she would frown and suck her teeth, talk of statins and beta blockers, and the importance of making healthy lifestyle choices. If she thinks he hasn't noticed she failed to answer the question she is sorely mistaken.

Jeanette is a widow; her husband Hugh, an actuary, died four years ago. A healthy man, who wouldn't have recognised his GP if he passed him in the street, he suffered a massive heart attack on the golf course aged 65, within weeks of retiring. They had been looking forward to their retirement, had planned to travel. They had particularly wanted to visit the cities in Eastern Europe - Prague, Budapest, Sofia, Bucharest. Jeanette had been a teacher, and only retired herself last year. She finds that she has no inclination to go alone to the places they had planned to together. She too has a son and a daughter, Robbie in London, Grace nearby, in the University town 12 miles from the village.

David and Jeanette had met, of all places, in the café in their local hospital. Rita had had an appointment with her endocrinologist- she has a thyroid problem, among other things-and he was waiting to take her home. Jeanette was there for a happier reason; her daughter Grace had just given birth to her third grandchild. Grace's husband had given her the wrong visiting hours, so she had an hour to kill before going to see the new arrival. The café was unusually busy, and there were no free tables. David had spotted Jeanette hovering, latte in hand, and had gallantly invited her to join him.

They were soon chatting, and found that they had a lot on common- in addition, that is, to a spouse with a serious heart condition. They both liked gardening and hill walking, and had taken up photography in retirement. David misses hill walking in particular, he says. Rita and he had often gone together, but her health no longer allowed it.

Well now, Jeanette says. She is a member of a hillwalking group, which meets regularly in the village. We're a friendly bunch, she says, always looking for new members. Would he…? Or perhaps he couldn't get away very often? He would love to, he says. His daughter often sits with Rita so he can have some time to himself.

At the end of the hour she looks at her watch. She should be getting along, her new grandson awaits! He hesitates, then asks her tentatively if she would perhaps be here tomorrow as well? His wife has a couple of appointments in the afternoon, with her cardiologist and with her orthopaedic surgeon- she also suffers from arthritis-so he will be here again. She would, she says. Grace had a Caesarean and would be in a least another two days. Shall we meet tomorrow? They agreed to meet in the same place at 2pm.

The next day he notices with pleasure that she is wearing lipstick and a rather jaunty scarf, presumably not for the benefit of her two-day-old grandson. He had been nervous, but somehow, when he saw her there looking around for him, his nervousness disappeared. The two hours go by in a flash, and before he knows it she is looking at her watch and saying she really must be going, her daughter would be waiting.

The next meeting of the hillwalking group is this Saturday, she says. Would he like to…?

Yes, he says, and she gives him the location.

As he watches her go he feels a pang of guilt. After all, isn't it a bit inappropriate to meet another woman while his ill wife is getting medical treatment? But, he reasons, it's not a date. Just a man having a cup of coffee with a woman.

As promised, the hillwalkers are a friendly bunch. Charlotte usually comes to see her mother on Saturdays; he tells her about the hill walking group, although somehow Jeanette gets left out of the story. She is pleased. That's great, Dad. It'll do you good to get exercise. And I know how you and Mum loved hill walking.

It is not until his fourth meeting that he realises that the group thinks he and Jeanette are a couple. They had chosen a walk that was a few miles out of the village, so they would need to drive there. David had offered a lift to a member of the group, and was driving Jeanette also. The woman made a joke about being a gooseberry; Jeanette had opened her mouth to speak, but David had merely laughed and changed the subject. But by then they had become lovers in truth.

He has Thursday afternoons to himself, as this is the day the nurse comes in to visit Rita. At first he'd stayed in, just in case he was needed, but the nurse soon told him that it wasn't necessary. You get off if you like, Mr Young, she said. All my other wives and husbands do. It's tough, being a carer; you need to look after yourself, too. So he had started going off for a couple of hours, sometimes for a walk, sometimes to a café, occasionally to a pub where he would make a pint and a half last the entire afternoon.

He mentions this to Jeanette during a hill walk. I'm free on Thursday afternoons, he says casually. Would you like to meet for lunch? They meet for a couple of weeks at the café in the garden centre on the outskirts of town. And then one day she says, Why don't you come round to the house next week, and I'll make us lunch there?

And so the following Thursday he goes to her house, to find her dressed up, in a pretty floral dress and make-up, as if she is going to a party.

Would you like a glass of wine? she asks, holding up the bottle hopefully. Not that I usually drink in the afternoons, honest! She gives a little laugh. She seems nervous, he thinks, and suddenly realises why. This makes him nervous too, and he gratefully accepts the offer of the wine. But when, after only half a glass he leans over and kisses her, he finds that his nervousness has disappeared.

At their age, it is generally thought that love is companionship rather than passion. Not for them; they are surprised at the intensity of their emotions. It has been four years for her, and even longer for him, despite the difference in their circumstances. It has been many years since Rita's health had allowed it. It had been a particularly cruel blow, the realisation that that side of things was over. He had even contemplated visiting a prostitute, but his innate sense of decency forbade it. Besides, their village didn't even boast a Starbucks. There was the nearby university town of course, but how did one go about procuring one?

Afterwards they lie in bed for a while, talking. It's just like riding a bicycle, he jokes, you never forget! Who are you calling a bicycle? she says in mock outrage, and they both laugh.

They start to meet regularly, on Thursdays and on Saturdays in the afternoon, although they rarely go hill walking now, preferring another mode of exercise. They occasionally snatch the odd couple of hours here and there; Charlotte works part-time and sometimes pops in in the afternoons and lets him away for an hour.

The guilt is ever present though. He is having an Affair; worse, he is cheating on a wife who is ill, who might not have more than a couple of years to live. What sort of man is he? He thinks of his daughter, and the nurse, imagining him doing something entirely innocent with his afternoons off; going for a walk, meeting friends for coffee. What would they say if they knew he uses the time to visit his mistress?

For she is his mistress, he supposes. The word is incongruous, and makes him think of a busty peroxide blonde in a satin negligee, rather than his Jeanette, an attractive 63 year old women in Marks and Spencer's leisurewear. The floral dress had been purely to "get him in the sack", she jokes. I'm not used to being a seductress, thought I should at least dress the part.

Six months in, he realises he is in love. He haltingly confesses this to her, one Saturday afternoon in her bed. Oh thank God! she exclaims. Not just me then.

Rita's angina is getting worse, and she now needs oxygen at night. Her cardiologist has begun to look even gloomier. If she was younger and fitter I would recommend surgery. As it is……she says no more, but does not need to. David nods. Just a matter of time then. He and Jeanette never refer to Rita' s death, preferring euphemisms; "When we can be together properly" "When we move in together." And even then, not often; there is something indecent in anticipating her end. She hardly ever goes out now, and keeps to her room most of the time- it is years since she and David shared a bedroom. He knows that soon she will need specialist care, and he will not be able to look after her at home. It will be easier then, of course. But many years ago, Rita had made him promise to keep her at home for as long as possible. And he keeps his promises. Besides, she is his wife, and he loves her. His love for Jeanette cannot change that.

The first time Jeannette comes round to his house they are both on tenterhooks. What if Rita comes downstairs? But she never does, although that doesn't stop him feeling guilty, entertaining his mistress while his sick wife sleeps upstairs. But he cannot just see the woman he loves on two afternoons a week. It is not enough.

Charlotte. He worries about Charlotte. She has met Jeanette twice. Once she had dropped in without warning, to find them drinking tea in the kitchen. He had introduced her as "a friend from the hill walking group". Charlotte had shaken her hand and smiled, but he thought he'd seen something in her eyes- a sharpness, a suspicion. And another time they'd been in the village, and had met her, coming out of a café with a friend. He had claimed he and Jeanette had just run into each other by chance, but there it was again, that look. What will Charlotte think when he moves into Jeanette's house with indecent haste?

They have already decided that they will live at Jeanette's house, which contains no memories of his former life. And he knows well that he is the subject of gossip in his quiet little cul-de-sac - he can see the curtains twitching. That's Her gone into number 17 again, Mrs Wilson at number 14 says sourly, and her husband clicks his tongue in disapproval. Shocking, so it is.

And Jeanette feels guilty too. She is a home-wrecker, a Jezebel, a scarlet woman. And her neighbours' curtains twitch as welll. The village is small; everyone knows everyone. She has seen the looks when David visits her, and she can imagine the comments. Carrying on with his fancy woman, while that poor wife of his lies dying. Disgusting. They should be ashamed of themselves.

People will come round in time, they tell themselves. And if they don't, what do they care? They will be together. They practically live together already; she is in his house most days, often stays the night. After all, they say to each other, so what if Rita does see her? Does it really matter now?

It is Saturday evening. Charlotte had been round earlier with her son but they have gone home. He no longer visits Jeannette on Saturday afternoons- there is no point, now that she comes to the house most days. Rita is lying down upstairs. She sleeps more and more these days; it is a blessing, he thinks. He phones Jeannette; she will be round in an hour, she says. What do you want for dinner? I'll cook tonight, he says. Can you pick up a few things on the way?

She goes to the supermarket, buys fresh vegetables, goats cheese, salami and basil. White wine tonight, she thinks; the weather is warm, a traditional British May heatwave to raise everyone's hopes, before crushing them again. 25 degrees today. They usually drink red, but who wants to drink it in this heat? A nice Viognier, she thinks, and buys two bottles, just in case. Although they will probably only finish one. They both find that, as the years pass, their tolerance lessens.

She lets herself into the house- she has her own key now. In the kitchen he puts on an apron, one that he'd bought for his wife many years ago. Kiss the Cook, it says, under the picture of a chef's hat. He did, too, for weeks afterwards. Cut it out, she'd said; I'll never get the dinner ready. A great cook she'd been, and a good baker too.

Jeannette pours herself a glass of wine and chats to him, while he chops and sautés vegetables and boils pasta. When the pasta bake is in the oven he pours himself a glass of viognier and joins her at the kitchen table. There is a newspaper open in front of her; she has begun the cryptic crossword but, as usual, is stuck after three or four clues. They fill it in with ridiculous words, a game of theirs.

The pasta bake is nearly ready. Jeanette sets the table for three, gets out a loaf of crusty bread, puts out a jug of water. David is frowning at the newspaper- why is that date so familiar? Then he remembers. He should have bought flowers; he usually does, although there seems little point now.

David goes into the living room, where Rita is sitting in her favourite armchair watching a game show, one of the American ones. A contestant is trying to answer a preposterously easy question, and Rita is laughing along. He puts his hand on her shoulder and tells her that their dinner is ready. She turns and looks up at him, as amusement gives way to mild perplexity.

"I know you, don't I, dear?" she says, with a polite smile. Patiently, he explains to her who he is, just as he has done every day for the past four years.

Ian Craine - Two Sisters At Their Windows

Maria never danced. She stood forever solemn at the upper window. A passer-by looking up might see the two girls staring at him. Magdalena would be at the big window of the *piano nobile* a floor down and across from her sister. To a stranger they might have seemed the same girl, diagonal copies or twins. But Magdalena, who was two years the younger, would not have stayed long at her window; unlike her sister she would have bounded and waltzed across the vast parquet floors in an ineffable celebration of girlhood. Maria was so shy and withdrawn that she would not go to school until Magdalena was old enough to join her, and so the younger, the cadet, accompanied and protected the elder. It was not that Maria was backward. She had a fine head for figures and took to the mathematical forms like algebra. She was just awkward and painfully shy so that she would almost blush at her own reflection balefully staring back at her from somewhere inside the gilt rimmed old mirror that hung in the hallway further extending the already vast house.

Their father was kind but remote and his health was in decline and he barely survived the girls' teenage years. It was their mother who organised their lives, moulded and made them into what they were and what they were to become. Hers was a strange and seemingly casual cruelty treating her daughters as if they were gaming cocks to be set upon one another for her separate amusement. She drew distinctions between them and emphasised what was already apparent enough. Magdalena had inherited her father's love and facility for ball games and she would take her sister to the beach and coax her into playing catch with the huge beach ball their father had bought, an oversized and gaudy sphere made up of arcs of blinding colour, lilac and lime, orange and vermilion. Maria did not know whether to catch it or kick it when Magdalena threw it at her. Both girls knew she could manage neither. Sometimes they were joined by friends of Magdalena and then Maria felt even more alone. Did she have any inkling of how her sister felt? Did she not know what it was like to be her sister, to be Magdalena? They were of the same stock, and all those agonies that Maria faced in life were felt just as harshly by Magdalena. But somehow the younger girl had learned to hide her pain from the world. That was the only difference. But Maria was not to know that as a child, and perhaps she never did. It was just that Magdalena knew how to catch a beach ball. It was as simple as that.

Hector Valverde lived down the street. He had seen the two girls standing at their windows, one diagonally above the other. Sometimes when Magdalena's friends had visited he saw girls at every window, a profusion of girls all gravely looking down on the world, looking at him. But mostly there were just the sisters so alike in repose, so different when animated. Maria seemed to be an image preserved on old film stock, or a freeze frame forever caught in one gesture. Gestures were alien to her, dangerous and terrifying projects that overwhelmed her. Her limited skills of self preservation, the thin and vulnerable carapace that protected her from the outside world, only allowed her one gesture, that blank and timid stare.

Magdalena was not like that and Hector Valverde understood the difference. He watched the girls at play on the beach and noticed how Magdalena would shield her eyes from the sun with an arm languidly stretched across her forehead. He heard her laughter and chatter within the walls of their big old house. She was gay; that was the word. She was gay in the old sense before *The Ballad of Reading Gaol* or whatever it was had changed the word's meaning but Hector Valverde could not for the life of him, and he tried, think of a word that better described Magdalena. Merry was not right; it sounded like Christmas and suggested the consumption of alcohol. Nor was she jolly; that word just made her sound fat and red cheeked. No Magdalena was definitely gay. In the old sense.

Occasionally Hector Valverde would talk to Magdalena. She treated him much as she treated everybody else, with a sort of temporary friendliness, an interest that would dissipate almost before he had said goodbye to her. Hector Valverde was not a shy boy but he was reserved and he kept his feelings to himself. But when Magdalena went away to university he realised how much he missed her and how he would count the days to her return. He no more knew what it was like to be Magdalena than her sister did. Magdalena coped with the world through a multiplicity of small and seemingly random gestures and felt pain as much as Maria did with her one permanent response. There was one pain that Magdalena knew now in her heart would be worse than any other, and that would be to lose Hector Valverde. So she did not seek to gain him, reckoning there could be no loss without prior gain.

The big house was quiet now. Maria, two years too late, went to university with her sister just as she had gone to school with her. Maria read mathematics, one thing at which she truly excelled. Magdalena read chemistry. Their father's health declined and he retired to his study to read and it seemed to prepare for his forthcoming death. Their mother sat bored and rigid now that she had lost her two daughters to provoke. She would barely acknowledge Hector Valverde if they met on the street as if she sensed that he had within him the power to make one at least of her daughters happy; happiness was not the design she ever had in mind for them. Magdalena and Maria returned for vacations and Hector Valverde at last asked Magdalena if she cared to walk with him. She did care. She cared very much and felt her heart beat frantically and the gay abandon of her earlier years began to slip away from Magdalena as she began to learn of love which she regarded as a serious and lifelong thing, a commitment. She sensed that Hector Valverde felt the same way, not consciously for he was not a young man given to such speculation. He was a practical and kind man and he disliked tension and unpleasantness so he was uneasy in Magdalena's house where he felt the spitting malevolence of her mother and the brooding nature of Maria. They were both jealous of Magdalena, both forever estranged from the happiness that despite them Magdalena could still just about embrace. It was happiness at a cost however, happiness forever coated in anxiety and the fear that it would come tumbling down about her. Hector Valverde was younger than Magdalena and the time came for him to go to college where he would study pharmacy which was the Valverde family business.

"Will you wait me for, Magdalena?" Said calmly but utterly sincerely.

"Yes".

What extremes of emotion were concealed behind that little word. She would wait for him, wait forever if need be. She would wait until Hell froze over. She inwardly cursed herself for the use of such a junk phrase, not fit for the scientists that they both were. Hector Valverde went to pharmacy college. He had exams at the end of his first year there. A week before the date set for them Magdalena's father died. She said that Hector Valverde must not be told for it would distract him from his examinations. It was the most selfless thing she ever did in her life. Now Hector Valverde was all that was left her, for she secretly hated her venomous mother and envious sister. Maria's shy childhood had been overtaken by her resentment of her sister's good fortune. Maria was her mother's semblance, two bitches now from the same poisoned litter more than mother and daughter. She would never marry.

When Hector Valverde qualified from pharmacy college he proposed to

Magdalena. She accepted his proposal. He was working now for a small wage in his father's business, too small a wage to offer prospects of their own house so he moved into the big old property and they adapted the *piano nobile* for their own purposes. The mother retired to her bed in peevish protest at this infusion of happiness and Maria sulked with her in the next room on the upper floor. For seven years the mother never left her bedroom; tray and commode supplied all her needs until she died. Within a month Hector Valverde's father was dead too. He succeeded to the business and worked in that compact pharmacy his father had created with its ornate counters and stands, the little individual wooden drawers each with its glass handle like the stopper from a bottle and a neat printed label describing its contents in Latin. There was a picture of Galen above the door. He and Magdalena lived a frugal life and if Hector Valverde was at last spared the barbs that emerged from the mother's mouth he still had to face Maria. He noticed that Magdalena was changing too. She seemed to be turning into another version of the mother. He realised that she could be as nasty to Maria (but never to him) as Maria was to her. It wearied him; he remembered his own mother and how calm and kind and beautiful she always was. People said he took after his mother.

Then Maria took the notion to go travelling. She wanted to see the world. An itinerary was minutely planned. She would travel the length of Asia and then see Australia and New Zealand where she would stay with an old friend from university. Hector Valverde noticed that Magdalena's moods changed. She seemed happier- fleeting remnants of her schoolgirl self returned. Maria packed half her belongings into a huge trunk and a taxi came to take her to the airport. In the weeks that followed postcards arrived. Then there were letters. There were strange allusions; she sounded a little hysterical, a little unhinged. Something was happening to her but what it was not possible to elicit. The last letter was postmarked Macao. Then there was the telegram. Maria was dead, some massive eruption in her colon.

Hector Valverde carefully watched Magdalena in the days that followed. Maria was her last relative. Magdalena knew what she felt but she could not tell even her husband. She felt relief- complete and undiluted relief that her tormenting and difficult sister was dead. Then it started. It was a muscle just below her right eye. It went into spasm. It twitched continuously all day and probably all night too. Hector Valverde tried everything he could. He brought home lotions and potions, balms and ointments. He read his pharmacopoeias. Nothing worked. He looked up for inspiration at the old print of Galen but none came. The eye continued to twitch. The doctors and the hospitals were powerless. They visited a Chinese acupuncturist who for a time succeeded in curing the muscle. But the twitch returned more intense than ever and the acupuncturist was unable to work his needles a second time. It was like a bacterium that had beaten back the last antibiotic that could ever reach it.

Sometimes of an evening Hector Valverde would open the big sash window of the *piano nobile* and smoke a cigar in the twilight. He listened to the clickings of the night animals that seemed to him like the souls of the recent dead reluctant to move away. He knew the terrible balance between resentment and guilt and the lives that are ruined by those complementary emotions. Magdalena had so resented her sister's bitchy ways. And how relieved she was at her death. He knew that; he did not have to be told. He knew too the guilt that Magdalena now felt not for anything she had done to her sister while she lived but for the relief she felt now she was dead. But what could he do? The twitch remained. Magdalena never danced again.

Ian Goh Hsien Jun - The Art and Science of Predicting Cherry Blossom Showers

"Why are you leaving your wife behind in Singapore?"

It is early March of 2018, and instead of the usual queries like "What are your strengths and weaknesses?" and "Why do you want to join our company?" I feel I'm being interrogated in the heart of Tokyo.

I pull at my collar as my interviewer, Mr Mori, fixes me with an accusatory stare from across the table, his eyes magnified behind horn-rimmed spectacles. The room we're in is a glorified walk-in wardrobe, with partitions on either side and a single lamp humming in silence from the ceiling.

'I'm sorry?' I ask, blinking in surprise.

'You're still married, yes? As indicated in your resume,' my interviewer states the question as fact.

'Y—Yes, but…'

In front of me, my application form is laid out in perfect rectangles on the otherwise spartan table. A passport photograph grins back at me, with a caption that reads, "Mr James Wong Li Yang." Could these sheets of paper encompass my life?

'Mr. Wong?'

'Katelyn — my wife — she's staying behind in Singapore. She has her own duties.'

'Hmph. And are you aware of *your* duties if you were to join our company?'

I dip my head, showing assent and respect.

'Allow me to rephrase: Mr. Wong, you are already thirty-nine this year. Our company has international offices, including Singapore. Why choose Japan? Why leave your family behind?'

'I I consider myself a risk-taker,' I say, too enthusiastically. 'It brings us out of our comfort zone, where we discover our true selves.'

I meant to be inspirational, but my interviewer purses his lips.

'Also, I came to watch cherry blossoms.'

Mr Mori tilts his head. '*Hanami desu-ka*?'

I nod. 'I've always wanted to watch cherry blossoms fall in Spring. I heard their showers are beautiful.'

'They are,' Mr Mori replies. 'But you are too early. *Sakura* only fall at the close of March. They are very fickle these days; difficult to predict.'

'I am willing to do what it takes.'

A smile creeps over his mouth — the first I've seen in this thirty-minute interview. 'I would recommend walking along the Meguro river. There is something special about the light as it falls upon the water,' Mr Mori says, before pausing. 'It is a shame your wife will not be here to appreciate it.'

Before long, we are on our feet and exchanging bows. I step out of the cramped office into the endless stream of commuters headed home to their families, to doting wives and kids, leaving this lone *gaijin* asking what the hell he was doing in the madness of downtown Shinjuku.

I take a deep breath and remind myself: no more sweltering classrooms back in Singapore, no more blank faces between glossy photographs of *prunus serrulata* in textbooks. No more waking up in the darkness of 5-am mornings, only stumbling past iron gates and grey buildings in the shadow of sunset.

No more Katelyn.

The interview plays in my head like a bad recording, along with the repeated question: "Can you really love two things at once without fucking it up?"

***

The catalyst for wanting to move to Japan occurred five years ago. Katelyn had insisted we attend the *Sakura Matsuri* festival at Gardens by the Bay during a rare break from her lawyering duties at Raju & Sons. But perhaps she thought that seeing a replica would placate my desire to drop everything and move to a foreign country to see flowers.

But something felt *off* as we passed the glass doors of the Flower

Dome and were greeted by wide pavilions, orange *torii* gates and a canopy of pink, red and white blossoms swaying above. A sea of spectators crashed into us, the rest of Singapore also having turned up for the spectacle, and we found ourselves jostling to get close enough to see, let alone touch a flower, the best spots already choked by Instagram enthusiasts.

I could sense Katelyn studying my mood as it soured. 'Nice, right?' she asked, squeezing my hand.

I didn't reply, my gaze drawn to a woman plucking a flower off a low-hanging stem before mangling the pink petals between her fingers.

'Yeah, nice.'

Like aunties manhandling mangoes at a wet market, why did Singaporeans always have to poke everything in order to appreciate their beauty? Perhaps we were used to seeing bougainvilleas hanging from overhead bridges or orchids pruned by the roadside, paying money to see freshly cut grass from other worlds. We continued through the glass enclosure, doing our best to appreciate the trees grown in imported soil, water falling from man-made mountains and *sakura* blossoms swaying between the intermittent blasts of air-conditioning.

We headed for the exit early.

Being a Geography teacher for the past ten years, I considered myself knowledgeable in the science of cherry blossom blooming. Few locals knew, for example, that we possessed our own brand of cherry tree the *tabebuia rosea* flower blossoming twice a year and possessing a lazy, sloth-like appearance in the local heatwave on Upper Serangoon. But somehow, we don't go travel to appreciate its "beauty", which resembles pink packets of tissue paper drooped over branches in a downpour.

The *real* cherry blossom is one of the ficklest flowers on the planet, requiring specific temperatures and enough sunlight to coax forth its delicate bloom. Even then, the *sakura* blossom only shows its face for two weeks before its plucked gently by the wind, spinning its last dance like a ballerina on death row. Millions of tourists descend upon Japan from March to April for this very reason, and why a teacher like me, shackled to the school holiday months of June and December, would never be able to witness a shower in his life.

Unless I did something drastic.

Back in our apartment, Katelyn and I were in the evening motions of styrofoam boxes on our laps, eyes glued to unfolding scenes of infidelity on Netflix, and speaking to each other only when we needed the salt or pepper passed.

I sensed a moment and leaned over. 'Still don't want to go?'

Katelyn flashed annoyance, but I couldn't tell if it was because the Korean actress on television just realised her boyfriend was cheating on her. Maybe I should have timed this better.

'Don't be crazy,' Katelyn said, her eyes glued front. 'You want to give up your career just to see some flowers?'

'It's more complicated than that,' I said. 'I've been stuck in this job for the past ten years. It's time for a change.'

'Why don't you buy yourself golf clubs?' she said, stuffing a french-fry into her mouth. 'Or get a new car *lah*. That Mitsubishi Lancer you like, right? Better than that *cui* Swift that's always breaking down.'

'But I've always wanted to live in Japan,' I persisted, staring at the four walls of our HDB flat. 'I told you before our wedding.'

'Go holiday *lah*? Why give up everything *likedat*?' she continued, not hearing me. 'It's not easy to find a job these days, you know?'

'Yeah, babe, but—'

'We've also got the mortgage to pay, my dad's bills, and *please hor*, our wedding and renovation loans still so big. I hope you didn't forget?'

As we fell silent, the girlfriend on television continued raging at her hapless boyfriend, now forced to fend off objects hurled across the room. I inched away from Katelyn in case she registered similar ideas.

'That's my point,' I said, my voice level. 'We should make big decisions *now* rather than *after* we get married, when we get tied down by—'

'Tied down by what, *huh*?' her voice dropped low suddenly.

'I just— Nevermind. Let's think about it, okay?'

She didn't reply, but I could sense dark clouds brewing behind her hazel eyes. In my profession, I could recite to you the life cycles of *rosa pouzinii* or predict weather patterns by scrutinising the sky, but Katelyn had always been a different kind of storm — fierce, independent, unpredictable — part of the charm for someone comfortable with watching grass grow.

Katelyn pushed her long, dark hair aside, hiding frustration. I placed my hand over hers, cautiously, but there was no squeeze, no affectionate glance, only the lingering quiet that lasted the evening. The on-screen couple ended their struggle in each other's arms, tearing off shirts and skirts, with awkward shrieks of "Bastard! How could you?" followed by "Kiss me, you idiot!"

***

Back in Tokyo, my apartment is located in the suburbs, in a grey three-storey building filled with green hallways and steel doors on either side. The entire place is the size of my old bedroom back in Punggol, with a toilet the size of a broom closet and the ceiling a victim of multiple, accidental headbutts. Where I eat, sleep and sit has become indistinguishable in the three weeks I've stayed, and tonight, my dinner consists of packeted potato salad, green beans and strips of shrivelled pork stretched thin over rice. If the view from my window wasn't blocked by concrete, I'd bet I could stare into the heart of another Japanese family seated around their *tatami* mat, chopsticks stuck into bowls of rice as the four walls of their flat force their stares back at me.

That night, I fall asleep, still hungry and dreading an interview in the morning. I dream of Katelyn's face framed by the glass walls of Changi Departure Hall, her hands pressed firm into the barrier, her dark hair hiding reddened eyes from the night before. "Are you really going?" she turns to me, half-asleep, tossing in bed, asking if this was all a nightmare she could wake from.

In my dreams, I always respond with a "Yes."

She turns and leaves, her eyes cast down furtive, her hair adorned with white blossoms.

The next morning, I open my front door in pyjamas and a pair of *totoro* slippers, and a Japanese woman greets me with a wide, immaculate smile.

'*Ohayogozaimasu*,' she bows. '*Ogenki-desuka*?'

I recognise her from random passes along the corridor, always dressed in a red jacket and matching skirt, a clipboard cradled in the nook of her arm. Her shoulder-length hair is pinned in place, glittering in the fluorescence of the hallway. I manage a "Good morning" before she starts speaking in rapid-fire Japanese, jabbing at her clipboard with a fountain pen. I blink with frenzied confusion, catching short phrases like "*uji*" (home), "*getsuyō*" (Mondays) and "*rīsu desu*" (lease).

When she pauses for breath, I shake my head rapidly. '*Sumimasen. Nihongo ga wakarimasen.*'

Her smile falters like a glitch in the system. 'Ah! *Gaijin desu-ka?*'

She rapidly scribbles on her clipboard, before she mouths the words slow and clear, as though speaking to a toddler. 'Y—You…' she says, her pen pointed at my chest. '…Trash.'

I blink in surprise. 'I'm sorry?'

'You. Trash… Throw…'

She mimics a forward rotating action with an arm, her fingers clutched as though hurling something elusive over my head. It dawns upon me: she's advising on special occasions for garbage disposal, with the Japanese being notorious for sorting their paper cups, plastic straws and aluminum cans into neat goodie bags.

'Monday, *o-kay*! Tuesday, *dame dame dame da*!' she crosses her arms over her chest, forming a giant "X" as a visual aid for the dumb *gaijin.*

'G*omenasai.*' I bow furiously, recalling the many empty bottles of *sake* unceremoniously chucked outside my door.

'*Ie, ie, ie*,' she replies, thanking me for my inconvenience with a pack of flavoured *mochii*, a Japanese sweet treat meant to reward children for their good behaviour.

I shut my door, already missing the nonchalance of Singaporean waste disposal. Back home, garbage vanished as soon as it went down the chute, and on rare occasions, refusing to go down with a "Have you thrown the trash yet?" or "Can you please clean up your own shit?" amongst other choke points in the first year of our marriage.

The next morning, as I pass my "neighbours" along the hallway, behind their stretched smiles and safe greetings of *ohayo!* and *genki-ne?*, I swear they're asking the same.

***

'So how did the interview go?'

A week later, Katelyn's voice is distorted on the main observation deck of Tokyo Tower, 300 meters above the ground. Her voice competes with the howling wind, both of which I find refreshing. It's the first time we've spoken in over a month, and the longest we've spent apart since the wedding.

Which interview was she referring to, though? Was it the English centre where I took an hour-long exam on grammar and spelling, only to find out they wanted a more native speaker? Or the translation firm that struck my name off simply because I hadn't bowed low enough as the Director walked in?

'Wonderful,' I say, raising my voice over the chatter of tourists. 'I think I have a shot.'

'Great,' Katelyn says, with a hint of disappointment. 'What were you applying for?'

I hesitate, slightly embarrassed. 'A tour guide.'

'James, what if you get rejected again?'

The wind presses cold on my cheeks, whips at the lapels of my jacket. 'Well, they said they'd get back to me in a week…'

The plan was to stay a month, or at least till the cherries blossomed. I brace myself for another of her lectures: for breaking an iron rice bowl back in Singapore; for thinking it was easy to survive as a foreigner; for the act of a husband leaving his wife.

'I miss you,' Katelyn says instead, her voice soft and barely catching the wind.

I pause on the metal railing, nudged between other couples admiring the sparkling lights of the city below, my mind racing through possible replies.

'I miss you too,' I say, finally.

'What's going to happen, James?' she asks.

'Well, I'm looking for another place to stay. I'll also need to—'

'I mean, what's going to happen to *us*?'

In the darkness, I picture Katelyn back in our apartment, her feet rooted to the ground instead of draped over my lap, shedding twice the number of tears from binging on K-dramas and mint-chocolate chip ice-cream.

'One step at a time? I haven't gotten the job yet.'

'I'm scared, James.' Her sigh echoes through a room filled with emptiness. 'Even if you *don't* get the job, I'm worried you'll stay.'

I've never heard her voice quiver like this, but I don't want to give an answer we might both regret.

'Have you at least seen the blossoms?' she asks.

'Not yet. They're taking their sweet time to bloom this year.'

'Well, I hope they're everything you've dreamt of.'

After the connection drops, I'm left with the city sprawled before me, like the ocean back home, when Katelyn and I were fresh undergraduates with a common love for skipping lectures and late-night steamboat suppers. Our dates had always ended with us staring outwards at East Coast Park, our hands clasped as the waves lapped at our ankles.

One of those evenings, I remember bending down on one knee.

Little did we know our futures would soon diverge: for Katelyn, marriage meant a new chapter in adulting, maybe a kid or two, and a bright future as a litigation lawyer; for me, it signaled housing loans, mounting renovation costs and the stark realisation of a life fenced in by rising tides, a sunset dipping past the horizon, never to return.

***

A week later, upon Mr Mori's advice, I find myself standing on the banks of the Meguro River, eager to watch cherry blossoms fall for the first time. The evening crowd has gathered, laying straw mats and baskets along the narrow canal running through the dense Tokyo suburb. The soft, gushing water has a calming effect as it shimmers under the glow of lanterns on either side of the river. Above us, a thick forest of pink and white flowers sings in unison each time a breeze ripples through.

I raise a finger to test the strength of the wind, estimating temperature and humidity, then gaze towards the legend of *sakura* only blossoming under a full moon's blessings. Right then, my phone chimes in my pocket:

Mr. Wong, I am pleased to offer you a position in our company. Please come in on Monday to sign the paperwork. Congratulations!

In that very first interview, Mr Mori had asked me: "What are your hopes and dreams?" and "What do you want to achieve in your life?", questions I realise people don't ask once they realise you're married, have kids or a stable job.

My fingers hover over the "Reply" button just as a chorus of exclamations sweeps through the park. '*Sugoi-ne*!' '*Kirei-desuyo*!' People point up as the white petals are taken by the wind, swirling over our heads as they perform their final dance of short, fleeting existence. The cherry blossom don't care for questions, nor do they worry about purpose or ambition; their beauty is simply stated in pink and white.

How does one predict the moment you meet the love of your life? I could talk all day about time standing still or the air being charged like electricity, but the truth is one simply begins to cry. I remember that same inexplicable happiness as Katelyn walked towards me down the aisle, her long, braided hair adorned with pink flowers. I remember pulling the white veil over her head and seeing her face blossom into a smile. I remember the shower of tears as the priest asked, "Do you take this woman to be your lawfully wedded wife?"

In that moment, I remember making a choice.

The following evening, I find myself looking for a familiar face at Changi's Arrival Hall. I see Katelyn, her delicate smile, her palm swirled against the glass, the other spread gently above as she waves towards me.

And I realise my search is over.

J W Voyce - Hold On

"I've missed your voice."

"Same. So, what else is new?—you're not yourself. I can tell that much."

"You can tell that over the phone?"

"Of course. I'm unbelievably intuitive."

"Yeah and super modest, I know."

"Use the nasal spray, Shan."

"I don't need it."

"You sound like you do. You're always so reluctant to take things that'll help you."

"Well forgive me for not wanting to put stuff in my body that I don't need."

"That's quite an ironic thing to say, under the circumstances."

"…"

"…"

I sighed. "This is just like when we were at that garden party, and they'd just cut the grass—"

"And your eyes were red, and streaming, and you couldn't stop sneezing—"

I chuckled. "And I didn't need it then, and I don't need it now!"

Jenna laughed. "See, that statement makes zero sense. Further proof that you should use the spray; you're not thinking straight."

"Just talk to me for a little while."

"Will you use the spray?"

"…"

"How about I don't want to talk to you if you're not gonna use it?"

It was hard to tell if she was joking. "*Please.* I feels like forever since I last spoke to you. I just want to know how it is there—wait, I forget, is there a time-difference?"

"God. How wasted *are* you?"

"No comment." It was difficult to argue with this; none of the lines of the room were straight. Anything l attempted to focus on became warped and wavy.

"And after all the lectures you used to give *me* about drinking too much—"

"Is my invitation still there? To join you?"

"Are you crazy? That's always been the plan. *But* you're actually not allowed to if you don't use the nasal spray."

I laugh. "Seriously? *That's* a condition now?"

"Yes."

"Well, it's pretty ridiculous one." I tried to look at the clock. It was too disorientating but I could tell it was still daytime. This was also obvious from all the light pouring in through the bay window. "Just tell me what it's like there at the moment."

"Oh. I don't know about that…"

"What? Why?"

"I mean, I could try and explain it to you. But it'd be about as comprehensive as trying to convey the beauty of an orchestral performance in a three-word description. Or as effective or fruitful as *you* trying to replicate The Twilight in the Wilderness from memory, left handed, using a worn-out magic marker."

"Fair enough. You know I'm no good at drawing."

"That was part of my argument."

"It's really that good?"

"Yes, Shan, it's really that good."

"But you can't give me any specifics?"

"Not really."

"I'm not sure I believe you."

"You don't believe it's that good?"

"No… I don't think I believe such a place exists."

We both laughed.

"I thought you were more open-minded than that."

"Yeah, I used to be. Maybe I'm jaded by experience."

"See, Shan, you're a terrible drunk. It just makes you grouchy."

"I just think, when the expectations are that overwhelmingly high for something, it's almost impossible for the thing to meet them."

"Well, you have to trust me then. It meets all the expectations."

"I just don't understand how it could."

"My, you *are* a sceptical Shanny today."

"It's also just simple logic. No matter how good something is, if you do it long enough, you get used to it. And then it becomes dull."

"All right. What about if there are so many things to try that you can't possibly get bored?"

"Do you *always* have to be so goddamn cryptic?"

Jenna laughed. "Isn't that why you fell in love with me?"

"Don't, Jen…"

"Isn't it though? You love how mysterious I am, and I love you for loving me, despite the fact I never give you straight answer to anything."

"If you really loved me you wouldn't have left."

"*Shan.*"

"…"

"You know that's not a fair thing to say."

"I know. I'm sorry."

"If I'd had any choice in the matter I—"

"I know." I felt sick. I was basically lying all the way back on the sofa now to try and combat the dizziness, but still felt like I was on a rubber dingy in the middle of a stormy sea. I closed my eyes. It helped. "Right, let's get back to why your argument is logically flawed…"

"…"

"Firstly, for every up there must be a down. That's basic science—"

"What do you know about basic science?"

"Shh. But I'm right. Equal and opposite reactions blah blah blah…"

"All right, back to *my* point then: what if you had so many things to do, that you start doing one thing, and you keep doing it until you become engrossed. Eventually you reach peak levels of enjoyment, and then once you're there, you simply move onto something else and become engrossed in that. No getting too used to anything, no boredom, no lull in between…"

"That's quite a programme they've got out there."

"Some would say it's the best."

"I don't think it's humanly possible—"

"I've been over this—"

"No—I was about to say, I don't think it's humanly possible to meet anyone as infuriating as you!"

"Aww. Thanks."

"Not a compliment."

"Sure it is. You're saying I'm unique."

"Fine… Well, despite how aggravatingly vague you're determined to try and be, I still want to join you there."

"And you can."

"I mean, I'm ready. Now."

Jenna laughed. "You're really not though, Shan."

"Why the hell not? I'm not doing anything worthwhile here. It's all just so boring. Work sucks, I don't want to see anyone, I'm not eating or sleeping properly."

"See, I told you. You're not yourself; the girl I know sleeps and eats like a giant panda."

"Yeah. I remember the stupid nickname."

Jenna giggled. "Shanda."

"Still not funny. Or the least bit inventive."

"How much sleep are you getting?"

"An hour here or there. Um, last week I think less than that… That's when I started seeing stuff."

"Seeing stuff? Damn it, Shan, you're hallucinating? Have you been to the doctor?"

"It's not that bad. To be honest, sometimes it's kinda nice. The whole out of body experience type deal. Like I'm barely even here, you know."

"I didn't know things were this bad."

"Well, I'm talking to you, aren't I?"

"Hey, what's that supposed to mean? You only talk to me seriously when things get desperate?"

"I guess that's pretty accurate, historically."

"You need to get a hold of yourself, babe."

I smiled. "Mmm. I like that. Call me babe again."

"I mean it. You need to be taking better care of yourself. And you can start by using that damn nasal spray."

"Oh yeah, priorities. Can't forget the nasal spray."

"Yeah. One thing at a time. Baby steps…"

"Oh my god, Jenna… Just — I mean… The count—the pollen… It's not — it's not even that high today."

"Jesus. Can you hear yourself? Does what you're saying even register? How incoherent you're sounding?"

"I told you. I haven't been sleeping."

"Forget that. How much have you *drank*?"

"Just… some wine."

"Yeah, and the rest."

"O.K. And—the rest."

"You know it's making me extremely unhappy, hearing you like this."

"You sounded pretty cheerful a minute ago. I thought you had a million things to do over there… Infinite things to become engrossed with. You made it sound like you were *perfectly* happy."

"Yeah. Well now I'm talking to you."

"Ouch…"

"You know I didn't mean it like that. Don't be so sensitive."

My head was pounding. With my eyes open again the room seemed to be throbbing sympathetically; inflating and deflating in partnership with my headache. It started to become harder and harder to keep track of my thoughts. "Look, Jen. I just don't understand why I can't just come out there now. You hear how miserable I am on my own. You *just* said it."

"Because you know that's not part of the plan."

"Oh, screw the plan. If you can just up and leave, I don't see why can't too."

"It doesn't work like that. I had no choice."

"Fine. But I'm pretty sure I've made my choice anyway."

"Shania, no, you can't…" Jenna's voice sounded different now. The lightness had faded from it. In all the years we'd been together I'd never heard her sound so serious. "Can you just listen to me? Do you understand what you're doing? You're going to ruin everything. I need you to just hold on. I've said you can come out here. Can't that be enough?"

"It's too hard. I thought I could do it, but I had no idea it'd be this difficult."

"We've done long distance before."

"C'mon. This is different."

"It's not that different." I heard her sigh. Some levity had returned and it made me feel a little better. Jenna was supposed to be the fun one, everyone said it about us. I was the one who dealt with all the serious stuff: chores, bills, long-term arrangements. She was the one who made a joke of everything. She stopped us from worrying, from stressing out too much, or from ever really acting our age. Whenever things started to go off the rails though, it was me who brought us back down to earth, not her. It sounds disgustingly cliched, but she was the Yin to my Yang. In college, when we met, everyone would comment on how perfectly opposite we were. And now, somehow, we'd arrived here: she was lecturing me. I found the reversal of roles unsettling. "You know, Shan, whatever you need to do to make things easier, I'm fine with it."

I frowned. "What do you mean by that?"

"You know. Go out more. See other people. Whatever. It's completely acceptable under the circumstances."

"No way."

"Yes way. You're in a slump, and that's putting it mildly. You know I've never been insecure; as long as you don't forget about little old me, I honestly don't care what you do."

"That's insane."

"It's really not. I'm sure other people have been telling you the same thing."

"I don't really care what other people have been saying. I think I've held on long enough. I'm ready to come out there."

"Patience is a virtue, Shan. All good things come to those who wait."

I rolled my eyes. "Any other worn-out aphorisms you want to say?"

"Um… Everything happens for a reason? It's always darkest before the dawn?"

I tutted, in spite of my smile. "But what if it's not as simple as you're making out? What if it isn't like you say it is?"

"I guess you're just gonna have to trust me on that."

"I just don't know how you can be so confident. Nothing is guaranteed. Things can change."

"They can. But I'm telling you as long as you follow my simple instructions, everything will fall into place. Take it from someone in the know."

"This is all sounding a bit airy fairy. You'll be talking about fate and horoscopes and crystals in a minute." I laughed, but my mirth wasn't genuine.

"Whatever. You're not going to remember any of this anyhow."

"What d'you mean?"

"I can tell how completely out of it you are. You're going to wake up tomorrow and forget we even had this conversation. But it's O.K., as long as I've broken through to some unconscious part of you, that's all that matters."

I was starting to feel bewildered as well as disorientated, like my short-term memory was failing me. I couldn't even grasp basic things. Like, when was the last time I saw my wife in person? Did she get a plane out there? I didn't remember going to airport… I really was a mess.

"Jen… Is it real?" I found myself asking, consumed with a peculiar doubt.

She howled with laughter. "Yes, you absolute space cadet—damn, I don't think I've ever heard you this goofy—yes. It's as real as it gets. And it doesn't even matter that you won't remember talking to me. All that matters is that you do as I say."

"O.K…"

"And that means you go and use the nasal spray *right now*."

"Jesus, back to the spray. You really won't let that go, will you?"

"Please. For me…"

"Fine! If it'll get you off my back."

Even though I couldn't see her face, I knew she was smiling. "Like I said, baby steps. Once you've done that, you're on your own. You'll have to figure the rest out yourself."

"Where is it?"

"You know damn well where it is. Medicine cabinet. Where else would it be?"

"I always thought—aren't anti-histamines better for—fine, for all the good it's going to do—but… can you please stay on the phone while I get it?"

"Of course."

I stumbled to my feet. The room was whirling around me. It took far more effort to reach the bathroom than expected. I closed my eyes when I approached the cabinet—I had no desire to look at my reflection. I opened it, keeping the phone in my other hand, and after a slight rummage I found the fabled nasal spray.

Two large blasts in each nostril. Ouch.

"I love you," Jenna said.

"I love you too."

The stinging sensation caused by the spray was nearly blinding. You're on your own after that, Jenna had said. She was right: I was suddenly alert, but also, suddenly alone. I looked for the phone in my right hand. Empty.

Things were making sense now. But the stark remembrance was heartrendingly painful. I walked back into the living room and found the phone, still plugged in. I lifted it out of its terminal, knowing what I needed to do.

"911, what's your emergency?"

"Hi." My own voice seemed much louder than before. It almost startled me. But it was also delayed and feeble; I really did sound out of it. "I've taken an overdose of pain medication," I said, trying to overcome the lag between thoughts and speech. It felt like talking with a mouth full of cotton wool. I listened to their questions. "Um, Oxycodone, Codeine… But I've also just taken a large hit of Narcan, through a nasal spray. Will that offset—" The person on the line interrupted me to tell me that that was good but they had more questions. I answered them. "Yes. About a bottle and a half of red wine… Several glasses of gin. I don't know how much exactly."

The ambulance was apparently on its way. "Just hold on, Ma'am."

Yes, *hold on.* That's all I needed to do. There was something vaguely reminiscent about the instruction, like I'd heard it recently. I felt foolish. I felt like one of those 'time-wasters' I always outwardly judged when I watched the reality EMT shows. Great—another thing to be guilty for.

What would Jen have thought if she could see me now? I looked up at the framed photo on the living room wall. It was such a good picture of us both. I looked somewhat aloof; I'd been glancing slightly away from the camera as it was taken, but Jenna was looking straight down the barrel. It always made it feel like she was staring right at you. It had been six months now. I needed to get a hold of myself. This wasn't me. I gazed straight back into Jenna's eyes in the photo. She'd be so angry at me if she knew what I'd tried to do. It was like it could almost sense this in the picture. She would've definitely tried to talk me around—but it's O.K., I didn't go through with it. I changed my mind.

I wanted to sleep. It felt like I hadn't slept properly in months. Truthfully, I hadn't. But I remained standing. I needed to be responsive for the EMTs, I needed to let them inside and then do as they said.

"Forgive me, Jen," I mumbled to the picture. If only I could talk to her one last time. Just one more phone conversation with her would've meant everything to me in that moment. I just wanted to tell her how much I missed her. Maybe it was good that she wasn't around tonight though. When she'd gotten ill, she told me I needed to live my life, live it with even more appreciation and purpose than before—to make up for her absence. I was still young, she'd said; I couldn't just give up. But I had. I'd not fulfilled any of those promises. I'd groaned when people said she wouldn't have liked to see me acting this way. A tear slid off my face and dripped onto my shirt. People always say stuff like that. People who didn't understand what it was like to have a part of yourself torn away. But it was true; she genuinely would have hated it.

I felt so nauseated. Why would I choose to make myself feel even worse than before? O.K., if I got through this, I'd start taking better care of myself. Baby steps. For her. And I'd tell them all of this at the hospital, when they inevitably questioned my mental state. I'd tell them it was a mistake, a moment of temporary insanity, and that It wouldn't happen again.

I looked at the little bottle of Narcan spray still in my hand. How strange to find it in the cabinet… I had no idea such a thing was even in the house. It must have been Jen's.

John Buckley - The Fitbit

You know how it is. You get dumped by your boyfriend, lose your job and are then told you're a fatty and at risk of diabetes or heart disease unless you lose weight drastically. So much for comfort eating; doesn't bring you much comfort does it? Or maybe you don't know how it is; maybe you are not that unfortunate, though I am not saying I was unlucky - I had brought it all on myself.

I admit I am not the easiest person to get on with. Alright, if you want the whole, unpleasant, truth, I am not - was not - a nice person. Looking back as far as I can see with my mind's eye, I never have been. I wasn't exactly a bully at school, but all my classmates steered clear of me which made me come on a bit strong when I got lonely. Then they avoided me even more. They had operated social distance policy around me long before a similar idea had ever occurred to Boris Johnson. Despite having all the right parts being in good working order, it took me two years after leaving school to get a boyfriend. When I did, I thought, right mate, you're going nowhere else and I told him straight what would happen if he so much as looked at another girl, yet he still dared do it. Men, eh? Well, I am sure he must have more than looked at her because I caught them in bed together. Angry? I think I may have broken his arm, but he was asking for it, right?

The same day - same ruddy day - I got called into the office at work, a beauty parlour. The boss said she could forgive me not being beautiful - cheek! - but I could at least smile and be pleasant to the customers and hadn't she warned me about it before? I said I hadn't come across a customer yet that was worth smiling at. That was when she handed me my P45. I think I may have broken her nose.

It all gave me quite a turn and I had a dizzy spell that worried me so off I went to the doctor's. He was one of these modern GPs who strongly recommended a non-Mars Bar low-cake high-lettuce diet and some healthy exercise.

He said: "You're obese."

"No," I said like a fool, "O'Brien."

"I mean you are *obese*, too fat, overweight, roly-poly," he said, labouring the point I think you'll agree.

I may have broken his computer.

Sorry. I'm getting into my story and I haven't even introduced myself yet. I am Miriam, nicknamed Miz by everyone, but it's not short for Miriam it's short for Mizmogs on account of me being short on smiles and good humour. I got labelled in primary and it stuck. In high school I was second from bottom in a like-ability poll. It was hurtful: I felt as if I was UK in the Eurovision Song Contest. The only person I beat was Snide Evans and he was the maths teacher.

But back to my story. I've been depressed, sort of, most of my life, certainly long before I knew what depression was. But this triple whammy - boyfriend, job, doctor - was a bit too much to bear and I kicked myself leaving the surgery for not telling the Doc about my not sleeping and let him give me some pills, the heavy stuff because oblivion seemed inviting right then and on the way back I was mulling over alternatives… the river (too cold), a bridge (too messy), carbon monoxide (asthma)… and I was driving on automatic pilot. We've all caught ourselves making the right moves without thinking about it because your mind is off on its own somewhere doing something else entirely and I'd turned into Johnson Street before I realised where I was and it suddenly registered I had just driven past a jeweller's shop I'd never seen before.

Odd. I thought I knew every shop in town but I'd never seen this this one before. There and then I made my mind up. I quickly pulled over and the car behind basted its horn and made me realise I'm a better driver when I am not fully conscious of what I'm doing. I got out and walked back to the shop. The sight of the jeweller's suggested a fitbit might be what I needed. Get one of them I figured and I'd have a choice: live or the other thing - and the other thing always seemed involve discomfort of one kind or another.

An old-fashioned bell over the door jangled as I entered and behind the counter was the jeweller. He looked very homely in a Bagpuss sort of way and in his hand he held, amazingly, a fitbit. Some things are meant to be, I thought.

"It's the last one," he said, without looking up. "It's exactly what you need."

Was he being sarky? I gave him a long look and thought about poking him in the eye, but he just slid the fitbit across the counter encouragingly. "Try it on, you'll never take it off," he said.

So I did and immediately the prospect of a new slimmer, healthier, happier Miriam conjured itself up in my mind. The jeweller smiled knowingly. I handed over £60 figuring if I was careful and looked after it I could use it for a couple of weeks then return it, say it wasn't working properly and get my money back. I walked out of the shop wearing it. His bell jangled. I remember thinking that's really cheery that, and when I got outside I decided I'd test out the fitbit straight away. I walked straight past my car and went home. I could come back for it later, but if I had slashed my wrists between times then the fact it was on double yellows would be someone's problem.

Steps taken 1,100 it said when I reached my front door.

Blood pressure 220/135 (high), it went on.

Heartbeat 180pm (high).

Weight: 15st 8lb (high).

That last figure got me. How would it know? I hadn't told it. Amazing what these gadgets can do nowadays.

Now, I'd heard when you bought a fitbit you tended to do the right things by it, try and please it and improve on the numbers by taking the steps it wants you to take. I didn't want to feel I was letting it down I walked back for my car and found I'd take the total over 2,000 already.

That night, I ran up and down the stairs a few times and when I'd recovered I drew the curtains and jogged on the spot until I was exhausted and in need of a burger and cuppa, but I forewent the burger. By bedtime the day's count was 3,205 steps. Hey, that's not bad, I said to myself and when I woke up I glanced at the fitbit on my wrist and it flashed a Good Morning message as if it has been waiting for me to open my eyes. I might have thought it a very clever had I not been thinking I was sure I took the thing off before getting into bed and put it on the stand next to my bed. Mustn't have done.

The day seemed keen for me to join it and I was just as eager. The sun was streaming through the window and there was probably some birds singing as well. I showered and went to my favourite room in the house: the kitchen. The idea of a challenge had set itself solidly in my brain so I had sweetener in my tea instead of sugar and toast covered in that plastic spread that says it tastes like butter, but if butter ever found out it would sue. I had numbers to beat. The challenge was everything!

I went for another long walk, well, I hadn't any work to go to had I? I power-walked when there was no one around to see me. The strange thing about walking in the countryside is that people you pass invariably smile and say hello. I had no idea why, but if you met the same people in the street they wouldn't give you a second glance and that has always been good enough for me. 'Good morning,' they'd chirp happily like a jeweller's doorbell and I was mystified. I didn't know them, so why were they speaking to me?

That night I pressed the button for my results:

Steps 5,600

BP 200/105 (high)

Heart 167 (high)

Weight: 15-3 (high) It may be high fitbit, but, wow!

Smiles 0.

Smiles!? What the… I stared at the screen in disbelief. How could… I mean what… That's not…

It preyed on my mind the rest of the evening. I heated a couple of meat and potato pies for my meal, but was so preoccupied with the fitbit's message I could only manage one.

You may think I was being silly and superstitious but I didn't take the fitbit off my wrist when I climbed into bed for fear that when I woke up it would magically be back on there. I was still bewildered when I lay down to go to sleep that night. Surely…

Good Morning said my fitbit the next day and off we went. It didn't really say it, there was just a message on the screen. There's a canal nearby and off along the towpath we went, Fitbit and I. I even took a bottle of water. Good Morning said my fellow walkers, 'Good morning,' I said, begrudgingly at first, but really when you get the hang of it, being polite is not that bad. When the next one came along I experimented with a smile and the one after that I actually spoke first. Good morning!

The good mornings turned to good afternoons and I found a pub for lunch and picked up a menu. Call me stupid if you like but as I wondered what I should have chips with I glanced almost nervously at my wrist, as if to seek approval. The word on the screen was: No. No what? Just No, in capitals. NO. So I sat in the fresh air with my soda water and salad and walked home.

That night I checked my readings:

Steps 10,574

BP 190/97

Heart: 150

Weight: 15-5

Smiles: 26

Pleasant Rating: 14.

My God! What else did it know? This was spooky, not right at all, yet it never crossed my mind to take the fitbit back to the jewellery shop. Even so it's one thing telling me my weight and counting my smiles, but gauging how nice I had been was sinister - and it had been stingy with my score! I fell asleep thinking about it: 14, out of what? I had to assume it was 100 and the next day my walks were full of 'Good mornings,' and 'afternoons' and I even passed the time of day with people who wanted to talk a little; I waved to folk on the narrowboats chugging past and I didn't think anglers sitting there hour after hour in their camouflage suits were stupid at all. Of course not.

At the pub a man about my own age, not bad looking in a Chris Hemsworth sort of way and, therefore, way out of my league, asked if he could share my table. I nearly said sod off, go and find your own table, but instead we started chatting. I was quite proud of my new skill. I'd never really chatted to anyone before. No-one's ever wanted to chat to me. It's good, isn't it?

That night by steps had gone over 12,000.

BP: 160/90;

Heart: 121.

Weight: 15-2.

Smiles 45.

Pleasant Rating: 52. Hey, Fitbit was beginning to like me.

I didn't take it of my wrist again that night and the next day I made my way to same pub and found myself waiting in case Chris Hemsworth turned up again. He did and he smiled and I smiled back and I shoved up on my seat and he sat down next to me and he didn't mind at all that the outside of our thighs were touching. It was as all as natural as anything. He said something funny and I laughed. Then I said something funny and he made a polite chuckle and I made a note to sharpen up on my sense of humour. His name wasn't Chris though, it was Danny.

I said, 'I'm Miz."

And he said: "Is that because you're not married yet.'

I thought, steady on girl, don't fall off your seat.

"Not miss, or even Ms, but Miz, short for misery. I'm actually Miriam, Miriam Obese, I mean O'Brien."

"I'll call you Miriam," he said and smiled. I smiled back. In fact, thinking about improving my fitbit count, I gave him two smiles. He asked me what I did for a living and I told him. We got on well. Two hours and three alcohol and sugar free drinks passed. We got on really well. We both said we'd try and do it again the following day.

This time I ran to the pub. I ran knowing all the time Danny wouldn't be there because nice things don't keep happening to a mizmogs. I rejoiced when he was and Fitbit clocked up the smiles.

We sat with our legs touching. My thigh was getting used to it. He said it was interesting that I'd worked in a beautician's because he was a hairdresser and was opening a new shop and maybe we should get together.

"Gerroffwithyer," I said.

"A partnership," he said, and I'm sure my thigh got warmer at that very moment. Something was going on down there at any rate.

While my mind can sometimes go AWOL, it can also get flustered. This was me, Mizmogs, fat and friendless sitting here with Danny Hemsworth and he was saying things that had two meanings. I was still overweight. Was I still clinically obese?"

"I can get down to 11 stone," I blurted and saw the puzzled look on his face. "Just saying."

"Have a think, call me."

"But I haven't got your number," I said stupidly.

"I'm going to give it you now."

Ooooh, I thought.

"Where is it, the shop?" I asked.

He said - and get this: "In Johnson Street"

I looked up into his eyes sharply. He sensed my surprise, or unease.

"An empty building, used to be a jewellers years and years ago. Do you know it?"

I shook my head. No, no, no. Well, actually yes. It might have closed down years ago but I went in it last week.

It was a hot day, but I swear I shivered and all the way home, little tremors up and down my spine. I couldn't Danny's words out of my mind. I went by way of Johnson Street wanting to see a jewellery shop, but somehow knowing it wouldn't be there and it it wasn't. The window was whitewashed and bore a sign: OPENING SOON: LOVE IS IN THE HAIR.

That made me laugh. I glanced at my wrist. Fitbit was still there, but it said nothing. What was I expecting? That it would say: Go for it, call him? I couldn't help it, I had to check the numbers there and then.

Steps: 10,940 - down a bit but I hadn't got home yet.

BP: 143/85 (near normal)

Heart: 89 (getting there)

Weight: 15-0

Smiles 67 - I grinned and it clocked up another, 68.

Pleasant Rating 87 - Woo-hoo! Then a new statistic flashed up.

FR: 91.

FR? What the hell was that? I flicked through the menu, tapping its tiny button for all I was worth. It would be there somewhere.

"Come on, come on, come on…"

Yes, there it was: FR - Fanciability Rating.

I let it sink in a moment, that a fitbit was weighing me up as if I was a sex object.

Well, good for it! It's just men that are not supposed to do that, or at least not tell you about it but I know they do. I think you'll find high-tech electronic gadgets can do and say as they please. I know I was getting fitter inside and out. I sensed it. People were getting to like me when previously even my boyfriend only liked me because I told him to. Men do not find me attractive: it's been a rule of my life.

Unless… unless… Nah. Never. No way. Surely? But… maybe… I took my mobile out of my pocket and started to dial.

John Sandry - The Man In The Dark

The man in the dark finally laid still. Perhaps this was acceptance of his fate. This was not at all how the man reacted at first. He had panicked when he had awoken alone in total darkness. Perplexed it seemed a shroud of impregnable dusk was over his eyes, blotting out every hint of shape. He could not feel a covering over his eyes and determined he was somewhere absent of light entirely.

Terror had detonated within him when his breath did not expire into the open atmosphere- instead it had reflected in a proximity far too local to his own face. Alarmed, this had felt as dangerous as coming too close to an otherworldly predator. The man did not understand what was happening. His head hurt, his wrist and ankles also pained. He tried to roll over on his side but met immovable resistance on both sides of his body. Trying to sit up was not permitted either. His disorientated instincts raced to every awful likelihood it could calculate. Every probability spelt doom.

This awful shadowland absorbed his adrenaline-fueled screams; he was not afforded a slither of an echo. Wherever he was in the void, his bellowing heart and voice were the only noise his ears could register.

The man in the dark learnt very quickly are certain things that break a persons' will; being unheard, no matter the volume of his cries was one. Another was to be held completely powerless to determine his own future. The man in the dark discovered this when he fought against unyielding surfaces denying his every move. There simply was no give in them, no matter the frantic exertions of his entire strength. The ache of his wrists and ankles; and their subsequent inability to perform any independent motions told him the bad news. The hard surfaces in all directions, the full darkness, the bindings of foot and hand could only mean he was incarcerated.

He learnt that there was a way to further increase the monstrosity of his incarceration. It was to bury the person beneath the breast of the earth. Breathing deep in order to suppress the overwhelming claustrophobia, he eventually calmed enough so have his sense of smell return to him. His nostrils were filled with the scent of the earth and grave soil. The pungent aroma was unmistakable. His mind made the calculations and the solution was right in front of him. He was buried alive. He was allowed only the knowledge that his future was a slow torture and then undignified death. It hit him hard and without mercy. All he could do was let the voracious soil digest and decay all his remaining sanity. The man in the dark was not exceptional. He was a regular man and quickly succumbed to the poisoned environment.

Delirium followed closely after this discovery.

The man in the dark did occasionally have moments of lucidity that were fluttering. Inevitably he would dive deep back into psychosis. In this state of derangement, he laughed at his plight- all rationality thrown to all points of the compass. The pleading impulses of survival were quickly forgotten. He was no longer a man in the dark- but undertook the transmutation into the dweller of the void.

The dweller of the void scoffed at time. It had been a thousand years- perhaps more since he had commenced his life sentence. He knew that the man he once was should have asked why he was in this subterranean sanctuary. The man would have cried and wailed in desperate despair. But down in the domain of the detritivore he, the inhabitant of murky eternity, was akin to a great worm who felt only the comfort of mother earth and her embrace.

Odd memories called upon the occupant in the void which made him uneasy. It was about the man in the dark. The occupant of the void endeavored to push the reminiscences away because the man's memories were a tangled nebulous and unwanted down here. What did pierce the veil despite his protestations- was the knowing that the man in the dark was not a good person. He had done bad things to worse people than he. He seemed to think they had put him where he was now. The inhabitant of murky eternity thought that he should really thank them if he ever could. He happily allowed his mind to trickle away from the surface dwellers.

A sudden terrible thought entered his awareness; what if someone was to attempt to liberate him from his pitch-black paradise? What if they wanted his to steal his solace, his clarity- Worse still, take his spot for themselves.

He would fight them! He was not sure how, for long ago had his body dissipated from reality. He was now just a consciousness in its rightful position. When in unconquerable night, there was no need for clumsy bodies, limbs nor senses. His will to life, and desire to stay should surely overpower any usurper. His mind was thusly put at ease knowing he was safe exactly where he was. No one would ever find him; nor want to come dig him up and drag him out. He returned to formless thinking.

The inhabitant of murky eternity was tersely bothered from the peaceful acceptance of his fate when a noise roused his senses. Vulgar thudding and unkind displacing of dirt came towards him in his shadow bound cocoon. His listened desperately. Panic and toxic fear returned to visit him. Scraping, scratching and snuffled rummaging filled the dank heated air.

His ears became antennae like that of an insect. Instinctively he was informed that he was no longer alone. Something had encroached upon his territory- looking to challenge him for his place.

Upon this detection, had heard a peculiar sound that astounded him. It was faint and weak; it rasped at a barely registered volume. It took a long-paused moment for the man in the dark to calculate within his fractured mind, it was not a hallucination of his own creation. He was then sure beyond a reasonable doubt. The sound, it had come from his own mouth.

The revelation that thunderstruck the inhabitant of murky eternity, was that he had not told the inbound intruder to leave and never return. He had asked- no begged- it to help him. He again, the man in the dark, had whimpered like a pitiful creature. He wished to be helped and cried appealingly to be pulled from his dirt hell.

There are moments when the most foolish or the insane can have moments of lucidity. This return to reality was enough to almost pull the man in the dark right back into madness again. It was much easier to process and accept lunacy over this true desperately despairing situation.

The man in the dark had been buried alive. The copper smell of coagulated blood roused his sensibilities like an ammonia stick to the fainted. The throbbing pressure upon his wrists and ankles indicated that he was securely bound. The penetrating smell of soil and root echoed the words he had heard before losing consciousness. "Put him in a pine box. Bury him alive for the beast to have!"

The blood had come from metal striking the back of his head and pressure tearing his scalp. The voices had come from the men he had double crossed at great personal loss to them. They had caught him when he had tried to run. They had punished him. The beast though was unfathomable. He did not understand what that had meant.

The continued ruckus coming from outside his pine box confines confused him. He would have no-one coming to his rescue. Everyone that he knew would leave him in place to serve out this punishment. Who then was coming to his aid? Were they coming to his aid?

As the excavating drew closer, a curious thing occurred to the man in the black. His directional bearings told him that he was facing up. His back was against the firm surface and his limbs could move ever slightly forward. The man in the dark swore that direction the intruder was coming from was wrong. His sanity may have begun slipping away again- but he swore that it come from beneath him.

The digging soon was ravenous- like an unholy fiend that had not eaten in days had discovered his scent. Excavating it struck through intricate webbing of mycelium and fungi. Tunneling it came through bone and elapsed remains of empires. Burrowing it snorted like a blind thing through microbes and micro fauna; no obstacle was to be a barrier for this menace.

The man in the black felt his stomach turn queasy instantly. He would have screamed, fought and attempted to escape- but it was no use. His oxygen supply was exhausted. He was exhausted. All that he could manage to do was lay there and listen.

The man in the dark was no longer alone. He had been found. Karma was delivered and the meal collected.

Karmen Špiljak - The Assistant

You don't expect someone to die at lunch, especially not when you're there for your first meeting with a big client. My boss, Kevin, insisted we arrive early to prepare.

The restaurant was almost empty, a large, dimly-lit space that left enough room between the tables to prevent eavesdropping.

'With Oxley, privacy is a must,' Kevin said. 'He fired his last PR guys, because they'd discussed details over the phone. On a train.'

'Let me guess. There was a journalist.'

'Isn't there always one? You can't be too careful, when you work with a business like Bert's.'

We ordered water. Kevin, who hadn't eaten any breakfast, cracked a breadstick between his fingers and devoured it.

'I've heard he has a new assistant,' I said.

Kevin lifted his index finger and took a long gulp of water. I waited for him to finish chewing.

'Keep her in the loop, Anna. Assistants are the first to know, when things go wrong.'

I eyed the remaining breadstick, but decided against eating it, so as not to spoil my appetite. As Kevin reached for it, there was a rustle at the door. We turned towards a large man in a business suit and a rather petite woman in long tweed pants and a silk blouse. She had dark bangs and cat-eye glasses, the kind reserved for artists and people with strong opinions.

'Here they come,' said Kevin.

We shook hands and exchanged pleasantries. A moment later, a waiter presented us with menus. Unlike Janice, who studied the content with an intense focus, her boss flipped through the initial pages. It appeared as if the idea of having a soup or a salad disgusted him.

'Ah,' he said. 'Roast chicken.'

'The best in town, according to the reviews,' said Janice, without diverting her gaze away from the menu.

'My wife keeps on nagging me to cut down on meat, but I keep on telling her. I can't look as if I'm on a diet, not in my line of business.' Bert said. Kevin let out a polite chuckle. The waiter took our orders and returned with the drinks, water for Janice and me, coke for Kevin and a quarter of red for Bert Oxley. He cradled his glass.

'So, what are we doing about the leak?' he said. 'Those vultures can't wait to eat us alive.'

'We'll start with a press release,' I said, 'to clarify the leak was an unfortunate coincidence and you're investigating.'

'The news will go stale in a few days. The world will move on,' said Kevin.

'They'll run out of names to call me. What was the last one again, Jan? Satan or killer?'

'I believe they referred to killing in general terms,' Janice said.

Bert pulled out his phone and read out loud, as he scrolled down.

'Just listen. *Dangerous* pesticides poison drinking water in Taiwan.'

He flung his hands into the air.

'As if it's my fault people don't read the instructions.'

He scrolled further down.

'Where's the last one, Jan?'

The muscles around Janice's eyes tightened. Slowly, she pulled out her phone. 'How long before AgroChems stop killing people?' she said.

Bert clapped.

'That's it. That's what we have to work with.'

'No problem,' said Kevin. 'We can spin this around.'

'I take it your lawyers are informed?' I said.

Bert licked his wine-stained lips.

'They're on it, alright,' he said. 'Bleeding me dry.'

At the sight of the waiter bringing our appetisers, Bert's mouth curled to the side. Foie gras for Bert, beef carpaccio for Kevin, smoked salmon for me and carrot and ginger soup for Janice. Bert pushed the pieces of salad to the side. The creases on Janice's forehead deepened, as he sliced the foie gras with his fork.

'The soup looks nice,' I said to Janice, in an attempt to engage her. She smiled at me and scooped a few pieces of fried ginger off the top.

'We need to put an end to this cancer talk,' said Bert, with his mouth full. 'The shareholders want this taken care of, so make it your priority.'

'Absolutely,' I said. 'We did just that with Infestex. From what I understood, you only had one case, right?'

Bert Oxley swatted the air: 'Ages ago! They couldn't prove more than that. Of course, others saw easy money and…'

Janice coughed, as though trying to clear her throat, or perhaps, to cover up an awkward situation.

'Everything alright?' I asked.

She put one hand in front of her mouth.

'I'm fine,' she said.

Her eyes watered. She patted her chest with a deer-like gesture, elegant and on the watch.

'You sure?' Kevin said.

'She's a rock,' he said. 'Aren't you, Jan?'

Her face turned paler.

'I'll be fine,' she said, in a choked voice.

Bert pushed Janice's empty glass closer to her. I filled it with water. She emptied it in a few gulps and beamed at me with gratitude.

'Good,' said Bert. 'It's bloody impossible to find a good assistant these days.'

Perhaps it was a trick of the light, but the colour returned to Janice's cheeks. Soon after, the waiter brought our mains. He presented Bert with his roast chicken and rosemary potatoes, Kevin with steak tartar and fries, Janice with pumpkin gnocchi and sage butter and me with a mushroom risotto. We waited for Bert to start eating.

I was grateful for a few moments of silence, to enjoy the rich, earthy flavour of creamy mushrooms in my mouth. Kevin delved straight into his meat and took a break to fill up on the fries. Janice cut her gnocchi into tiny pieces, then chewed each one with pursed lips. Bert moaned with pleasure. I avoided looking in his direction, so as to gain some time to eat without having to talk.

It was a few moments afterwards that I became aware of a peculiar silence. When I glanced back up, Bert was glaring at me. His eyes were wide open and stood out from his round face. Perhaps some risotto had escaped the spoon and landed on me? I examined my shirt for food waste, but found none. Bert's face was flushed.

'Too spicy?' I said.

Only then did Janice turn to Bert. The sight of him unsettled her.

'Don't worry, Mr Oxley,' she said. 'I'll get your pills.'

She reached into his jacket pocket.

'What kind of pills?' I asked.

'For his heart.'

Bert's eyes glistened with tears. He struggled to say something, but couldn't. With remarkable calm, Janice searched through his pockets.

'Maybe he forgot them?' I said.

'I put them in myself,' Janice said and tapped over his pockets. 'Mr Oxley, where is your nitroglycerin?'

Bert tried to say something, but couldn't. He clutched onto his heart and staggered to one side like a drunk, before falling down. I rushed to his side and frantically searched through his pockets.

'Call an ambulance!' Kevin shouted.

Janice leaned closer to Bert. His mouth opened and closed, as his eyes darted from Kevin to me and back to Janice. All he managed to get out was a strangled 'Ssssh…' His eyes shot with blood.

Saliva gathered at the corner of Bert's mouth and started to ooze. His eyes bulged. Everyone in the restaurant was looking at us, paralysed by the shock. The waiter informed us the ambulance was on the way.

Janice tapped Bert gently on the cheek. 'Mr Oxley? Blink if you hear me,' she said. Bert continued to stare at the ceiling.

When the ambulance took Bert away, I stayed behind with Janice.

'I don't get it,' she said. 'The pills were in his pocket.'

'Maybe he lost them?'

She shook her head.

'I checked before we left. His wife insists he has to carry a spare, but he…'

'Did he change his jacket just before he left? Kevin sometimes does this,' I said.

'Maybe.'

Janice's face was pale. Her hands were still trembling, when the waiter brought us some brandy. I downed mine and ordered another. Janice sat on the stool and stared blankly at her glass without touching it.

'I remember putting them there, before we left.'

'He'll be alright,' I said, but when my phone rang a few minutes later, restlessness nestled into the pit of my stomach. Kevin was calling to tell me Bert Oxley had died of a heart attack. Janice understood what happened, before I told her.

'I'm sorry,' I said. 'Will you be alright?'

She nodded, her eyes hollow, as though she was retreating into a blank space behind.

'I haven't worked for him for that long.'

'Still. I'm sure he…'

They say not to speak ill of the dead, but I struggled to think of something positive to say about Bert. I signalled to the waiter for the bill.

'Janice, would you like to share a cab?'

'Thanks,' she said. 'I'll be alright.'

Despite my attempts to pick up the check, Janice insisted on paying for the brandy. She unzipped her purple purse, made of fake leather. As she pulled out her wallet, something rolled over inside her bag. I pretended to brush a piece of dirt off my pants, so I could take a closer look.

There it was. A tiny bottle of pills with Oxley's name and thick black letters spelling 'nitroglycerin'. Janice caught my gaze and held it for a few moments. There wasn't even a hint of surprise on her face.

'You know what,' she said. 'I'd love to share that cab after all.'

Kate Bramhall - Another Lost Day

The summer of 66 was eternal.

Mandy had spent the first few weeks of the holidays drunk. Mandy spent most weeks drunk. Eileen sometimes hated Mandy for being drunk, and sometimes Eileen simply didn't care. Mandy and her daddy argued a lot. Sometimes about Mandy being drunk. Sometimes about Daddy being drunk. Sometimes about nothing. Sometimes about everything.

Eileen tried to stay out of their way, but that summer the heat was so exhausting that she could not last more than a couple of hours in her box-room. The little bedroom - well it had a bed in it - at the back of the two-storey terrace house, was a heat trap. When the room got too much, but the communal area of the house was too hostile to enter, she would sneak down the stairs and creep into the garden at the back. It wasn't really a garden, not like the gardens she'd seen on the nice streets, streets filled with beautiful trees and perfect front lawns; the houses she'd stare at through the dirty windows of the bus when she had to accompany Mandy into the town. That didn't happen often, Mandy only went into town if she had to see one of her friends about their dogs. Or if she'd heard of somewhere she could earn some 'easy money'. Eileen didn't know why she was so interested in dogs, or how money could be easy, money was money, but she didn't mind going with Mandy because she loved looking at those lawns. Sometimes, there were children playing on them. Once she saw a small chubby boy jumping around on a weird metal pole with a big spring and footholds. The boy was laughing and bounced so hard his glasses flew right off his face. Eileen could see, what looked like, his mother and father behind him, they were smiling. They reminded her of the front cover of a book she had read at school, Shopping with Mother, or it could have been Play with Us. That had made her happy. The memory of the book. She'd wiped at the smear on the window as the bus had passed them, hoping to see them for just a few seconds longer. But just then Mandy had smacked her hand down into her lap.

'Don't pissin' touch that, you dun't wannna get covered in crap.'

Eileen had not looked back. The family disappeared behind her and she had never seen them again.

Eileen's back garden was like a wild forest. Not big, but it was long. She liked to imagine sometimes that she was a courageous explorer out on an expedition. Discovering new lands and old lives. Out she'd set, into the mass of brambles, grass as tall as a grown man and thickets of winding weeds that choked everything to death.

One day, earlier that year, when Mandy had passed out drunk on the settee and burnt their dinner, she had asked her Daddy about those weeds. She was sat on his knee eating a bag of crisps. Daddy had taken her to the darkies shop on the corner, specially to get them, after he had tried to wake Mandy up and thrown out the burnt chips from the oven. Eileen liked the corner shop, but going there always made Daddy swear a lot. When they'd returned he'd sat her on his knee to eat and stroked her hair while glaring angrily at Mandy asleep.

'How are they weeds, Daddy? They have such pretty big white flowers on them.' He'd looked at Eileen for a second, wiped the salt from her chin, and sighed.

'I don't know smudge; the world is bloody weird.' She smiled at him, appeased with his answer.

'And sometimes pretty things can grow from crap.' He added.

Eileen remembered that day because later that night, when Mandy had finally woken up, her and Daddy had had a really big fight. She had sat up and listened to them, on the landing outside of their bedroom door; pulling at the pealing wallpaper. She wouldn't get in trouble for it, it had always been peeling, half of it was missing in big teardrops going up the walls, always had been. Through the wood and cracked paint Daddy called Mandy 'a useless fat cow. Then without pause Mandy called Daddy 'a pathetic old hunt whose sick didn't even work'. Whatever that meant. Then the banging and thumping began.

So, she'd sat there, on the threadbare orange carpet that looked like a weird swirly sea, bright orange in some spots and dark and stained in others. Sat on her orange sea, pealing at the teardrop paper and listening to the screams of hyenas rearing up for battle. There was no light on the landing, there was a hanging light fitting, but no bulb, Daddy had taken it out a couple of months before when the bulb had blown in another room. When the landing got so dark that the shadows threatened her, she stood and calmly walked across the landing and away from the worsening situation. That was a phrase she had learnt at school. No one wanted to make situation worse.

Eileen had made her way down the dark and cluttered stairs and filled a bowl with cold water from the kitchen sink. She couldn't find a cloth but did find a couple of her Daddy's dirty socks in front of the fridge. With her tools in hand she had gone onto the living room and cleaned up the pile of congealed cold sick at the side of the sofa. She knew if Daddy had gone downstairs and seen that again it would definitely make the situation worse.

Standing now, looking at the weeds in the garden reminded Eileen of that day. She looked away and continued into the brush. Deeper and deeper she explored. Further and further went the muffled sounds of angry voices. She imagined she was in the Australian Outback, a wild place she had also learnt about at school. Mr Scott had told her how it was full of savages that hid and waited for you, so they could slice open your head and peel off your scalp. Roger, a scabby little boy, had told Eileen that he had had an uncle that had travelled to Australia and for 15 cents he had bought a licence from the post office to hunt the savages. He seemed to know his stuff. Only he had used a different word, Eileen wanted to say aubergines but that didn't sound quite right.

Further and further Eileen foraged. The deeper she went the cooler her skin became, the shade from the tall grass protecting her from the sun. Eileen sat down. It wasn't dirty, the ground was too hard for mud. Her tummy rumbled. She hadn't had any breakfast, and from the sounds of the native savages inside there would also be no lunch. Perhaps even no tea. Today was looking like a lost day. Sometimes they had lost days. On those days there was normally a lot of shouting, a lot of hiding, and at some point, a hug. Eileen hated the hugs perhaps the most of all.

On a lost day Mandy would always discover Eileen, wherever she was hiding, she would find her and hug her. Then, either through hysterical sobbing or hilarious laughter, she would say 'Oh Eileen, honey, I'm sorry. I guess this will just have to be a lost day.' It was always one or the other, tears or laughter, but the one thing that never altered was that the words always floated to Eileen on a bed of Gin breath. Once Eileen had accepted her fermented words Mandy would dance off merrily or collapse on the floor in a ball of sadness.

Today was a lost day. Eileen could feel it. And so could her tummy. She raised herself to her feet and stood on tippy toes to examine the landscape. She looked around expectantly. Looked for a passing chaeta or deer she could kill and roast on a fire. Her eyes settled on Barbara's apple tree. She didn't like stealing apples from Barbara's tree because Barbara was nice, but the thought of entering the house and encountering the horrors inside was too much. Besides when she'd checked the kitchen two days ago there had only been some old mouldy bread in the cupboard, and an open tin of half eaten beans in the fridge. She'd eaten the beans for tea yesterday, so she knew there was nothing left, all that would happen if she ventured inside would be they'd corner her and drag her into their fight. Eileen was often dragged into their fights. Mandy would grab her wrist and drag her around the house while she shouted at Daddy that they were leaving. They'd run feverishly around the small damp house grabbing useless knickknacks and dirty clothes and shoving them into wrinkled carrier bags. Screaming, screaming, always screaming. Daddy would be on their heels shouting back. Matching insult for insult, decibel for decibel.

They never actually left though. Or, on the odd occasion Mandy did actually make it out the door she always seemed to forget all about Eileen at the last minute. The door would slam, Daddy would slump in his chair with a beer, and Eileen would be stood at the foot of the stairs clutching a carrier bag containing a few crumpled pairs of pants, her little red toothbrush with the broken handle, and a dandy comic she'd found on the bus once. Daddy never came to her, so she would usually wait for twenty to thirty minutes, just in case, and then quietly climb the stairs back to her little corner of the house. She would unpack her bag. Put the pants back on top of the pile in the corner, the comic back under her mattress, and she would sleep. Mandy usually came back after a few days. Though her record was two weeks.

The apples looked good.

Eileen moved slowly through the overgrowth. If she went too fast one of them might notice the movement from the window. They probably wouldn't, they normally saw nothing but each other, but they might, Eileen couldn't risk that.

Near the tree she got low to the ground and started to feel around with her hands. Her hand moved slowly over dirt. Mud. Moss. A worm. Bits of plastic. Old battery. Squashed can. Then it was there. She closed her hand around the pole and pulled it toward her. It was quite long, about 6ft or so, at the end there was a small wicker basket. The basket was old and flaky, Eileen had found it in the street last summer and brought it home. Eileen brought a lot of things home with her, they always came in handy, they were her treasures. Those that she didn't keep as toys often became useful for practical things, like this basket. It had had many lives she imagined, once it had been bought new, treasured by some lady who used it to hold her wool or materials, who had it pride of place in her home to show off to her neighbours when they visited. Then, perhaps, when it had become old and weathered, she could have given to a poor relative, or to the boy collecting for the homeless. Then it was no longer a prized possession to be admired, but a trusty old favourite that was always reliable for holding the potatoes or the firewood. Then the paint flaked further, and holes began to appear. That was when it was taken out and left, left at the side of the road to be taken to a rubbish tip or torn apart by dogs. That was when Eileen came in. She had seen that basket, hidden it behind her back and the placed it behind the old settee in the garden. It stayed there then. It stayed there for a good month or so before Eileen was struck with an idea, a brilliant idea. And right then, that basket had purpose again. The basket was her apple catcher. All she had to do was slowly raise the pipe, so slowly it would not warrant attention, from either her house or Barbara's, place the end over a nice juicy apple, then, with a few swift jerks, the apple would break free of the tree and roll down the pipe into her treasured basket. Bruise free. Lunch.

Eileen took another furtive inspection of the landscape above the long grass. All seemed quiet. She raised her pipe.

Slowly.

Slowly.

Slowly.

Slowly.

'And what do you think you're doing, missy!'

Eileen jumped and the pipe fell from her grasp. There standing only a few feet from her, on the other side of the brick wall that separated the terrace gardens, was Barbara frowning at her disapprovingly.

'I weren't doing nothin.' Eileen tried to look innocent, but her cheeks were as red as the big rosy apple still dangling above her. She was just about say that she had just been playing a game, trying to catch butterflies, when a tremendous crash sounded out behind them. She spun round to stare at her house, and so did Barbara. When Eileen turned back to face her neighbour, she found the woman staring at her with a look of sadness.

'Are you hungry, girl?'

'No, I had a massive breakfast and Mandy will have a big lunch planned.' Her face grew from red to crimson, Eileen hated lying.

'Really' Barbara said smiling 'well, I was just cooking a hotpot, it'll be done about now, I thought you might like some.'

'But I've eaten.' She replied with less conviction.

'I know you have, dearie, but just in case you're still hungry.' She bent over the wall a little closer and whispered, 'I won't tell if you don't.'

Eileen looked back at the house. It had gone silent since. Silence was never a good sign.

'Okay, that would be nice thank you.' She said, slipping over the wall, 'Not that I'm hungry mind.'

The hot pot was amazing. She could not remember anything, ever, tasting as good in her life. She sat at a small, doyley covered, semi-circled, table in the corner of the kitchen and ate two helpings eagerly. As she ate Barbara watched her.

'You know, I think I may have too many apples this year. Usually I make good use of them, plenty of jams and crumbles, but this year I just don't have time.'

'Uh huh.' Eileen muttered as she scooped up some spilt hot pot from the doyley with a hunk of the bread.

'Duya like apples?'

Eileen stopped, looked up. Was this a trap? 'Not really.' She lied.

'Oh, that's a shame, I was going to suggest that you could help yourself. If you ever got peckish between meals.' Barbara turned and started clearing pots from the side leaving the statement hanging.

'I don't think Mandy would like that.' She said. 'Who is Mandy?'

'My mother.'

'Why don't you call her mother?'

Eileen stopped scraping the bowl for a second and looked up, thinking. 'I don't know.' She concluded.

'Ok, but why wouldn't your mother, Mandy, like you eating apples?' 'She says we're not bloody beggars.'

Barbara nodded and turned her attention back to the sink. Eileen could sense she was frowning.

'Well, just remember the offer is there, missy.' Eileen didn't answer.

She chewed slowly. With each swollen she knew she was a step closer to going home. Yet every second she stayed sat there, the monsters next door grew. Became less bearable. Became uglier. Fiercer. Eileen didn't want to go back. The kitchen was warm. The kitchen didn't bite.

'You got kids, misses?'

'Yeah, I got two of em. Grown now o'course.' She picked up a cloth from the counter and dried her wrinkly, suds covered, hands. From a cabinet she grasped a photo and took it over to Eileen.

'This here is Carol, my eldest, lives over in London.'

'Wha dus she live there for?' Eileen was instantly fascinated. Imagine that, London. 'She moved there in sixty. Met a man. Always the way, missy.'

Eileen sat looking at the photo of this strange creature. Could this have been Eileen in another world? Could she ever do anything so brave. Maybe she could find Carol, if she ever managed to run to London, find Carol, explain that she was Barbara's friend and seek help. She wanted to ask Barbara where Carol lived exactly. Specifics, number, street, postal code. But that might sound weird.

'Does she live near the queen?' That was the closest she could think of.

'Well, pretty close. You're never too far away from nothing in that London, they go everywhere under the ground.'

Eileen resolved to come back sometime and push Barbara for the facts. The absolute facts regarding Carols whereabouts.

'What about your other kid?'

'Billy. He's a teacher over in Birmingham. Good boy, he comes and visits me when he can.'

Eileen nodded and looked down at her empty bowl.

'Well I guess I better head home. Mandy will be wondering where I am.'

'Yeah I'll bet.' Barbara stood with her. 'But if you do wants those apples, or maybe the odd sandwich or owt, just let me know.'

Eileen looked up at her, fear and embarrassment across her face.

'It'd be doing me a favour really. I gets a bit lonely here, and I'm always getting too much food, I'd hate it going to waste.'

'Well I guess I might be able to sometimes.' 'That's settled then.'

Eileen managed to sneak back up to her room without being discovered. Her father and Mandy were too busy making up by that point. Music was on and they had begun laughing. Awful, loud laughing. There was no real difference between the screaming and laughing, either way Eileen knows it is still another lost day for her.

Malina Douglas - The Secondhand Smile

No, not here, he thought, looking at the shops of Gillingham High Street. People trundled back and forth with dour expressions. Not one of them was smiling.

He turned onto Green Street which was really more brown and grey, and passed the Sewing and Knitting Centre. An old woman glowered at him. *No business here.* He wondered if his worn leather jacket and black skull cap looked shifty to her. Or maybe it was his eyes. People often seemed to cringe from his gaze.

He turned, and stepped into a slim lane.

There, easy target. A youth walked with a bouncing step, headphones in his ears, and a big foolish grin on his face.

Simon pressed himself to a stone wall and took a little hooked rod from his inside pocket, lined up the hook with the edge of his target's mouth, and with a deft quick swipe drew the hook through the air to his satchel.

The youth's smile vanished. He shook his head, frowned a bit as if to wonder why he was suddenly so unhappy, and walked on as if nothing had happened.

Simon smiled to himself, a cynical smile, a nasty smile. The smile of a man who earns his bread off other people's smiles.

Serves 'im right, thought Simon to justify himself. In his skewed sense of the world, he assumed that just as many bad things should happen to other people. After all that had happened to him.

It had to be that way for his suffering to make sense.

Sly Simon, they called him. Others called him Simon the Swindler. He detested that.

It revealed too much of the truth of who he was. Not who he always had been. Not the little boy who had skimmed rocks and flown paper airplanes, who had never said a word against another child but got teased by them anyway. It was the truth that cruel circumstances had led him to become. Driven by the urge to swipe and swindle and cheat everyone he could get away with, to set right the scales that constantly tilted away from him.

He walked, scuffed boots slapping the pavement, narrowed eyes watching.

Turned down a side street. *There.*

In an antique shop like a rat's hole, crammed with the detritus of untold lives, was a little bent man who rasped "pardon?" when one spoke to him, who paced and tisked and tutted about his shop. He polished medieval weapons, dusted the Phaistos Disc, and wiped down statuettes of a shepherdess, a bulldog, and a gnome.

The door jingled.

"Oh, it's you."

Horace looked up to see a man in a dark trenchcoat with a broad weathered face and stringy dark hair. He gave a sort of grimace that could be taken for a smile but wasn't.

"Not wasting your smiles on me, are ya Horace?" Simon spoke in a thin, reedy voice.

"You might swipe them off my face and sell them back to me."

They both laughed at this, Horace with a deep hoarse laugh, Simon with tinny laugh, the kind that grates on the ears.

"What have you got there for me then?"

Simon grimaced.

"Fresh crop o' smiles." He opened his leather satchel and Horace peered in. Gave a low whistle.

Horace regarded him. Looked as if he was about to ask a question but thought better of it.

"Right-oh," he said instead. "I'll take the lot."

He took out a velvet drawstring bag and Simon tipped the smiles in. Horace glimpsed the semitransparent outline of mouths until he pulled the string shut. I really should stop doing business with him… but then again smiles are a renewable resource…

Horace took out a finely embroidered Morocco leather wallet and handed Simon a pile of notes, which he crammed into the inner pocket of his trenchcoat.

The door jingled and an old woman entered, her face pinched in an unpleasant look.

Both men froze for a moment, then Simon strolled away from the counter and pretended to inspect an African death mask.

The old lady flicked through a rack of fur coats, pulling her lower lip up with derision at each one.

"Don't you have any fox skins," she asked. Her voice was thin and sour as vinegar.

"Unfortunately, we don't," says Horace in a voice aimed to express condolence despite actually caring very little.

She turned to leave.

Horace timed the words perfectly.

"Perhaps you'd like a smile?"

She paused. "A smile?"

"Yes," said Horace. "I've got a selection right here."

"I've already bought a set of teeth… I supposed I could get a smile to go with them." She cast a glance to the door. "Especially on a rotten old day like this one."

"I have just the thing for you," said Horace. He reached under the counter and pulled out something between his fingertips. It was slender and barely visible, but glinted with an array of colours as it caught the light.

He lifted it up to her.

Simon watched as her dour look turned to curiosity and wonder. Horace released it and it drifted towards her face. When it landed on her lips, they widened into beatific smile.

She turned her head this way and that. Stood up straighter.

"That's…" She said as she searched for the words, "that's *lovely*!"

"Any time, Madam."

"I feel marvelous. Thank you, sir!"

She walked away with a light, gliding step.

Simon gave Horace a satisfied nod and stepped out of the shop. The door dinged as he closed it.

***

Now, he thought, *time for the fun part.*

Simon was not very good at enjoying life. What he most enjoyed was the sense of oblivion he gained when he escaped it.

He walked through the glossy green doors of the Frog and Toad. He tended to run into problems in pubs so he was always looking for new ones where nobody knew him. He stepped in and blinked as his eyes adjusted to the dim light. Took in the maps and grainy photos on the walls, a few lonely men and a dart board.

He wasn't sure how it started. It was sometime during his second pint of London Pride. Or was it the third? But an old pockmarked man was having a go at him, and he was defending himself. He hated having to defend himself but somehow he kept getting himself into situations where he had to. He didn't get very far until he heard a gruff voice behind him, and there was the barman, saying, "time for you to leave." His arms were folded across his chest. There would be no arguing.

"I hope you fall in the gutter and rot there!" Said Simon to the old man.

"You'll get what's coming to you," said the old man shaking his fist. "I swear it!"

Simon muttered something vile and slammed the door behind him.

Cold rain stung his face. He pulled his trenchcoat tighter across his body and dug his hands into his pockets. The trenchcoat was like his second skin, his armour. He felt like shelless hermit crab without it.

Maybe he's right, thought Simon as he walked away. *Can I really keep getting away with this? Nonsense!* He shook his head. *Course I will! I could get away with murder! They don't call me Sly Simon for nothing.*

He walked on, swaying a little. Made it home and passed out on a single mattress surrounded by dirty and wadded-up clothes.

Simon woke with a dry mouth and a headache and the old man's curse ringing in his mind.

Hogwash! He told himself. He was expert at lying, especially to himself.

He changed his clothes to a different shade of black and slid on his trenchcoat.

It would be a good harvest today.

It was Sunday: good pickings. His target: Hillyfields Park.

He pulled off the smiles of children eating ice cream by the sand pit. They dropped their cones in the sand and wailed. Stole the smiles off a couple who were strolling arm and arm who then turned on each other and unleashed a torrent of built-up resentment. Snatched the smile off a lady sunning herself in the grass who suddenly frowned, stuffed her blanket in her bag and stomped off.

If he could, he would steal the sun from the sky, divide it into packages and sell it.

When he was satisfied that the majority of the park's visitors were either frowning, snarling or walking off with blank apathetic faces, he strolled down Gardiner Street to Gillingham High Street to steal some more. Two ladies exiting a charity shop, arms heavy with shopping bags. Their smiles stolen. A small boy tugging at the hand of his mother, pointing to a shop display of toys. Simon took away the look of childlike wonder till his face was as blank as a toy soldier.

His satchel was bulging but Horace's shop was shut by now. He turned down an alleyway, taking a shortcut home.

He knew it was a dodgy place but it was a place he often lurked himself, standing in the shadows with his back pressed to a brick wall, swiping smiles from foolish random people.

Out of the dim light, a teenage boy was walking towards him. Baggy sweatshirt on, cap pulled low. *He looks well dodgy,* thought Simon. *But then, so do I.*

Simon felt queasiness in his stomach. The kind of feeling he got when he saw the fishheads on his mum's stargazy pie. He pushed it aside as silly; reminded himself he'd been there dozens of times.

But the figure was getting closer, and Simon's hands in his pockets were sweating.

The figure increased his pace.

Simon hesitated. *Should I turn back? Don't be silly!* He told himself. *He'll go right past me, it'll be fine.*

The youth increased his speed and charged straight into him, knocking him to the ground. He grabbed Simon's satchel and ran down the alleyway, spindly legs flying, trainers smacking the pavement.

"Hey," called out Simon. "Thief!" Before he could move, rough hands pulled his arms back behind him and stripped off his trenchcoat.

"Stop," bellowed Simon. "Get off me!"

Someone dropped his arms and took off. As he struggled up, hands scraped and knees aching, he saw two figures running down the alley, one in his trenchcoat, the black cloth flapping as he moved.

By the time he reached the mouth of the alley, they'd disappeared.

Simon cursed the empty streets.

The old man was right.

***

The boy kept running, heart racing, feet pounding, eyes wide as a rabbit. Dashed into Hillyfields park. Stopped, panting. What kind of catch had he got today? Could it be as good as the purse full of cash and jewellery he'd snatched last Saturday night by the station? If there was cash, it wouldn't be much. It was a pity people didn't carry around more of it these days.

He opened the satchel, anticipating something good, something he could sell and buy new, flash trainers with.

It was empty.

He cursed.

His friends caught up with him, panting. One was in his usual red sports jacket, while the other was wearing a faded, oversize trenchcoat.

"What's in there, Jake" asked the boy in the trenchcoat, tugging at the satchel.

Jake's expression was downcast. "Nothing."

"Chuck it away then!"

He tugged it back. "No, I feel like keeping it."

The boy in the trenchcoat was digging around in the pockets. "Not much here," he said. "Hang on…" He fished out a small metal hook. Frowned. "What's that," asked Jake, snatching it away from him. He pretended to pick his nose with it. The other boy laughed. He was smaller than Jake and Eddie but made up for it with his dexterity. His pockets were brimming with stolen sweets.

Eddie reached deeper into the coat and pulled out a wad of cash.

"Woah!" he said.

"Give it 'ere!" Said the smallest boy, darting his hand out.

"No, I found it!"

They squabbled over the cash for a while, eventually dividing it between them, the finder secretly taking the most. The metal hook they chucked in the bin.

Jake parted ways with his friends. When he was sure he was alone, he opened the satchel again. He caught an edge, a glimmer of something. He peered in. There was something there—msomething hazy and indistinct. No, many things. They were floating upwards and out of the bag. Passersby walked right into them and began grinning.

A young woman bore a sour look, premature winkles furrowing a face that should have been smooth. She was hunched over a pram, walking slowly. One of the wispy strange things landed on her face. Her mouth burst into a beaming smile and her whole face transformed, looking once again youthful. The baby waved its tiny fists. She straightened and walked on with new vigour in her step.

The face of a shriveled old man lit up. He straightend his back and walked with a sense of purpose.

Jake looked between the old man, the young mother, and the wispy things floating up from the satchel. He blew them back in, snapped the stachel shut, changed direction, and set off at a fast walk.

***

He reached Gillingham Station. It was a typical Kentish afternoon: pale grey sky and light drizzle. He looked around at the people on the platform: slumped and sad looking, irritated, or pacing with barely-disguised ire.

He decided he was done with stealing. He was sick of the guilt that clung to him and couldn't be washed off. He liked the burst of positive energy he felt when he made people smile. He wanted more of that.

He opened the satchel. Watched the smiles float out and the faces transform as they landed.

A scrawny, pale-faced teenage girl was slouching with a hood pulled low and staring into the floor. When a smile landed on her, her mouth stretched into a brilliant grin, transforming her face to something beautiful.

The last one landed on Jake's mouth and he smiled—a huge smile that lifted his heart and set his eyes glowing. He couldn't remember the last time he'd smiled like that.

He couldn't tear down all the grey buildings. He couldn't pull back the curtain of clouds and make the sun shine. But he could change the way both he and others felt about it.

The beaming girl turned her eyes on him. Smiling back, he walked towards her.

Matt McCabe - The Token

The clinical fluorescent lights of the 'Supa-Save' hummed their monotonous drone high above Tom Walkers head as he stood pondering in the tinned food aisle. Tom bit his lip in confusion as he stared at the two items in his hands, a plain white can of 'Supa-Save' own brand diced tomatoes in his left, and a slightly more exotic looking name brand in his right. He turned each one over in turn, weighing up the ingredients and nutritional value of his two options as the busy hubbub of the supermarket carried on behind him.

This one is cheaper, he thought, *but, this one has more potassium.* He sighed, it was quite the quandary for Tom, in fact he was so engrossed in the seemingly essential comparison that he didn't notice the young woman in the dark zip-up hoody enter the aisle he was in. Nor did he notice as she slowly slid the zipper down, reach in, and remove a large thick metal pipe whilst striding purposefully toward him.

As the young woman brought the pipe down on Tom Walkers skull, his last thought was whether the extra 6g of protein was worth the extra money the name brand tomatoes cost.

The attack took less than 20 seconds in all but by the time she was finished the young woman was out of breath, heart pounding, knees weak, and with the final strike she collapsed into a heap on the floor next to her victim, her face and clothes covered in the rich warm blood of Tom Walker.

After allowing herself a few seconds of heavy breathing, the young woman composed herself and moved to sit crossed legged in front of the motionless body. She reached into her purse and withdrew a silver token the size of large coin and held it tightly in both hands as she bowed her head, and waited.

By the time the police arrived, a small crowd had gathered at each end of the aisle, teenagers on their phones taking photos for 'the gram', housewives trying to catch a glimpse to use as fodder for their Friday night drunken stories with the girls, some of the older shoppers just seemed annoyed they couldn't get to the tinned foods. The general manager of the store made his way through the crowd, the police following closely behind. "There" he said pointing at the murderer, "looks like she's cashing in".

The lead officer walked towards the woman and knelt down in front of her. "I'm officer Wheeler, I understand you'd like to perform a token exchange?" the woman raised her eyes to meet his, and nodded quickly. The officer could see her face properly now, she couldn't be more than 20 years old, pretty, with big blue eyes staring out from under her hood. "Little young to be cashing in aren't we?" asked the officer. The eyes just kept staring back.

The trip to the station was quiet, the woman sat in the back of the police car, handcuffed until the token could be verified for authenticity. There had been a spate of counterfeits recently, not so sophisticated that they could fool the equipment back at the station – the government had made sure tokens were damn near uncopiable - but certainly good enough to trick a desperate buyer who needed a second token. Something told Wheeler that this one was genuine though, she'd done everything right; she'd used a crowded place with plenty of witnesses, waited with her victim for the authorities, and most importantly made sure she'd displayed her token prominently.

Seventeen years. Seventeen years since 'The Token Act' had been introduced thought Wheeler. An unthinkable solution to a growing problem back then of a huge increase in anti social behaviour. Cyber bullying had become so rife it had become impossible to police, revenge porn too, divorce filings due to adultery were up nearly 80% in the three years before the introduction, it seemed as though people had just stopped caring what others thought about anything they did. Businesses were no different, 'deals' had disappeared as had loyalty cards, prices had been hiked as far as they could, the poorest in society died at an alarming rate, something had to be done.

Wheeler could still remember those days, he was still in police training when the government had brought in the tokens, at the time he was one of the few who wanted to try and fix the troubles from a position of power. Looking back he could see that was futile, he never would have been able to 'make a difference' and he wasn't exactly a saint. The tokens - as much as he'd hated the idea at the time – had worked.

The premise was simple, each citizen over the age of 18 was given a silver token which entitled them to kill one other person also over the age of 18, with absolutely zero legal implications. You only got one token, you could only use it once, on one person – no exceptions. The idea behind it was that the threat of someone using their token on you would stop the nefarious behaviour that had become commonplace. Would the average person be mean to their waiter if there was chance they'd get a fork through the eye? Would they steal a parking space if they ran the risk of getting mowed down in the car park? The powers that be had hoped not, and amazingly, it had worked. People had started being nicer to each other, treating each other with respect, the increase in anti social behaviour had taken a huge U-turn with other crime following suit, albeit with more *legalised murder…*

Wheeler and the woman pulled up to the station, he switched off the engine, climbed out, and opened the back door. Walking into the reception the desk sergeant greeted them, "Hey Dave, what you got?"

"Token exchange" replied Wheeler, "I'll take room four", the sergeant buzzed them in, saying to no one in particular "They get younger and younger".

"You want a drink? Tea? coffee?" Wheeler asked the woman as they sat down on well worn armchairs he mused probably used to be orange, facing each other across a small wooden table.

"No, thank you"

"Ah so you do talk?" said the officer with a wry smile. The woman didn't reciprocate. "Ok, so as I said back at the supermarket, under article 8, section 2 of *The Token Act*, you need to formally acknowledge the exchange of your token for the homicide of…"

The woman cut him off before he could finish, "Tom Walker"

Wheeler paused. "Yeah. Tom Walker. So you did know him then?" The woman nodded. "It's just that usually with people your age, *cashing in* tends to be a more… impulsive, decision"

"No. I knew him"

"Right, well as I say, you need to formally acknowledge that you're exchanging your token for the murder of Tom Walker, we'll verify your token, get your signature, then you're free to go".

"Don't you wanna know why I did it?"

"Well, as per the act, you're under no obligation to tell me. But if you need to – want to talk about it…"

The two looked up as the door opened and a junior officer walked in with a battered looking machine the size of a credit card reader with a coin sized slot at the top, "DS said you needed the authenticator?"

"Yeah I'll take it" answered Wheeler. The officer handed over the machine and left as Wheeler reached into his top pocket "I'm just going to do the authentication ok?" the woman nodded as he slotted the silver token into the machine and pressed a small button on the side, the LCD screen on the front lit up displaying the words;

'Authentication Process - 0%'

"This'll just take a minute." Said Wheeler, putting the machine on the table, "You were saying you wanted to talk about why you did it?", before the woman could answer Wheelers phone started ringing, he sighed, "Sorry, I'll just be a second" he stood up turned around and answered the call, "Wheeler here".

"Officer Wheeler, this is Doctor O'Shea from Green Hill Surgery"

"Uh, yeah hello how can I help?"

"Well it's just that we have Mr Walker here, and, well the officer that brought him in said he'd been exchanged?"

"Yes, that's right"

"But Officer Wheeler... he's not dead?"

"What? That's impossible, I saw him with my own eyes?"

"Well he took a hell of a blow to the head, but he was unconscious, not dead, we expect him to make a full recovery"

"I see, ok, thanks for letting me know" Wheeler hung up, "looks like you didn't quite finish the job with Mr Walker, he's still alive" he said over his shoulder, locking his phone.

"I didn't try to kill Tom" replied the woman standing up.

"Huh, I don't understand?", a *ping* sounded from the table, Wheeler looked down and saw that the authenticator had finished processing. The screen read:

'Authentication Process - 100%'

Token Authenticated

Citizen 5839637

Miller, Amanda

In the next moment Wheeler felt the cold steel of the woman's handcuffs dig hard into his neck, the shock causing him to fall backwards, his hands flailing. "I didn't try to kill Tom you idiot, we're in love." Her tone had changed now to one of power and she pulled with all her might as the officer writhed helplessly. "He let me attack him to make it look like I was exchanging, so I'd get the chance to be in a room with *you*… Dad" Wheelers eyes widened with realisation. "Don't say you don't remember, 20 years ago you fucked my mum and ran off into the night without a second thought. I've known since I was seven years old who I was gonna use my token on, you slimy fucking piece of shit!", with the final word she gave one last hard thrust and heard a short sharp satisfying *crack*.

Tentatively she loosened her grip and let Wheelers body slump off her and onto the floor while she lay there panting. Composing herself, she got to her feet and straightened her clothes, sitting back down to wait for the other officer to come back. Revelling in what she'd accomplished she looked down, let a small smile creep over her face and thought to herself, *I did everything right.*

Michael Noonan - The Mystery Tour

Joe deliberately walked past the bus stop on Fell Street, on his way to the pub, on Sunday evening; though it took him a bit out of his way. It was difficult to believe that it was just one year, to the day, when it had happened. When the bus had departed, on such a seemingly routine excursion; though never to return. Time hadn't brought any closure or explanation; and it was still an utter, inexplicable mystery, that defied logic and reason.

He could still picture Howard and Trevor, in the pub, when they had first discussed the subject. He was sat with them, at the same table, just by the slot machine. They were, all three of them, old friends and drinking cronies. Their conversation seemed to be of virtually no consequence or importance at the time. But it would change everything.

'What are you looking at?' said Trevor, to Howard, who'd had his nose in the local paper for the last few minutes.

Howard pointed a forefinger towards a paragraph of small print in an advertisement column. 'Just reading this advert, about a mystery tour leaving Fell Street at nine o'clock next Sunday morning.' He paused. 'Due back at nine thirty the same night.'

Howard handed him the paper so he could scrutinize the ad.

Joe, who was also a workmate of Trevor, was a more phlegmatic and down to earth character than the other two. Indeed, he could be quite caustic and judgmental at times.

'A mystery tour!' he scoffed. 'What's mysterious about anything round here?' He shook his head and laughed to himself. 'Where d'you think you'd end up? Transylvania?'

Yet Howard was not to be downcast. 'I've never been on one before. It should be a laugh.' He turned to the others. 'How about you lot?'

'I'm game,' said Trevor; ever eager to assimilate new experience.

Joe pondered the froth on the top of his beer. 'Well, I've been on one before. Ended up looking round a rundown church and a heap of old ruins on a hilltop. The only mystery about it was why I even bothered going on it in the first place.' He took a leisurely sip of his drink. 'So you can rule me out, lads.'

'I don't know,' said Trevor; a man whose genial, optimistic outlook was an abiding feature of his character; 'maybe this one's different. After all, a mystery can be anything.'

'I wouldn't bank on it.'

Thus a minor fissure had developed between Joe and the others, though they had known each for over thirty years.

Joe walked across town to see a relation that same Sunday morning the mystery tour was due to start. He deliberately made a small detour along Fell Street to see the party embark into the unknown. He had a feeling of rather smug condescension at having made the sensible decision to exclude himself from that ridiculous excursion and considered that his two compatriots were about to be taken for a ride in more ways than mere mileage.

The old, dilapidated coach, which had seen better days – 'mystery tour' emblazoned on its destination board – revved its engines, then pulled away from the kerb. He noticed his two mates sat by the window, next to the back seat. He waved an arm. They turned, recognized him and waved their arms in return. Though he couldn't help feeling that they looked rather sheepish and ill at ease. Perhaps they were beginning to realize that it wasn't quite the bright idea they imagined it to be under the stimulus of mild intoxication.

The coach chugged its way around a corner, on route to who knew where? A heavyset man in his fifties ran down, panting heavily, towards the stop from which the bus had left.

'Dammit,' he blurted, 'it's gone without me.' He leaned against the pole of a streetlight, and got his breath back. 'They could have hung on for a minute or two?'

'Take it from me, mate, you haven't missed much. I've been on one before. And it was a waste of time.'

The man gave him a far from flattering look. 'That's as maybe. But I'd like to have found out for myself.' Joe went on his way. The stout man rested against the pole for a few more minutes. Then he turned on his heels and trudged back the way he'd come, with forlorn, heavy steps.

The coach lumbered down the high street, made a turning, drove past the gas works, then across a cast iron bridge that spanned the canal and pulled itself beyond the last straggling suburbs of the town until at length the greenery of the rugged countryside came into view.

The clear, sunny weather, in which the coach had set off, was no lasting phenomenon; and an hour after departing a thick dank fog descended from the sky to smother town and country alike in its damp, clammy embrace.

'Well they've certainly chosen a day for it,' said Joe to himself, almost maliciously, as he looked out of a window of his flat into the dirty grey mist that enveloped the town.

It took all day for the fog to lift and clear from the streets. At ten fifteen Joe made his way to their local, the Silver Lantern, to see if the lads had dropped in for a few drinks after their mysterious excursion. But there was no sign of them.

'Probably too embarrassed to show their faces,' he muttered to himself. 'Pint of bitter please, Reg,' he told the barman.

The next morning at the council office where Joe worked, there was no sign of Trevor. Though he had an exemplary attendance record. Nor, was he later to learn, had he rung in to excuse his absence.

'Well this is a mystery,' he told himself.

After work, on his way home, he picked up the local paper from a street vendor, as was his usual routine. Yet he was taken aback by its lurid, black headline.

MYSTERY OF THE MISSING MYSTERY TOUR PARTY.

He read on, his hands anxiously clasping the paper. It appeared that the coach, due back at nine thirty the previous night, hadn't returned. There had been no contract between the driver and the coach operators – or for that matter, between the passengers and their families.

At home Joe switched on the regional television news for an update. The story featured as a prominent item.

The coach hadn't as yet been sighted. There was no knowledge of where any of the passengers were, even though the police had made an extensive search of the 'mystery' route the coach was to have taken and had interviewed local people concerning the matter.

All the while police switchboards were jammed with anxious calls from mothers, fathers, sons, daughters, lovers, relatives and friends of the missing, desperate as to any clue concerning the whereabouts of the party.

In the Silver Lantern that night the mystery of the missing coach was almost the sole subject of discussion. Joe cocked an ear and overheard a typical snatch of conversation from an informal little grouping at the bar.

'Well I think the driver might have lost his way. Remember how thick the fog was that Sunday? You could hardly see past the end of your nose.'

'For all we know the coach could have fallen into the reservoir below Crag Lane? That's a dodgy place at the best of times.'

'Well gents,' another ventured, in a more jocose, light-hearted tone, 'it was supposed to be a mystery tour after all.'

'In that case they've certainly got their money's worth,' added a fourth voice, to the general mirth of the gathering.

Joe got himself a fresh pint. 'I told them not to go,' he told himself gloomily; 'but they wouldn't have it.' He lifted the glass to his lips and downed a generous measure.

The next day the mystery was partially explained. A bus, of the description of the missing vehicle, with 'mystery tour' on its destination board, was found by a local man, walking his dog, near a lonely, little used country road several miles beyond the route of the specified mystery tour. The coach had pulled off the road and was partially hidden behind a screening of bushes.

News was relayed to the police. The vehicle was examined and found to be the missing coach. Yet though the coach had been found, there was no sign of the passengers and the driver.

Inside, there were half eaten sandwiches left on the seats, discarded crisp packets and emptied cans of beer. The radio was still on, with a hit record from last year blaring out to the disembodied air.

'It's like the Mary Celeste,' said one bemused copper to another.

A few local people, living in their isolated cottages and farmhouses, were interviewed by the police but had nothing of significance to disclose. Footprints were examined, but they petered out in the grass and moorland beyond. It was as if they had all disappeared from the earth.

Descriptions of the driver and passengers were circulated through the press and broadcasting media in order to alert the public and jog memories. There was a plethora of replies, but unfortunately nothing that constructively aided the police in that most baffling and mysterious inquiry.

The police made a special point of delving into the background of the driver, to see if that held any information that could begin to crack the case. But they drew another blank. He was a sound family man, with no criminal record, a clean driving license, and he had been employed as a driver by the same firm for the last twenty years. Indeed they described him as an exemplary employee who could always be relied upon to do his job.

By then the whole town was bestirred almost to the point of hysteria, by that inscrutable story. Indeed it had become not merely a local, but a national sensation.

'Things like that just don't happen in places like this,' insisted one irate fellow worker to Joe, in the rest room during the morning break. 'I mean we're living in England, not Haiti.'

'At least it's put us on the map,' said another worker, who welcomed almost any development that bucked the dull routine of mundane reality.

'It might have put us on the map,' said Joe, with an undercurrent of anger in his voice, 'but what about Trevor? Where the hell is he on the map now?'

Reporters, and television and radio crews, descended in their droves onto the streets of the town. Local and national news personnel were joined by people from overseas networks and papers.

Joe himself was collared at one point as he walked to the betting shop, and found a microphone thrust before his mouth.

'I waved them off in the morning,' he informed the interviewer, 'and I expected them back in the boozer that night. But I haven't clapped eyes on either of them since. As for what's happened to Trevor and Howard?

You tell me?' He shook his head and his voice became heavier and more emotional: 'I only know that I've lost my two best mates and I'd give anything to have them back again.'

Each new dawn emerged with the townsfolk expecting at least some glimmer of a clue as to the whereabouts, or the fate, of the missing people; but each morning they were cruelly disappointed. The police, despite all their efforts, hadn't unearthed the scintilla of a lead.

That awesome mystery edged out everything else from the town's consciousness. Even the prospect of a vital cup game the local football team were to play at the weekend, and which in other circumstances would have galvanized the enthusiasm of the populous, all but faded into insignificance when compared with that sinister enigma.

In the taverns, clubs, restaurants and coffee bars, explanations concerning the enigma of the disappeared mystery tour coach party became even more bizarre and unreal.

'Maybe they've just had enough of life in the town?' ventured a typical barroom know-all one night in the Silver Lantern, within Joe's hearing. 'Perhaps they decided to get out and start again somewhere, all under the guise of going on a mystery tour?'

'And who could blame 'em,' added someone else, of a distinctly jaundiced disposition.

'It could all be an outrageous leg pull,' suggested another interlocutor. 'They might be lying low on the moors somewhere, and then, after a few more days, when they've milked it dry as a publicity stunt, they might simply stroll back into town and say, fooled you.'

'No,' growled a fourth character as he shook his head. 'That's impossible. Someone would have seen them by now. Thirty odd people can't simply disappear, into thin air.' There was a look of incredulity in his eyes. 'If you ask me there's something unearthly and supernatural about all this.'

Other ideas floated to the surface, such as kidnapping and mass murder. One member of the informal think tank even dragged down elements from the stars in an attempt to cast some light into the cloudy opacity of that mystery.

'Y'know, I think they could well have been abducted, taken, by creatures, Aliens, from beyond our Solar System. Yes; that's my solution to this mystery.'

The outlandish claim was met by shaking heads and inebriated laughter.

'Yeah,' another jibed; 'and I suppose it's the same Aliens that are cutting the corn circles.'

The days went by. Yet there was no sign of the passengers or the driver, despite a nationwide search. Endlessly, during that time, Joe wandered what could have become of his two mates. But the immutable mystery was like a brick wall against which every vain speculation broke into powdery fragments. In his sleep he would dream of them shouting and beckoning to him from across the bleak moorlands. He would rush in panic and trepidation towards them, only for them to recede before him like insubstantial spectres, leaving only the darkness and the wind's mournful cry. Not awake or asleep could he escape the mystery.

He walked the same grey streets to and from work. They seemed even greyer and colder now, without Trevor and Howard, his pals from way back to his old schoolyard days. The days seemed longer and gloomier than he could ever remember.

No doubt the controversy surrounding the disappearance would itself dissipate in time. Even sensations had a finite shelf life. The town would be left to drift back into its normal, indifferent, mundane existence. And now a whole year had gone by, with no one the wiser, about how or why it had happened. Without its missing souls the town seemed a sadder, smaller place.

They say that time goes by quicker, the older you get. But that year, without his two old friends, had seemed like an age to Joe.

He felt distinctly downcast and gloomy after walking past the bus stop, and he went to his local that night, to drown his sorrows.

He listened to all the standard speculation about the disappearance – that had been further stimulated by the fact that it was the first anniversary of the disappearance - though much of it was stale, regurgitated stuff. As the minute hand approached last orders he felt particularly desolate at the galling absence of his two mates.

He picked up a fresh beer and sipped a mouthful through the froth. He turned to a fellow regular: 'Y'know; I wish to hell I'd gone with them.'

Mike Tibbs - Hibernation

Tortoise had just completed her evening stroll in the grass before bed, making one last dandelion leaf disappear into her leathery face, when she heard Hedgehog coming out of his first hibernation. She had been up and about for some days now putting her weight back on, and was eager to update him. A seasoned hibernator, she had starved herself for days before her big sleep, drinking only water while Hedgehog had eaten as much as he could. His first big sleep had been interrupted once or twice and he'd spent a few days rearranging his bed, only to find the leaves too damp and uncomfortable. He'd then tried sleeping in the empty grouse house, but found that he couldn't quite relax in a place with a door that large and decided to brave the damp. Unlike Grouse's house with a single door, Hedgehog's house featured an offset pair of entry holes which larger animals could not get in.

Not everyone survived the winter. Grouse had not returned since getting restless one late August afternoon and taking to the air, and Owl and Sparrowhawk had both succumbed to the sickness that had taken some squirrels and most of the rodents. The gardens would be justice free if not for the corvids. And there was a new menace in the gardens to be wary of, a tortoiseshell cat that had everyone's defences up.

"We are safe enough here while Dog is out and about, but the cat is stalking the gardens day and night. Sometimes it sleeps inside the bird table at dawn as though waiting for breakfast. It has taken a young blackbird already." Said Tortoise. "The chick was last seen waving a wing with Cat's jaws clamped around its throat, being carried over the fence back to its own garden."

The other big news was the activities of the humans, or rather, the lack of activity. Beyond the gardens, for as far as anyone reported, for the first time ever in Tortoise's memory, most of the humans were in hibernation. Only some of them behaved as normal, the rest remained inside their homes. It was a major topic on the dawn chorus and evening howl. No one knew why but it was evident in the lack of disturbance, in the cleaner atmosphere and drastic reduction in noise from cars. Normally the humans were obsessed with their machines. Those humans who did carry on, patrolling with dogs once or twice daily, kept an unusually large distance apart from one another. Some had taken to wearing muzzles. It was not just the dogs reporting this but birds too and seagulls ventured inland from the seaside to hunt rats and pigeons because there was less human food to steal. The seaside had been practically deserted since winter. It was reported that fish were returning to waters that had previously been too dirty to survive in, fewer floating machines carrying people were being used (an item of news of no concern to anyone but those who travelled beyond the gardens), seagulls in particular, boasting of their exotic travels across oceans, whatever they were. Of course they knew of fish because some of the gardens stocked ponds with them to entertain local cats and feed visiting herons.

Soon after hibernation, a large rabbit was brought out from the human house and installed in what had been Grouse's house: a shy, clueless thing that was unlikely to last very long in the garden without human intervention. Being good hearted and curious in equal measure, Tortoise had ventured over and introduced herself. Later on, Hedgehog acknowledged the new resident without approaching close enough to scare it. The respect for strict social distancing was innate since getting too close to predators got you eaten.

Tortoise was the oldest and wisest inhabitant of the garden, at least ten hibernations older than Hedgehog, who would perhaps only experience another one or two. She had known Hedgehog's mother and grandmother, even his great-grandmother and perhaps even further back than that.

The same human family had occupied the house all that time; her earliest memories were when the humans that were now adults had been very young, handling her almost daily and tormenting her with pieces of cauliflower. Now she was fed pellets almost daily but handled rarely and left to forage among the flowerbeds for her favourite dandelions. She was scooped up to be confined to quarters during the noisy grass cutting ceremonies and the odd health check but that was the limit of her interaction with the humans these days. Generally she was well provided for and left alone.

Beside the conundrum of the first human hibernation in living memory, it was a cause of anxiety that the gardens were being eroded to make way for more of the humans' needs, gardens were shrinking, trees and hedgerows were being cut down and became extensions to existing buildings, patios, spaces for more cars and decking areas. More than half of the houses that used to have bushes, hedges, lawns, flowerbeds and even trees had been built on or been paved or gravelled for cars to be parked on and the animals were powerless to do anything about it. There were precious few places to nest in anymore and many types of birds that Tortoise knew by their calls as a youngster had just disappeared. The dawn chorus was always keenly updating as to which roadside hedges and trees were disappearing, news that made no difference to the permanent garden dwellers. There were not as many gardens in the world and they were reducing in size, seemed to be the point of the announcements. This sort of knowledge was beyond the comprehension of the garden dwellers, what could Hedgehogs or Tortoises or anyone do about the end of the world?

"Toilet training," announced Hedgehog to the entire assembled evening court to an uncomprehending silence. Then laughter from Magpie, who was acting as judge and evidently had no grasp at all about proper court procedure or the law. Tortoise wearily turned her head, she had faith in Hedgehog. Maybe she was wrong but she recognised an intelligence in him that was beyond that of his ancestors, at least all the generations of Hedgehog she had known. But this was falling on deaf ears.

The garden courts had evolved over many generations and was still evolving; anyone could propose a bill for consideration. Few did, because there was always a risk, and there was always a cost. Strictly speaking, the garden court was not the correct place to introduce Hedgehog's proposed legislation to, but Hedgehog and Tortoise were using the courts primarily to get the bill discussed in the dawn chorus, proposing changes to the laws of nature were never easy and rarely successful. The best outcome they could possibly hope for would be an amendment.

There was a natural avian bias in all court proceedings, unavoidably because circuit judges were almost exclusively birds and more often than not, birds of prey. The laws of nature were universally applied and the birds covered the widest territory, ensuring consistency in rulings across different regions. They communicated the updated laws among themselves and coverage of any changes across the land were reported accurately (given the avian bias) via the dawn chorus. The evening howl was another source of reportage with a more earthbound slant (albeit with a canine bias). News topics were not necessarily covered in the same way but by paying attention to what was being reported everyone could make their own judgements.

"If it pleases the court," she interrupted. "If I might suggest that we ask the house animals, Dog and Cat to explain the concept." It was no good, the laughter was out of control now, and Tortoise almost began to wind her neck in, when Dog barked once for order. There was some ruffling in the tree branches above, then silence as the tortoiseshell cat, who had been quietly creeping along the top of the fence lowered her tail and swished it suggestively.

"What our mobile cactus plant is alluding to is the benefit and influence that comes from cleaning up our habits." There was a silence, again, and it might have had the desired effect if not for the fact that it was broken by the coughing up of a furball.

Dog added helpfully, "When we live in houses we learn to control where we take a dump. The humans value this highly, they really don't like it if we crap where they live."

"They have a special place in the house to go and I have always said that the main purpose of the daily patrols is so that we get to crap outdoors. The collection business is more to do with this obsession than all the other theories."

"So what you are proposing is that we learn to crap in specific places then?" Uproar from the feathered carrion eaters again. "I shall make a habit of only crapping on cars after the humans have spent the morning cleaning them." Pigeons were already engaged in this sport, it was well known that the trees near the car wash were the favourite roosting places for adolescent birds who enjoyed car spotting.

"The proposal to the garden court, in a nutshell," summarised squirrel, "is that we endeavour to become the best individuals we can be and that might influence the humans. After all, they are capable of outstandingly benevolent behaviour as much as their wantonly destructive behaviour."

"Exactly," said Hedgehog, who with the help of Tortoise, brought the matter to court, an inalienable right that every animal had in the gardens, though many were consumed by the justice process, particularly when Owl had been the judge. "Influence them by what we do. They are clever, they watch us and they learn from us."

"And we have demonstrated that they can be influenced," Offered Dunnock, who then explained to the court the phenomena of bird table performances increasing the frequency of bird seed being brought to the table.

It was Crow's argument that swiftly defeated the motion. "While there is no doubt that human behaviour is the cause of all the environmental destruction," he said, "the humans already exhibit the greatest obsession with self-discipline and hygiene and that could be what compelled them to interfere with everything and mess it up. So how will making them even more obsessed encourage them to leave things be?" And so Hedgehog's proposed amendment was defeated. Laughed out of court, according to the next morning's dawn chorus with its typical feathered bias.

"The amendment was defeated but that doesn't mean you were wrong," said sparrow later on. "Just that you were unable to convince the court."

"Magpie was unwilling and unable to control the court," Said Dunnock, "And it descended into chaos."

"As corrupt and tyrannical as Owl had been," Tortoise said, "at least he exerted control over court proceedings."

Even if the bill had been approved, it was not obvious how the humans could be persuaded to stop expanding their territories with mess everywhere from their machines and their constructions. But there did not seem to be any way a Tortoise and a Hedgehog could have any influence there, especially now that the laws of nature were never going to be amended.

"What's the point of it all anyway?" asked Rabbit, "Humans just do whatever they want regardless, I was inside with them all winter and now they have put me out here."

"The closer you get to Hedgehog, the more points you will discover." Said Tortoise, who had been inside too when she was a hatchling.

The argument that humans could not be made to change their behaviour was weak, especially with the undisputed testimony of Dunnock, and in light of the recent human hibernating behaviour, which Dog referred to as "lock down". It wasn't quite a hibernation as they humans were still awake and active behind their walls. And every few days before dusk they came out to the front of their homes and made a brief commotion before returning to silence.

Was it possible that the humans had already begun to curtail their expansion? Maybe that was what this lock down was all about. It was certainly having a noticeable positive effect on the gardens' way of life.

"Well, thank you for your support regardless. It was too much to expect, even impossible, but we tried anyway." Hedgehog said and went sniffing for some slugs on the way home. At least his own house would be safe and well ventilated if not tidy; he actually preferred it a bit messy, it felt lived in.

There was no way squirrels would be convinced that modifying their behaviour to obey new laws of nature was in their interests. "It's not natural and even if it is we're not doing it." Was their attitude and regardless of any law being passed they wouldn't comply anyway. They were only in court positions because they needed to keep abreast of the laws pertaining to nut running, in which they were heavily involved. The few cases of vandalism to bird feeders that reached the courts were never proven, even the law was not clear in this regard. As one of the many corvid beaks had put it in a decisive court case: "If a squirrel proof bird feeder could be defeated by squirrels then by definition it was not squirrel proof." The case had collapsed and the squirrel defendant had hopped. No squirrel had ever been prosecuted since squirrels and Magpies got involved in the court process.

Hedgehog spent little time ruminating about the court defeat. He had spent enough time and effort with the humans, and with the world, and now he would simply be the best Hedgehog he could so that if he could find a mate and have hoglets of his own that would be better prepared for the world. He had caught a scent in the air and now, more than anything else, he wanted a mate.

Rats were gradually returning to the gardens, if only to bring their high pitched news of more dumping of human detritus along lanes where previously only dog patrollers ventured, the rats had made new nests amongst the discarded furniture, although there was precious little additional food to be had there, but like everything else it just had to be explored. Dog had explained they called it fly tipping, but there were no more flies there than anywhere else, and Dog couldn't even catch a fly let alone tip one.

In the undergrowth, well out of sight of the humans, the rats had successfully gnawed away at the base of a fence, and made a small hole near the post, where they could squeeze through. Hedgehog persuaded them, for the good of their teeth, to open the hole a little more, and gained access to the next garden. Overnight, more new holes were made and enlarged, a little larger than necessary for rats, but too tight for a fox or cat, just perfect for Hedgehog. He easily convinced the rats they needn't be confined to just one or two gardens when they had travelled all the way from the fly tip, they could now explore all the adjoining gardens. And so could Hedgehog.

It took a few nights but Hedgehog's efforts were eventually rewarded with access to the seventh garden, beyond where the tortoiseshell cat lived. There he followed the scent under a pile of rotting logs by a compost heap, as safe and romantic a setting as he could possibly wish for, when he finally met up with the female Hedgehog of his dreams and presented her with the mouthful of leaves he'd been carrying. Courtship was a fairly prolonged and noisy affair that involved much circling and rhythmic puffing and snorting, and attracted the attention of another male Hedgehog who had to be chased off but still lingered somewhere in the undergrowth of Tortoiseshell Cat's garden. Having endured the synchronised breathing, singing and dancing, he persuaded his mate to come and visit his house and they spent that night and the next few days and nights in each other's company, moving between one home and the other, rearranging the leaves and eating whatever centipedes, worms and slugs they sniffed out on their way. After a few days, the romance wore off and the Hedgehogs parted back to their own gardens. Between bad tempered rows, she promised him that she would bring his array of babies back for a sniff in a few weeks when they were able to walk, and he promised to pop over to smell if she was doing ok from time to time.

Part of Hedgehog's charm was that he seemed unaware of the effect his example had on some of the other garden dwellers. His casual and unassuming way with the rats, effortlessly persuading them to help him. The same way Tortoise felt compelled to use her considerable experience to help him prepare for court, because she sensed something in him, plus he was so cute. She remembered the way the humans had provided him with his home shortly after he had appeared on the patio.

Tortoise had noticed that Hedgehog never defecated inside his house, and never close to a food tray or water bowl; a behavioural trait that none of his ancestors adhered to. Her own habit was now to go in the corner of her burrow, an area that the humans came and dug over every once in a while.

Just because it would never become a law didn't mean it couldn't become a habit.

The Ruminant Kind - M.E. Hills

A doe and her fawn made their way through the woods, picking their way carefully toward the lake. Their hooves twisting, ripping the grass with every step. Coated with sweat. Eyes wide but soft. They were alone. Perhaps the herd was near. Perhaps they were lost. Perhaps they had left.

The mother encouraged her child forward through the cattails toward the black water to drink while she stood guard, cautiously chewing the grass in her mouth, pausing at every snap of a twig. The fawn did not look up once. Sucking furiously at the water. A flurry of midges circled its head. Its mouth dipped perfectly into the moon's reflection on the lake, rippling its milk out to the bank.

From across the lake Cat held her breath, she could feel every pine needle beneath her bare legs imprinting into her flesh. Before long, a distant siren urged the doe to move on. Her fawn was thirsty and continued to drink. She nudged her baby softly. How strange for the fawn to be so resistant. This wasn't any normal kind of heat. The doe must be thirsty too. But she no longer felt safe. When the fawn finally lifted it's head, it gazed at Cat with sleepy eyes, water dripping in pearls from its chin. It looked at her as though it had known she was there all along. As the sirens wailed in the distance, the fawn unphased, yawned and staggered backward through the reeds and disappeared into the wood. Leaving just the rippled moon on the water behind.

As the night air dripped like treacle around her shoulders, Cat squirmed into a new position, unable to sit comfortably cross legged and plucked at her top. She squeezed her eyes shut and tried to focus on her breath, but as always, focusing on her breath just made her feel too conscious of it. Like the intrusive thoughts that come to her head before she sleeps, bullying her into thinking about what colour the inside of her eyelids were; the thought of concentrating on her breath only panicked her into a distorted hyperventilation. "Fuck Yoga" she said, lunging for her phone.

AMARA: Be there in 10, two dickheads won't leave

It's always the way. The one night you want to close up early. Tonight was particularly sticky. The kind that makes you want to wash and wash and wash your skin. This was no night to be stuck behind a bar with two dickheads that won't leave.

Cat could not bear any kind of heat. She must have been from some Icelandic place in her previous life. She heaved her breasts up to relieve the discomfort. She wanted to be something anonymous, scuttling across the floor of the sea, the same colour of the sea. Something hard. Neither prey nor predator. Does such a thing exist.

When she was younger she didn't know how to swim properly, but would instead sink to the bottom of the pool, releasing the air in streams from her nose, open her eyes and stare. At the legs. At the plasters. At the coins. She can't imagine a level of peace greater than that. It isn't weird for a child to do that. As an adult, it would be unacceptable. She reached into her bag and began to roll a joint.

***

Amara foolishly began cleaning down the bar an hour before it shut. There had been only one customer since 9pm and on a Monday night it was rare to get a walk in after 10. But anyone will tell you that cleaning early will only ever invite people to come in. She was one glass wash away from full clean down when they came in. They were the kind of nondescript middle aged men that came into bars at this time of night and caused annoyance. They could be in their 30s or their 40s - it was always hard to tell. White skin. Bald or Shaved heads. Salmon pink polo shirts buttoned up over too tight jeans and a firm porcine belly hanging confidently over the top. Loud voices, louder laughs. Cat would say "those brexity kind of guys" and immediately Amara would seem to know exactly what she meant. Amara always knew what Cat meant.

On this occasion, Amara was in the office when the men walked in, and it was Satskia who had to serve them. Begrudgingly polite, she asked them what they wanted as they swayed red-eyed at the bar, pressing their bellies into the counter. One was larger than the other, with a shaved round head, every feature on his face seemed to bulge as though he were being squeezed from the middle. He leaned over the bar toward Satskia, so close that she could smell his sour, cidery breath.

"How long until last orders darlin?"

"Twenty minutes," she replied without a beat, "what can I get you?" The second man barged across his friend and drummed his tattooed fingers on the bar, "we'll take two pints of Aspalls each."

"Okay," Satskia replied, tightening her smile, "but when it gets to 11 im going to give you plastics so that we can close."

"Alright darlin," the first one slurred as he staggered back, lowering his eyes to her chest, "we'll see."

As soon as the men had sat down at a table, Satskia wiped her hands on her apron and walked over to the office where Amara was counting receipts. "There's two guys here that came in just now by the way."

Amara slammed the till shut, catching her finger but barely noticing. "For fuck fucking sake I'm meeting Cat tonight, what did they order?"

"They got two pints of cider, each."

"You're kidding me man," Amara shook her finger and stuck it in her mouth. "This shit always happens when it's my day off the next day. Did you give them plastics?"

"I told them i'll make them pour their drinks into plastics in twenty minutes." Satskia looked down at her feet, knowing full well she wouldn't be able to make *anyone* do anything.

Amara raised her eyebrows in irritation, if it was her that had served them she would have just told them to piss off the moment they walked in.

The smaller of the two men winked at Satskia as she slipped out of the office. Satskia was the kind of girl who always walked with a hip sway, even when she didn't want to. Men catcalled her all the time. Her flame red hair and pale skin drew attention to her, her deep, throaty Czech accent didn't help either on nights like tonight. She started wearing more and more heavy clothes to try and cover her body. She couldn't walk down one road without being shouted at, but whenever she complained the rest of her friends would either tell her to simply "never go out alone then" or tease her for bragging. "Oh no! Men won't leave me alone! I can't help being so HOT!" But Satskia was never bragging. She didn't know what she was doing that was making it happen more to her than anyone else. What was she doing that made her stand out? Even with her baseball cap on, head down and a fast walk - she would get stopped. She took it all in good humour, but with every day she walked to and from work, she became a little more anxious, her heart beat a little faster, and her courage shrank a little smaller. Was she supposed to just pay half her wages in cabs instead? Satskia stopped complaining about the men to the others. She worked in a bar and she was a woman. What could she expect? In years to come, Satskia would entirely stop leaving her apartment.

Satskia pretended she hadn't noticed the men staring at her, and continued pretending to clean down the already clean bar.

"Bet you get a lot of tips don't you?" He slurred from his table. He was at least a head shorter than his friend but looked twice as menacing. His face was rat like, with a persistent grin, and tiny black eyes like a pair of cloves pressed into a ham. "Scuse me, I'm talking to you."

Satskia put the bar mop down and scratched her head. "Uh not much, I mean we do but we share them. People don't tip as much these days in general."

The bulging-eyed man slapped his hand down on the table, nearly knocking over his pint. Satskia knew she shouldn't have served them. It was a mistake. These men were extremely drunk.

"I never tip," he bellowed, "It's your job to serve, why should I pay more for you to do the job you're already supposed to be doing?!"

"I guess that's why it's up to you…" she shrugged. She could feel her cheeks glowing like an induction stove. *Amara please please come out of the office you fucking bitch.*

"Ohhhh she's fiery isn't she?"

"Yeah I love it!" the larger man had turned his chair to face Satskia. His Legs spread open as wide as they could go. "Where are you from then? Russia or something?" His drunk red eyes had that glazed look that she knew too well. It was the kind of look that terrified her. All the blood in their brain had either been scrambled or gone to their groin. In the prickling silence, it was as if all three of them were weighing up Satskia's implication.

Like the snap of a twig that startles the deer, Amara stomped out of the office, slapping the door shut, breaking the frozen silence. "Alright guys, time to make a move, we are gonna shut now." She swiped two plastic cups from the stack on the bar and rolled them on the table towards the men and turned back toward Satskia, rolling her eyes.

"She said you were closing at eleven. It's still ten to." said the larger one.

"Well I'm closing now. Please pour your drinks into the plastics and leave." Amara snapped, sliding herself behind the bar towards her phone. Satskia couldn't understand how someone could be so at ease in confrontation.

"What if we aren't ready to leave?" said the rat, "what are you actually going to do if we don't?" He looked so smug Amara could have spat poison at him. She leaned across the bar, looking him dead in the eye.

"Well I would have to call the police. Who are next door. But I don't *really* want to waste their time, so…"

Satskia looked at Amara. The police station next door had been closed for years, and besides, the last time the police were called, they said they couldn't send anyone out on priority unless there had been a physical threat of violence.

The rat looked at his friend, "I don't think she would even call the police, and besides what are the police gonna do?" he jeered, "we aren't doing anything wrong. So I think we are going to stay here, and enjoy our drinks" he sharpened his gaze on Satskia, "and our company."

Amara unconsciously ushered Satskia behind her and picked up her phone. "Fine, ill call them now then" she sighed. Pretending to dial 999, she texted Cat.

***

CAT: No worries. x

Cat thought that was probably the text she had sent the most. No worries No worries. But really there were so many worries. So many worries all the time. Cat worried about Amara, who hated being worried about. Amara had been running that bar for as long as Cat had known her. She treated it like her home. She guarded it like a fox over its den. Ah but the den seemed to invite troubled strangers much too often. Amara was always kicking people out, and sheltering people in. She was as fierce as she was kind. But no one ever thought Amara was kind, only Cat. Other women disliked Amara. She was more self assured than most. Less apologetic. She never tried to fluff up a harsh sentence. Most of the staff were scared of her. But like the truest of kindnesses, Amara's kindness was silent, so no one ever heard it.

Amara was one of those rare people you find in hospitality that aren't there because they failed at whatever it was they wanted to do, but rather that she had found her great passion was in that very job. People often quietly pitied Amara; as for years she continued to serve drinks and wipe tables, while hundreds of others came and went. But she considered herself one of the lucky ones. It was never a limbo for her. She didn't want to do anything else. She came here to work in a bar. She did it well. And so that's what she did.

When Cat met Amara, she was 19 and Amara was 24. Cat has wanted to be everything a person can be. An animator. A vet. A psychologist. Much to Cat's frequent disappointment. All of these jobs required actually doing something. It wasn't that she couldn't do any of those things if she tried. And it wasn't that Cat was lazy either. But instead she felt consistently incapable of anything at all. She could never muster herself to work harder than she already was by just living on autopilot. Surely just existing was hard enough work as it is. How is it that so many people are capable of both existing *and* excelling. Cat found it hard simply to exist for as long as she could possibly remember. It was as though a dark fog was slowly closing in over her head, preventing her from exceeding a maximum usage of energy each day. With every action, the fog would close in an inch further. Some mornings the fog would already be over her eyes before she even got up. Getting out of bed felt like lifting a boulder with a floss string. Other mornings the fog would be nonexistent. She would wake up and set her intentions. Look up online courses, go for a run, deeply inhaling the juicy air, laughing at the birds, seeing friends, dancing, dancing, dancing. She knew how rare these days were and crammed them full, as though if she could only run fast enough she could gain enough momentum to simply coast once the fuel had run out. But the fuel always ran out too soon. So it goes. So it goes.

She took in a small puff on the joint that she didn't really want and inhaled it with the rest of the syruppy night air. She wanted Amara to be here now.

***

"Police please." Amara flicked her phone onto silent with her finger while holding it up to her ear. "Yeah hi, I have two men at my bar that won't leave. SE15 5BS. I will. Thank you. Yes I do have CCTV. It live streams to the -" *fuck*. She thought she had put the phone on silent but now it was ringing. Can she still pretend she's on the phone to the police? Can a phone still ring when you are on the line? Maybe they were too drunk to notice.

Sitting up from his drunken stupor, bulge-eyes pointed his fat pink finger at Amara, knocking the table with his bulk "She's not even on the phone the sneaky bitch!"

"I told you, didn't I?!" The rat's smile grew even larger as he stared at the women. "They can't do shit."

The rat continued to grin, his long pestiferous yellow teeth glistened from his tiny mouth. The air in the room was throbbing. Nothing was happening and yet the moment was so charged. It felt silly in the way a dumb nightmare feels silly but only after you've woken up. Why were you scared anyway? And now these two women stood with their fight or flight systems flaring up and perhaps for nothing. Two men with alcohol coursing through their veins. All this powerlessness. All this potential. What were these men going to do? What was the next move? Was there one? Would they just have to wait until the men got bored. All this powerlessness. These men only had to sit here and not leave and that was enough.

Amara stood with her mouth slightly open, staring at the men that sat before her. To Satskia it looked like she was panting. The room had a pulse. Amara shut her eyes and filled her lungs with breath and screamed, "JUST FUCK OFF!!!!" at the top of her voice. The sound ripped through her entire body like an avalanche.

The rat finished his cider and staggered to a stand. For a minute, the pulse stopped.

"I'm only messing with you. Jeeesus." Slapping the puddle of his friend who was now beginning to drool on the table. "Come on mate let's go". The two men crashed through several tables on their way out before they got to the exit, fumbling and slapping the push-bar before finally leaving.

The moon hung oddly low in the black swell of the sky. It was not quite full. It must have been waxing. Cat thought it looked like a balloon. As if a child had let it go on purpose, for it to float up and bounce off of the sky's ceiling and just stay there. It was extremely bright. Brighter than Cat had ever seen before. Out of breath, she paced towards Amara's bar. Eyes wide but soft. This wasn't any normal kind of heat. She told herself repeatedly not to worry. As she approached the bar, through the alley of empty oil drums and cigarette butts. Two men walked past her. One more drunk than the other. Swaying like palms in the thick heat of the evening. One of them turned his head towards her. Her face dripping with sweat, gaunt with worry.

"Lighten up," he said.

Neil Walker - Rebecca & William Zero

November the 6th, 1975, plays no significant part in anyone's life, unless, by some freak coincidence, your date-of-birth or wedding day happened to fall on that Friday. Or, and this carries a much stronger probability, you've attached greatness to an event widely labelled as 'shambolic'.

It was 8:35pm at St. Martin's School of Art when time and place cavorted to ignite pleasures previously unheard of, a coming together of car crash proportions lasting thirteen minutes in all.

Those were the opening lines of my last letter from William. Not your typical content, but then we weren't family, lovers or friends. More an encounter thrown together over two showery days, exchanging two pieces of correspondence each. End of story. Except the story didn't have a definite ending, and so, by default, lives on.

It took place in mid-August 1989. I knew rain was on the cards as I'd just passed A-level Geography with a grade 'A'. But it was far too sultry to be lugging a coat around and a blouse should be spared the indignity of submitting to a cagoule.

I'd been searching out a type of dragonfly when the downpour set in. The nearest refuge was under the laden foliage of two mature sycamores. And from there I watched William drag himself over to the neighbouring tree. He stood as if under a shower, raising a bearded chin before sweeping back wet hair with the fingers of one hand. The other hand was holding an orange which appeared oversized due to his physique. Arms, on show through drenched white shirtsleeves, told of a man fleshless and bird boned. Black trousers sagged heavily on scuffed brogues, and, using his free hand, he tugged up the waistband before adjusting himself. His attentions then turned to the orange. With teasing actions, he stripped the peel in one piece dispatching it into a bin midway between the two of us. The smell of warm rain smothered any lingering fragrance and, as William trundled back to his tree, I drew on memories touched by the scent of zest.

St. Martin's that night was a 'year-zero' moment when amateurs elevated hormonal insurgency above the middle-aged meanderings of professionals. After instigating the mayhem, the Sex Pistols left the scene of their first gig the same way they'd arrived, by the back door. It would take another year for them to assume the mantle of media pin-up boys, a year spent plastering their ransom-note demands across the face of popular culture.

William's clothing and full beard spoke of a youth out of step. Hallucinogenic colours were nailed to Manchester's mast. Onboard were clean-shaven pirates barring the odd goatee chin. William had cut himself adrift, the dislocation underlined by a peeled, uneaten orange dripping rainwater from a shirt sleeve.

- Rain's clearing.

Why I came out with the statement, I really don't know. William looked across at me unmoved and, shamed by my dumb spontaneity, I walked off.

From September, Manchester was to make way for an English Literature degree at York. The lives of the Wordsworths were presently lighting little torches; siblings trudging around Lakeland tarns with cold pork and notebooks stuffed in their pockets. They helped burn off the veil shrouding Manchester life, revealing the allure of wasteland grasses, the honesty of allotments and the writerly urges of an eighteen-year-old local lass. I wrote down names of tree-lined streets I'd failed to notice before and coloured over grey existence by meditating on fate. It seemed whatever direction I chose, Alexandra Park lay in wait.

That first awkward encounter was no different, except it had started with an iridescent blue dragonfly leading me a merry dance to the park lake. The thing couldn't have understood the point of the exercise flitting as it did between pedalo relics bobbing corpse-like on turbid water. The siblings, seared with migraines, could be seen heading for the nearest bed. My own sensibilities felt a park this size had to contain a more inspired dragonfly.

The first Pistols' gig is a beacon, without doubt. But a nation taking punk heritage to heart smacks of a people resigned to impotency, collectively blowing cobwebs off treasured memories when the hours are dragging. History counts for nothing unless it harbours an incisory presence. And how deep it cuts depends on whether we've borne witness to history in the making.

I wasn't at St. Martin's that night, and the graceless dimensions of this are all-encompassing because I insist on having been there, transported beyond a Charlie Bucket bedtime and mum's goodnight kiss to live through a moment when four lean teenagers unleashed themselves for a feeding frenzy.

The next day was another humid affair but framed on a grander scale with the burgeoning *cumulonimbus* adding pure menace. It was a day for Mary Shelley's gothic prose rather than the miscellany of Dorothy Wordsworth's journals.

I kept busy in the park, picking off yellowing leaves, snapping leafless branches, deadheading tainted roses. Yet, come early afternoon, the only thing playing on my mind was a wasp sting below the right elbow. It murdered, a red swelling with constant shooting pains. Mary's voice was insistent though, this was the administering of white lightning, the propagating of a transcendental moment.

By the time I found William sat on a bench, hunger and thirst were also toying with an altered mindset. I looked longingly at two oranges, one of which he was already peeling. He lifted his head to see whose shadow had infringed on his personal space, his eyes asking why. The eyes were the standout feature, scary translucent green, while marked bone structure lent symmetry to a parchment-coloured face. The tangle of beard I was sure hid an angular jawline. At a guess he was early twenties with shaving already beyond the pale, and he wouldn't have thanked you for gifting him a comb. I placed him buried in a vale a country mile behind, his ruined encampment devoid of mirrors, only the lure of oranges drawing him to town.

- You're eating oranges again.

He nodded reluctantly while splitting the orange in two and removing white tails.

- D'you mind sharing your bench?

His hand gesture spoke more of indifference than acceptance, and only when he offered me half his orange, did I take my place. He'd no doubt been adjusting himself of late, so I cleaned the orange with spittle before separating the first segments. Each was sweet and loaded with juice, and I finished before he did:

- That was a seriously good orange.

I walked over to a water fountain to rinse my hands and on returning watched him savour the last two segments avoiding spills with tender bites and sucks.

- When do we get to eat the other one?

A smooth Irish accent warmed his first words:

- Going home.
- Not much to sustain us on the long road to Ireland. You know there're thunderstorms on the way?
- I know.

He displayed a shoddy anorak dug from underneath his trousers.

I went on to express my love of weather, garnering the odd grunt in response, yet the rumblings of approaching thunder gave voice to the fact both of us were badly underperforming.

For thirteen bewildering minutes, a spray of lyrics and insults are directed at me full-on. I'm ten-year-old Billy Zero, the first convert baptised by Johnny's slanderous kiss, a kiss sealed with the residue of beer and phlegm. Johnny and I have reached an understanding.

The plugs are pulled after five vainglorious songs, but this is only the beginning. As iconic statement, the safety pin is peerless, and while chasing along streets aside wide-eyed urchins, my bloody lips proclaim London is set to burn.

- You ever heard the saying: 'There's a bird born to everyone'?

My question only succeeded in painting a frown on William's brow.

- It's an Irish saying I heard someplace. If you search the sky, you can find a bird born to you, that flies and sings for you alone.

We both trawled the heavens for signs of life. Beyond a circling vulture that didn't count, all else was bubbling cloud and a cloak of rain enveloping the horizon.

- There's one.

William nodded at a distant seagull, no doubt on its way to Blackpool, or Featherstall Road rubbish tip for richer pickings. He told me seagulls didn't sing, something I already knew. Our eyes broke contact. Repositioning his body, he slumped forward once more, refocusing on a point across the open parkland where boys were playing football.

Our best moments are lived in playgrounds, bouncing off each other, tumbling headlong, righting ourselves to start again in earnest.

The Pistols fomented a dark magic petrifying those on playground duty; industry promoters as statuesque maypoles for a new generation whirling in the void; a generation X spewing out brazen emotions before resting their heads on the cold, soiled floor.

During playtime at Seven Stars I caught glimpses of emotions. Peering through bars, I saw chances for connection go swirling by in a myriad of colours.

St. Martin's is the illogical extension. For while the most incendiary band on God's earth provoked reactions above and beyond, that same band has me shadowboxing inside an illusion, knowing I can't be hurt if nothing is real.

A scintilla of hope remains that something compels me to leap the encroaching chasm. But hope comes in consequence of a life half lived, and a scintilla of hope of a life all but extinguished.

William broke his gaze and asked what music I was into.

- Good stuff, of course. I like dancefloors, so House. But at home I listen to other stuff. Talking Heads are great, as are New Order. And you?
- You know neither of those groups nor a thousand others would have made it if it weren't for punk.

I told him he didn't look like a punk, to which he answered the best punks came camouflaged. A nascent smile was playing on his lips, a smile he was trying to suppress.

- D'you have a punk moniker?
- William.

Well, at least it confirmed he was an early-nineteenth-century Romantic.

- Mine's Rebecca. Isn't that just too beautiful for words? You like your oranges.
- They make me happy.
- You need oranges for that?

- Well, they help.

He looked embarrassed. I looked at my legs and told him there were so many ways of getting a buzz out of life.

- But oranges produce the neurotransmitters, dopamine and serotonin.

It was news to the rest of us loved-up on 'E' in deepest *Madchester*, unaware the local greengrocer was our man.

William's three long words spun around in my head and left me saying nothing. I was thankful when the first fat drops began falling out of a bruised sky. Our early-nineteenth-century moment had arrived.

- I've got a wasp sting telling me something gigantic's about to happen.

I met his perplexed silence by suggesting we head for the sycamores. He made no move to follow me, even with splashes littering the bench.

- You should get yourself a wasp sting, William. Beats serotonin any day.

To which he said he had to go and set off towards the open parkland.

- But the trees, our storm?

He laboured on, his fading form diverting round the discarded bikes of boys still at play, boys laughing in our rain.

I looked back at the bench whose ghosts were already being washed away; a girl with a wasp sting below her right elbow, a boy artfully working orange peel. A boy sat on a dire anorak, except the anorak was real. I could touch it, hold it, run with it, sprint the entire length of a deranged path smashing my way through a Manchester brick wall. And once at his side, we would throw ourselves at the onslaught of heavenly violence bound for an encampment more bedraggled than ever.

The view from my fortress includes bird-less evergreens. They render the eyes soulless. Disinfectant sterilises the smell of fresh-cut grass. The irony is not lost since no heel digs the turf here, no stud tears up root, no foot crushes a single blade. On the rare days I ploughed through muddy affairs, you could taste the earth, the ball all but forgotten in a riot of play.

Those cuts collected on footballing knees were worn with honour. The razor cuts on arms are hidden in disgrace. Each one serves to mark off another day lost. Only mum's kiss resists a deadening touch, a tingling sensation warming the left cheek, fading with first light, resurrected in sleep.

It was no good, my legs and breath were giving way, still some distance from William. The deluge had passed but drumrolls continued, gods playing out the soundtrack for Primrose Bank, an estate with neither a bank nor primrose to its name. The high-rise William entered was home to a school friend, and having lost him in the building, I sought out Rachel. Her mother, Cath, answered the door:

- You're drenched to the bone, girl. Why aren't you wearing your anorak?

She went off to fetch a towel.

Cath was a sweet woman enduring a bad-tempered husband. A heavy mood descended whenever he was in the room. It was Rachel's turn to endure him today, in his Mr. Twirly ice-cream van. The kids on my estate knew him as Mr. Twatty.

Cath being Cath, she insisted I slip on a bathrobe and dry my clothes on a portable radiator. She brought me a cup of tea with a plate of shortbreads and I sat next to her on the sofa, snug in the robe with a towel round my head. We chatted happily about my upcoming university adventure. And then I asked about William.

- Oh, you mean William of Orange.

She said he lived with his mother. The father, long gone, had been a prominent dealer, chased off by good and bad alike. The mother was quiet, same as the boy. And like most on the estate the boy didn't seem to have a job or much about him.

- You don't know the flat number? He left something behind on a park bench.
- He left you behind. Stupid boy. But then is there any other kind?

She went off to make a phone-call, leaving me eating the last shortbread and admiring the room's photos. She returned in no time, catching me holding a black-and-white portrait of her, youthful and joyous.

- That photo fills me with bitterness. Number fifty-one. But if you ask me, stick to your own boys on the Coppice.

I made my excuses, hastily throwing on damp clothing while thanking Cath profusely. Her final words, as ever, left me smiling:

- For God's sake, put your anorak on. If he doesn't like you in it, he's not boyfriend material.

I ran off up to the fifth floor. Pressing the doorbell, I felt the wasp sting inflame. The smell of disinfectant hung around the adjacent lift. A planter next to the front door had long since relinquished its choked, sunless plant. I told myself modern-day escapades were like this, having to contend with precincts, car parks and stairwells, places where time either dragged or raced, and little served to inspire. Breeding grounds for bitterness. I pressed the bell one last time, but no-one stirred. I wanted to rain fists on a door less than gigantic, but someone had beaten me to it.

I went to the park the next day but couldn't find William, nor the day after. On the third day, I hand-posted the anorak with a note, address included. He wrote back apologising as I had done. He talked about his need of a catalyst, asked if I had one going spare that didn't involve wasps. I answered with a letter about a punk whose motto should be: 'Attack the Day', and whose camouflage might prove useful unless it locked away what was living inside.

It wasn't until I was at university, in November, that a second letter arrived forwarded by mum. It contained a piece of writing entitled: '*Senseless*', the envelope handwritten in ransom-note lettering. What I read left an impression in so many ways. My response tried to make light of it, easy quips about the envelope leaving our postman hospitalised, about York's Punk Studies course needing an eminent professor. Although his response never came, Rachel's did. William and his mother had gone back to Ireland.

As I said at the beginning, a story held in suspension, the intervening years still flavoured by mid-August '89. And to this day, I make a point of downing tools late afternoon. On the desk, beside pen and paper, sits a fruit bowl for oranges. Teasing away the peel infuses the paper with perfume, an interlude for thinking about the words on the page. I don't know if William continued his writing. I like to think the rubbish-tip seagull was the making of him. I can't say that dopamine and serotonin have been the making of me, but I can remove the full peel of an orange without breaking it.

Waking from sleep, falling asleep, these are the tumultuous events. All else is quietness in a walking sitting waiting stupor.

Except today the beating heart is unsettling the void. The more attentively I listen, the louder it becomes. And then faster, a pulsebeat speeding after wild hearts; youths crashing through evergreens, ravaging the turf, with screams so primordial that walls twist and snake. Flailing weaponry frees me of chains, liberated from that in which nothing is of note, save for today being November the 6th.

Patrick Eades - What Lies Beneath

The man first saw the bandaged woman as he began to unsee his wife. The Spanish apartment they moved into looked out over the Bay of Biscay, and also the balcony below, where the bandaged woman would sunbake. The man would peer over the edge of their small balcony and watch as the woman would remove layers of clothing, to expose a body wrapped entirely in white bandages, except for a one-inch strip for her eyes, and two little holes for her nose. There were no holes for the mouth.

'It can't be burns,' his wife snapped at him, like he was an idiot, 'They would heat up in the sun and become inflamed.'

His wife knew many things: the amount of time they could afford to rent the apartment before their money ran out (19 weeks), the number of grey hairs on his head (now in excess of 50), and a passable grasp of the Spanish language. She did not know how the bandaged woman ate.

One day the bandaged woman's eyes caught the man staring down at her. She waved a bandaged limb, and he scampered back inside. He felt a flush that could not be explained by the morning sun.

His wife had drawn a timetable of activities: to walk to and swim at Playa Xago in the mountains, a dolphin spotting cruise, a scuba diving lesson, and a pottery course taught by a local artist she had once seen in an art magazine she subscribed to. The man understood the activities to be mandatory. He would try, but he held little hope that even the potter could re-sculpt the crumbled ruins of their marriage.

***

They passed the bandaged woman in the hallway as the man lugged two misshapen clay pots up the stairs to their apartment. The bandaged woman struggled with her shopping bags, their weight cutting into the creases of her elbows, forming a small crevasse in the bandages.

'Help her!' his wife said.

He placed the pots on the floor and rushed over to the woman. Unlike his wife, he had yet to conquer the Spanish language, and had to mime carrying the bags himself. The woman said nothing, but the man could have sworn he detected a smile underneath the bandages as she let him take the bags. Up close, there was a sweetness to her scent, like fresh baked cinnamon scrolls.

'Why do you think she can't speak?' the man asked his wife in bed that night.

His wife snorted, a sound he used to find adorable. 'Why do you assume she has anything to say to you?'

He rolled over, admiring the clay pot on his bedside table. He would paint it red, he decided.

***

The following morning, the man woke to muffled conversation drifting into the apartment. He opened the sliding door to the balcony and peered over the railing. His wife sat across from the bandaged woman, a plate of fresh pastries between them. Snippets of the one-side conversation drifted up to him.

'…our marriage counsellor suggested this…'

'…he'll never understand, you know?'

When she returned to their apartment, she carried a plate with two small pastries left amongst a smattering of crumbs.

'Why didn't you talk to her in Spanish?' he asked her.

'What makes you think she's Spanish?'

'Well, she lives in Spain.'

'So do we. We're not Spanish.'

He let out a sigh, and blew out the fuse of an argument he didn't have the energy to fight.

***

The next few weeks the man overheard all the reasons their marriage staggered towards collapse. His wife spent her mornings chewing the ear off the bandaged woman over pastries and coffee, and he spent his mornings peering down at them and wondering what lay beneath the bandages. He couldn't tell if she meant for him to listen in. His wife would return full of good spirit and Pestiños, but as soon as he opened his mouth to speak, her smile would fall away into a frown, and she would chastise him for never listening.

Whatever they had hoped to achieve by moving to Spain felt beyond the man's reach. He felt grateful they had no children, no one to explain this mess too, no awkward family gatherings where he would have to fake civility and friendship with a woman who had stolen the best years of his life. No strings attached, just the frayed edges of what could have been. Perhaps if he had spoken up earlier, the wounds that grew and festered between them may have had a chance to heal, but it was too late now.

He prepared two jugs of Sangria for their midday lunch, and awaited her arrival home.

***

'There's another woman, isn't there?' his wife said after they had finished the first jug and he had told her.

'What? No. There's no one,' the man said. *There's not even us,* he thought.

'I've seen the way you look at her, undressing her with your eyes. I bet you'd love to unwrap those bandages and check out what's underneath, wouldn't you?'

The man shook his head and rubbed his palms across his eyes. He wouldn't tell her about the dreams he'd been having. He dreamt of the bandaged woman standing on the edge of a volcano, and the heat searing out of the crater began to set her bandages alight. He shouted at her to come down from the edge, where he could douse her flames, but she remained a burning statue against a soot-filled sky. He cried and screamed, but could do little but watch as the fire engulfed her. Still she stood, even as the embers petered out and turned to ashes. A cool breeze sprang from behind him and began to blow the ashes off the woman. He waited to glimpse what lay beneath, but he woke before the reveal.

'We're not getting any younger, and we're not getting any happier. We're not what we were before…' he trailed off, unable to speak of her (or him; it had been too early to tell).

'Alright, prove it. Let's go downstairs and take her bandages off, and you can tell me then that it's not her.'

He drained his glass of Sangria and stood. 'You're being ridiculous.'

'I'm the ridiculous one? I sacrificed my job, said goodbye to my friends, my family, all to come her for you, for us. I know you still blame me; I can see it in your eyes.'

That blow knocked the wind out of him. The truth packed the strongest punch.

'Fine, let's go. If that's what you want, then let's go and see her.'

He turned and marched out of their apartment, his wife trailing behind. He paused outside the bandaged woman's door, tried to steady himself with a few deep breaths. His wife reached passed him and knocked on the door like an angry parent.

Knock-knock-knock-knock.

The door opened a minute later, the woman's eyes wide with surprise.

'May we, come in?' his wife said in a mixture of broken English and hand signals.

'She still hasn't spoken to you?' the man asked his wife as they were led into the apartment.

'No. How could she, with her mouth bandaged up so tight?'

The woman stood facing them, the pale afternoon sun streaming in through the balcony window cast her shadow her against the wall.

'Can you…' his wife said to the woman, miming unwrapping the bandages from the top of her head.

The woman shook her head, *no*. The shadow trembled.

The man felt his legs wobble, as if on the edge of a cliff—one step further and they may plummet into oblivion.

'She doesn't want to,' he said.

His wife turned to him, stared into his eyes with an intensity he hadn't seen since they made the decision, eight years, three months and fourteen days ago.

'I need you to tell me this time; do you want to?' she asked.

The man closed his eyes, he could still picture the bare white walls of the doctor's office, a poster of the human body with all its bones and muscles and organs the only decoration. The doctor waited for an answer, his wife—eleven weeks pregnant—waited for an answer. They already knew what their decision would be, they made a pact before she fell pregnant not to bring a child with a serious disability into the world. They agreed to make the decision before the emotions of pregnancy messed with reason and logic. The question was: did they want to know the results of the test? Did they want to make that decision? He searched his wife's face for a clue to guide his response, and came up empty.

Her voice snapped him back to the present. 'Do. You. Want. To. Know?'

'Yes.'

His wife approached the bandaged woman and drew her in for a hug. The embrace lasted long enough for the man to try and remember the last time he had held his wife that long. He couldn't.

His wife drew back from the embrace and looked into the woman's eyes. After a moment's hesitation, the woman nodded. His wife's hand found the end of the bandage tucked in behind the woman's ear, and she began to unravel them.

The man could barely stand, the crashing of his heart against his chest all but knocked him off his feet.

The top of the woman's head peeked out into open air, like a chick bursting through its shell. A shaven skull revealed itself first, but as the bandages fell away from the woman's face, the man wondered if he was back in the dream. Her face was an angry red, as if consumed by fire, but when he looked closer, he saw it wasn't burns, but mountainous eruptions of pustules and abscesses. He could smell cinnamon again, it wafted out from the ointment lathered over her skin. Tears streamed down the woman's face, flowing over and through the ridges and craters of the old and the new. His wife—focused on her job, kept unwrapping the woman, exposing shoulders red and raw.

'Stop!' the man called out to his wife.

His wife stepped back, and let forth a sob as she caught sight of the woman's body. The woman shook like a leaf in a storm.

The man moved in and drew her into his arms, his own tears fell from his chin, a small tributary to the river cascading down the woman's face.

He had told the doctor yes, all those years ago. He thought that would please her. The doctor informed them it was more than a 90 percent chance the baby had Down Syndrome. They did what they had agreed upon, and she was no longer pregnant. They told themselves it would be fine, they were still young, they had plenty of time to try again. Now time was no longer on their side.

'I'm sorry,' his wife said.

The man pulled back from the bandaged woman and turned to look at his wife. He took her hand, and together they wrapped the bandages back around the woman.

'She must be deaf,' his wife said, 'God. What were we thinking?'

'I don't know,' the man answered.

'Should we leave?' she asked.

Before the man could reply, the bandaged woman reached out a hand and placed it on his wife's arm.

He felt cool fingers grasp his own arm, and looked down; there was nothing but his own bare flesh and memories of a dream. As he stared back at his wife, he wondered how he had grown so far apart from the only woman he had ever loved.

'I think we should stay a while.'

Peter Hankins - Glimpsing Her

I got that feeling of being watched, but I couldn't look round. I was playing *Columns*, the ancient video game, a bit like *Tetris* only not. When the trominoes start falling faster, you cannot afford to take your eyes off them. But I am good with peripheral vision and I noticed a smallish woman standing just where I couldn't quite see her, looking sort of sideways at me.

Your eyes don't work the way you think. People assume their visual system is giving them a broad, detailed, *CinemaScope* kind of image, but actually the only thing we see really clearly is a tiny patch right in the middle. It's the bit that uses the *fovea*, the only decent bit of our retinas. The rest is hopelessly vague and out of focus but you don't notice because you always point your eyes right at the thing you're interested in. Our brain maintains the illusion of a fully-detailed picture by flicking our eyes around quickly without us even noticing, using the fovea to check a few things and guessing the rest.

With a bit of concentration, though, you *can* switch your attention to your peripheral vision, the blurry bit round the edges. By doing that I could look at this woman without moving my eyes off the falling trominoes; unfortunately, that only gave me a weirdly blurry impression of her. She looked smallish, young, and dark-skinned, but that was just my brain's guesses; when I moved my eyes and foveated her properly she would most likely look a bit different as well as a lot clearer.

But she didn't. Having crashed out of the game with a mediocre score I swung my eyes towards her. She disappeared completely at once. All I could see was the white, neon-lit wall of the library. Nothing. Nobody there after all. A little spooky; but we all get these wrong impressions of what's around us sometimes; like I say, it's ninety per cent the brain guessing and sometimes it makes big mistakes. Here's the thing, though; when I looked back at the PC screen, she was back again in my peripheral vision. *And she was trying to get my attention.*

Normally you'd dismiss something like that as a little mental quirk; maybe you were just a bit tired or spent too long staring at a screen? Time to pack up and call it a day. But I decided to go with it a bit, partly, I admit, because I was proud of having trained myself to use peripheral vision. I always thought it would come in handy one day, though I thought it was going to be in games or something. Anyway, I made an effort to pick up what she was doing, and all at once – I was sure – she started using sign language.

Now I couldn't see her clearly even with my best efforts, and every time I thoughtlessly turned my head towards her a bit she winked out of existence. She had to exaggerate her movements to a ridiculous degree before I could recognise them, and even then I might be imagining what she was doing. But I happen to have a deaf cousin who signs and I'd made the effort to learn it properly. I started signing back and we got a laborious conversation going.

Her name was Amalia. It turned out that she could only watch me in *her* peripheral vision too. Otherwise, as far as she could see, the library, actually full of people, was empty. She couldn't see anyone else. Something really weird had happened to her; all the people and animals had disappeared, quite suddenly. It just happened one day for no reason.

How can I explain this? I didn't get it fully clear myself for a while. Her world was now empty of people. For Amalia, it must have been a bit like those films where everyone has been killed by radiation or some disease, and you're the only survivor. You can go into shops and take what you want, help yourself, do whatever you like. Everything's great till the power and water go and the zombies or the biker gangs arrive. Or maybe it was more like those stories where you've got the magic watch, or whatever, and you can stop time and walk around in a frozen world, interfering with people – except, for Amalia, there were no people to interfere with. No people in a little area all around her, just big enough to stop her ever seeing anyone. The funny thing was that the effect of this person-free zone was temporary. Ordinary life was actually going on just outside that bubble of hers, and when she moved far enough away from any point, normality was restored there and resumed its course. Nothing she did in her bubble was permanent. So, for example, she could go into a shop - no-one there, obviously - take a chocolate bar and smash the window. Then if she went a good way up the road and came back, the glass would now be intact, the same chocolate bar would be available to be taken a second time, and there might be small signs that the shopkeeper had actually made a couple of sales since her last visit. But the shopkeeper would be gone again.

It was the cars that bothered her most. As the bubble moved around, cars came into it and as soon as they did, the drivers temporarily disappeared. If she walked down a street, it would be full of empty, freshly-crashed cars, and she would hear distant bangs and smashes as the drivers blinked out of cars somewhere ahead, at the edge of her bubble. Gentle crashes, mostly – this was city centre traffic that was hardly moving anyway most of the time – and everything was restored once she moved far enough away. Obviously no-one was ever hurt; but it was disconcerting, and she was afraid that some vehicle would somehow end up hitting her or exploding beside her, though in fact the crashes were always far away from her.

She'd been living like this for six months. She said the loneliness was the worst. She especially missed Basil. Her dog.

I tried to come up with a better way of communicating, but it was no good. The only thing she could see in my version of the world was me, and the only thing I could see in her world was her. And we could only get that far by squinting at each other. I couldn't read anything she wrote down, for example, even if the letters were huge. We couldn't hear each other.

That first time signing with her, I got exhausted quickly, and said I had to go home. I was beginning to worry a bit about what the library staff might think, too – though it probably wouldn't have been the first time they'd had some bloke sitting on his own in a corner making weird gestures. Amalia didn't want me to go; after six months alone, she was desperate not to lose contact, but when I promised to return next day at the same time, she reluctantly agreed to break off the stilted conversation for the time being.

I got a burger on the way back to my room and ate it in front of *Starship Troopers,* but my mind was on Amalia and her peculiar predicament the whole time. I already thought the phenomenon must have something to do with quantum physics, but it didn't really make any sense. I spent a couple of hours on the PlayStation before bed, but that didn't really distract me either.

Then just as I was about to get into the grubby duvet nest that served me as a bed, I caught a flicker of something out of the corner of my eye and my heart leapt. I scanned around with peripheral vision, but it's not much good if someone is trying to hide. I signed into empty space with more certainty than I felt, telling her I knew she was there – and she stood still so I could get a fix on her.

'You followed me home?' I protested. She told me it had been incredibly difficult, just using peripheral vision. She lost me twice but finally picked me up coming out of McDonald's. She hadn't been able to sneak inside the house with me but had – I couldn't believe it - taken a selection of big power tools from a local store and demolished my door. She said it didn't matter, and I suppose she was right; in my world the door was still intact, and once she moved far enough away, it would be restored in hers, too.

But hell, creeping around spying on me? I objected. I told her I didn't like having people in my chaotic little studio flat anyway, unless I'd had chance to clean. Did I have friends round often? No, I said; look, I'm an online kind of person. I have friends all round the world, but we don't meet up in meatspace. I had trouble signing 'meatspace' and she didn't understand 'irl' (in real life) either, so I ended up saying 'face to face'. I think it came over as 'I never meet anyone'. She said it was a pity. Aren't you a student, she asked, like an undergraduate? Don't you have lots of parties and things?

I really didn't want to go into that. I'd been ill the first week of University and sort of missed everything. After that, I didn't really know how to make friends. You can't just turn to someone in a lecture and start talking to them. Can you? I hate all that small social stuff, anyway – at parties I was always the bloke standing next to a group of people and pretending he was part of the conversation, or eating crisps very slowly in the kitchen as if that was really all he wanted to do. I mean, don't get me wrong, I'm not some sad git who can't deal with humans. I know all the people on my course and we have normal conversations and friendly interactions all the time, in seminars and what not; I just never made particular friends at Uni. In meatspace, I say again; I've got loads of friends online, I mean real ones, not like Facebook friends. And look, I'm perfectly happy, not crippled with anxiety or loneliness. The truth is, the extroverts have taken over our society and imposed their shouty, let's-all-hug values on us. It's not acceptable to be someone who's comfortable with solitude and silence. But the truth is, there's nothing wrong with being that way.

Actually, my real problem with her invading my privacy was that five minutes more and she would have been watching me have, like, private pleasure time; but obviously I couldn't tell her that. She said she was sorry, but I couldn't possibly understand what it was like to be completely alone for six months and then have just a slender contact with one person. If she lost touch, she might never see anyone again. She promised to go and break into the empty flat downstairs with her power tools and sleep there so long as I swore to be up and ready to talk to her at 8.30

We developed a routine over the next few weeks. We spent at least an hour talking every day, usually more. She told me all about her family (two brothers, three sisters) and how much she missed her Mum. I told her that last time I went home my mother spent half an hour shouting about what a useless wanker I was and why couldn't I bring some money in like my pond-life nob-head brother instead of wasting my time doing stupid exams that I thought made me so bloody clever.

One day we decided to try contact, I mean to see whether we could touch. We edged into position in my room a bit awkwardly, standing up to keep it formal (because I called it a micro studio flat, but honestly we were basically in a bedroom and if we could touch each other, I mean…). Amalia reached out towards my shoulder and… nothing. Her hand passed through me. We could see, but we couldn't touch, hear or smell. I felt pretty sad about that, actually.

I thought we should bring in other people – this was potentially important science, after all - but for some reason she wouldn't allow me to tell anyone. She said if I did, she would disappear forever, and though I didn't really believe that I did as I was told. I had to admit there was a good chance I would just make myself look like a nutter if I told anyone about it all, anyway. Perhaps I *was* a nutter? I had no objective evidence that any of this was anything more than my imagination.

I had a sort of a theory now, though, which I attempted to explain to her. Quantum mechanics says particles exist in indeterminate states which get resolved one way or the other when they're observed by a conscious mind. The 'many worlds' interpretation says that the particles go *both* ways, splitting the future path of the universe into two. So we thinking beings are constantly taking the universe down more and more branching paths. Somehow Amalia had done a branch that didn't carry the rest of us with it. She was sitting on a little spur off the main pattern. She should be isolated forever, but I hypothesised that tiny numbers of photons could leak across the infinitesimal distance between her world and mine. In the fully-lit glare of our world, you couldn't normally detect them, but in the thin coverage of peripheral vision they had a chance to register. Like, if you're looking for a very faint light, it helps to turn the others right down.

By a fantastic stroke of luck, she and I had happened to see each other out of the corner of our eyes. Maybe people actually get stuck in little spurs off the main world quite a lot, but most people who get into a branch like that never see anyone and just live out their lives in their bubbles. That was sort of depressing, though I admit I thought I could have coped with it a lot easier than someone like Amalia. Being able to take whatever you want from any shop is pretty good compensation for never seeing anyone, from a certain point of view. People like me might as well be invisible half the time anyway, for all the impact they have,

Amalia asked if I thought the theory was really true, and I told her I wasn't even sure it made sense. A tighter, more rigorous hypothesis might be that it was all down to fairy magic. Or the nutter idea, probably the most parsimonious explanation of all.

But she wasn't imaginary. We got proof in the end. She showed me a picture of herself. She led me to a hospital where on one ward they had labelled pictures of all the staff, and there she was. A nurse. Amalia Macall. Till then I'd never had a straight look at her; she was younger than I thought and had a sharp-witted look I'd missed altogether. Her hair was shorter, but she was taller, and she had amazing brown eyes. And a broad, friendly smile.

The funny thing about that is, if my theory was true, there would be another, normal Amalia still working on the ward, the one my Amalia split off from in that unfortunate quantum event. I wasn't brave enough to ask if she was there.

Ultimately, we decided we had to get her out of her solitary timeline, somehow. I thought we just needed to shut down her consciousness completely for a while and she would reboot into the main world. One of the main worlds, I suppose. *A* main world. Sleep clearly wasn't enough to do it – there were residual shreds of awareness while you were asleep, I guessed - but between us we identified a drug that would safely put her out completely for half an hour, and of course she had no problems accessing it.

We arranged a final dinner. I went ahead and ordered while she was far enough away, so that when she came in she could actually get her pizza. Then we ate together for the first time. I must have looked like the saddest git ever, talking to his imaginary girlfriend. But I didn't care any more.

At the end of the meal, we went to the park. She lay down on a bench, smiled, and took the pills. They worked. I'd meant to sit by her the whole time, but after a while I sort of lost her. No matter how I swivelled my head and scanned my peripheral vision, I couldn't pick her up. I wasn't sure what that meant, if anything. We'd arranged that if the pills didn't do the job, she'd come to my place as usual.

Long story short, she never showed up. It was only then I sort of realised what we'd probably actually done. I'd never see her again. I went to the hospital and this time I asked to see her; she was there, she was fine, she was normal. It was weird to be able to look straight at her. But as far as she knew now, she'd never met me. To her now, I was a disturbing weirdo, faintly threatening and probably mental. There was no way I could start talking about glimpsing her in the library. She looked me right in the eye and there was nothing.

Philip Charter - Ludgate Circus Crossing

You watch the tiny people on the street below scurry across the road. It's good looking down from twelve storeys up. The only person you know on a higher floor is a management consultant — a career so feckless that you considered becoming a one just so you could advise your colleagues to get a more useful job. Perhaps that's why there aren't many skyscrapers in The City of London. They'd just fill them with more management consultants.

The people on the crossing fizz across the street like electrons bonded to their phones. Two of them bump into each other but there's no reaction. You're fed up with *your* phone. Most of the notifications display your boss's inane questions or pictures of your friends' ugly babies. Was there ever a moment when we had the perfect balance between life and gadgets? Maybe sometime in the nineties, you think. Beepers, that was it. Useful, but not too intrusive. You make a vague plan to start a Mennonite-like sect which caps technology at a 1994 level.

The intersection is a four-way crossing like they have in Japan. Frowning lawyers and investment bankers juggle coffees and copies of City AM, all seemingly one ball short of a full set. A young upstart crosses on an electric unicycle. The Council can't decide if they should go on the pavement, the cycle lane or straight to the bottom of the bloody Thames. In spite of the chaos, you love the crossing. In fact, you spend a good portion of your day watching the action.

After this morning's rubbernecking, you'll be late with the financial projections you're preparing for Scotch-Bright Sponges. Your boss doesn't really give you a fair crack of the whip. He'll roll his eyes and use this as another excuse to keep you on the accounts nobody else wants. He didn't even acknowledge your joke about doing a 'clean job'. Get back to your desk now.

Without a decent bonus this year, your life plan will come tumbling down. You've got five years tops before your Tinder account stops getting any right swipes and your bosoms are lost under curtain folds of flab. By that time, even Pervy Pete in the local off-licence will have stopped asking you out.

Outside you see a painted face among the crowd. The Clown. You hate that guy. Why can't he get a real job like the rest of the country? He might be French. They have whole colleges devoted to clowning over there. You wonder if he lives in a squat in New Cross and cooks dinners for a rag-tag bunch of activists and penniless photographers. Look at him, prancing around with his lame routine. And the costume! Curly hair bulging out of the swimming cap, white gloves and a stripy t-shirt. What a joke.

You've had coulrophobia (the fear of clowns) ever since one threw a bucket of glitter over you at Jenny Bartlett's seventh birthday party. You had an asthma attack, then you had a panic attack. It was so upsetting that you forgot to take home your party bag and missed out on a miniature My Little Pony and some top-notch cake. You were coughing up sparkles for days. How can anyone like clowns? They're devious. At least the ones at the rodeo get a few wallops from the bulls.

An alert pops up on screen. Barnaby is probably on the move. The cat-cam seemed like a fantastic idea at the time, but it's become a time-stealing bandit. It did help you discover why the spider plant in the lounge is dying a slow death. Barnaby pisses on it. You watch him stretch his furry legs, march around in a circle, spray the poor plant, and flop onto the rug as if he's been shot with a tranquiliser dart. A job well-done. You make a note in your online calendar to move the plant to the balcony. Another entry informs you that there is a Dawson's Creek marathon on E4 tonight and that the jam roly-poly in the fridge will be out of date soon. What a Friday night.

Down below, Antoine (you've given him that name even though you've never met him) is pissing people off as usual. Last week you saw a woman smack him with her handbag. It made your day. His act consists of jumping in front of people, pretending there's an invisible wall between them, then thrusting his hand out for spare change. He only gets a few seconds before the lights change and the stampede begins.

You sometimes think about keeping statistics on the crossing. For example, the number of times people fall over (none so far today), the percentage of men wearing pink shirts, or the estimated hourly income of Antoine. He probably earns more than you, the bastard. It's already 11:25 and the report document is still sitting open on your screen, waiting for the show to start. Maybe you could write a light-hearted article about life in The City of London accompanied by the crossing stats. One of the free papers might publish it. You might even get a date out of it.

It clouds over and you sense a shitstorm coming. There won't be any play in the test match, and without cricket, the partners will have nothing to talk about. They'll come round the office and flirt with all the women under thirty, which of course excludes you. You may as well be fifty in their eyes.

Coldplay groans out over the radio in their depressingly successful way, and the wall of windows separating the office tower from the street turns grey. Workers around you pull on cardigans and suit jackets, even though the dry office air remains at a strict constant of nineteen degrees. You find yourself looking out the window again.

The rain performs a drum roll on the roof and lightning flickers in the distance behind St Paul's Cathedral. At the crossing, Antoine sits in the middle of the road. What's that silly French bugger doing now? You press your face to the cold glass window to get a better look. There's no traffic and all of the pedestrians have scarpered. He's sitting on the ground, his white makeup running down his face, and his bushy hair slicked down by the rain. He must be freezing.

Can Antoine see you staring from all the way down there? Yes, he's definitely looking. Then he points! He mouths your name, then, lifting his hands in front of him, he does his little glass wall routine, miming the invisible barrier.

You reach out and touch the window in front of you. "Me?"

Still sitting cross-legged, Antoine rises up and hovers above the ground like a levitating Buddhist monk. This is too much. Why doesn't he do *this* trick for the punters? It looks so real and not a single person is there to see it. You fumble for your phone to record him, but you drop it in the kerfuffle. You've cracked the screen. Bugger!

"Quick. Come and look," you say to the three stooges nearby.

Bald Barry glares at you as though you're a cockroach in his sandwich. "Shhhhh."

When you look out the window again, Antoine has floated higher. He must be two meters above the ground. How is he pulling this one off? It's better than his mime routine, that's for sure. The tapping of computer keys and the drone of Chris Martin continue in the background and you begin to accept that it would take more than a rocket-powered clown for anyone to tear their gaze from ever-changing algorithms on their computer screens. No one will believe you without your phone, which is now leaking inky fluid across its screen.

After a few seconds, he raises his arms and blasts up into the air as if he's a pressure cooker that's had its valve purged. Wet through and with white gloves pointed to the heavens, the clown shoots skyward, increasing in speed. Your mouth hangs agape. Antoine flies up, getting ever smaller. You can just make out his stripy shirt and red boots. This is not going to do your coulrophobia any good. You strain your eyes to see, but Antoine has disappeared into the clouds.

A lightning strike pierces the sky in front of the office. The sound is thunderous and your heart jumps up and down like it's on a trampoline. People finally look up, grumbling in mild surprise, then go back to their typing. You're speechless. You couldn't say anything anyway. They'd think you are mad.

After what happened, there is no chance of you getting any work done. That report will get written when pigs— when *clowns* fly. You slump into your ergonomic computer chair and drink a whole bottle of peach flavoured fizzy water in one. *Christ on a bike.*

You go to the toilets to assess your sanity. The broken strip light above the mirror buzzes and flickers on and off. Your mind wavers between putting the whole incident down to the fact you skipped breakfast, and requesting the number of the nearest psychiatrist with an available appointment. There's no way you can casually drop a gravity-defying circus performer into a conversation. "Did anyone watch Eastenders last night? No? Well, did anyone see Chuckles the Clown turn himself into Apollo XV on the crossing?" Even eating the double-chocolate cake bar in your handbag doesn't bring you back to the real world. When you look in the mirror, a palid woman with flat hair and hollow eyes looks back. You splash water on your face, but it makes your foundation run like Antoine's makeup. The wicked witches in accounts give each other a look when you emerge from the bathroom. *Someone's been crying again.*

Your expensive pedometer watch beeps at 1 pm: only two-thousand steps so far. In the last hour, all you've done is work on your crossing statistics spreadsheet and buy another Halloween costume for Barnaby online. You've scoured the street for signs of Antoine without success. He's probably rocketing over the English Channel by now, squirting water onto passing seagulls with his trick flower.

At lunch, you discover that you can access the Tinder App through your computer. No matches. The chicken in your Caesar salad tastes of cardboard; the lettuce is soggy and tastes the same. The croutons might actually be made of cardboard.

Although you *have* to get that report done before lunch is over, you can't resist going down to the crossing to do some detective work. It's still overcast but the rain has stopped. Perhaps Antoine left a scorch mark from his bum-based jet fumes you think, but there's no sign of your French friend when you get down there.

You wait at the lights then participate in the scrimmage, charging towards the opposite corner, dodging the groups of tossers with spiky hair and Bluetooth earpieces. Even though you go back and forth several times, you see no trace of clown makeup or modelling balloons. What were you expecting, his business card and a box of coloured handkerchiefs? Then you remember that you're wearing a pink shirt and that by crossing so many times you have compromised the statistics for today.

"Excuse me," you say to the kiosk vendor a few meters from the crossing, "was there a clown here earlier?"

"I see a lot of clowns around these parts, darlin'." He laughs a toothless cockney laugh.

Everyone's a comedian today. "No, an *actual* clown, you know, white face, swimming cap, looks terrifying."

"Like this fella?" He points to a top-shelf magazine covered with tissue paper. A man wearing a clown mask hovers menacingly behind a naked woman. The title reads *The Naughty Circus*. Brilliant, more nightmares.

Your heart's racing like the little green man on the traffic light when there's only five seconds left to cross. "Never mind," you stammer.

The old man laughs as you leave.

As you take the lift back up to the twelfth floor, you check yourself in the mirror — even worse than before. For a split second, the masked man from the porn magazine flashes up behind you with his evil grin. Your whole body tenses with the shock and your legs give out. When you can bring yourself to open your eyes, you scoot around to face him but he's not there. You ride the last five floors with your bum stuck to the carpet.

The doors spring open and the lunchtime secretary at the front desk peers into the lift, wondering why one of the firm's top financial analysts is sat on her arse, having a panic attack. You consider doing a forward roll out of the lift (and possibly finishing with jazz hands) but you doubt that you can pull it off, so you dust yourself down and mumble something about yoga stretches to the secretary on the way back to your work station.

Something is waiting for you on your desk when you get back. *Mon Dieu!* It's a full report folder with the Scotch-Bright logo on it. You check the overview on the first page. It's perfect — Helvetica New, twelve-point, cells aligned right and colour coded. As you flip through the quarterly figures, you see that everything is exactly as your boss would demand. Just as you ask yourself who could have done this, a Post-it note flutters out of the file onto the desk. It reads:

When I told my manager I wanted to quit accountancy and become a clown he said I'd have some big shoes to fill.

It *must* be him. How can it not be? As long as there is nothing funny about his calculations, you're happy to pass his work off as yours. You scurry towards your boss's office and knock on the frosted glass.

"Step right up."

What fresh hell does he have in store today? You compose yourself.

"Come on then!" he barks.

When you enter he sits behind his desk, puffing his chest and twizzling his moustache. "Ladies and Gentlemen, our brightest analyst."

"...Scotch-Bright." You hand the folder to him, praying he'll look at it later. "Sorry it's late."

"Hope you've scoured it for errors?" he says.

That was *your* joke, and he's passing it off as his own. Typical. "Err, squeaky clean, Sir."

He lets out a roaring laugh. "Excellent."

You smile and turn to leave.

"Wait a moment," he says. You stop, with your hand on the door. What's he seen?

"What do you think of this?" He reaches under his desk and pulls out a black top hat. "Taking the clients to Ascot tomorrow. Decent or what?" He nests the hat on top of his bald head and twists his moustache again. It's uncanny, he's just missing the red jacket.

"Very handsome, sir," you reply, then you run for the exit.

Now that ordeal is over, you can focus on the crossing at Ludgate Circus for the rest of the day. Your phone bleeps. The screen is still damaged, so you can't see the entire message. It's a Tinder match. You rush to log in on your computer screen.

Jacques, 38, London: *Girls say they want a guy who is funny and spontaneous, but when I tap on the window at night dressed as a clown it's all screaming.*

The picture that accompanies the message looks vaguely like Antoine without his makeup.

You decide to play along: *It'll take more than one joke for me to get over my fear of clowns.*

Jacques replies. *Did you like the report?*

So it *was* him. Today has been so confusing you feel like you've bet your sanity on a game of three-card shuffle. You sit and stare at the screen. A minute passes.

Jacques: Are you still there?

You: Is any of this real or is it a trick?

Jacques: Let's meet and I'll show you all my tricks.

Your texting wit has deserted you. Today has been exhausting. Are you going to go on a date with a street performer who has a working knowledge of financial reporting software, access to your office space and the ability to fly?

Jacques: ...6 pm at the crossing?

He might have tickets to *Cirque du Soleil* at the Royal Albert Hall, but then again he might drag you into the sewers of New Cross, murder you and serve you up to his squatmates.

Then you notice it. On closer inspection, the pink of his collar peeking into his profile photo. Be honest, you've always admired men who are in touch with their feminine side. This one wears makeup too. Your fingers start tapping.

You: I suppose you won't reveal the secret of how you pulled it off…

Jacques waits for a bit, then sends three emojis — a rocket, a crying laughing face and an aubergine followed by a question mark.

You smirk. If a guy can't impress a girl by obtaining a superpower and doing a spotless job on a complex report, then what is it going to take?

You: All systems go.

Six o'clock is only a few hours away. You'll leave the jam roly-poly and you won't watch Dawson's Creek tonight. How exciting. You bring up the crossing statistics sheet. Your finger hovers over the Recycle Bin icon. *Are you sure?* You hit delete.

Rachel New - Compliments and Appreciative Platitudes Season Two

Josie

WARNING: YOUR RELATIONSHIP WILL REACH RED ALERT STATUS WITHIN 24 HOURS IF YOU DO NOT INITIATE ONE OF THE PRESCRIBED BEHAVIOURS.

I switch my phone off and on again. Uninstall and reinstall the app.

ESTABLISH AN EMOTIONAL CONNECTION USING ONE OF THE FOLLOWING BEHAVIOURS:

SCHEDULE A DATE NIGHT AND PLAY THE RELATIONSHIP DILEMMAS GAME

RESOLVE THE DISCREPANCY BETWEEN YOUR CREDIT CARD BALANCE AND YOUR PARTNER'S PREFERRED LEVEL OF FINANCIAL SECURITY

INITIATE SEXUAL INTIMACY

I sniff loudly. Why isn't there an app to detect off-putting odours in a partner? Research has shown it to be a significant factor in frequency and quality of intimacy… hasn't it?

I check my bank account and look away quickly. Then I open the dilemmas game module to carry out a risk assessment on its potential to create novel forms of conflict.

WOULD YOU RATHER BE RICH BY UNLAWFUL MEANS OR POOR BUT HONEST?

It's going to have to be the sex.

***

Ben

CURRENT RELATIONSHIP SATISFACTION LEVELS ARE STILL BELOW AVERAGE.

GENERATE A DETAILED BREAKDOWN OF YOUR RELATIONSHIP PARAMETERS

OR

SELECT FROM A LIST OF SUGGESTED BOOSTER ACTIVITIES

The door opens abruptly. A tray of freshly-baked muffins and a pot of tea are placed on my lap. I check the app again.

BRING YOUR PARTNER BREAKFAST IN BED

JOIN YOUR PARTNER IN HER ONLINE MEDITATION CLASS AT 08:00

WRITE YOUR PARTNER A POEM OF APPRECIATION IN TODAY'S POETRY WORKSHOP AT 10:00

Can I tick off the first one if I'm the recipient? Too late – it vanishes from the screen and is replaced by

CLEAR UP THE KITCHEN THOROUGHLY WITHOUT BEING ASKED

***

Josie

In my superior bubble of serenity after meditation class, I discreetly place the standard government-issue mouthwash, floss and anti-viral shower gel on the bathroom windowsill. I know from previous feedback on the app that a more direct approach is counter-productive. Data indicated a moderate negative correlation between length of verbal hint and desired bathroom behaviour. Not to mention the mediating effect of depleted ego on bedroom behaviour. I have definitely moved beyond the illusion of control in my relationship.

WOULD YOU RATHER HAVE A RAW ONION BREATH KISS EVERY HOUR OR A TUBE DOWN YOUR THROAT FOR A MONTH?

I press a few buttons to get to the sex tips module.

WOULD YOU LIKE TO WATCH YOUR TOP TEN SEXUAL ENCOUNTERS FROM THE LAST YEAR?

Sometimes "top ten" just means "only ten".

GENERATE FIVE NOVEL WAYS TO AROUSE YOUR PARTNER, BASED ON RECENT PSYCHOMETRIC ASSESSMENT.

I decide to make a mid-morning sandwich while I listen. No onion, obviously.

***

Ben

I listen to a podcast called "Surviving the Final Lockdown: Did you move in with your lover too early?" while clearing the kitchen. I wonder how the app would react to us sleeping in separate rooms for a while and acting out the early stages of dating – the time before you've had sex, when you're on your best behaviour and actually listening. When the dilemmas game was fun and the sex tips hot.

YOUR DESIGNATED OUTDOOR EXERCISE SLOT WILL BEGIN IN FIVE MINUTES. PLEASE SELECT A ROUTE AND MODE OF TRAVEL. DELIVERY OF YOUR NEW RUNNING SHOES IS IMMINENT.

I grab the shoes from the drone whirring outside the window and walk out through the automated sun protection sprayer. I need to work on my sanity protection plans.

***

Josie

When I finish my virtual visits to my allocated vulnerable adults, I can't help noticing that the art things have been cleared away, which pleases me. Each new fad seems to bring with it a frenzy of online shopping – although that's preferable to the time he gate-crashed my new origami circle on *Whiz*. ONE shared hobby is quite enough, thank you.

WOULD YOU LIKE TO SET UP THE SHORT, MEDIUM OR LONG VERSION OF THE SEXUAL FOREPLAY PROGRAMME FOR TODAY?

I check my schedule. An audio-only meeting with my boss at 12:00; experimental philosophy seminar on Whiz at 14:00; designated exercise slot at 16:00; retreat pod with aromatherapy massage booked for 17:00. I'm not making any decisions before 18:00. And that's only if Ben is back from replacing fox-chewed electricity cables.

***

Ben

After my run, I scan the route plan for the day's jobs and pack my rucksack. It'll be much easier now my bike is fixed.

WOULD YOU LIKE TO SET UP DELIVERY OF:

RANDOMISED SEXUAL TIPS (INTERMEDIATE LEVEL)

COMPLIMENTS AND APPRECIATIVE PLATITUDES SEASON 2

A WEEKLY SHOPPING CART OF SMALL PERSONALISED GIFTS

I select them all. Way easier than the poetry workshop, anyway.

TIP #328: Try a symbolic gesture in the bedroom that recognises your partner's passions. Personalised examples for you:

Passion: Order. Gesture: Remove all items of clothing from the floor.

Passion: Philosophy. Gesture: Arrange silk underwear on the bed in the shape of a question mark.

***

Josie

After my massage I take a shower. The bottles are back in the cabinet. Does this mean they've been used or is this our new way of communicating?

YOUR PARTNER REQUESTS A MEETING WITH YOU IN THE BEDROOM AT 21:00.

I accept.

I'm not sure whether to be concerned or slightly aroused when I get a rare sighting of a neatly-folded pile of his clothes on a chair.

WOULD YOU RATHER HAVE A PARTNER WHO CORRECTS YOUR GRAMMAR OR ONE WHO NEVER CLEANS THE BATHROOM?

I don't think the dilemmas game and sex tips modules are synching today.

***

Ben

I'm halfway round my route. I check the app.

PLEASE COMPLETE RATINGS ON YOUR RELATIONSHIP PARAMETERS FOR THE DAY.

I select mostly 3s, with a couple of 2s for perceived costs and personal autonomy.

PHYSIOLOGICAL MEASURES INDICATE ABOVE AVERAGE LEVELS OF AROUSAL. IS THERE ANYTHING YOU WISH TO ADD?

I type in "anticipation of sexual intimacy".

The app calculates my overall relationship satisfaction score. The weekly times series graph shows a modest improvement.

YOUR NEXT GOAL IS TO INCREASE YOUR POSITIVE TO NEGATIVE INTERACTIONS RATIO.

I check the compliments and appreciative platitudes tips for inspiration.

***

Josie

WOULD YOU RATHER HAVE THE PERFECT RELATIONSHIP ONE DAY A FORTNIGHT, OR A MEDIOCRE ONE EVERY DAY?

The app needs updating. If only there were that luxury now.

I change the bed linen and put some wine in the fridge. I notice the coasters on the coffee table are at odd angles again. I decide to leave them. A pile of tidy clothes was enough for me. Really.

I select "medium" from the foreplay options.

***

Ben

WOULD YOU RATHER HAVE A GOOD RELATIONSHIP WITH A REPLICA OF YOUR PARTNER OR A POOR ONE WITH THE ORIGINAL?

"I thought this would be your kind of question," I smile as she enters the bedroom. "I know you like a bit of philosophy."

"Hmmm, yes, interesting – relationship quality at the expense of authenticity. What would happen to the original, though? I don't want to kill him off." She thinks for a minute, possibly contemplating methods of doing so. "Is this the app's suggestion for foreplay? Maybe the dilemmas game and the sex tips modules are synching again. I like it, though."

She's wearing the new silk chemise I'd chosen earlier today, in pale blue. She stands still, completely absorbed by the two choices.

"Umm… I'm not here. I've moved out and started my quaration. I'm sorry," I say.

Immediately, her expression changes. She focuses on me - my image on the computer screen - as if for the first time, and then looks away. "Oh. You're not actually here… I didn't notice."

***

Josie

I thought we had resolved the question of him entering a quaration. Three weeks' quarantine followed by moving in with a friend (or "friend" – I didn't like to ask) for a minimum of six months was a big step.

I type *WHAT TO DO IF YOUR PARTNER WANTS A QUARATION* into the app.

IMPLEMENT A SEPARATE BEDS STRATEGY TWO NIGHTS PER WEEK

INCREASE NUMBER OF COMPLIMENTS AND APPRECIATIVE PLATITUDES BY 20%

ATTEND A SIX WEEK COURSE ON RECOGNISING YOUR PARTNERS' GOALS AND VALUES

SCHEDULE A MINOR CONFLICT RESOLUTION SESSION WITH ONLINE SUPPORT

I look back at the screen. "Is it too late to reverse?"

"I'm afraid so. I think we both know it's too late."

"Was it the coasters?"

"Not really."

"When did you finally decide?"

"Only really when I'd finished work today. I wrote you a goodbye poem, though."

"I'll read it later."

"OK."

"I'll have lots of good memories from our time together."

"Was that from *PRODUCTIVE ENDINGS*?"

"No, *COMPLIMENTS AND APPRECIATIVE PLATITUDES SEASON 2*. I definitely recommend it."

"Well, thanks for leaving the flat tidy."

"No problem. Good luck."

I sign off and take a deep breath. Then I install the LOCKDOWN FOR SOLOS app.

Richard Hooton - The Secret of My Success

IN the beginning was the word…

…*And that word was promise,* thought John Stead as he sat at his sturdy old oak desk, holding up a little white pill that seemed to sparkle like a diamond under the strip lights. To him, and thousands of others, it was no less valuable.

'What's your secret?' he whispered to it, as an artist would to a muse.

That first meeting a year ago with the client wearing a pin-striped suit and an easy grin flashed into John's mind.

'I promise you,' the stranger had said, 'this deal will transform our lives.'

John had laughed at the cockiness, at the arrogance of youth. Until it saved his manufacturing plant. He kissed the cross held on a gold chain around his neck. *You are my help and my deliverer.* Still, something troubled him. That old enemy, doubt, gnawed away deep inside.

John's fingers drummed the desk. He glanced at the clock. Almost ten. Nearly time for the client to return and fulfil another promise.

What does the bible tell us? His mind searched for the right phrase. *But if we hope for what we do not see, we wait for it with patience.*

Breathing deeply to settle himself, John winced at the bite of a headache above his right eye and prayed it wouldn't develop into a migraine. Rummaging around a drawer, he couldn't find any paracetamols. He looked at the pill. *Not an aspirin but might help. It is called the miracle drug.* He swallowed it down without water. *Certainly won't harm. No reports of side-effects or addictions.*

His phone emitted the short buzz of an internal line. He pressed the flashing red light.

'Keeley?'

'Mr Beale's here to see you, Sir.'

John rubbed his hands together. *Bang on time.* 'Good. Send him in.'

He felt like a child on Christmas Eve. A sharp pain flared behind his brow. Another deep breath. Needed to calm himself to deaden this headache.

The door opened.

'Mr Beale for you.'

He looked just as when they first met: same sharp suit, crisp white shirt, black skinny tie. Rake-thin and that glint in his eye exuding promise. He smiled at Keeley as she closed the door.

'Please ask your staff to call me Bob.' He outstretched a hand. John rose, shaking it vigorously. 'No need for formalities now.'

'Will do, Bob, will do.' John gestured at a chair in front of his desk. 'Grab a seat.'

Bob sat, one leg casually crossing the other, his smile spreading like sunlight at dawn. 'Must say, you're looking well, John. How are things?'

'Good.' The headache felt otherwise but John didn't want to grumble. 'Extremely busy. Just taken on new staff.'

'The devil finds work for idle hands.' Bob chuckled, running a hand through his thick, glossy hair.

'It's all good,' said John. 'Helps the community. Spreads the wealth.'

Do not grow weary in doing good.

John handed over a bundle of papers. 'We're meeting all production targets.'

Bob gave them a cursory glance. 'Rapid growth, just as we promised.'

John's headache was dulling. *Really is a miracle drug.* He felt sharper. Saw the opportunity. 'And there was something else you promised.'

Bob raised an eyebrow. John took a silver blister pack from a packet on his desk, pushed a thumb nail through the stretch of silver with a satisfying pop and pulled out its hidden treasure, the fruit of their labours. He held the pill up between them.

'Which of the ingredients and their combination in this little beauty make it so life-changing?'

'That's not important.' Bob's smile was set. 'All anyone need know is that it works.'

John followed Bob's gaze to newspaper cuttings pinned to a corkboard on the wall. "Wonder drug saves lives", screamed one. "New pill increases confidence", read another. "Happy pill boosts brainpower", ran a third.

It's certainly effective. This pill, so small and fragile between his fingers, made people feel clever, confident, happy. Made them feel better. About themselves. About life. About everything. Sales struggled until the media called, then thousands began taking it and business boomed. They'd even got the backing of doctors and celebrities. It was a phenomenon.

Who, on finding one pearl of great value, went and sold all that he had and bought it.

'Priceless publicity,' said John.

'I can't be responsible for what journalists write.' The smile was a Cheshire cat grin. 'Though I can show them the results of positive trials over lunch.' A pause. 'The one's we paid for.'

John laughed. 'I'm dying to know the secret of my success.'

Bob's eyes scanned the floor. 'Think of it like the Colonel's special recipe or Coca Cola's secret formula. What's life without a little intrigue?'

John's laughter stopped. He fixed his eyes on Bob's. 'I need to know.' His voice was plaintive.

'Look around you, John.' Bob gesticulated to the office window, which overlooked the factory floor. John walked over to what was his viewing platform to the hubbub below. 'Remember how it was before I arrived.'

The night before that first meeting, John had stood in the same position and stared at a dusty factory where machines with nothing to manufacture had ground to a halt, a dwindling workforce trudging between them waiting for inevitable redundancies. The contract for the cancer drug they'd been producing had gone to another firm who'd undercut them at renewal. When he'd plunged the building into darkness with the click of a switch he'd felt he was casting out the light for the last time. Bankruptcy. Unemployment. Repossession. He'd shivered in the cold draft that blew through his office.

And they will look to the earth, but behold, distress and darkness, the gloom of anguish.

'Now look at the transformation.'

Workers in pristine white lab coats milled around machinery amid a mechanical hum. Thousands of little pills tumbled along metal chutes on their path to creation, falling into large cylindrical holders that span them at dizzying speed. Thriving. Successful. Wealthy.

And God said, 'let there be light,' and there was light.

'What more do you need to know.' The smile broadened further. 'Just keep producing as we pay you to.'

John turned. Doubt's side effect, fear, was now eating away at him too. The same as during those sleepless nights when the pill wasn't selling and he thought he'd made a terrible mistake, only his lifelong religion keeping him anchored. A phone call hung heavy in his mind.

'Speaking of journalists,' he said, 'one contacted me yesterday. Claimed he was working on a story about a woman with cancer who'd declined chemotherapy. She'd placed her trust in our pill instead.' He noticed Bob's lips twitch in the corners, a tiny wavering in the strength of his smile. 'But it wasn't working.'

Bob shrugged. 'We don't claim to cure or prevent disease.' He brushed a speck of dirt from his sleeve.

'But people are taking this to combat health problems.' John rolled the pill between thumb and forefinger. The headache had not only returned but was now behind both eyes.

'It's not medication.' Calm but firm.

'Those headlines. We're marketing this as a miracle drug…'

'We didn't write those or claim that.' Bob wagged a finger like a teacher to an unruly pupil.

'…that's helped thousands.'

'It won't help everyone.'

'He said she was dying.'

That phone call now filled John's mind. A chill had crept up his spine at the journalist's words. "She'd thought she was doing the right thing." He'd detailed the disease's effects, making John feel sick. "There's no hope for her now." John had searched for the right response but shock had muted him. "And there are others. I'm compiling a dossier." *How was this happening?* "What will *your* firm do about it?" The journalist had demanded answers. "I'll get back to you," was John's weak reply before shakily hanging up.

Bob exhaled so loudly, as if the pupil was too slow to grasp the lesson, that it jolted John back into the room.

'We're not pharmaceutical, John. What did you think they were?'

'We just manufacture your pills. We don't formulate them. You said they were scientifically proven.'

'They are.' Bob's expression veered between bemusement and amusement. 'In a way.'

John's widening eyes locked onto Bob's. 'What the hell does that mean?' The doubt and fear lurched inside him. 'Is this harming people?' Guilt joined the swirl of emotions.

The one who doubts is like a wave of the sea that is driven and tossed by the wind.

'It's safe for consumption.'

'That journalist said there were others. People taking it to relieve depression who've…'

'It's not an anti-depressant either.' Bob casually pulled out his wallet. 'Look, any reporters call just put them through to me. They should bother the proprietor, not the manufacturer. I'll deal with them.' He took out a gold-embossed business card and placed it on the desk. 'New card. I've changed my number.'

John peered at it with disdain. **Robert Z Beale, sales director**. 'What on earth does the Z stand for?'

'Oh, it doesn't. I put it in for effect. Adds an air of… mystery.'

John had been expecting reassurance that would relieve the journalist's words. Instead, he felt more disconcerted than ever.

John glared at Bob, then the pill. 'So what is this?'

Bob stared back. 'We're categorised as a dietary supplement.'

'Who's approved it?'

'It doesn't need approval. It's not prescribed. Read the small print. It's *not* medication.'

John grabbed the packet, clutching it as if a prosecutor holding up vital evidence. The print blurred in his swaying eyesight. 'Damn well looks like it.'

'Admittedly, we make it look like medication: the packaging, the style, the wording.' Bob leant back in his chair. 'It's just presentation.'

'Someone must regulate it.'

'The product's a food supplement. The Food Safety Act and Food Supplement Regulations apply. Basically as long as it's safe to eat we're fine.'

John's eye caught an advertising poster, mounted on the wall, its glossy white paper yellowed and fraying around the edges. 'You've made claims.' He pointed to it.

'What? "Boost the immune system" or "keep the mind healthy" or "maintain a healthy body". So vague, John. There's nothing on there to worry the Advertising Standards Authority. How would you prove or disprove them?'

'Somebody must.'

'The European Food Safety Authority looked at the claims of thousands of different supplements and 80 per cent didn't stand up to scrutiny. They're still sold.'

'So what *is* in this?' John threw the packet. It struck Bob's chest then dropped into his lap. He didn't flinch.

A knock on the door made John jump.

'Come in,' he barked.

Keeley entered. Hesitated. 'Coffee, gentlemen.' She placed two steaming mugs on the desk.

'Why, thank you, Keeley', breathed Bob, his eyes on hers. White teeth gleamed. She blushed.

'Just leave us be,' snapped John. 'No interruptions.' Concern shadowed Keeley's face. John tried a reassuring smile. *Mustn't show anything's wrong. Don't want to alarm the staff.* It faltered in the corners.

Bob tossed the packet of pills onto the desk and stood up as Keeley turned for the door. 'Let me get that for you.' He winked. His eyes lingered on Keeley's figure as she left. John frowned. His headache pounded.

Be sober-minded; be watchful. Your adversary the devil prowls around like a roaring lion, seeking someone to devour.

Bob returned to his seat and took a sip of his drink. 'You know, I read about the health benefits of coffee only this morning.' He held the hot mug carefully. 'Provides a mental boost, speeds up reactions, lowers the risk of cancer and diabetes.' That smile was back. 'Try some, John. Even combats baldness.' John touched his bare scalp. 'Though I guess it's too late for that.'

Do not resist the one who is evil. But if anyone slaps you on the right cheek, turn to him the other also.

They sat in cold silence. 'I won't be part of anything untoward,' said John, finally breaking it.

'You're an integral part of the process.'

John sank in his seat. *Too hot. And this damn headache.* He undid his shirt's top button. 'I'm not comfortable with any of this.'

'Look, John, I'm sorry.' Bob held up his hands. 'I should have been more open with you.' He cocked his head as he tried to meet John's downcast gaze. 'We really need and value you.'

John toyed with his cross, dangling on its chain. 'I thought we were making something worthwhile. Doing good.'

For we walk by faith, not by sight.

'Come on, John.' Bob's voice cajoled. 'The beauty industry has been charging a fortune for products for years with no proof they work. Do you think they really reverse ageing or make your wife more beautiful? There is no excelsior. It's just clever marketing. Tapping into a need.' Bob nodded his head. 'Trust me.'

'Trust you?' John waved the pill. 'You need to tell me exactly what's in this.'

Bob stayed motionless. 'A little Vitamin C.'

'Anything else beneficial?' Sarcasm flooded John's voice.

'We recommend fresh air and exercise after taking the pill to speed up the metabolic process. They always make people feel better.'

'The ingredients?'

'They're all as cheap as possible.'

John looked aghast. 'So what the hell is the magic ingredient?'

'A magician never reveals his secrets.'

'Tell me now.'

'Very well.' Bob looked him in the eye. 'You see…'

John edged forward.

'… A magician never tells because it's all an illusion.'

John stiffened. 'Come again?'

Mischief glinted in Bob's eyes. 'Come on, John. Magic doesn't exist.' John stared at him. That horrible chill was back, now prickling his neck. 'There is no secret ingredient. It's a placebo.'

John thumped a fist onto his desk. 'You said it was scientifically proven!'

Is that a smirk, hidden in the smile? 'Every researcher knows a placebo works.'

'It's a con.'

Bob placed his hands behind his head. 'The power of suggestion. Tell someone something works, they'll believe it and hey presto, it comes true.'

A slither of disgust wriggled in John's stomach. 'It's outrageous.'

Bob laughed scornfully. 'It's business. The art of selling.'

'People take it instead of medicine.' John clutched his skull and stared at the ceiling. That journalist's words were ringing in his head. 'It's putting lives at risk.'

'It's just making people feel better about themselves. All in the mind. Water into wine. Mind over matter.'

'You're tricking people into false beliefs.'

Bob ran his teeth over his lips as he raked long fingernails down his designer stubble. 'Look at your religion. Have faith, John.'

John leapt to his feet. 'You're nothing but a worthless snake oil salesman.' His chair fell against the floor with a sharp crack. 'All you're missing is the Stetson.'

Bob's face darkened. His smile twisted into a snarl, a flash of anger in his eyes. 'You wanted to know,' he hissed.

John raised his fist.

The anger of man does not produce the righteousness of God.

John's fist dropped and unfurled. He picked up his chair and sat back down, trembling, those words haunting him: *"I'll ask you again, what will your firm do about it?"*

'It's wrong. I'll go to the authorities.'

Bob shrugged. 'I've told you. We're doing nothing wrong.'

'Then I'll call that journalist back. Expose this sham.'

Bob snatched the pill from him. 'Then everything you have will be ruined.' He crushed the tablet between smooth fingers. 'It'll all disappear.' It crumbled into dust on the desk.

'Are you threatening me?'

'There's no need to threaten people, John. Just give them a vested interest. Again, look around.'

John sprung from his chair and paced to the window. At the far side of the factory stacks of large cardboard boxes packed with thousands of pills awaited delivery. *Thousands of useless, fraudulent pills.*

He shook his head. 'Why me?'

'I knew you'd believe in it. No questions asked.'

'You knew I was desperate.'

John looked down on his workforce, busying like ants. White face masks, hair nets and latex gloves covered their appearance. He imagined their faces when handed P45s. He'd been their saviour when securing this contract. The giver of employment, security, fulfilment. *How will they react?*

John returned to his seat, stared at the little heap of fine powder on his desk and felt as if it were his bones crumbled into ash. 'So the secret of my success… is a lie.'

Bob rose. 'Just enjoy the good times.' He pushed his chair under the desk. 'No-one else need know.' He waved a hand as if swatting a fly. 'Anyway, these decisions are above you.'

People's lives damaged, devastated, destroyed. 'Could I live with myself?'

'Whatever. I'm done here.' Bob opened the door. 'I'll leave you to dwell on things.' He flashed that grin. 'I'll see myself out.' And he was gone.

John sat alone in his office, accompanied by just the background drone of machinery. He thought of how many times people had asked him the secret. He'd just smiled. *Dumbly, it turns out.*

He picked up the telephone receiver. Looked again through the window, where the wide expanse of white walls and shimmering chrome stung his eyes. There were no belongings or human touches. Just cold, clinical, perfunctory.

The dial tone beeped urgently.

He saw the workers. And pills churning through prosperous machines rumbling with life.

John put the receiver down.

He took another pill from the packet. Stared at its blank dullness. The cold metal of his crucifix twisted between frantic fingers.

A deluded heart has led him astray, and he cannot deliver himself or say, "is there not a lie in my right hand?"

The headache wasn't going. John's hand hovered over the phone, tears welling.

Rob Dorey - Past Imperfect

1

"I think you'd better leave," muttered the old woman, recoiling from the table, the colour draining from her face. Her abrupt movement shattered the silence in the room and caused the table to rock slightly, sending the pack of tarot cards scattering onto the floor. Nearby candles flickered, sending demented shadows dancing around the room. The cards had not startled her, however. It was the large crystal ball into which she had been staring intently just moments before.

"Please, leave now," she repeated, her tone now distinctly unfriendly. "I can't tell you any more, the reading is over. Now, please GO!"

The old woman appeared to be struggling to avert her eyes from whatever she was seeing in the crystal ball. Leaving the cards where they had fallen, she crossed the room and turned on the light, breaking the atmosphere, illuminating the sparse, old-fashioned furniture. Then she blew out the candles one by one.

Susan Turner stared at her, shocked at the sudden curtailment of what she expected to be a forty-five minute reading. She glanced at her watch. Barely twenty minutes had passed. Susan had been sceptical of visiting the woman at first, having been determined to search for a scientific, medical explanation, but she could not deny that certain things that had been said no-one else could have known about, and she had just begun to feel as if after so long, she was getting close to some kind of answer.

"You *can't* stop now!" she blurted out, tears welling in her eyes. "What did you see? I've got to know what's happening to me. Tell me!" She left her chair and caught the woman's arm, looking pleadingly into her eyes.

But the old woman shook herself free with a sudden strength that Susan hadn't expected from someone so frail.

"I can't help you," she repeated, motioning Susan towards the door. A black cat appeared from somewhere and brushed against the woman's legs. She fumbled with a small purse and brought out coins, pressing them into Susan's hand. Her wrinkled hands were shaking.

"There," said the woman, opening the door. "A full refund. Don't come back here, do you understand? I've got no more to tell you."

"But I have to know what you *saw*!" persisted Susan, through her tears.

"Keep your voice down," hissed the woman, almost forcing Susan out into the corridor. "I saw nothing, do you hear me? *Nothing*."

With thc door safely shut, the old woman felt suddenly dizzy, her heart pounding in her chest. Breathing deeply, she sat at her dressing-table and peered at herself in the mirror, reflecting on what had happened.

A face had appeared in the crystal ball, its expression one of pure evil. She had felt its presence in the room, reaching for her mind. If she hadn't ended the session, anything might have happened.

She fumbled for a packet of cigarettes and lit one, her heartbeat slowly returning to normal. Then she wrapped the crystal ball in its shroud and put it away carefully. No harm could come to her now. Nonetheless, she reached into a drawer and brought out a bottle of whisky, unceremoniously taking a long swig without bothering to get a glass.

For she knew who the face was.

Detective-Sergeant Goldsmith of the Kings Cross police department had seen enough. Yet again, he had felt that he had seen these injuries before, *somewhere*, but not on a recent case, that was for sure.

He nodded to the medical team, who moved forward to cover the body until forensics arrived. A distant siren heralded the approaching ambulance. Rain continued to fall heavily from a leaden sky.

Goldsmith took out his radio, punched buttons and waited for an answer. Three of his men were taking a statement from a tall man with gold rings on his fingers.

"Hello, Control," he said, at last. "I'm here. I'm afraid it's number three, definitely. Another girl, another prostitute. Dead for approximately five hours. No witnesses, but we're questioning the pimp." He paused while questions were asked on the other end of the line.

"Yes, sir. The same hallmarks, the same type of injuries. Looks as though we've got a serial killer on our hands."

2

"Before we go any further," said Dr Jack Gooding, hypnotherapist, "let me just make sure I've got this right. You're suffering memory lapses and you want me to take you back to a point just before one of them so that we can try to fill in the missing gaps, is that right?"

"That's it," nodded Susan Turner, eagerly. "It's getting worse. It's happening outside now. It never used to. I black out and then when I recover, I'm somewhere else and I can't remember how I got there, or what I did in between."

"And the longest black-out was, how long?"

"Almost two hours. I started to wonder if I was being abducted by aliens!" She laughed nervously, without humour.

Dr Gooding smiled. "Well, you'll certainly need a full course of treatment, but we can discuss that afterwards. For now, we'll put you under and see what we can discover. You have your notebook with the dates and approximate times of the black-outs?"

The young woman brought out a notebook from her handbag. "I can't have this happen at work," she went on, with a note of desperation in her voice. "I'm a nurse."

Wasting no time, Dr Gooding settled her on the couch and began his standard procedures. When Susan Turner was successfully in trance, he switched on his recorder and began his questioning, regressing her step by step to a point just before the latest memory lapse.

"It's ten-thirty at night, September 3rd," he said, speaking slowly and clearly. "Where are you, Susan, and what are you doing?"

"I'm going home," said the girl, drowsily. "I've just come off duty and I'm tired."

"Are you near the hospital?"

"UCH, Accident and Emergency. I'm walking to the tube with some friends. I've decided to go to Euston. They're going to Euston Square."

"Are you carrying anything?"

"Yes. A bag with a coat and one of my uniforms in it. I'm going to wash and iron the uniform at home. Also there are some reports I was going to finish."

"Okay. Now, Susan, we're going to move on. You've just said goodbye to your friends. They've gone to Euston Square. It's ten-forty. What are you doing now?"

For the first time, the girl hesitated, frowning. "I'm crossing the road, walking towards Euston Station. It's not far. I'm starting to feel dizzy. I must be really tired… I…"

"What's happening, Susan?" prompted Dr Gooding, his curiosity piqued. This had to be the beginning of the memory lapse.

"I'm standing still. People are looking at me. I feel bad…" Again, the woman hesitated, stirring slightly on the couch. He waited for her to continue but she said nothing.

"What's happening?"

"I'm walking. I'm feeling good now. I've got a job to do."

The doctor glanced at her, puzzled. Her eyes were wide open, looking straight at him from the couch, although he knew that she was still deep in trance. But he thought her voice sounded different, deeper. He noted his observations.

"I thought you were going home, Susan."

"Soon. But there's a job to do first."

"Where are you now? What is the job you have to do, Susan?"

"I'm going towards Kings Cross. I have to find someone."

This might help, thought the doctor. He might be able to use the name of this person when Nurse Turner was conscious to help trigger her memories.

"Are you meeting a friend, Susan?" he asked. But to his dismay, she laughed without humour, her mouth curled contemptuously, almost into a snarl. Something about the expression made him feel uneasy. He felt that even under hypnosis, she was changing before his eyes.

"No," she said, vehemently, "not a friend."

He took her forward slightly, to a point fifteen minutes later.

"What are you doing now, Susan?"

"I'm waiting. In a yard. I've put my coat on over my uniform." Her voice was definitely much deeper, almost guttural. Sweat had broken out on her brow. She began to stir on the couch, turning back and forth. He wondered if he would need the nurse to restrain her.

"Who are you waiting for?"

"Shh! Someone's coming. I'm following her."

The doctor began to feel alarmed. "Who is it?"

"She's very young. High heels. Short skirt. She can hear me. She's turning, saying something, smiling. She's relieved. She thought I was a man. I'm walking towards her, there's something in my hand. Now she's scared…"

"Oh no," he breathed, and pressed the buzzer on his desk. As he did so, the woman gave a piercing scream and slipped from the couch, falling heavily to the floor. But even as she did, her scream gave way to hysterical, evil laughter.

"What have you done, Susan?" he asked, quietly, knowing full well.

"I'm not Susan!" cackled the woman. "You know me as *Jack!* Jack the Ripper."

Ros Levenson - So lucky

'You're so lucky!'

That was Kwame, first to chip in as usual on the Friday night Zoom calls that the younger members of the sales team had instituted at the beginning of lockdown, when they could no longer meet for a drink to start the weekend. It had seemed like a great idea at the time, but as there was now so little to talk about, it seemed like a burden. No-one wanted to be the first to suggest abandoning the calls, and no one wanted to take a unilateral decision to be absent as that very absence would ensure that the rest of the group had an interesting topic of conversation, so the calls limped on.

Kwame's remark was aimed at Petra, who was, so far, the only other person to have joined the conversation.

'Why am I so lucky?' asked Petra.

'Well, it's been so hot and you've got a garden. I just have to work in my bedroom with the laptop balanced on the chest of drawers. I'm hot, it's stuffy, the window hardly opens and my back hurts. And my osteopath won't see me even though I've been going there every six weeks for two years.'

'Yeah, you're right, Kwame, I am lucky,' replied Petra, but when I bought this flat you said I was going into exile in Zone 3. You didn't say I was lucky then. You said - and I quote - "Haha, you are going to live in the boondocks."'

Petra's defensive waspishness was brought to an end as Annalisa joined the conversation, followed by Jake and Ben.

'Hi guys,' said Kwame. 'Petra was just giving me a hard time.'

"*Play nice, children*" – a message appeared in the chat box. It was Annalisa making her mark as usual.

'Why does she do that?' wondered Petra. She kept it to herself but thought how stupid Annalisa was. The whole point of these wretched Zoom calls was to have a conversation, and that woman spent her time tap-tapping away at the keyboard.

Another message flashed up.

"Carolina has joined the meeting"

'Hi.'

'Hiya.'

'Hi, Caro.'

There was a chorus of greetings. Carolina launched into a speech about why she was late. Even online Carolina liked to make an entrance. Even for a Zoom meeting that required zero effort to attend – zero – she was always late. And she always had a trivial reason that no one cared about. This time Carolina explained almost in real-time that her Amazon delivery had just been posted through the letter box. She had had to wipe it down and then there was the packaging to dispose of.

The group settled down for the long haul. Annalisa and Jake altered their settings so that they could not be seen. Petra assumed that they had probably gone to make a coffee or invent a cure for cancer or something. They knew that once Caro got going they had a full ten minutes before she would draw breath. Then she would fiddle about changing her background settings, as though anyone cared whether she sat in front of her Ikea Billy book cases or by the rim of the Grand Canyon.

At last, Carolina stopped and her putative audience resumed their places in the call.

'So what have we all been doing this week?' Carolina asked.

There wasn't much to report, and those who had anything momentous to talk about had very likely announced it on WhatsApp anyway. Someone's cat had fleas. Someone had watched a re-run of Sex and the City and wished they hadn't. Two or three people had made banana cake and there was an unfathomably long conversation on 'Why banana cake?' The store cupboard and fridge were loaded with rotting unused food, so why had banana cake become the universal favourite for this flurry of home baking?

Just to move the conversation away from banana cake Petra admitted that she had won the Premium Bonds twice in one day.

'It was yesterday, actually. I was going to throw the envelope away unopened, but something stopped me. Then I saw I had won twenty-five pounds, Then I looked at the bumph in the envelope and there was also a note about another winning Bond, this time for a hundred pounds.'

'You are so lucky,' chorused the members of the sales team.

'Yes, I suppose I am,' agreed Petra, while thinking to herself that they all earned about the same amount of money. If chose to she spend her money on Premium Bonds and her colleagues spent theirs on Versace T-shirts or on white powder to stick up their noses, was that luck?

Jake, who spent most of his time reading online articles from the Guardian and the New York Times on the pandemic changed the subject, as he always did, to the latest news on Covid 19.

'Do we have to talk about this again?' whined Ben.

'No,' replied Jake, offended. 'but I thought you'd be interested in this.'

'Go on, then' replied Ben. Annalisa posted a smiley face into the Chats.

'Well, since you ask,' continued Jake, 'I was going to tell you about the new Covid antibody test, You can get it at the chemist to see if you've had the virus. Loads of people have and they don't even know it.'

'I bet Petra will be one of those. She's so lucky,' said Kwame.

The conversation dwindled after that and everyone logged out. Petra decided to clear her head and post a letter. It was a birthday card that she needed to post to her friend in Leeds. As she walked to the post box, she thought to herself 'Why do they always say I'm so lucky?'

And, although the younger members of the sales team would never know this, those were the last thoughts that Petra ever had, as the young man driving his brand new Mercedes A Class took the corner at speed and knocked Petra high into the air.

Rosemary Barry - Ivy, Mary and Me

Ivy Lilian Vernon was born on 31st July 1912, in Charlton in North Kent, the younger of two children. Her father was a school master and her parents had met teaching in Sunday school at the local Wesleyan chapel in the closing years of the 19th century. It was a comfortable lower middle class home where education both at school and at chapel Sunday School was highly valued. She was a bright youngster and at the age of 10 Ivy won a scholarship to nearby Blackheath High School.

Despite the upheaval caused by the family move to Bromley and the need for her to travel further each day to school she passed 'Matric' with exemption at the young age of 15 which gave her automatic admission to University should she wish to go. There were only three respectable options for someone of her class and upbringing; teacher, nurse or secretary. She definitely didn't want to be a teacher and even less wanted to be a nurse so at just 16 she enrolled in secretarial college and at 17 began her working life in the British office of The Irish Times just off the Strand in London.

She turned 18 in 1930. Not that that was a significant milestone for her, 21 was coming of age then, but because of the significance in the national psyche of the decade that was beginning. Ivy had taken photographs since she was 15 and joined a local camera club, played tennis at an old school friend's tennis club, and enjoyed weekend house parties into the north Kent countryside. Wearing a daring just above the knee divided skirt she cycled up to 70 miles with a cycling club and rambled with a rambling club at weekends. It was the freedom of the new era which she was embracing. An outdoor era. The 'new moderns' when young men and women could indulge in healthy outdoor activities together and unchaperoned.

Her parents at the end of the summer term had taken her from the age of ten on holiday to fashionable seaside resorts including far flung Grange over Sands on the edge of the Lake District which was to kickstart her life time obsession. While her parents walked demurely along the promenade or sat fully dressed in deckchairs on the beach, Ivy and her maiden Aunt Daisy who always came along, played tennis and crazy golf. When she was older she gave this up and joined her old school friend's family plus another family each summer for two weeks somewhere at the seaside, often Devon.

In 1914 an amazing chap called TA Leonard launched an organisation he called the Holiday Fellowship. He had started out as a Congregational pastor who took his first church group on a trip to Ambleside in the Lake District in 1891. He formed the HF as he felt that the original Cooperative Holiday Fellowship was becoming too middle class and he wanted a greater sense of internationalism. His approach was to encourage working people to admire the natural world and develop themselves and was greatly influenced by Christian Socialism. The HF concentrated on renting houses and promoting the intellectual and social interests of the party who were resident at the time. There were organised walks by day and activities for the evenings. So, during the 1930s Ivy had two holidays each year. One in June with the HF and another later in the summer with her two adopted families. Fresh air and fun in abundance.

And then there was the Women's League of Health and Beauty. This was founded in 1930 by Mary (Mollie) Bagot Stack. Originating from a few private exercise classes it soon grew into a mass movement, riding the zeitgeist. It was an early example of franchising with teachers and organisers being trained by Mrs Bagot Stack who then set up their own centres. One of the first was in Bromley and the young Ivy was an ardent supporter.

It was a complex organization and very much of its time. The exercises which combined yoga-like poses with some basic keep fit were explained in detail in her 1932 book *'Building the Body Beautiful'*. What was revolutionary was the skimpiness of the identical costumes to be worn. Very, very short gym knickers and sleeveless white V necked silk blouses to allow maximum freedom of movement. There were also mass 'demonstrations' in huge public arenas like the Royal Albert Hall and Olympia of synchronised rhythmic movements to music. Ivy took part in an Indian Club routine at the Albert Hall.

This was a tricky time to be mobilising young women to demonstrate identical 'keep fit' type exercises en masse in the open air and there were unfortunate comparisons with Arianism and the Hitler Youth movements. A reading of Mrs Bagot Stack's book would have quickly dispelled this idea as despite the many serious sections with photographs of prescriptive exercises her writing style is hilarious. Among the high flown prose she is able to laugh at herself. Something that dictators and adherents to the far left and right seem to struggle to do.

It wasn't only exercise, there was a philosophy behind it, also of its time. It was designed 'for business girls and busy women to enable them to conserve and improve their physique'. It started with the firm belief that 'pride in the body is an essential foundation on which to build life and character'. To quote Bagot Stack 'Health represents peace and harmonious balance in the innermost tissues of mind and body. Beauty seems to me to represent this idea carried out by every individual, by humanity universally. The ideals of your League when shared universally must help to root out the weeds of self seeking, misunderstanding and hatred which lead to war'.

But in 1939 war did come, The Irish Times office in London closed and Ivy was relegated to a job in the typing pool at Woolwich Arsenal and further did her 'bit' with nightly fire watching back home in much bombed suburban Bromley when she wasn't cowering with her parents under the stairs whilst her older brother was doing his 'bit' as an army driver and mechanic.

Constance Mary Hutcheson (known as Mary) was born on 13th June 1910 in Nuneaton Warwickshire, the second of four children. She won a scholarship to Chester City Grammar School where she enjoyed hockey and tennis. After leaving she enrolled at the Cheshire County Teacher Training College where she studied art and specialised in the Secondary age group.

Whilst at college she became involved in the Student Christian Movement (SCM). Formed in 1889 this is the oldest Christian student organisation. Beginning as a loose network of Christian students dedicated to missionary work overseas, it later broadened its aims and membership to include values of openness, inclusiveness, radicalism and an open and challenging approach to the Christian faith. It was very effective during the early years of the 20th century influencing the growth of ecumenicalism and playing a vital role in the formation of the British and World Council of Churches and also the National Union of Students in 1922.

On qualifying she obtained a position as an art teacher in Lichfield where she stayed until 1940. In 1935 she joined the Wolverhampton branch of the Oxford Group which became in 1938 Moral Re Armament (MRA). This was an international moral and spiritual movement. Its founder the American minister Frank Buchman could see what was happening in Europe and felt that military rearmament was not the answer. At its inauguration in East Ham Town Hall in London he said "the crisis is fundamentally a moral one… the nations must rearm morally. Moral recovery is essentiality the forerunner of economic recovery." Daphne De

Maurier in her book of stories '*Come wind come weather*' wrote in the dedication to Frank Buchman what they are doing up and down the country in helping men and women solve their problems and prepare them for whatever lies ahead will prove to be of national importance in the days to come.'

During the war some HF centres were requisitioned by the government and used to accommodate troops but a few remained open and Ivy continued to take her hiking summer holidays. In 1946 she spent a week at the very basic and rationed centre at Langdale in the Lake District followed by a week in the more luxurious and recently opened Monk Coniston on the shores of the lake, leased from the National Trust. During that first week she had met Edward (Ted) Pursglove a recently demobbed and shy south Londoner who had had an HF holiday recommended to him by a work colleague. He had thought that a walking holiday in the Lake Distinct might involve walking round lakes and suffering severely from vertigo was nonplussed to discover the mountains. Trying to get nails for his city shoes in the local village led to some amusement but somehow a shared interest in photography and joining forces to play table tennis in the evenings led to a holiday romance which resulted in marriage in the autumn of 1947. Ivy was 35. She gave up her job three months later and in 1950 a son was born followed in 1952 by a daughter.

While Mary was attending her MRA meetings in Wolverhampton she met Ernest Whitehouse and they married in 1940. She was 30 years old and left teaching to bring up her three surviving sons.

In 1959 Ivy and Ted moved out to the north Sussex countryside to an old farm worker's cottage in the middle of nowhere that needed renovating plus had a large overgrown garden. Ted cycled into the nearby market town each day to catch the train to London and Ivy cycled the 7 mile return trip twice a week for shopping. She made jam and chutney and grew flowers and raspberries which she sold at the door and at the local WI market. They turned a walk-in cupboard off the kitchen into a dark room and despite money being tight had their own enlarger. She was always there when the children came home from school and at the weekend there were family rambles, blackberry gathering, wild flower identification, tennis and badminton in the garden and table tennis on the kitchen table. They were members of the Ramblers Association (one of TS Leonard's initiatives) and Ivy was a stalwart member of Friends of the Lake District (also founded by the amazing Mr Leonard).

In 1953 Mary returned to teaching. The day before the coronation of Elizabeth the Second she broadcast on Woman's Hour as a 'loyal housewife' and also wrote an article for the Sunday Times on homosexuality writing as to how that a mother might 'inadvertently' pressure her sons towards that orientation. From 1960 she taught art at Madely Modern school in Shropshire where she also took responsibility for sex education. This was incredibly enlightened for the times. Attending a girl's grammar school myself in the late '60s our sex education comprised a talk on periods in the first year, drawing diagrams of the male and female reproductive organs in 'O' level Biology and an excruciatingly embarrassing Q and A session with a blushing young Biology teacher in the fifth year plus a lot of girlie sniggering and passing round of Bond novels.

This was the swinging '60s and Mary was shocked at the moral beliefs – or lack of them – of her pupils. She saw this as linked to the declining moral standards of the British media, especially the BBC. In 1963 she wrote requesting to see Hugh Greene the network's then Director General. He was out of the country but she managed to secure a meeting with his deputy Harman Griseman, a Roman Catholic. In 1964 she launched the 'Clean up TV' campaign appealing to the women of Britain. The first meeting in Birmingham Town Hall had 2,000 attendees prompting The Times' correspondent to comment 'Perhaps never before in the history of Birmingham Town Hall has such a successful meeting been sponsored by such a flimsy organisation'.

Interviewed by the Catholic Herald for its Christmas 1965 issue Mary explained that she thought the BBC loaded its programmes in favour of the 'new morality'. Greene defended the right of the corporation to be ahead of public opinion and went on to ignore Mary blocking her from taking part in BBC broadcasts. In 1965 the CUTV campaign was relaunched as The National Viewers' and Listeners' Association as this was felt to be less negative and was supported by a variety of leading politicians. The group continued to campaign against a number of television programmes from news bulletins covering the Vietnam war and comedies to the work of Dennis Potter and even some episodes of Doctor Who.

Mary was a prime mover behind the 1971 Nationwide Festival of Light. which was a Christian initiative intending to unite young people to take a stand against the permissiveness of the day and challenging the nation to 'recover the pure idealism of Christ, the light of the world who taught that real love always wants what is best for others and defends the weak against exploitation by the corrupt'. That late September I was a few days into my time at a teacher training college on the south coast and travelled up to London to join my home church in Trafalgar Square. My Baptist church had hired a double decker bus to take its young people and others. Just days before, beacons had been lit on hilltops all round the country – the Festival of Light. It was an amazing experience to be among around 50,000 mainly youngsters like myself next to those famous lions listening to celebrity speakers like Cliff Richards. Then, we marched peacefully en masse to Hyde Park for a rally and a concert.

It's a pity that a Gay Rights group went to such lengths to disrupt the meeting in Westminster Central Hall a few days earlier and that Rolling Stone magazine was so proud of vilifying and insulting the speakers, attendees and organizers of the Saturday event. I was just 19, had a steady boyfriend and my friends and I were no prudes or naive crackpots. The excesses of the 1960s had been just that with the 'free' love and drug culture. I had enjoyed being a child of the '60s with its new freedoms especially after the bleakness of the decade before and done some crazy things and enjoyed rock music and worn garish clothing and pelmet skirts. We were normal, everyday youngsters who could appreciate and wanted to join in with the message of the Festival of Light. A dialogue would have been good rather than the provocations and childish delight in disruption that made little difference anyway, there were too many of us.

The following year I travelled up with members of the college Christian Union to a similar but smaller event. Upset at the lack of publicity I wrote an impassioned letter to a national newspaper decrying that young people causing trouble were given publicity but when they gave the word 'demonstrate' back its true meaning they were ignored. My letter wasn't published. In 1973 instead of rallies a flotilla of small boats was assembled to sail down the Thames with banners. In Hastings near where I was now living I took part in what we called the 'Hastings Festival for Jesus'. Nine churches as diverse as the Salvation Army, The Church of England, Pentecostal, Baptist and Catholics worked together over nine summer weekends with each responsible for a Friday and Saturday night coffee bar, a Sunday afternoon beach service and a Sunday evening service in their own church. I was there for all nine weekends and so was a young lad who I went on to be married to for 42 years.

There have been criticisms of the efficacy of the Nationwide Festival of Light and its lack of achievements with the 1970s carrying on as they would have anyway. But it did bring thousands of young people of different denominations together in a new way where we would find out about working in a common cause that would have been unthinkable only a few years earlier. I am sure it had a more lasting effect than those on the outside realised.

Mary went on to other causes. Among other things she complained about swear words in Brookside, accused Gay News of blasphemy and importantly set up a petition against paedophilia and child pornography signed by one and a half million people which led directly to the Protection of Children Act 1978. In 1980 she was made a CBE.

In 1986 Ivy and Ted moved from Sussex up to north Essex near Colchester. Ted died there in 1989. In 1991 at the age of 79 Ivy won the cup for best in show in the photography section at the local horticultural and craft show against strong (and much younger) competition of over 20 entries. Her winning picture? A lake in the Lake District. She celebrated her 80th birthday on a family holiday complete with rucksack and walking stick by hiking along the notorious rocky and steep waterfall walk in the Brecon Beacons. She died near Colchester in 1997.

Ernest Whitehouse died near Colchester in 2000 and Mary in a nursing home in Colchester in 2001. She was 91.

In the 1990s I saw a listing like you get in national newspapers headed 'Today's birthdays'. Among those for June 13th was Mary Whitehouse. Just that. Unlike the other celebrities she needed no description, no explanation she just was – Mary Whitehouse.

For my imaginary tea party I would invite Ivy and Mary. I would leave them with a plate of cakes and their shared love of snooker to discuss the relative merits of defensive play and who was likely to be World Champion this year and slip away to make the tea.

Sagamba Muhira and James Page - Out of Africa

Life is always a journey. I am now an Australian citizen, although I was born in the Democratic Republic of Congo, and it was there that I grew up. I am also a refugee from the Congo Wars. My home is and forever will be now in Australia, and my journey to Australia has been long and complex. Yet it is only now that I am beginning to understand this journey.

The region in which I grew up was North Kivu, a province in the eastern part of the Congo. North Kivu is highland country, with good rainfall, large inland lakes, extensive forests, rich pasturelands, and a cool climate. Almost anything will grow there, and normally people have plenty to eat. If one had to choose a part of Africa in which to live, then, at least under normal circumstances, one would logically choose North Kivu.

The small town where I lived, Sake, is on Lake Kivu, and about half an hour from the regional city of Goma. From Sake one can see a blue line of the Virunga Mountains in the distance. Our name for these was "Crooked Teeth", due to their jagged appearance. There are active volcanoes here, and sometimes at night we could see the red glow of eruptions, accompanied by a "boom, boom" of exploding lava.

My father (Papa) owned properties nearby to Sake, where he concentrated on raising cattle and growing crops. My mother (Maman) also worked on these properties. I was the eldest of the children, with two brothers and a sister. We also had many cousins in Kivu, as well as cousins and relatives over the border in nearby Rwanda. It was a good place to grow up, at least on the surface.

The underlying problem for our country was that we were ruled by an incompetent, corrupt and ruthless dictator, President Mobutu Sese Seko, backed for a long time by western powers. The country suffered from serious inflation, the breakdown of basic services and institutions and increasing ethnic tensions. My parents tried to deal with the ethnic tension through working hard to be friends with people from all the different ethnic groups. For a while, this succeeded.

What changed everything for the worse was the Rwandan Genocide in 1994, when close to a million people were massacred. My province of Kivu is next to Rwanda, and because of this it was not unexpected that millions fled over the border into my province during and after the killings. Unfortunately, those fleeing into Kivu included many of the perpetrators of the violence, as they feared retribution from a new government which had taken over in Rwanda.

This was not a war as it is normally known. It was difficult to identify a front line, as fighting forces criss-crossed vast areas of the Congo. And there were many irregular militia involved in the conflict, as well as forces from many nations. It was often difficult to understand who was fighting who. The nature of the war meant that civilians were often killed, merely because they were members of the wrong ethnic group.

What made things worse was that soldiers were often not paid. Thus, to survive they needed to extort money and food from the local population. Agriculture gradually came to a halt. Famers could not get their produce to markets, due to roadblocks. In any case, there was little point growing crops if these were only going to be stolen. People began to starve. Some took to the nearby jungle, and attempted to live from jungle fruits and jungle meats, a very uncertain prospect at the best of times.

What was this like for me personally? For us kids, war was at first exciting. There were soldiers everywhere. They would sometimes let us look at their weapons, and we were impressed. At one stage I found a live grenade, and took this home, keeping this for a time under my bed. I had no idea how dangerous this was. Needless to say, when my Papa found out, he promptly removed the item from our house.

One incident, however, changed my personal view of war quite dramatically. A group of us were returning to Sake, and we had hitched a ride on the back of a pick-up truck. Soldiers stopped the pick-up truck, and ordered three of us, all of the same ethnic group, to sit by the side of the road. One soldier recognized me, and this undoubtedly saved my life. I watched as the two other young boys of my ethnic group were taken away, and then beaten to death.

The fighting continued, and things continued to grow more and more chaotic in the Congo. For a short time, I left school and started a new life as a coltan trader. Coltan is a rare mineral mined in the Congo, which is used in mobile phones and computers. I was growing taller, and, wearing a suit, I could pass for someone much older. There was much money to be made but it was also very dangerous. Soon after my Papa found out about this venture, however, I quit and returned to school.

Thus far I had escaped injury myself, but this too was to change. In December 2004, a minibus I was travelling in was ambushed on the way back to Sake. An old man of my ethnic group was taken off the bus, and beaten to death in front of us. I almost escaped, but the soldiers caught up with me, and beat me with clubs and rifle-butts. Afterwards, I also realized that they had used either machetes or bayonets, as I still have the scars on my fingers where I tried to shield myself.

What I can remember from the beating is lots of blood and some bones sticking out of my legs. I passed out, and the soldiers left me for dead. My crime was that I was a member of the wrong ethnic group, and the soldiers saw me as an enemy to be destroyed. I was, however, fortunate in that there was an MSF (Doctors without Borders) patrol passing by later that afternoon, who picked me up, gave me emergency treatment, and took me to Goma Hospital.

In a hospital one would normally expect to be safe, but not so now. It was commonplace for patients to be put to death, because they were of an undesirable ethnic group. What saved me was that a local Catholic priest visited the hospital, and he paid money to the staff to ensure that I survived. Even then, the priest feared for my safety, and as soon as possible took me away from the hospital to a safe place in a nearby village.

One of the remarkable things about war and violence is that even when you think that things cannot be more chaotic, then they become still more chaotic. I could not go back to Sake at all, because the violence there made that out of the question. I was safe for a time at the nearby village, but eventually the priest told me that I needed to flee the Congo entirely. I agreed, and he paid for a place on a pick-up truck, which took me to the Congo-Uganda border. Fortunately, I was not stopped at the border, and I walked, on crutches, into Uganda.

The years following were a mixture of ongoing uncertainty and struggle for survival. I spent years in various refugee settlements, and a considerable amount of time as a homeless refugee. Even in these settlements, there was no real safety, as the ethnic violence so prevalent in the Congo had spread there as well. You feared for your life because others would consider you to be of the wrong ethnic group, and thus a threat to them.

One positive at that time was that, by chance, I was re-united with my younger sister, who was also in a refugee settlement in Uganda. She was the only remaining member of my family of origin – all the others were presumed dead. Western countries often like to accept family units in their refugee intake, and thus both my sister and I were offered humanitarian visas to enter Australia, and to make our new home here.

Needless to say, like most Africans, we knew very little about Australia. We knew that it was sunny and hot, and given much of Africa is also sunny and hot, this encouraged us. We knew about the strange animals here, such as kangaroos. Strangely, we were also familiar with many Australian trees. Eucalypt trees have been planted widely in Africa, although I only became fully aware of this when in Australia I saw eucalypt trees everywhere.

Flying to Australia, and landing at Brisbane Airport, was a little surreal. We had never flown before. There have been many challenges in adjusting to a new life in Australia. However we were free and safe. I am now living and working in Queensland, with a wonderful wife and two beautiful children. Australian is my new home. But I will never forget my origins, and where I've come from. Out of Africa.

Samiha Ali - Cave of Anguish

It all started with the spin of a bottle.

Robbie invited his five high school friends over to his parents' lodge for the weekend.

"You sure your parents aren't gonna be back?" Casper asked several times with persistent paranoia, wiping away his forehead sweat with his arm over the spine chilling stories they were sharing.

"I told you. They're *abroad.* Whole place is ours, pussy." Robbie bopped the back of his head.

The teenagers sat in a circle with a lamp and an empty wine bottle in the middle that Tom found while exploring the kitchen. This was their winter half-term. No parents, no nagging, no rules.

For Robbie, 'dares' were much more exhilarating than 'truths', as he wasn't sure if people even told truths anymore. The bottle spun to Tom this time, and Robbie grinned before blurting, "Dare you to kiss Jade."

Tom licked his lips, eyes shut, thinking he was about to kiss Jade but she ducked.

Hang on, this feels bristly, he thought. He opened his eyes, "Bro, what the fuck?"

His lips met Elliott's cheek instead; the teens broke into a hysterical collective cackle.

They moved on and the bottle spun to Casper.

"Oooooh, Casper ghost!" Robbie teased.

"Quit calling him that," said Maisie, Casper's crush, in defence.

"Let's spice things up. This is getting boring." Robbie continued, "So y'all heard about that cave in the woods here—"

"We're not meant to go there," Casper quivered.

"*Nobody* knows what's in there. But you're going in there, unless you're too… pussy."

"Don't force him, man." Elliott became concerned.

"Yeah, we're only here to have fun." Maisie agreed.

"What ya pussies sayin'? This *is* fun." Tom sneered.

"Even my *baby* brother wouldn't be shitting himself." Jade provoked Casper.

Everyone, except Maisie and Elliott, made chicken gestures at Casper, chanting 'Casper ghost' repetitively.

"If you do it, we won't ever call you that. Promise. Right, guys?" Robbie offered.

"Uh-huh," they all said.

"K, I'll do it." He blushed a little, wanting Maisie to perceive his bravery. "But you assholes better come with me."

"No shit, wouldn't want you to lie that you went," Robbie smugly remarked. Maisie had a queasy feeling about this. She read social media theories of some cave being off-limits to visitors, but it wasn't apparent why. Nonetheless, they grabbed their coats and scarves, marching their way through the snow, beginning a forty-minute hike. Robbie kept pushing Casper in front, warning him that if he backed out and fled, they would out-run him, tie him up and blast him on Instagram.

They made it near the cave, seven metres away, stopping on the side path to catch their breath. There, they noticed a small abandoned bike, its metal rusting, and spider webs encasing its tire, it was covered in moss – *but they didn't dwell on it…*

"Where's your phone?" Tom asked.

Casper showed him, and Robbie snatched it away, "It'll be more daring this way."

Jade high-fived Robbie, "Good idea."

He whimpered, "B-b-but… I won't be able to see."

"The sun's still out. We'll wait here. You're only going inside for five minutes. We'll keep count. Then rush back out. Easy-peasy!" Tom pressured.

"I believe in you, Casper." Maisie mumbled, thinking that the sooner Casper went into the cave and came out, they could head back to deflate the theories.

"Only for f-f-five minutes," he reluctantly agreed, separating away from the group as the blackness of the cave engulfed him. In he went, his heart pounding.

***

"Guys. It's been like twenty minutes." Maisie said, in trepidation as the sunset peaked.

"I'm calling the police." Elliott announced, whipping his iPhone out. "Shit… no network."

"No! My parents will *kill* me."

"What now, Robbie?" Tom asked.

"We'll go in. Idiot probably got lost or found gold."

Maisie deprecated, "That's suicide. I'm staying in case he comes back."

"Suit yourself, hoe." Jade giggled, tagging along with the boys, seeing the whole thing as a heroic rescue mission.

Elliott turned on his phone's torch so they could see.

"Casper?" They all yelled, while taking steps to venture their way through. The cave's walls glistened; they weren't sure if it was crystals or simply ice.

"Casper ghost, where are you?" Robbie jokingly shouted.

Elliott prodded Robbie's ribs with an elbow, "*Don't.*" This was getting serious for Elliott. He hoped Casper was okay, knowing it was a bad idea, all for a vacuous dare to "prove" something.

"Guys, there's like three entrances back here," Tom announced.

Jade crouched, putting on her own phone torchlight, "*And* there's footprints." She examined, "Casper's size. I think he went this way."

They'd seen plenty of horror movies by now to know that the idea of splitting up was ludicrous, especially now that they were on a lead.

"How big even is this cave?" Robbie wondered.

"Like any of us would know." Elliott rolled his eyes.

The teens walked for what felt like hours. They felt disorientated, as the cave sucked them further in, each secretly worrying if they'd ever make it out.

"*Ah!*" Jade yelped.

A rat scurried across to the other side.

Elliott put a hand on her back, "Relax." He looked at his battery. "I'm gonna turn mine off, I'm down to fourteen percent."

Their steps became heavier, as the steepness of the path beckoned, and the crystals on the wall lighting their way became an enchanting sight. They continued to yell for Casper.

Suddenly Robbie tripped over what he thought was a lump of log, Jade's torchlight flashed out, revealing the decomposing limbless torso of a little child.

The group froze in shock, then Jade puked, dropping her phone.

"N-n-no way, this has got to be old p-props, right?" Tom stuttered.

Maggots squirmed and penetrated through the child's stomach moulding a gaping hole in the rotting flesh, while flies swarmed the child's hollow eye sockets.

Robbie noticed a wristband on the ground and picked it up, putting it in his pocket – "Casper's. He came through this way. C'mon, we're getting closer."

Tom held Jade's hand, caressing it, as he kicked the torso insolently out their way, believing it was a prop intentionally put there to justify unconfirmed social media theories.

"Do we have to go through this way?" Jade groaned as they came through another entrance, not wanting her designer jeans to get muddy. The teenagers would have to crawl their way through the gap, heads ducked down, it was simply too murky to navigate any other entrances.

"We're getting close, come on!" Robbie rushed.

The teens helped each other get down, Jade being the last to be picked down by Tom, they continued walking deeper inside, until they came across a campfire. Here was the hairy back of a topless man, with a ladder by his side. An adult! Maybe a cave explorer who could lead them out.

"Sir?" Elliott asked. He repeated again but the man hadn't turned around, instead he continued making slobbering, salivating noises. His food perhaps?

"I got this." Robbie pushed him back and took a few steps closer. "Excuse me, sir? We're a bit lost. Have you seen our friend, he—"

The man turned around with an eldritch grin, blood smeared all over his mouth, standing up to offer them a leg to eat as a tease.

Their jaws dropped.

He was eating burnt *human* leg.

They looked up.

Casper…

His lifeless body dangled with a rope, mouth duct taped shut, eyes wide open, and his pupils dilated. The side of his head had been crushed with brute force, his left leg freshly sliced, and his other limbs still intact for now. On his far right was a cage containing a small skull, most likely from the corpse of the child they had stumbled across, kept here as a souvenir. The heinous atrocity they both had been through was too traumatising to imagine.

It was in that moment they realised a psychopathic cannibal indeed lurked these caves. How many lives had he viciously claimed?

Outside, Maisie heard the sharpest screams of her life, as the cold breeze caused a spike in her goosebumps. This was a definite call that the group were in immense danger.

She sprinted back to the lodge, every second meaning the difference between life or death, her lungs burned as she yelled for help. In that secluded area, nobody could hear her despair. Once inside, she dialled for the police.

***

Before Jade could turn back to run, the psychopath lunged at her, grasping a lock of her hair. She screamed in agony, knowing this was the final moment of her life, as his knife lodged inside her mouth, muting her scream forever.

He tossed her to the side like a rag doll to sadistically slice up for later.

Tom stood still witnessing Jade's murder. Paralysed in shock, his mouth quivered and his knees trembled hard against each other while tears dropped off his expressionless face. Elliott budged him to snap out of it, but Robbie grabbed him by the shoulder signalling there was no time to save him – they *needed* to flee before they met the same fate.

As the two boys bolted, Tom's scream in the background sent chills down their spines, his terrorising final words echoed: "Guys, w-w-why did y-you leave me? Help me, g-g-guys!"

"He got Jade and Tom!" Robbie cried, begging this to be a crazy nightmare, as they kept running. They halted to the stop of a dead-end maze of rocks obstructing their way. They had no idea which route they had taken to get back to the entrance, it was just too dark and foggy to see.

Elliott hissed. "Shut up! It's kill or be killed. I've got a plan." He saw the rocks as weapons to strike the psychopath. They needed to work together to get out.

The screaming stopped; the reason was obvious.

No mercy.

The psychopath was now coming after his next targets; the two boys with darkness and time against them.

"You can run but you can't hide, kids." His hysterical laughter echoed from metres away.

Elliott devised a plan quickly, whispering rapidly into Robbie's ear.

Lunge on him, tackle, seize the knife, head-butt him, you're the bigger guy, I'll take him from behind. He separated from Robbie, hiding behind one of the rocks in anticipation of the attack.

He couldn't do it.

He just couldn't.

Instead, Robbie urinated a pool and fainted, hitting his head on the way and slouching against the rock.

"Shit. Shit. Shit." Elliott furiously whispered, quickly turning off his phone and having to rely on the faint light emitted from the crystals.

The psychopath crab-ran, with the silhouette of his shadow getting longer as he encroached the boys' territory, "I see you, boy."

Elliott ducked from the side, hoping he'd seen Robbie instead.

"This is no fun, you're sleeping. I want to hear you scream." The psychopath shrugged. "Oh well. This'll be quick." He swung his knife from up high to stab Robbie's head precisely, but just before he had the chance, Elliott came out from hiding and leaped on his back, strangling his throat.

"Agh!" The psychopath choked.

"Fuck you!" Elliott dug his nails deeper into his throat, skin peeling, his fury boiling on the murders of his friends.

The psychopath swung around in circles, stabbing Elliott's shoulder from behind in an attempt to get him off. Elliott yelped in pain. It just wasn't enough. He sustained another deeper stab in the shoulder, this time the knife penetrated further into his ligaments until the pain became so unbearable that he had to let go. Elliott fell flat on his back and before he had the chance to roll away or get up, the psychopath flung his entire body onto him to trap him, fatally and grimly stabbing him all the way up his throat before he could push him off. The life quickly drained out of Elliott's eyes, mirroring the blood from his throat. "Hahaha!" he crackled a high-pitched demented laugh and taunted. "You tried, little kid! You tried *me*!"

He knelt beside Elliott's corpse, ferociously stabbing his stomach, the blood bouncing out like a fountain.

Robbie started to gain some conscious, opening his eyes half-way while holding the side of his head to numb the soreness. He covered his mouth, trying not to let out a scream, as he witnessed the psychopath stabbing Elliott's stomach. The sound of blood and organs squelching with each thrust of the knife was enough to make him throw up, but he couldn't. Robbie failed him, yet he was the only one alive, for now.

This shouldn't have happened, I should've been the one dead, not them, he thought to himself.

Was it too late? Should he give up? But if he surrendered into his defeat and continued to play dead, the psychopath would forever haunt these caves and claim more lives for his sadistic pleasure and repulsive lust. It was time to fight back, he had to avenge all of them. He began self-soothing, calming down because his fear was an obstruction that wouldn't help him at all. He rubbed his eyes harder, squinting for anything around he could use as a weapon. Elliott was right, it was kill or be killed – if he made a quick run for it, he would risk being caught. He had to do this quietly, hitting him with a blow he wouldn't expect. The psychopath and Elliott's corpse were three metres away from him, just a small gap in which he had one last chance. He found a medium-sized rock by his side, stared at it, then looked ahead to calculate his rate of survival. If he could just pick it up, stealthily and cautiously, then deliver the final blow on the head, he could finally get out. There was only one way to find out. He heaved himself up, taking quiet cover under the psychopath's loud laughs, gripping the rock with both hands. It was heavy but he couldn't risk dropping it. Sweat and tears rolled down his cheeks.

Don't give into fear, he kept mindfully telling himself.

Carrying the rock, he waddled quietly. Just two more steps. He was close. The psychopath continued to laugh. The psychopath felt a presence behind him, immediately turning around to see Robbie fearlessly lunging the heavy rock at his face with a hard blow.

He'd done it.

It was over. He kicked the psychopath's corpse off Elliott's body, crouching down and crying hysterically.

"I'm so sorry, I couldn't save you! You deserved better! I freaked out at the last second!" His hands shivered, stained with the blood of his best friend.

Robbie heard the faint echoes of police sirens from a direction. He didn't have his phone but recalled having Casper's phone which he confiscated earlier, if only he could take it all back and had never suggested going down here. He turned it on to navigate the area more clearly, as he scurried and tripped. Jumping and crawling back up from the entrance they all came from, he continued to follow the sound.

He was close to the entrance. Police sirens had never felt reassuring to him until now. He saw the light of many police officers' car headlights and a rescue team getting ready to head inside.

He saw Maisie, and she ran over to him.

"No, stay here!" the police officer held her back.

"Robbie, what happened? Where are they? Is that blood?" she quickly asked, her face turning purple with concern.

"Maisie…" he faintly whispered. He was exhausted and traumatised.

Five police officers surrounded him. "We came as quickly as we could. What happened down there? Are there any survivors?"

"They're all dead… he killed them all!" he choked on his tears. Maisie's chin wobbled, hoping this was another one of his sick twisted jokes. "I tried my best."

"Slow down, take a breather. We're here to help you." An officer put a blanket over him. "Who killed your friends?"

Robbie tried to ease his breathing. "This psycho. He eats people. I killed him though. He killed all my friends, they're all gone! We saw a kid too. He died a long time ago. Oh my fucking God, I can't…" His breathing increased, he hyperventilated and looked up at Maisie who looked away, she couldn't bear to look at him. He got his arms out, craving her comfort, but she screamed no and pushed him away.

"This is all *your* fault! It was his idea we come here. All for a stupid dare."

"I know, I made a mistake and I'm sorry!" Robbie wailed, not expecting Maisie to throw him under the bus like that when the night was as horrifying as it was. "But we were all trying to look for Casper, I had good intentions! None of us knew what was fucking down there, so give me a fucking break!"

"Now, now," the officer tried to calm her down, "I understand your anger, but this isn't fair on your friend, he—"

Maisie screamed louder again. "I'm *never* forgiving you! You dickhead, this is all your fault, all your damn fault!" She shrieked with the misdirected anger of somebody who didn't know what to do with themselves, it was irrational, and he knew deep down that she didn't mean it.

The officer ushered to his colleague with his eyes to take Maisie away in the car to relax, whilst he handled the distraught and broken Robbie in the other car.

"Where are your parents?" he asked him.

Robbie shivered.

What would his parents think?

Started with a bottle spin, ended with disturbing emotional laceration.

Sean Sheehan - Insects

'Do you like insects?' inquired the little girl.

Darting eyes in an angelic face dominated by a sweeping smile the little girl had stopped Mary, a plump twenty-five year old worker at Talbots supermarket. Twelve year old Veronica was out shopping with her mother who was in a queue for customer services; the supermarket was quite busy.

'Do I like insects,' smiled Mary taken aback by the question. 'Well to be honest their very small and I don't think about them much… but I like ladybirds!'

'Their orange!' she replied her eyes blazing with excitement.

'There are lots of different types of insects… ants, bees, cockroaches, centipedes…' Mary said racking her brains to think of all the different categories.

'Moths!' the little girl declared with unrestrained excitement. 'Have you ever rode a bicycle on a bumpy road?'

'Well… no I haven't actually,' Mary replied startled by the question.

At that moment her mother left the queue and re-joined her daughter. The little girl waved at Mary as she exited the store. Talbots supermarket was a large supermarket, occupying a vast space. High ceilings looked down on row upon row of products ranging from foodstuffs, cleaning materials to clothes. Mary worked on the self-service section with her friend Daphne, a tall broad shouldered young woman distinguished by her Goth make-up. They both shared an unlimited curiosity about other people and had a vivid imagination. Their imaginations were nourished in the main by popular culture. Their cultural reference points were The X-Files, Buffy The Vampire Slayer and Star Trek. Mary also had a liking for film versions of Dickens, particularly Great Expectations.

They both took a break in the staff canteen. There were news reports on the TV that a twelve year old boy had gone missing in the local area.

'They still haven't found that boy who's gone missing,' remarked Daphne.

'No, poor thing,' replied Mary. At that moment a tall, thin young man approached their table. Henry was what some people would describe as a nerd and possessed a repertoire of obscure knowledge. He had a tendency to ask questions that only he could answer. This afforded him great pleasure.

'Afternoon ladies,' he said breezily sitting next to them. 'And how's things on self-service?'

'Busy,' replied Mary.

'Well I have a question for you. What is entomology?' he asked his face beaming. Mary and Daphne looked at each other puzzled and were unable to provide an answer. 'Well its a branch of zoology that's given over to the study of insects.'

'Well it's funny you should mention insects because today a girl asked me if I liked insects.' At this Daphne jumped in.

'Did you see that old film last night on TV… The Naked Jungle with Charlton Heston?'

'Wow… yeah. Brilliant!' replied Mary. At this she turned to Henry. 'What is Marabunta?' The smile disappeared from his face; he had clearly never heard of the word.

'I don't know,' he replied crestfallen. Mary had brilliantly turned the tables on him.

'Marabunta means an army of ants on the move who destroy everything in its path. Charlton Heston plays a plantation owner in South America who's threatened by an army of ants.'

'So it's Charlton Heston versus an army of ants… got it,' said Henry.

'Exactly.'

'So how does he defeat the ants?' inquired Henry.

'He floods the area around the plantation and wipes out the ants,' replied Mary.

'But get this… as the the army of ants are advancing through the jungle they send out a scout…' added Daphne.

'That's right. An advanced guard to check out the area. That's intelligence for you!' said Mary.

At that one of their colleagues, Brenda, passed the table. She approached Mary and bent over.

'There's ants in the Ladies toilet!' she declared. Mary, Daphne and Henry looked at each other.

'Marabunta!' declared Daphne.

***

The music spread over the length and breadth of Talbots.

'I just can't get you out of my head

Boy your loving is all I think about

I just can't get you out of my head'.

Mary and Daphne had worked at Talbots supermarket a number of years and got to know the regular customers. One of these customers was an elegant older lady, a retired barrister. Always beautifully dressed she displayed exquisite old world manners. Contrary to the stereotype of the elegant, clever barrister she was friendly although this was counter balanced by a sinister smile.

'There's Mrs Roberts,' observed Daphne.

'Always elegant,' replied Mary.

'Is it true that she was jilted at the altar?' inquired Daphne.

'Yeah. All set to get married. Everything arranged. She was literally waiting at the altar standing beside the priest, the church pews full and the bride-groom didn't turn up', said Mary.

'Like that character in Dickens,' replied Daphne.

'Mrs Havisham, that's right. Her life stops after she's jilted,' said Mary.

'I saw the film on TV the other week… the clock stops in her dining room, the wedding banquet is still on the dining table, including the wedding cake and it is covered in cobwebs,' said Daphne.

'And a spider walks over the table,' replied Mary grimacing.

After a few minites Mrs Roberts entered the self-service area where Mary and Daphne worked. She purchased some alcohol so Mary had to authorise the purchase on the self-service machine. Mrs Roberts took a shine to Mary and always had a chat with her.

'Thank you my dear,' the exquisite manners of Mrs Roberts on display.

'That's alright,' replied Mary.

'Quiet in here today,' Mrs Roberts observed.

'Very quiet,' replied Mary.

'And have you found yourself a suitable young man to marry yet?' she inquired jokingly.

'Not yet,' said Mary, an embarrassed expression on her face. At that Mrs Roberts moved closer to Mary, adopting a confidential manner.

'You must always dangle a man,' Mrs Roberts declared.

'Dangle?' replied Mary, looking interested but puzzled.

'That's right.' Mrs Roberts was now warming up to a subject that clearly excited her passion. Suddenly the sinister smile came into full view. 'You make them fall in love with you, then you walk away. You break their heart!'

At this she collected her shopping and took her leave. Daphne came over to Mary.

'What did she say to you?' Daphne inquired.

'She talked about men… you must always dangle a man… then when he falls in love with you… you break his heart!' said Mary.

'Just like Mrs Havisham!' declared Daphne.

***

Each month a small middle aged man would shop at Talbots. Casually dressed, small in stature he had watery eyes and sometimes spoke to Mary. He had a very distinctive nose, bulbous in form. He would approach the alcohol section furtively and fill his basket with bottles of brandy and whisky. Mary was returning from the staff canteen when she passed the alcohol section. He would sometimes talk to staff. The man smiled at Mary when he saw her and he approached her.

'A person in my shoes does not like the C word,' he said as if taking Mary in his confidence.

'The C word?' inquired Mary looking puzzled.

'Cirrhosis… cirrhosis of the liver, it's a killer. Over the weekend my cousin decided to give me a lecture on the subject. So when you see me heading for the alcohol section you should try to steer me away from it… toward the fish counter or the bakery maybe.'

'Ok, I'll do that,' replied Mary. At the same time Mary couldn't help notice his basket full of bottles of alcohol.

'Today however I'm celebrating,' he declared.

'What are you celebrating,' inquired Mary.

'My unbirthday,' he said cryptically.

'Unbirthday?' said Mary looking puzzled.

'The three hundred and sixty four days of the year that are not my birthday!' he declared much to Mary's amusement.

At that he and Mary walked the short distance to the till area. A number of staffed tills had long queues except one that had a short queue.

'That's a short queue,' she advised the man. But the man stopped and stared at another man who was standing in the queue.

'I know that man… he's an undertaker. I won't stand behind an undertaker in a queue. It may change my odds of living a long life.'

At this he took his leave and joined another queue. Mary joined her friend Daphne in the self-service section.

'See that man in the queue there, the small, bald middle aged man with broad shoulders?' Mary inquired.

'Yeah,' said Daphne.

'Well, the guy who's fond of alcohol wouldn't stand behind him in a queue because that guy is an undertaker,' said Mary.

'Well some people are superstitious,' replied Daphne.

'That undertaker looks like a large beetle,' observed Mary.

'Since talking to that girl you've got insects on the brain,' replied Daphne.

'That's it… he looks like a deathwatch beetle!' declared Mary.

***

The following day Mary was passing the fish counter when she saw the girl who was fascinated by insects. The girls' mother was engrossed in a conversation with another woman, who was her neighbour. Mary stopped and the girl smiled at her.

'Hello,' said Mary.

'Hello… do you want to see my insects? the girl replied. Mary laughed.

'You've got some insects?' inquired Mary. The girl removed a jar from a bag she was carrying.

'Look,' she said holding up the jar. 'Spiders and caterpillars… see.'

Inside the jar Mary could see a number of insects crawling around. The girl then returned the jar to her bag. She continued.

'I saw handbags over there.' She pointed to an area near the entrance. 'When I grow up I'm going to get a handbag… women have lots of little thing in a handbag and I'm going to put my insects in it!' Mary laughed. 'If you go to Mayflower woods near the big Oak tree there are lots of ladybirds there.'

'Ok,' replied Mary.

'Last week I went to Mayflower woods with my friend… it's a secret.'

At that the girls' mother broke off her conversation with the woman she was talking to and called her: 'Veronica'. The girl waved goodbye to Mary and re-joined her mother. Mary went to the self-service section and re-joined her colleague Daphne.

'I saw that little girl again. This time she had a jar of insects with her. Strange girl. There's something going on there.' She paused.' I have got a day off tomorrow. So have you. Fancy a picnic!' Mary inquired.

'A picnic?' replied Daphne.

'Yeah… we could go to Mayflower woods,' said Mary.

'Why not. It's a chance to re-connect with nature… and study insects!' Both Mary and Daphne laughed.

***

The following day Mary and Daphne ventured out to Mayflower woods with their picnic box. A sunny day, when they arrived at the outskirts of Mayflower woods they were met with the sound of birdsong. As they moved into the woods the sound of birdsong was ubiquitous. They followed a curved path, passing gnarled tree branches. They saw a butterfly hovering over a hedge. Mary and Daphne stopped to study the butterfly.

'Is that the painted lady?' asked Daphne.

'Could be… I'm not sure. Wow have you been researching butterflies?' replied Mary.

'Well I did google butterflies.' At that the butterfly flew off. 'And one colourful butterfly was the painted lady.'

They both looked at the butterfly fly off. They continued to follow the curving path, the leaves brushing past their bodies. They walked over a branch of a tree that blocked the curving path. At one point they heard the sound of a twig breaking. The sound was some distance off. They saw the contours of a dark figure and both Mary and Daphne, instinctively, stood still.

'It's a deer. Keep still,' whispered Mary.

Two minutes later the deer was gone. Mary and Daphne looked at each other; a look of wonder suffused their faces.

'Wow. Awesome!' declared Daphne.

'Definitely awesome,' affirmed Mary. 'Let's find a spot where we can have a picnic.'

'Ok, replied Daphne.

They saw a sign The Big Oak Tree and an arrow, so they headed for that. When they arrived at the Big Oak Tree they stopped and removed the food from their bag. They suddenly heard approaching footsteps; and from the branches and undergrowth emerged a little girl. The same girl in fact who shopped at Talbots with her mother.

'Hello, you're the ladies from the supermarket,' the girl said recognising Mary and Daphne.

'Hello, it's Veronica isn't it,' said Mary searching her memory.

'Are you here on your own?' inquired Daphne.

'Yes, I live next to the woods,' Veronica replied. Mary and Daphne looked concerned.

'We'll take you back to your home if you like,' said Mary.

'After I've collected some insects.' She held up a jar. 'Then I'll go home', said Veronica.

Mary and Daphne looked at each other and shrugged their shoulders. She continued.

'There are insects everywhere,' she said with unrestrained excitement. 'Look there's a spider's web,' she said pointing to a spider's web underneath the branch of a tree. 'Watch'. She unscrewed the jar and removed an ant from the jar and guided it on to the spider's web. The ant struggled in the web as the spider advanced toward it. Then the spider overwhelmed the ant. 'Look its eating the ant.'

Mary and Daphne watched this grisly scene and grimaced at each other. Veronica watched the scene with intense interest. Then she turned to Mary.

'Have you got cobwebs between your legs?' she asked as if it was perfectly normal to ask such a question.

'No, I have not!' replied Mary, startled and shocked.

'Sit down, we've got some spare sandwiches,' said Daphne. All three sat down and tucked into the sandwiches.

'So what's the fascination with insects?' inquired Mary.

'Well they're small and some are fat and some are skinny and they all have different shapes. Beetles are different from ladybirds.' She paused to eat her sandwich. 'Sometimes I talk to trees. Do trees know the alphabet?' Veronica inquired.

'No!' replied Mary laughing.

'There's something in my shoe,' exclaimed Daphne with a look of alarm on her face. She took off her shoe and out ran a beetle.

'It's a beetle! exclaimed Veronica, a look of joy splashed over her face. 'Do you put blood on your lips?'

'Blood?' Daphne looked perplexed. 'You mean lipstick. Yes, I do,' replied Daphne.

'Mummy says that everybody has an angel watching over them and that angels live in heaven. Heaven is far away up there.' She points upward to the sky. 'Can you get there by aeroplane?' she inquired casually.

'I don't think so', replied Mary baffled. She looked at Daphne.

'I don't like insects. When you go underground… when you're as dead as a doornail… they eat you, they eat flesh. I once had a cat Napoleon. It died and we buried it in the garden. Later I dug up the ground but the insects had eaten him all up,' declared Veronica, to the evident surprise of Mary and Daphne.

'I tell you what, why don't we take you home to your mum,' said Mary becoming uneasy about the turn in the conversation. Daphne looked at

Mary, clearly in agreement.

'Stephen stole my watch! exclaimed Veronica suddenly.

'Who's Stephen?' inquired Mary.

'My friend. I was collecting insects. First he said I was ugly and then he stole my watch. I pushed him and he banged his head on the ground. There was blood from his head and he didn't move. It was an accident.' Mary and Daphne exchanged horrified glances.

Veronica walked over to an area to the right of a large tree, behind a tangle of branches and bushes. There was a small piece of level ground that was broken by a small mound of soil and leaves. Mary and Daphne followed Veronica. She knelt down beside this small mound of earth and looked at it vacantly. She moved some soil and there appeared a human hand. Next to it a caterpillar moved slowly. She picked up the caterpillar. Mary and Daphne stared at the hand in horror. The mystery of the missing boy was solved.

'The insects will eat Stephen just like they ate Napoleon,' Veronica said matter of factly.

Stephanie Rybak - Transmogrification

It's all a mistake. I wasn't supposed to come back as a cat. Wasn't supposed to come back at all, in fact. I'd been given the most wonderful welcome and told "Well done, good and faithful servant" and I was looking forward to an eternity of bliss when that trainee dispatcher of souls made a mistake and I found myself inside Mamma's belly, but with all my human consciousness intact. I didn't realise I was a kitten at that point, but I did suspect that I was being reincarnated. I couldn't see anything, but began to feel other bodies jostling against mine. Was I going to be reborn as a triplet? Was there no way of putting this right? I tried *in utero* prayer, but that didn't work.

Then one day, the pressure became intolerable and I felt I just had to get out of there. It seemed my siblings were of the same mind, because we all strained and struggled and eventually emerged from our confinement, still blind, but no longer so squashed. I felt something like a great wet towel wiping me repeatedly: I later came to know that feeling as Mamma's tongue. I opened my mouth to try to explain my existential predicament, but all that came out was a pathetic little mew. That startled me: it was my first clue that I had been reborn as a kitten. The next was that I was very keen to suckle from Mamma and found that her teats were surrounded by fur.

Various people cooed and took liberties with my person and I was grateful to Mamma for seeing them off. My eyesight came gradually in my third week and I looked at my siblings. There were six of us, all black with patches of white in different places. I had white socks and found myself thinking, "Please don't call me Socks!" adding as an afterthought, "or Mittens!"

My siblings and I went through the usual snuggling and play-fighting of any litter of kittens. I found myself quite schizoid about it. On the one hand, here I was, with my human consciousness trapped inside a kitten's body, on the other, my kitten's body relished and learned from all this contact – and anyway, what's not to like about cuddling kittens? My favourite was my sister with a face that was half white and half black.

After about four weeks, the carer began to wean us. I wondered where I would go after that and hoped desperately that it would be to a good home. Various people came to look at us. I made a point of scratching any I didn't like – and biting them if they persisted, to be on the safe side. Then a woman called Paula came in. She had a pleasing, low-pitched voice and made no sudden movements. She watched us carefully for a bit, then picked me up. She smelt good and I liked the way she held and stroked me, so I turned on the charm, snuggling against her and purring.

"Wow!" said the carer, "You're the first person he's liked!" They didn't tell her that I had scratched and bitten most of the others.

"I'll take him!" she said impulsively, and I licked her hand. "Oh look! It's almost as though he understood! I'm going to call him Descartes."

Paula came back to collect me when I was eight weeks old. I found myself a little sad to be leaving Mamma and my siblings and wanted to explain to them what was happening, but I couldn't. I suffered the indignity of being put into a cat-carrier and then strapped into the front passenger seat of Paula's car. She talked soothingly to me, assuring me that everything was all right and we'd be home soon. I sat there, quietly noticing that she didn't change gear soon enough when accelerating.

I had taken a gamble in choosing what I suppose I must call my owner. I didn't know whether she had a cat-hating boyfriend or sadistic children at home, or whether she lived in a top-floor flat, but I was in luck: she lived alone in a ground-floor flat with a garden. There was a cat-flap, but Paula must have been told that she shouldn't let me out for two weeks, so I sighed and sat by the cat-flap to let her know that I was disappointed it was locked. The flat was not bad, except that she had put down laminated flooring, which is much less comfortable to lie on than carpet. I therefore made a point of laying claim to all the soft surfaces: the sofa, the armchair and, most importantly, her bed. There was some initial resistance to that, as she tried to convince me that the cat-bed she had bought was a better place for me to sleep. I graciously consented to nap there from time to time, as long as she accepted that her bed was now also my bed whenever I chose.

To some extent, I found myself thinking like a cat. I noted that the sachets of cat-food were supermarket own-brand, so I showed Paula what I thought of that by sniffing at my bowl then scratching the laminate, as if I had trodden in something nasty. She went up a grade with the next Ocado delivery, but the food was still mid-range, so I continued my hunger-strike, just eating crunchies, until she relented and bought me the top-of-the-range brands. These I wolfed down, both because I was by now very hungry and to make a point to her.

I had been 81 when I died and I had grown used to having a limited range of movement, so, despite the frustrations of my new state, it was exhilarating to have the physical flexibility of a kitten. I revelled in leaping, stretching and pouncing, though the human prefect in my head kept me from climbing up the curtains!

Paula was a writer and spent most of her day at her laptop, not taking the recommended breaks, so I decided to enforce them by asking for a cuddle every half-hour or so. Sometimes she would put me on her lap and go on typing around me, but it was much better when she moved to the sofa and put her feet up and I sat on her and snuggled under her chin. Those cuddle-times were the moments when I felt closest to being human, because I suppose Paula is the sort of woman I would have enjoyed cuddling when I was a man. I did try to speak to her about my predicament, but it still came out as "Meow!" I wondered if I could gain access to her laptop to type something for her, but she shooed me off it in the day-time and always turned it off and shut the lid at night.

One evening, a friend of Paula's called Joanna came round for a meal and they were talking about me, confident that I couldn't understand them. "I'm taking him to the vet next week to get him donc, poor little thing!" said Paula. I freaked out and rushed round the flat, thinking only of escape, but the cat-flap was locked for the night. This time, it was the friend who commented that "it was almost as though he understood!"

When Joanna came to leave, Paula walked back out to her car with her. The laptop was still on, so I seized my chance. There was a Word doc open, so, working with one paw, I managed to type "please dont cut my balls off" (shift, and so upper-case, apostrophes and exclamation marks, were beyond my feline competence). Paula came and lifted me down from her desk, then her eye fell on the screen. For a moment she froze, then she burst out laughing. "Oh Joanna, honestly!" she said aloud and sat down at the desk. I made a fuss, yowling and pointing to the appendages which I was so keen to protect, but she ignored me and wrote an email to Joanna.

There was a ping a bit later, presumably when Joanna got home, and a few messages bounced back and forth in quick succession. Then Paula went off to the bathroom, saying, "It's not funny any more," under her breath. I leapt back on the desk and typed, "paula its me descartes". She came back and was shocked rigid: "I'm going mad!" I got back on the desk (no sudden movements) and approached the keyboard. As she watched, I typed "i am a man in a cats body". Paula was shaking, so I typed, "its ok cuddle me". She gave a stifled scream, rushed to her bedroom and shut the door on me – something she never normally did.

What she did not shut on me was the laptop. I managed to save my document, then laboriously typed:

"paula, you are not going mad. this is real. i was a man. i died. i was supposed to go to heaven but a dispatching angel made a mistake and sent me down to earth again without wiping my memory and I was born as a kitten. it has been so frustrating. perhaps now you know about it we can have a meaningful relationship. you can read me what you write. you can talk to me intelligently. you can cancel the appointment at the vets. please. cogito ergo sum. descartes aka ken brittan, b 13 jan 1939, d 14 jan 2020."

It took me a very long time to type it and then I kept touching the space bar every few minutes for the rest of the night to keep the computer from going to sleep, so that I would be able to open the document in the morning.

I thought I should keep things as normal as possible in the morning, so I started yowling to be fed at 6am and she started yelling at me to shut the fuck up. So far, so normal. When she finally emerged, she looked at me warily, as though trying to work out whether she had dreamt it all. I wove round her feet for a few moments to reassure her and then jumped up on the desk and opened the document I had typed with such effort. She looked scared rather than appreciative, but read what I had written.

She turned to me. "Did you write this?"

I nodded vigorously – not a natural movement for a cat, so all the more convincing. Come on, I thought, ask some more yes/no questions!

"Is it true?" A bit feeble, but OK, she was in shock. I nodded some more.

"Am I going mad?" This time I shook my head as emphatically as I could.

She sat down and googled "ken brittan" and found a few entries, one of them being an obituary, with the dates I had given.

"Is this you?" she asked. I looked at the screen and nodded. "I need coffee," she said.

I was keen to read the rest of the obituary, so coaxed the tracking pad to send the cursor over to the right of the screen to enable me to scroll down. She saw what I was doing and gave a muffled yelp.

Paula brought her coffee back and sat on the sofa. Normally, I would have jumped on her lap at this point, but I thought she might feel odd about that, now she knew I was a man, so I observed social distancing. When she had finished her coffee, she turned to look at me.

"So you're really a man?" Vigorous nodding from me.

"Your name was Ken Brittan?" Nod.

"What am I supposed to do about it?" *Ask yes/no questions for a start!* I thought. Failing that, I pointed in as human a way as I could at my imperilled testicles.

"You really do understand! OK, I won't have your balls cut off!" At that, I leapt onto her lap and snuggled against her. She stroked my head: "I don't think I've ever said that to a man before!"

We spent the next few days adjusting to our new mode of being together, with Paula knowing I was a man and me knowing she knew. This showed itself in little things. She now shut the bathroom door. At first, she seemed unsure about me snuggling against her breasts, but eventually accepted that was what happened if a cat sat on your lap, so let it pass. I think we both found it comforting.

After a few days, she had another dinner guest, a conceited young man called Jonathan. Everything about him put my back up. Paula had spent hours getting the meal and herself ready and she seemed nervous. They had what was clearly supposed to be a romantic dinner, then moved over to the sofa. I was trying my hardest to think how to derail the rest of the evening and had almost determined to make myself barf on the duvet when Paula went to the bathroom. While she was there, Jonathan sent a text. When he went to the bathroom himself, he made the mistake of leaving his phone on the sofa. I was on it in a flash and opened his texts, meowing urgently for Paula to look. She resisted for a moment, but only a moment, then saw his most recent outgoing message: "About to get laid!" When he came out of the bathroom, she handed him his phone and his coat and said, "You had better correct that last text!" as she pushed him out of the front door.

The next day, Paula moped a bit, but the day after that, she was in the mood for a serious conversation, so she put me on the desk, with her laptop pushed back from the edge so that I could access it more easily.

"OK," she said, "Where do we go from here? The options would seem to be

1. keep this a secret between us
2. tell the world
3. find some way of using your unique situation, without explanation. You could be a TV or internet sensation!

What do you think?"

I thought for a moment, then typed: "dangerous to tell world or be freak show. cant predict what theyd do. might take me to lab or try to make me spy."

"You're right. I might not be able to protect you," she said. "What do you want to do with this unexpected extra life of yours? Or extra nine lives?" At least she was relaxing enough to joke about it now.

"read novels on kindle" I typed. "eat sheba, purina, roast chicken and prawns. lie in sun. and why don't we collaborate on a story about me. you could pretend it was fiction."

And that, dear reader, is exactly what we have done.

T.H. Kunze - Ionisation

I'm so happy for them! And I can only hope—

Decaying flotsam, washed in and out on her tides of consciousness.

I'm so happy…

A dull crackle has Eve pull focus, stare at the fire, its feeble glow now all but lost to the shady whispers of candlelight. More coal in the bucket, but… She shrugs up her tartan blanket, seals the cocoon tight from the inside. No time to be wasteful.

…for them!

The voice in her head jars, sounds hysterical, savage even. It probably didn't at the time. Darkness amplifies normality's echoes. Yes, she knows. And what could be more normal than the news? Reporting on the engagingly febrile couple who had ham-fisted their way into the final of a cooking contest, against all odds, where their jittery antics stultified rivals and stormed the minds of a gripped nation. As so vividly expressed by the viewer reaction intended to wrap the piece.

…And I can only hope—

Hope what? Even two hours later, she can't stop wondering what the woman in her flowery robes had aspired to, ablaze with compassion. A spark snuffed out in the blink of an eye, when life froze silent and night fell inside, to the shivering smile of a Hunger Moon.

Savouring the un-dead air, Eve sucks in its rooty scent, refuels her starved senses. Going out was a good idea, despite… Everything.

The faint, grinding hum of what must be an emergency generator grows louder to fill the night with a promise of primal urgency. She stops, swipes back her hood and tracks the sound to somewhere near the village square, its inky crown of gables still half a mile away. In the distance beyond, a lone pair of headlights flares up, slicing through starless skies as a car sweeps along the Dundee road. Driving had somehow struck her as inappropriate. And unsafe.

Ten minutes later the Restless Ram swings into view like a faithful constellation, lush amber ripples spilling from its dimpled windowpanes as if to flaunt the wisdom of an electric backup. And no doubt the tills were ringing as usual, too.

Eve straightens, enters the light-splashed throng, instantly gagged by a wave of staleness suffused with the spiky odour of compounded human presence. Most are clustered around half-a-dozen tables, their faces animated yet inscrutable. None look familiar. Nor should they. Once stabilised she skirts around a group of guffawing males to reach the bar with its posse of taps beckoning, bright as runway beacons.

'Gin and tonic, please.'

The young barmaid nods, eyes wide, probing hers. 'How're you doing?'

'Me?' Eve shrugs nervously. 'I'm fine. In the dark, like everyone else. Well…' She motions at the gleaming counter. 'Almost everyone else.'

'Dark?' A bemused smile. 'Oh, you mean our shiny new taps. That's all part of our claim from Scot2O, after their pressure spike and the burst pipe fiasco. Still stuck with those noisy dryers outside, but… There you go! I'm Gemma, by the way.'

'Eve. Thank you.' She pulls off her slouchy cap to a wheat-blonde cascade. 'So, any idea yet what caused this?'

'Nothing confirmed. But they reckon—'

'Cyber attack,' rasps the bearded man beside Eve. 'Some heavy-raging industrial virus, I'm guessing. Like Stuxnet on steroids.'

A stocky brunette behind him leans into view. 'Yea, makes sense,' she asserts in Estuary English. 'Probably them Russians. Because we slammed their poison scam. Not to mention, we got Trident.'

'You mean, you lot got it,' her neighbour jibes. 'We're just the sooks chilling your missiles up here.'

'That's a bit rich!'

With no reply from fellow drinkers Eve's attention turns to the resonant Glaswegian chops erupting from one of the rear tables.

'…No power, satellite or telecommunications. And yes, that includes sub-Atlantic optical cables. In saltwater, their electric repeater stations get fried like battered squid.'

'Thought those relays were bomb-proof?' someone asks.

'Maybe. But tinsel wrap to a solar storm. And we're talking full-bore geomagnetic wipeout here.' A dry laugh. 'Like, better world – cancelled!'

'Good,' sighs Eve, into a tense silence. 'At least it's not man-made, then.'

Nearby eyes home in on her like startled gunsights.

'What's wrong with *you*?' the brunette asks with a caustic inflection.

Eve unplugs, gaze slumped, retreats to the safety of time's trickle, until faces dip and hushed local conversations resume.

Then a tap on her shoulder.

'Cosmic justice beats hi-tech bedlam, eh?' His voice is softer now, but the Glasgow patter remains distinct. 'Looks like some of us aren't up for it, though.'

Sharp, deep-set features, bisected by the skewed shadow from a flat-brimmed hat. A straggly black goatee nestles roguishly between the tips of his coat's sweeping fur collar.

'And you are?'

'Proxi,' he smiles. 'Join me for a fag outside?'

Eve ruffles up her scarf against the February chill, accepts his proffered cigarette. Across the road, two young women in short sleeves peer at them between hasty puffs, their clutched phones the limp impediment of habit, stroked once more, sullenly, before both return indoors.

'Seems to keep them warm, at least.' Proxi grins after them. 'Hyper-dependency. I find the whole concept fascinating.'

'Scary, more like.'

'They're greedy wee monsters, aye. But wiped out by the mere blink of a star, like I said.'

'Right…' She seeks his dark, almond-shaped eyes, briefly. 'In there – were you somehow saying you saw this coming?'

His puzzled frown quickly resolves. 'Nah! I just know most folk connect best with people, not spooky science. So I wasn't surprised by their reaction to your gaffe.'

'Oh, that…' she bristles. 'Well, I only spoke my mind.'

'Then I'm glad.'

'Really? That puts you in a minority of one. You must be some kind of philosopher.'

'Hardly.' He flicks off some ash. 'Just a keen observer. Comes with being a painter, I guess.'

'Nice! Oil, or acrylics?'

'Oil. It's more forgiving. And waiting two days for layers to dry suits me. More time to think, and "philosophise".'

'Lucky you. All I ever seem to think about is how to stop thinking. Mostly about work, useless people…'

'The daily grind.' Proxi scowls, strokes his beard. 'I self-ejected from that. But it's been tough.'

'Wish I could.'

'Moral obligations? Or the other M?'

'I'm a search engine consultant. So, take your pick.'

'Could be both,' he says, deadpan. 'You help the good guys get top ranking, right?'

She laughs bitterly and looks down at their spectral shadows soaking up the tarmac's pale-orange glow. 'I'd best be heading home, I think.'

'Local?'

'Pretty much. Rented cottage, two miles up the road. You?'

'My very own caravan, on a friend's farm nearby.'

'Ah.'

'Ah?'

'Nice chatting,' she says, turns briskly, slinks off into a crack of darkness.

The letter flap clangs her awake the next morning. Breath pumping, context floods in: Proxi, daylight, cold… And it's gone nine-thirty. She bolts up, cursing, until the discovery of her defunct mobile flips a switch, re-renders a red alert in pastel shades of pink.

Curled up on the damp doormat, actual mail, much to her surprise at a time like this. Or maybe not – yet another smart-meter offer, and a TV Licence reminder. She crumples both with a steely sense of satisfaction before padding across to the kitchen, lifeless but for the dull pinging from a leaky tap.

Catching sight of the gaping fuse box cover in the hall stops her dead. Probably forced open by last night's blow-out. She walks past, eyes down and shivering, heads for the bedroom to get dressed.

'Didn't expect to see you today,' her boss says listlessly, one hour later.

'I'm amazed to see myself sometimes,' Eve replies in passing, makes for a free desk beside the broken vending machine. 'But home office tomorrow, electrons willing.'

'What?'

She doesn't have the heart to explain. Pointless, just like the whole idea of turning up in the first place. Power here seems to have been restored, though who knows for how long. But the network problems are clearly taking their toll on her colleagues. Far from the hoped-for morale boost, their shiftless platitudes and hollow jargon reek of desperation and defeat; broken spirits, held captive in the fortress of unimportance. When their feckless banter descends into hip-shot quotes from old gossip columns she gives an excuse and leaves. Few seem to notice.

On the drive home a triptych of panoramic billboards bears down on her as if for the first time. Presiding over a retail centre near the city's outskirts, their bold, ferociously upbeat message shines out like a blowtorch on the wasteland of her tangled thoughts.

She squeaks an angry U-turn at the next junction, doubles back, parks up at random, just another binary dot on the concrete matrix. The vast iconic building before her gleams with motionless perfection in the crisp afternoon light, integrity and purpose fully intact. Unlike the slow shuffle of returning shoppers with their pinched, tight-lipped expressions that suggest indifference, revulsion even, at the bloodless salute from a toppled knight.

Slammed by a raw gust, Eve trembles, vindicated, and eager to escape. But an open filling station near the exit seems too good to pass up.

'Hi there.' The attendant grins infectiously from behind his notebook screen. 'Cash only, please. Card reader's borked.'

She nods, counts out notes.

'You were lucky – we're almost out.'

'My first bit of good fortune for the day,' she says and shoots him a smile.

He returns it, gaze lingering. 'Mind if I ask your name?'

'I thought telemarketing's been put on hold?'

'No, nothing like that.' His fingers wiggle. 'Real names help me believe in my characters, you see? I'm a writer, when I'm not, uh…'

'Working, is the common term. And I'm Eve.'

Three keystrokes. 'Perfect! You're in my first novel now. Thank you.'

'No bother. Good luck, and…' She recoils, shakes her head. 'And thanks for reminding me.'

'Of what?'

Streaks of mint-green and white shimmer through a skeletal stand of beeches near the crest of a gentle escarpment rising from the river's opposite bank. Reassured, Eve drives on slowly towards a narrow bridge, then follows the private road that winds past watchful Highland cattle and up a slight incline where she pulls in behind a mud-spattered old Picasso.

The short walk along rutted tractor tracks leaves her breathless with indecision.

'I never told you my name!'

The words ring so hollow from her mouth, seem lost to reason. Until their earthy echoes drip back at her, plumped by mossy boughs, rain-soaked bark, and hope.

'It's Eve, right?' The barest smirk on Proxi's sculpted face.

'How did you—'

'Gemma told me.'

'Ha! The barmaid? She must be dancing. I asked her directions.'

'To here?'

'Uh-huh.'

'In that case…' He fixes up his bunched ponytail, steps out onto the glossy carpet of winter leaves. 'Welcome to my hideaway, Eve.'

Her gaze skips along the web of drooping branches with his sizeable static caravan seemingly enfolded in their midst. 'It's magic. But how…?'

He thumbs at the river in mid-distance. 'Major flood, some years back. Gertie got swept up here somehow. We just had to nudge her into position. The trees don't seem to mind.'

'Gertie?'

'That's right. Fancy taking a peep inside?'

The surprisingly spacious interior is partitioned by a central kitchenette awash with neatly stowed utensils and supplies. To its left, convertible living quarters, their home-made, rustic elegance offset on the right by the explosive anarchy of Proxi's studio.

Drawn in, Eve feels like sliding down a spinning kaleidoscope, stops halfway, turns.

'It's OK,' he prompts from the doorway.

A tall, spiry easel proudly marks the eye of the storm, bears its canvas to the mottled late-afternoon light. She steps up to it delicately, waits for the shadows to melt…

The haggard, angular features of an old man, cast in pivotal focus against the violent blur of whirling detritus; discarded paragons of civilisation, their ghostly-green statues, sigils, portraits and parchments the dead phosphorescence of borrowed energy, uprooted and hurled outwards at the pulsating blue fringes of night.

'It's so intense!' Her hand leaps forward, retracts in awe. 'Does it have a title yet?'

'*Ionisation.*'

She swallows, probes his ocean-blue gaze for clues. 'I've heard the term, but…'

'It's basically a transformation process at elemental level. Usually of atoms, turned into ions by losing or gaining electrons.'

'Is it dangerous?'

'Not inherently.' A knowing glance. 'But this sudden, often dramatic change of identity requires a powerful catalyst. Like lightning, nuclear explosions…'

'Or a solar storm.'

'Yes.'

'Of course!' Her voice needs time to steady. 'It's a metaphor, right?'

'Most art is, but—'

'And those idols and legends here, the make-believe greatness – that's like all the hyped stuff I used to watch on TV, and always felt more empty after. If that makes any sense?'

He nods emphatically. 'The painting's icons are meant to symbolise vicarious pride. That false sense of personal fulfilment we derive from the legitimised achievements of others. It's like a drug these days. And a sad substitute for our own neglected self-esteem.'

Just the softest of tugs before she feels a knot uncoil inside. 'It's like… like a thread that doesn't lead out of the labyrinth, but back inside.' Her eyes blink back tears, find his. 'But I think I felt it snap, last night. When the lights went out.'

Proxi draws near, his gentle touch on her arm the brushing wingtip of long-lost certitude.

'I think only *your* lights went out,' he whispers.

'I don't… How?'

'Probably by your own doing. And for a good reason, I hope.' He steps back, studies her face calmly. 'Looks like it worked.'

Struck by a warm electric tingle, Eve can only watch as her fingers reach for the canvas, rake wilfully across its deep sea of colours, but come back dry.

Yvonne Barker - 3 Syllables

Dangerous – 3 syllables

Turn around – 3 syllables

Don't go there! – 3 syllables

If only she'd known how dangerous he was she wouldn't have got involved. If only she'd known what she was going to find when she went to his house, she would have turned around. If only she had known the consequence of her actions she would have walked away – not gone there.

But she didn't know. She did get involved and she did go there and unfortunately there would be a consequence – even though she didn't yet know what that consequence would be.

Her friends had asked if she was happy because they said that she didn't seem herself since she'd started seeing him, and that if he was making her unhappy then she deserved better. But what is better? If someone says the weather is better today: how is it better?

Is it hotter for someone who likes to sunbathe?

Is it cooler for someone who can't stand the heat?

Is it raining following a period of draught?

Is it dry after prolonged rain?

Better for – 3 syllables.

Better for one person is not necessarily better for someone else. Better for her was being with a person who humiliated and ridiculed her, who blew hot and cold and made her emotionally and psychologically vulnerable, rather than being on her own.

Better for her was accepting a holiday destination that didn't appeal in the slightest, instead of suggesting going to a place of her dreams.

Better for her was sitting with him through a film that she knew she would hate – and did, rather than watching a film alone that she had been desperate to see.

Better for her was eating liver that she couldn't abide because he said it was full of iron and she looked anaemic – even though she didn't know she was deficient.

Better for her was drinking green tea because he said it was good for weight loss – even though she had never thought she needed to shed the pounds.

Better for her was wearing clothes that he liked her to wear instead of what she felt comfortable in.

Better for her was going out with him, when she would really like to see her friends.

He told her where to go, what to watch, to eat, to drink, to wear, and who to see. It was better for her to do what he told her to do or she would have to face his wrath. It didn't seem worth it to say no. She didn't feel worth it.

She has friends – 3 syllables.

"Did you notice how he tried to avoid her being on her own with us? When he went to the bar she went with him to help him carry the drinks. When he went to the gents, she followed him to the ladies."

"That was surely her choice though: she didn't have to go and help him, or decide to go to the loo at the same time."

"Well I got the feeling that she didn't have much choice if she didn't want to annoy him. He'd either warned her beforehand or she knew what would happen if she didn't conform, and thought it best anyway."

"You could be right: she was always vulnerable but she certainly doesn't seem like the same person since she started seeing him."

"If a person can be described as 'a human being regarded as an individual', then she's not even a person anymore because she isn't functioning as an individual. She is single in the sense that she isn't married; but she isn't single in the sense that she no longer seems to be a separate entity, with an independent existence. She appears to be an extension of him and is only capable of functioning within his parameters."

"It doesn't seem a healthy relationship –

"What's your take?" – 3 syllables.

"I agree." – 3 syllables.

"Worrying." – 3 syllables.

"Yes, we need to try and get her from under his spell. Let's invite her out on Friday – girls only: the three of us haven't been out together without the boys for a while. Shall I ring her?"

"Good idea, let me know what she says."

***

"What did she say?"

"She's busy all weekend – with him. I suggested the following weekend but they're away. I got the impression that she will have an excuse for any subsequent weekends or invitations that don't involve him; and we can't talk to her when he's around."

"What are we going to do?"

"All we can do is keep in touch and let her know that we are here if she needs us."

"Not if, when!" – 3 syllables.

"You're right" – 3 syllables.

"Monitor?" – 3 syllables.

"Yes for the time being, but if she continues being uncommunicative then we'll have to go round to hers to talk to her, and hope that he isn't there."

***

"Have you ever thought about looking him up online?"

"You know I don't do social media."

"Well I have, and it makes for very interesting reading."

"Ominous?" – 3 syllables.

"Very much." – 3 syllables.

"Tell me more." – 3 syllables.

"Apparently he was in a relationship with a girl whose friends accused him of all sorts of nasty things."

"What sort of things?"

"Stalking, unreasonable jealousy, humiliation, manipulation. He would lead her on – sending flirty messages, but then wouldn't be interested in meeting up. Then he would come on really strong and serious, convincing her he would be the perfect partner, but when she succumbed to his charms once more he would go cold again and leave her wondering what she had said and done."

"Breadcrumbing?" – 3 syllables

"Love bombing." – 3 syllables

"Plays mind games." – 3 syllables.

"Exactly. Then it turned more than nasty – it became a tragedy when his girlfriend killed herself. Her friends said she was vulnerable before their relationship, but even more so afterwards – she became enthralled by him. They tried to tell her he was no good but she wouldn't listen."

"Sounds like us." – 3 syllables,

"Trying hard." – 3 syllables.

"Fruitlessly." – 3 syllables.

"Yes, the girl's friends tried and failed: but more was to come out of the woodwork – it transpired that a previous girlfriend of his had also taken her own life. She too had been vulnerable before meeting him and became more so under his control. We have to get our friend to see exactly what he's like before she becomes completely brainwashed. Let's go and see her."

"Together." – 3 syllables.

"Without him." – 3 syllables.

"Help her see." – 3 syllables.

***

She sat on the kerb and retched, but didn't puke – though the regurgitated contents of her stomach would not have looked out of place surrounded by discarded take away containers, fag ends and fly infested dog shit.

She stood on shaky legs, made it to the car and drove home, trying desperately to concentrate on the road instead of what she had just seen.

She wished she hadn't told him it was all over. She knew that he wasn't right for her and that he was a manipulator – that he'd controlled her.

She thought she'd been brave and that by ending the relationship it would make things better.

Better for – 3 syllables.

Better for who? Hanging himself was not better for him. Finding him with a rope around his neck because of what she had said to him was no longer better for her. If she hadn't called time on their relationship he would still be alive, and she couldn't live with that.

***

Her friends were never able to tell her what they'd discovered on social media – they couldn't tell her because she couldn't listen. She couldn't listen to anything ever again.

If they had known that he'd enticed her over to his house under false pretences – apparently under the guise of talking things through – to try and convince her to change her mind when she'd told him it was all over, they would have said:

"What a shit!" – 3 syllables.

If they had known that she'd gone home to kill herself after seeing him strung up from the ceiling they would have said:

"Poor darling!" – 3 syllables.

If they had seen him remove the noose from around his neck, and unscrew the hook from the ceiling, then sit down and calmly watch TV after she had run out of the house, they would have said:

"Murderer!" – 3 syllables.

***

If she had known her friends were going to come and find her she would have told them:

"Don't come here!" – 3 syllables.

"Turn around." – 3 syllables.

"Unpleasant." – 3 syllables.

Consequence – 3 syllables

Printed in Great Britain
by Amazon

48619882R00175